# THE
# OPERA HOUSE
# BALLET

JOSEF OTEIM

Tellwell Talent
www.tellwell.ca

ISBN
978-0-2288-0448-2 (Hardcover)
978-0-2288-0446-8 (Paperback)
978-0-2288-0447-5 (eBook)

*For Eleni. Half of me was made for half of you.*
*For Joel, whose imagination was integral.*
*And to the bulletproof kid . . . You did this.*

There's a cabin in the woods
That we dreamed about as children.
Another life
Another way.
Away from humans
Away from the stench and filth of city life.

When we got older
We forgot about dreaming.
We forgot about ants and caterpillars
Frogs and snakes in white plastic pails
And the fun 900 numbers.
We forgot about baseball.

We've done things to make you cry
But you've made men on earth go mad with sadness.
And we're so desperate for your love
But you make us pass away alone in silence.

-Oteim

# 1

*November 9, 1997. Marion Black's bookstore. Sudbury, Ontario*
*10:42 a.m.*

The preacher sat on a wooden chair in front of a row of burnt-down houses somewhere in one of Detroit's wretched west side ghettos. The photo, taken during a cultish religious movement he helped bring to fruition in the mid-80s, portrayed humility and penitence. A tattered wooden cross hung from a string of beads in his right hand, and his wrist was bent delicately, suggesting confidence, cool and a Christ-like resolve.

Dale Potoniak loathed the preacher and his books. This one was just as effective, by way of its sheer size, as the preacher's cover photo was at enticing readers to sympathize with his idiotic "God wants you to be rich" faith doctrine. Regardless of his unorthodox claims and blatant "repurposing" of obscure, handpicked verses in scripture, sixty thousand God-fearing people lined up at his events each night, filling stadiums for nearly a decade, paying a hefty forty dollar fee to get in. The preacher claimed God would return it to them a hundred fold if they would *only believe.*

"Brothers and sisters . . . The Lord almighty says that that which you've freely given—that which you've given from a servant's heart, from a heart that's free of doubt and selfish intent, will not only be given back to you—but I will open up the floodgates of heaven and pour out so much blessing there won't be enough room in your bank accounts for it— Malachi 3:10— can I get an 'amen'? I didn't hear you! I said can I get an 'amen'?"

Tithing plates were passed around at the end of each service accompanied by emotional praise and worship music. Men, women, mothers, fathers and children emptied wallets, purses and piggy banks like they had a fix on a winning horse—and no one doubted a man who could preach like that, take a cover photo like that, or write a book so appealing to the greedy devil in all of them.

The preacher pocketed millions in tax-free cash while his most hardcore followers went bankrupt financially and spiritually, blaming themselves for a lack of faith. Either way, it was desire that destroyed the hearts of men.

In June of '92, the preacher was caught diddling a fifteen year old male model in the back of a stretch limo and was instantly disgraced by the church and media. He was charged with statutory rape, possession of cocaine (there was an ounce of pure on the front seat), and felony assault for striking a female police officer in the face. He did two years in prison, where he befriended an eighteen-year-old hacker doing six for cyber crimes. On the day of his release, the preacher stole a notebook filled with handwritten code from the kid's cell. Ten months later, the first social network on the web, Chatmates.com was officially launched.

Chatmates.com was quite rudimentary at first. Users could create basic personal profiles and gain access to a limited amount of group text and private text chat rooms. Within a year, streaming video technology emerged and it changed everything. Chatmates.com became the first website in history to offer a high-quality, live-streaming video chat option. For the first time ever, people could talk to each other across the globe, face to face in real time.

In December of '96, the preacher sold Chatmates.com to a competitor for a billion dollars and disappeared for a while. A couple months later, he was found dead in a hotel room in Bangkok, Thailand. Suicide. The autopsy revealed fatal amounts of heroin and cocaine in his blood, and blood tests confirmed he was HIV-positive.

Dale shook his head and slid the book back onto the shelf. He skimmed through several stacks of books along the edge of the narrow bookstore aisle, accidentally bumping into an old grisly-looking fellow who'd been searching for a copy of *Bad Eyes* on the lower shelf. The old man shot Dale a dirty look, but he was already busy flipping through Bert Conrad's new poetry anthology.

Bert had recently received the prestigious five-star rating in *Re-Think* magazine, and Dale was curious to see what all the fuss was about.

A Fox, Frozen in the Headlights

In the summer she raises flags
And cannons blast worldwide
The silent war still rages inside her mind
The individual against the herd
The individual against nature.
We are all wretched things
Who dance and tilt
When the piano plays
Oh now you've got soul, poor devil?
Now you've found your groove?
The dance of ruin
For men and beasts.

-Bert Conrad

Dale closed the book in disgust. *Cannons blast worldwide? Pfft. What fake, fabricated horseshit.* As far as he was concerned the poem was shit, and Bert Conrad was a talentless twat. A local rich-kid wannabe trying to act a part. The brooding type. But Bert was the son of Howard Conrad, owner of *Re-Think* magazine, and that meant he had connections, which meant the spoiled brat was given a pass by other local writers on account of those connections, which they all, including Dale, desperately wanted to exploit.

Dale slid Bert's book behind a copy of *Down Low* and made for the door.

*11:13 a.m.*

Dale stepped outside. It was snowing lightly and cold as he walked down Durham Street looking for a bench where he could sit down and smoke.

A pigeon walked by. Dale ripped a chunk off the granola bar he had in his pocket and threw it on the ground. "Enjoy it," he said, gazing listlessly at the peculiar brown bird. ". . . Enjoy the silent nothing."

Dale lit a cigarette, pulled the tattered notebook from his coat pocket and began to write.

Enjoy the silent nothing

A calm ocean

Tomorrow's storm

A violent vision

And then—

The wonder of shattering.

He took a puff. The pigeon had disappeared along with his gift, but now there was a black crow going mad in the street, pecking wildly at a mangled ball of aluminum foil.

Try to find a reason

Amid this chaos

Try to live a second outside yourself

Without a chance to survive.

We were shooting heroin that night.

Oh god—

She was scratching her arm.

And I never stopped doing you wrong.

A homeless man pushing a noisy shopping cart approached Dale's bench from the left. Dale took inventory of the man. He didn't appear to be crippled or handicapped physically, wasn't a raving madman, nor did he appear to be suffering from an illness of any kind. He was around Dale's age in his early thirties, and when he asked Dale for a smoke he used plain English without slurring or stuttering the words, which led Dale to believe the man was either a drug addict, simply too lazy to get a job, or was one of those content-to-be-a-parasite types. Either way he didn't need or deserve another freebie from a guy like Dale who was fighting to survive himself. There were plenty of missions and social services willing to continue enabling this sub-human, bottom-feeders lifestyle.

Dale shook his head in disgust at the sickening smell wafting toward him from the bum's filthy clothing. "Fuck sakes, man. Have some dignity why don't you. You smell like shit."

The bum shrugged and reached into his pocket, pulling out a flattened rollie. "Well, you got a light then, bud?" he asked gruffly.

Dale looked up at him, confused. "But—you just asked me for a cigarette. Fuck outta here, man."

The homeless man swore, muttering something about the system before walking away with the wrinkled-up unlit smoke stuck to his chapped bottom lip. The rattle of his rusty shopping-cart wheels on the sidewalk a caution to passersby about life in the fast lane.

Dale went back to writing.


If I could learn, not to hide, but to harness my contempt
Then that might be a powerful weapon.


He looked up a minute later to make sure the bum was a safe distance away before pulling out his pack of cigarettes again.


To learn to smile
When I'm trying to tear apart with my eyes

Or to stare off ignorantly

When knives penetrate the heads of my enemies

From a vicious, vicious place.

Dale finished his smoke, crossed Durham Street, and went inside the Mine Eyes Café to find a table for his blind lunch date with a woman named Jane St. Marie. A mutual friend named Minnie Calloway thought they would be good for each other seeing as they were both writers and "kind of looking, but not for anything serious."

Dale was hesitant, but Minnie had insisted. "C'mon, Dale. Might do you some good to get off that computer of yours for awhile. You spend too much time on that thing anyways."

Dale still told people that he was a poet and novelist, but he was mostly just blogging and freelancing then, making a little money here and there writing articles for various travel, music and theatre publications. His high standards often prevented him from earning income, seeing as men's lifestyle magazines were all the rage at the time, and he wouldn't dare lower himself to writing at *that* level. He earned the most money through public speaking engagements at creative workshops, seminars and literary events, and he had a fantastic ability to command an audience once his nerves settled. He released his first novel in 1993 to a well-deserved and devoted national readership, but his recent works had garnered little in the realm of national, provincial or even local success, which Dale blamed on a lack of intelligent, free-thinking readers out there, nothing more. Dale felt as though he belonged to an elite group. Those last few living disciples of an aesthetic art form and solitary lifestyle, who had ignorantly been labelled *starving artists* by the same shallow, money-hungry trendsetters controlling the media and the Internet. The same people who allowed, and even encouraged, the Bert Conrads of this world to operate and succeed. So, Dale often resorted to using the Internet and his blog as a platform to strike back at those critics and so-called writers with cruel, scathing, and often ruthless attacks of his own.

Noted, the world Dale grew up in was vastly different to the one he existed in now. Before there was Internet and streaming video on

Chatmates.com, before the forums, blogs, chat rooms, dating sites and free porn, before there was access to unlimited and uncensored information. A time of library cards, books, phone calls and mailing letters, a time of encyclopedias and face-to-face flirting. A time when men went to strip clubs or prostitutes for kicks, and paid small fortunes for live personalized shows like the ones suddenly available at the click of a button on the World Wide Web. A whole generation of VHS-watching, magazine-gawking adolescents became men in the mid to late '90s, and their sexual appetites were literally transformed, essentially supercharged, by the Internet's limitless ability to stimulate, satisfy—and provide an increasing degree of kink, filth and fetish as their preferences evolved beyond just beautiful woman with fake breasts, nice bums and shaved everythings. That was just the beginning; and Dale's interest in this emerging virtual fantasy world, even as a self-professed traditionalist, was well above average.

Jane St. Marie was a writer too, but poetry and fiction were more of a hobby than a vocation for her, even though her first novel received several awards when it was released in 1994. Her true passion was journalism, and she was a highly sought-after writer for her work in environmentalism and sustainability, human rights activism and the arts. She currently wrote for a syndicated news, arts, culture and lifestyle magazine called *The Carriage*, and her freelance journalistic work was regularly featured in many of Canada's top publications. In the past five years she'd been to Tibet, Tijuana and the Middle East— twice. And during the course of her short but illustrious career, she'd been shot at by diamond lords in Liberia, summited the northeast ridge of Everest without oxygen, and nearly died after contracting malaria in a Gambian refugee camp. A week ago she received an elite member frequent flyer card in the mail after returning home from a forty-week-long stay in China. And she was a born-again Christian.

*The Mine Eyes Café*
*11:42 a.m.*

Dale was early and chose a table with a street view so he could see Jane coming and people-watch later on if their conversation got boring.

Jane arrived ten minutes late, at 12:10 p.m., which would have been grounds for a roasting, but Dale let it slide because she happened to be a very attractive and suggestively dressed young woman in her prime at twenty-seven years of age. Jane wore a low-cut white blouse that revealed the right amount of cleavage, and her slender legs were squeezed into a pair of tight, form-fitting black jeans. Based on the vague description that Minnie had given him over the phone, he'd assumed Jane would be a stuffed-up, boring Christian-careerist in a grey skirt-suit, but she wasn't. She was a total knockout. Her wavy natural brown hair, almond-shaped blue eyes, long thick lashes and high cheekbones were all very appealing. He even liked her downwards-sloped nose. Dale glanced at her breasts as she removed her coat, hoping she wouldn't notice. He'd expected so much less and was aggravated now that he'd agreed to meet her here for their first date.

Jane smiled and said, "Hello," then reached across the table to shake hands, but Dale was busy staring at the stained stippled ceiling. The Mine Eyes Café was an okay "coffee and a bite to eat" type of place, but it had a certain "sad motel diner from the past" vibe that made Dale feel uncomfortable. The fluorescent lights flickered overhead and the age-old flamingo-coloured paint on the walls had faded and peeled away in several spots. Dinged-up, wobbly cafeteria style chairs had been covered in a tacky fifties-era mint green poly-plastic, the look of which made Dale nauseous, and the staff working there were all over-the-hill folk singers or painters who'd missed their given windows. *What a fucking shithole*, he thought, unintentionally ignoring her.

Jane cleared her throat loudly. "Hi. I'm Jane," she said.

Dale finally snapped back to reality. "Oh right. Sorry about that. I'm Dale. Nice to meet you, Jane."

*12:17 p.m.*

Jane babbled on and on about anything and everything that came to mind. "I'm a Christian . . . I'm a vegetarian . . . I travel the world for a living . . . I'm a writer . . . I work for a magazine called *The Carriage*. Have you heard of it? Mainly I write arts and culture pieces, but I love writing poetry. Oh, I published a novel in 1994—you might've heard of it. Kind of a true-life, avant-garde, art-noir type think-piece with a spiritual twist. Stylistically, it's like Ola Kant mixed with—well, your stuff, I guess. It got five stars in *Re-Think* magazine, which I was really proud of at the time. But I'm dedicated to my career in journalism and the magazine world now . . . What are you thinking about, Dale?"

He didn't hear a word after—

*Ola Kant.*

Dale had fallen madly in love with Ola after seeing her on stage at the Elgin Street Opera House, playing Wilhelmina, in an opera of the same name that she'd written and composed entirely by herself. It was just over a year ago, and it was the most spectacular thing he'd ever witnessed. Ola was a vision of absolute beauty, and Dale's heart was immediately filled with longing, lust and an unbreakable devotion to her and her amazing talents. She was the most ingenious poet, writer and composer he'd ever seen grace the stage. A true artist. A delicate, curly-haired blond beauty with the saddest eyes and the most heart-wrenching, angelic sounding soprano he'd ever heard. It was as if her voice had come from heaven, her hallowed words etched by the hand of God on flaming tablets floating high above her pretty little head.

It was Ola who extended the invitation that night, and they had a torrid, drug-fuelled love affair in her subterranean home following the performance.

*About a year ago . . .*

*September 2, 1996. The Elgin Street Opera House Presents: Wilhelmina. Sudbury, Ontario.*
*9:02 p.m.*

*Darkness . . . Curtains . . . Lights!*
*Enter Daphne*

DAPHNE
*Praying silently in her flower garden*

JOSIAH
*Lurking about nearby*

"With lips like yours,

There's no need to speak.

In cities of silver,

You are the atmosphere,

In a world of snow."

DAPHNE

"Is his love so rare in peace, as it flowed so fair in war?

Poor gentle flesh,

There is no answer.

I don't know anything—

Anyway,

I don't care.

It doesn't matter.

Suddenly, I feel free."

JOSIAH

"Here we are, alone.

Dancing under lights for serpents.

Your voice I cherish,

Your throne inherit,

A dancing doll— from jeweled hair, to black, to dawn.

What we have won't last forever— what is will not always be.

I'll spend tonight in roses and steel beams of broken glass, blowing bubble-gum kisses filled with my love for you."

DAPHNE

"Josiah, you fool. You speak as though you are an expert, yet you know nothing of true love . . .

Why here?

Why this far from home?

Why here?

Why alone?

Why, why, why?

Why so nostalgic about those days?

Why those songs?

Why so comforting to reminisce?

Why so fond am I?

Why so old now?

Why so hard to die?

Why waiting?

Why then and not now?

Why, why, why?

Why lessons?

Why teachers—students?

Why books?

Why work and no play?

Why tomorrow and not today?"


*Enter Wilhelmina, Daphne's licentious lover, singing softly*


WILHELMINA

"Life's been turned upside down,

Angel hair, angel eyes, in this devil town."

JOSIAH
"Angel hair?"

WILHELMINA
"Angel hair, bleeding from my dear Daphne's hands."

JOSIAH
"You're a fucking kook, Wilhelmina—
Daph . . ."

*Josiah reaches for Daphne's hand*

"I want to forsake this madness,
And let the laughter ring.
I want to be the servant,
I want to be the king.
From my bleeding heart,
To the end of time—"

WILHELMINA
"The sportsman that spent his life training,
But never took the field!
The hunter with perfect aim,
But no heart for the kill.
The man of dreams,
who never sleeps.
The man of flight,
Who will not fly.
The man of wisdom,
Who will not write.
The singer with the voice of beauty,
Who cut out her tongue.

The carpenter who will not wound a tree.

The artist,

Who will not make manifest their pain for all to see.

The doctor,

Who holds the cure,

The miracle worker who will not touch,

The heavens,

Kept contained,

In the name of saving face."

JOSIAH

"I never once claimed to be a hunter!

But I would return every day from the killing fields to trade my gun for a brush,

The mud for city pavement,

The dirt for something better.

Two kinds of hands—

Only one capable of mercy.

Every man has a purpose and he must diligently seek it.

I must go,

To the edge of the unfamiliar wilderness, for you, Daphne."


*Josiah darts off stage*
*A flirty Wilhelmina approaches a forlorn Daphne*


WILHELMINA

"As birds sing songs that enjoy laughter."

DAPHNE

"When you said, 'a bird', he wept."

*Josiah responds from behind the stage curtain*

JOSIAH

"You're both birds, but even birds build nests when it's time to stay awhile!"

DAPHNE

"Something I can't comprehend!

Oh Willa. It's this fog-eaten life. Will I ever shiver?"

WILHELMINA

"I could tell you about the world as it is,

But little child,

Close your ears,

You may not like what you hear."

*Wilhelmina begins running her fingers through Daphne's hair*

"If I wasn't so ugly,

You could probably hide your beauty,

But until I can appreciate you,

My soul is alone.

Through the ice beneath my feet,

Through the spit between my teeth,

I broke the diamond,

It shattered once,

Its name meant nothing,

It became more special now that it was broken.

It was what it was intended to be,

Before it froze

On that cold night,

And took on unintended form.

Blasted by wind,

Ripped by ice and the dark,

The streets claimed it,

Gave it structure,

Gave it ego,

Gave it name and purpose and form,

A perverse breath of life,

And I set it free.

I crushed it underfoot,

And I left it waiting for the warmth of morning.

Men are smashing forms of beauty,

And writing poems about it all the time.

Poems that no one will remember,

Or even understand.

Days are like rivers of ice in my veins,

And my heart grows colder with every new season."

DAPHNE

"As I dream,

Minstrels quietly play a chorus of strings,

But all these things are sad to me.

Eternities wait,

And Cupid's woeful wounds cause my lowly heart to break,

And eyes to cry, as he plays his holy tunes."

WILHELMINA

"I have a bad name among evil.

When I think of you, my wicked heart still thinks it's young.

Your art is your soul mate—

Your lover.

All others are friends.

An art in itself, our love.

Within the ruins of time,

Daffodils spread wings of purple,

And shine like the mountains.

Forget the marketplace,

Where they steal and lie and try to sell your soul back to you.

It's all deception and

I'm so sorry for allowing it in."

DAPHNE

"Your plastic shoes,

We should bleed together on the avenue.

There's something in the mud for you,

These veins—

These veins are filled with love for you."


*Josiah returns, stealing the moment*


WILHELMINA

"They may know *you* by name,

But I've written better books

So they'll worship *my* fame."


*Josiah kneels before Daphne*


JOSIAH

"Abolished my profession,

Surrendered my possession,

Made an image, but cannot hold to it forever.

Done harm to you,

I guess I'll say goodbye.

Elision means sounds left out,

I made my baby cry.

I have no kinder, gentler means,

I've seen your face inside my dreams.

Ceremonies for a chosen few—

There's more to life than just you two."


*Wilhelmina begins laughing*
*Daphne cannot help but join her*


DAPHNE
"Poor boy.

Resting in his palace alone,

Raising children that dance for crumbs,

Your song is like a string boat,

I know it comes together in the end, but—."

WILHELMINA
"Lines are crossed and the animals smile.

In holes they dig

Sewers for themselves,

Another home in

The sewers they live

Where no civilization is."

JOSIAH
"Razor blades on every raindrop,

Ripping into my face, dear Daphne!

Silver bells, silent night,

Now I'm ready to die."

*Wilhelmina plunges a knife into Josiah's back and he falls dead at Daphne's feet*
*Daphne gazes into Wilhelmina's eyes longingly*

WILHELMINA

"The thirst for liberation

Will drive a nation to madness,

And armies of thousands

Become after-thoughts overnight

When they can shout under their own moons,

And are free to roam in the halls,

As slaves they built for kings.

Wear your scar like a memory,

Inside you remains the morning eye,

Bound to die in the strangest colours,

Still we hide away

The sad, sad morning.

Run with me,

I will lay you in roses,

And lust for your fairness

We can dance over Paris.

Magnify the moment,

Pond lily,

These rotting leaves pay well for fire."

DAPHNE
*Looks down at Josiah*

"Some men bleed a lot from open wounds, don't they? Whether they are old or new. Why did we start digging graves the day we were born, Willa?"

WILHELMINA

I sat a thousand nights under the same white moon trying to comprehend my own similar convictions—

So fear of death,

I just came down to the fasting spot."

*Daphne and Wilhelmina kiss each other passionately*

DAPHNE

*Down at Josiah again*

"At his enemy's knee,

He was ready to die."

WILHELMINA

"But you're still beautiful,

And you're not alone while you lose your mind.

Shallow Main Street

Talks of visions to me.

Eager faces towards the sun,

Rising over distances I've been.

I've seen your face in the marketplace,

All over town is where I'll be,

Wishing you a constant farewell

For a voyage to everywhere.

Why we can't muse,

And be each other's gardens.

Your flames,

And my design

Seem incomplete in close proximity.
I'd rise at dawn,
And fill a great page
With words to compliment,
But only come the noon dismay,
The torment,
The absurd response to work,
No retributions made—
You followed me,
And I followed you,
And for once we had a name—
For once.
For time and time again and gone,
Long night and lonely days
I walked alone.
Without your glove,
Without your skin,
Without your skin,
Without your glory,
Without your shining eyes.
Your hand in mine,
Your fingertips,
Your fingerprints,
All over this map of mine.
And my design is flawed,
By the brutal truth,
That it's incomplete.
So what can I do to make thee whole?
I wonder when I might see,

That you loved me like this,

Broken—

Just as I was . . .

I hope I die where it's beautiful."

*Curtains.*
*Applause . . .*

*Behind the opera house. A back alley after the show*
*10:58 p.m.*

It was snowing, and she saw him standing there. "Are you waiting for someone?" she asked.

He turned, and the first thing she noticed was his hair. It was long, dark and wavy, unlike hers, which was naturally curly and only looked good when she cut it short. Her tight blonde ringlets had made her feel insecure and boyish growing up, and she'd often fantasized about having hair like his, especially when she was a young girl.

"I—I was just waiting here hoping to see you, Wilhelmina. I—I wanted to meet you in person. My name is Dale Potoniak, and I wanted to tell you that what you did up there tonight was . . . just amazing. I haven't felt this alive in a long time."

"Aw thank you, Dale. My name's Ola. Ola Kant . . . I really like your hair."

"Pleasure to meet you, Ola. I like your hair, too."

She shook his hand and shivered. His skin was so cold.

"You're freezing."

"I'm okay . . . Can I tell you something?"

"Of course."

"You did something to me tonight, Ola. I can't describe it, but you did. Your voice, and . . . I don't think anybody's written anything more perfect— like, ever. I consider myself a good writer—well, I did before tonight, but—fuck. How did you write that?"

She felt guilty for feeling proud of herself. "I don't know, but I'm glad you enjoyed it. I worried when they told me only half the tickets sold tonight. I put so much work in and nobody—"

"Bulletproof man stomping around now. At the beginning of his life, at the beginning of his first love story. Bulletproof and invisible now. Always a cartoon, always a dream come true . . . That was . . . you . . . are a genius . . . Sorry that was really fucking weird, wasn't it."

She laughed. "No, not at all. I'm flattered, really. Thanks."

"Would you have a drink with me tonight? I know this place nearby that—"

"Sorry, I can't . . . I hope you didn't—"

"No, no, not at all. I totally understand."

"I don't mean it like that, I just really need to be somewhere right now, so—"

"It's fine. Don't worry about it."

". . . Hey listen, if you're not doing anything later, you should come by the old Kingsway Bingo Hall. We can talk writing, and I'll introduce you to my friend Christine—Daphne."

"Really?"

"Sure, why not."

"Yeah? When? What time should I—"

"How about an hour? Just walk in the front door, turn left and you'll see some stairs. Go all the way down. It might look abandoned, but it's not. Well it is, but it isn't, if you know what I mean."

"Yeah of course. That's great, Ola. Sounds perfect."

She smiled and waved then walked away.


*12:02 a.m.*


Dale reached the top of the Lloyd Street hill and saw the old bingo hall below him on the corner of Lloyd and the Kingsway.

The red brick building was covered in graffiti and most of the windows had been nailed or boarded shut. Some were covered in black cloth that beat in the wind. He approached the main entrance, taking caution to avoid stepping on any broken glass or other trash scattered about the twisted path.

The heavy steel door popped open like it was on a spring and banged loudly against the wall inside.

Dale stood in awe in the main lobby of the bingo. The floors, once carpeted in a lovely ruby-red floral pattern, were now covered with a layer of grey dust, and the walls were covered in graffiti and slogans like, "I came here because I couldn't handle living with a loose cannon anymore. She was just too hard to please."

Dale's eyes adjusted to the light inside and he moved slowly toward the centre of the huge rectangular lobby. He noticed a confection stand to his left, still open for business. A make-shift sign indicating there were hot dogs, pop, ice-cream bars and cigarettes for sale there, and two people—a middle-aged man and an older woman were tending the counter. Both were unkempt and dirty-looking and wore the original dark-red circa-1950 bingo uniforms, along with hats to match. They looked dreadful and sleepy, and paid no attention to Dale's prolonged stare. He wondered if they'd even noticed him come in.

Dale's gaze swept right, away from the confection stand. His wonder quickly turned to shock, as he saw what was once the main bingo hall. It looked like it might have been an old theatre before, but the roof had collapsed and there were no lights inside so it was hard to tell. He imagined all the hours people had been spent in there singing, laughing, smoking cigarettes and having their dreams crushed, missing letters, numbers.

He walked toward an exit sign at the back left corner of the lobby, indicating a stairwell, that upon closer inspection, descended to unfathomable depths. The ceiling in the stairwell was Styrofoam that had been white once, but had turned an awful hue of brownish green from a century of stale air, mildew and cigarette smoke. The walls were a strange-looking stone, glimmering emerald green at the bottom, changing to a sickly institutional green near waist height. Some sort of glazed concrete perhaps.

He proceeded down the first flight of stairs and recalled in horror the stories he'd heard about places like this downtown where intravenous drug users congregate and squat. Surely Ola wasn't one of *them*, he thought, making a mental note not to touch anything unless absolutely necessary.

There was a rusted metal door at the bottom of the second set of stairs with a worn-out "members only" sign on it. Dale heard voices and decided to investigate. The room was quite big, but lit by just a couple fluorescent bars on the ceiling which made everything inside slate-blue.

The hot smell of urine suddenly stung his nostrils, and he realized his suspicions were true. There were at least twenty people inside, all partaking in, or preparing for intravenous drug use. *Their hideous faces.* Only one of them, a girl, noticed a change in the air as he stepped inside. She glanced up for a second, made eye contact, then looked away again without saying a word. She sat cross-legged on the concrete floor, and looked cold and tired, hungry. Dale figured her for twenty-five or thirty, but couldn't tell for sure. She might have been a lot younger, and would've been pretty before all this.

There were a few of them prostrate amongst the filth, and he took care when stepping over their bodies and the dirty needles strewn between them.

He saw blank, tortured eyes. *Blank.* So blank, tortured and sleepless, like tired human batteries running off some perverse, human version of mosquito blood-lust. The complete and utter torment in their hollowed out black eyes. Some of them could be mistaken for dead, even. It was as if for a moment there was no one. Only the sin, only the death, only the disease. *To carry the weight of the world. Christ on the cross, looking into the future, into this place, into the hearts of these ... into my heart.* But no one here was innocent. They chose to stay here, and they'd wasted their entire lives hoping to remain unjudged, and lived for years in this darkness, quietly praying for salvation and dreaming dreams of white light while on the nod.

For a split second, Dale forgot why he'd come here in the first place. *Ola.* She was waiting for him somewhere in the depths below, but he felt a strange urge to sit and stay with these people, like a curious kid in a cemetery. But there was more to see, so he turned around and headed back to the stairwell.

Dale stood expressionless— motionless—for a while, at the top of the next set of stairs looking down. He needed a cigarette, so he reached into his pocket for his pack and a fold of matches, taking a long drag before continuing his descent into the darkness.

Halfway down, his mind began to drift. He saw a twinkle, a poem, a ballad for the girl who looked up. It floated by like a banner on a plane and read, *With baby in arm, I might try to clothe you. Before you lay your head down, know this . . . You lay in your own ash, frozen, in an expanse of abomination and potential.* Suddenly his legs would not support the weight assigned to them. He dropped the cigarette and fell forward, but a flicker of light from a single bulb below him lit the path a little further.

The staircase ended. He'd reached the bottom. *Go all the way down.* The floor was wet and muddy, a mixture of scum and slime from leaking pipes and trash left behind by those dwelling in the bowels. To his left and right were corridors that went on for about a hundred metres in both directions, both with several doors on each side. Images of what he might encounter if he opened a few of them flashed though his head and he shuddered, but managed to keep his wits about him. If it wasn't for a few halogen bulbs on the ceiling still flickering their pale yellow light, it might have been a completely different story.

Dale's heart skipped a beat. He heard voices and faint conversation in the distance. Pleasant-sounding, amidst the most unpleasant place he'd ever been. They were pretty-sounding female voices, and he walked slowly in their direction, pushing open a creaky door. He tried adjusting his eyes to the darkness inside as if there was actually light inside to adjust to. There was. A tiny light. So tiny he barely noticed it. It looked like a candle in the middle of a empty baseball stadium. So faint and small, but glorious and friendly feeling amid the desolate blackness. It was far away, maybe fifty feet to the right, and that's where the voices were coming from. Dale tiptoed, but there was broken glass everywhere, making his presence obvious to anyone—or anything within earshot. A gust of cool air passed directly in front of him and every hair on his head stood up. His body stiffened into a singular muscle and his eyes bulged from his head like a spider-hawk.

He made a mad dash towards the light and the voices he'd heard. They were close now, and he could make out certain phrases.

"We are so ugly when we argue . . . Beauty lies in ruins, and you are everywhere . . . I have yet to meet a John the Baptist . . . Never trust a dead guy." Things like that.

Dale felt better knowing they were human and could speak his language. He took a deep breath, turned the knob and pushed the door open. He'd found the boiler room.

"Hey!" a voice in the shadows screamed.

Dale was scared shitless and jerked his head to the right. His eyes adjusted to the light and the voice produced a face. It was Ola.

"To never shed a tear for you, in darkness let me live. Forget your cares and love me, in darkness let me give. Leave your life, your life to me, but never let me go. Just sit and wait just one more day, the pageant and the snow . . . Until I've soaked in so much sin, my soul is rotted from within—but now I'm ready. This place is wrong in every way, but you—you are beautiful."

Ola clapped her hands. "Well done! But is that all there is? Is that how he meets the girl?" she asked, greeting Dale with a smile.

"It has to be," Dale answered, astounded by her beauty.

She stood up and took him by the hand, guiding him toward the light where Daphne sat. "Christine, this is Dale. The guy who was waiting for me outside after the show. Dale, this is Christine. Better known as 'Dear Daphne.'"

"Hey," Christine said, uninterested. She was busy cooking up.

"I can't believe you actually came," Ola said, plunking back down on the floor beside Christine. "I didn't think you'd actually come all the way down here just for me."

"Are you kidding? I'd do anything for—"

"Aww, you fucked it, Christy. Give it here, I'll do it," Ola said, grabbing the lighter and spoon from Christine's hands.

Dale sat down beside Ola. "What's it like?" he asked.

"What's what like?" Ola said, moving the lighter side to side beneath the silver spoon. The brownish liquid inside began to bubble.

"Heroin," Dale answered, softly.

"Wanting is pure bliss and eternal," Christine said, with a tired smile. "Satisfaction is temporary orgasm of the mind, body and soul. It's highly addictive. Loss is a freezing of the part of you that cares. Numbed until you can forget and live more afterward. Gain is coincidental and quick. Spent, used, smoked, snorted, shot up— it's fast. A day, sometimes less, but it's beautiful. Even the day after. Some days you can ride the wave into another dark night and days that float by like grace. Some days you shutter in disgust, face reality and become real again. You see it for what it is. You see what you are and you want to kill yourself on the way here. To be a junkie is one thing. To know what you are, and the sudden dawning of that reality on you can be a scary thing. Saddening, but sometimes satisfying. Trying to defy what you are—I always have to say, 'what you have become,' in this instance, along with the previous statement—but to embrace the meaninglessness and dwell in the darkness daily, living opposite of everything the world admires becomes an almost sickening Zen. A nirvana reached by few, touched by many, but turned away by those who cannot see the beauty in the destruction of themselves."

Dale looked at Ola, raising his eyebrows.

"Like she said." Ola giggled. "So—you wanna try?"

"Oh shit, I uh—" Dale stammered.

"No pressure," Ola said.

"No, I know. Sure. I mean, yeah. What's one time right? But—"

"But what?"

"The needle is clean, right?"

"Of course. Christine just opened this one. See— the wrapper's right there. You can go first if you want."

"Okay," Dale said, looking nervously at the needle.

"Here, baby. Like this. You tighten this around your arm and pull the ends real tight . . . There you go. Nice. You got good veins."

"Ouch!" Dale cried, as the needle pierced his skin.

"It's the end of summer, and you feel pain when I bring you roses?" Ola squeezed the stopper slow.

*Heroin.* "Whoa . . . Your blessed needle. Breaking into innocent melodies . . . Canvassing for a purpose we all had once. Sour and sad. A note in your voice, I float on stages with silk and black . . . Oh my god, that feels good."

"My turn," Christine said, grabbing the gear.

"Face to face with the creature, and it made him feel strange," Ola said, kissing Dale softly on the cheek. Dale weaved side to side, his eyes half open, a contended smile. "Now me," Ola said. "They say suicide is painless. Tell me lies."

*3:13 a.m. Heroin.*

A small battery-operated radio played opera arias and minor symphonies nearby. Ola and Dale lay side by side on Ola's bed, which was nothing more than a plastic mattress and some blankets on the concrete floor. Christine had retired to her own room in some other part of the building shortly after taking her hit.

"I wonder what it felt like looking down from the cross," Dale whispered. "The nails are in—hands, feet. They've hoisted the tree or post or pole into the hole and—I imagine it being mostly agony—mostly physical pain. The kind that can't be ignored, but for a moment he must have had a realization, an acceptance, and then wondered . . . and then—I don't know."

"They have crucified me. Messenger of love. Giver. The hope for peace. They shunned the light because it exposed all the dirty little secrets in their hearts. I spoke and they would not listen. They wanted soft pillows and a way to heaven that didn't include pressure or pain. They crucified me and now my life is over. And I don't know what's going through my mother's head. She must be so sad—but knowing humans, I bet she's wishing it turned out some other way. That this was some other woman's son up here on this cross. Why did it have to be him? Why did it have to be *my* son? Why was I chosen to bear a martyr? Aware that this world could not but kill that which would set it free." A tear fell from Ola's eye, but Dale couldn't see.

"I went to Bell Park the other day. There was a madman behind a statue, chasing pigeons and swearing at them. He was spitting at them. Apparently they were an inconvenience to him somehow. Somehow he'd justified spitting on the birds . . . He's hit the nail now and there's no turning back. He's tasted blood, and he's felt the mad universe scream for more. He's joined along in some sad solitary march to another Calvary here in this present age. 'This too will kill me,' he screamed."

"I let go of those romantic images a long time ago. I walk with my head down and my hands in my pockets now. I don't even listen to music anymore unless it's behind closed doors. And I don't get too close to the streets anymore—not like I used to. I look, but not for long, and I don't get too close to buildings anymore . . . When I see a picture I like, I walk the streets and everything smells the same. Sometimes I get a hint of spring and my heart jumps, and I feel my feet getting antsy, but usually I just keep walking along with my head down . . . I'm not going that far . . . Nothing's too exciting these days and that's the way I like it. I don't want to get too close to these streets and those images anymore. They get me going—and for what? For nothing . . . I like it like this. Slow. I feel good right now, but soon I'll need a good cry. I'll need to break it all back down—all that music I've hidden away. All those back pages and stories I never wrote—they'll get revisited. I'll get on my knees, on my face, right here, right now and kiss the dirt, sleep it off, shake it off. These streets will wake you up, break you up, shake you up, let you live, let you breathe. I'm going to open my eyes on a hot sunny day and go take it all in, smile, sing. It'll be a day for images, and a day for loving and everything will come together in a triumphant circular motion tying together the spring, summer, fall and winter with the holy knot of love. And I won't bother with these mental parasites . . . I know salvation is right there. One cry away. It could come raging in to change the season, but I like things the way they are right now. Quiet, calm—like this aria. But this too will come crashing down. Listen. It always breaks to pieces. It always goes back to nothing. That's where you should always be, Dale, but you like to get too close to these ideas, I can tell. You're black and white, but don't tell me black is white just because you find the truth too hard to see."

"About your voice—I'd die for you. And the nature of truth leaves no room for doubt, but images aside, you're the one I've tried to be. When you saw me by the window, I was praying on my knees. I witnessed you floating by the bar, beside the stairs . . . My eyes were captivated by your jewellery, and your plain black dresser drawer, left open from the night before, revealing a corset and a letter to your fantasy lover."

"Feeble prayers and feeble desires for synthetic things we do not require. This too shall pass and in time will go by the wayside by the power of the eternal word."

"Sometimes I want to take your words and wash myself in them until I drown. Ola, I've been searching my whole life, and now I've found you"

"I do not doubt our connection, I doubt my ability to keep it. I do not doubt our immortality, I doubt my familiarity with the current state of mortality. I do not fear death, but what a horrible punishment—eternal pain. What a horrific threat to keep us in line with. We may feel that we've suffered for love, but love would never cause us pain."

"I could carry you in my arms and you'd never have to cry about bad dreams. You could bring me your sadness, I could take away your broken heart. I can take away everything you've ever wanted gone, but I don't know what that is—do you?"

"I can't be what you want me to be, but you might like what I become. I don't understand the hesitation, why I can't be motivated for us. My hands are tied behind my back and my time is spoken for. I write by candlelight every night and it's easy to love beauty like that. It's easy for men like you to fall in love under these lights . . . It always makes me sad when I think about the '60s. It's always sad to see a candle burn out. But always remember that there's a dancer dancing where others just watch. There's a singer singing where others just watch. There are people just watching, off somewhere else, robbing themselves of the majesty of now."

"I'm sure they're lonely too, when they go to sleep. We're not the only ones."

"The truth is, I don't want to die. I'm afraid that I won't say what I should to whom I should . . . I won't do suicide, but you can't—won't stop me from dying inside."

"Ola—"

She was crying now. "No. No more, Dale . . . I need more drugs."

*4:32 a.m. Cocaine.*

"Every junkie is a blemish on my soul!" Ola screamed, thrashing about the room in a hysterical rage. "Oh my god the father, please! What did we ever do to bring about this disease? A rock-hard killer eating at my knees as I beg for mercy! So perverse in nature, yet truly hiding nothing. Bringing forth people's ugliness. Fucked up twisted whores, camel people, brick world, moose people, square world, klink, chlink, freeer, gleerr, weeeer! Poor fish! I left him to die in a fishbowl in China . . . I just want to be beautiful. Not to boast or brag. Not to you, not for her or for any other reason I can think of other than when I look at myself on camera or on film, or in the mirror, I want to feel the way I feel about you—for myself. I want to be glad it's me. I want to feel jealousy that it's me. I want to be so beautiful that I can love myself."

"You are beautiful. More beautiful than silver. We're meant to go through this life in twos—"

There was violence hovering in the air around her like pestilence. Something from her past was eating her alive, and only she could hear the accusers hideous, guttural snarling. But Dale recognized the shame of innocence lost. "I'm just a little girl," she cried.

"Ola . . . We're meant to go through life in twos."

"I'm just a little girl . . . It feels like my heart is breaking."

*5:48 a.m. Comedown.*

"Sleep baby, sleep," Dale whispered. Ola writhed on the bed and he knew in his heart there was no God out there watching out for her. There were tears in her tanzanite eyes. This poor girl who knew she was a long way from home. He knew his eyes had now seen the worst depravity this earth could spew out, and all he could do was hold her little head and let her cry, her curly blond hair pillowing his cheek, as they shared a moment more intimate than anything he'd ever imagined possible. *She never sleeps. She is a pale, pale white. And in the eyes of a fatherless child did I see the tears of absolute sadness. She's still out there waiting in the dark for her daddy, somewhere.*

"The sky is so ugly today," she said quietly. "It hurts to be alive. Every sound is so wrong when the drugs are gone and my heart . . . my heart is breaking.."

"Shh, dearest. You rest now . . . Would you like to hear a poem I wrote just now?"

"Please."

"I would close my eyes tonight,

And sleep away the aches,

Sleep away the modern life,

Sleep away the shakes.

I'd rest with you tonight,

And just lie—lie in bed,

Lie away the fast life,

Lie away the dread.

Candles, umbrellas,

There's nothing more for me,

Than the sound of your boot heels,

Clicking on the street.

Looking the way you look right now this very instant—

Coming home to me—

I'll take that.

My queen kissed me, I'm better now,

But she's been betrayed by a careless kiss.

Our master plan was dear to my heart,

There is nothing built that won't fall apart.

Sea to sea you shine like heroin,

Poison me, I'm happiest when we're skin to skin."

For a brief moment, Ola smiled. "After all this time, I realized you gave your life for mine. And I'm godless without you. You know how the colours are gone from us now. I wish I could shine like you do, Dale. Why do I hate the sun? Hate who I am. Every day I write another suicide note, speak wisdom, babble about nothing—waste away. Jesus Christ, you said you'd be by my side forever . . . What a funny life. Lots of pain, lots of suffering, all for those we love . . . The thought that is nothing masquerades itself in the public places of my mind. The thing I feared has come upon me, and then we fell in love. The thing I fought so hard to avoid became comfortable and warm, and so it goes with time, and so it goes with being and just surrendering to what is . . . You need to ruin this, until I finish you." Ola sat up and did the last line of cocaine, then lit a cigarette and laid back down.

*Why did you teach me to carry the world when I see a broken heart?* "Ola, I'm afraid of you. More so of myself—what I'd do for you. I'd let you have it all . . . All of my pure. I feel like I'm falling into you. And as for the brokenness . . . The cracked wall sounds like a million children crying. All without hope, falling towards an uncertain glamour. You are mine and I'd take you home with me. I'd let your crack grow in my own life, and prolong the legacy of your father before you. Even though your destiny has you disgraced, on your knees at the foot of a flag you once despised—begging, even loving the potential they have sold you, your brokenness will become health and your filth will become clean. You will be washed in the blood I claimed was nothing. Maybe your crack will grow from my garden, and when you've reached the top we can meet in the middle, and I can show you your brokenness. " He wanted to hurt as she did. He wanted to feel her pain, like it would somehow bring them closer together.

She kissed him.

*There is a Judas.* "It was written in your eyes," he said, "while we made something you won't talk about. The poison has you, and now it's licking at my skin. I can't stay here and wait for you to realize that . . . But what if you could forgive me for leaving? I remember you said your heart was breaking and now I'm stealing from the dead. I wonder how that gets punished." Dale stood up. "I'm sorry I didn't hold you longer. I should've stayed forever, but I want to hide face and save tomorrow for another sad. I'm sorry I didn't kiss you like a real man."

"I always knew it would end like this. In your arms, and my tears."

"Come with me," Dale pleaded.

"Baby, I've told you like a million times. I cannot follow you today, and it won't change tomorrow . . . There's this feeling you get when you're about to leave a place—not homesick, but you miss the person you are at that very moment because you like what you've become in that place . . . If I came with you now, would I be free? If I left this place, would I be happy? If I picked up and just set out, could I find someone to love me?"

"I love you . . . I love you."

"Who do you love—me? Sin? You sin and my heart is cold. You can deny the truth, but you cannot deny the power of the truth. It's not about *what* comes out of a room, but *who* comes out of a room."

"Some people live in homes, most people live in prisons. I found a girl who lives in pine tree cellars and alleyways. I thought I died and went to heaven tonight. This— it—she—can't be real. You can make a paradise inside these walls, Ola, and it'll be great for a while, but you might want to step out for a minute—and then what? Does it really matter if life just keeps us preoccupied?"

"Forgetting that I feel horror? I'll never feel like that willingly. I'll never let you lure me in, and I'll never say yes when I want to say no. I'll never feel ugly again and I'll never be contained. I'll never be so helpless. I'll never stay when I should walk away and I'll never be yours because sometimes I am born into the day, reborn to a new experience. Eyes wide open like a newborn baby. But over time I recede back into familiar darkness where ignorance is okay. I rise and fall, but life is lived or not at all . . . We either live by inspiration or die from boredom. And it's not worth living if you're not living free. I'll never let you have power over me because of my guilt. I will always forgive myself. I won't allow you to remain in me. I won't remember you or hate myself for loving you like I have tonight. I will not give you the honour of living in my mind. I will go on without you. You don't even exist on a page yet. I have a gift and I don't know how to use it, I have a drug—I just abuse it. No matter where I go I can't escape myself. Laughing at the maniacal hallucination . . . Like I said before, the channels change so quickly you'd barely have time to get accustomed to the static."

"I never thought I'd laugh like this in September."

"The confusion continues, but you'll learn the cosmic laugh that only a raving lunatic can get below when he gets to know the mystery behind the whole mad comedy and its design. Now all we have to do is live and die and fill, fill, fill, fill, fill the time."

"Who are you? You're so unique."

"Just a girl who's had a lot of lazy days, and I never grow tired of dreaming of my next one."

"Light?"

"Light."

"Whilst thou not weep this day, for the locusts of death pour hence to your shores. From the darkness emerge a fallen arch angel crying forth her blasphemous words. She tears till blood doth spill forth, and spirits seep from wounds so deep. Should I fill mine eyes with fruit so sweet to touch and eat, or will thou grant my lips one last unholy kiss?"

"With your flesh exposed you may have one wish—but first, ask me a question.

"What?"

"Ask me a question."

"About what?"

"Anything."

"Okay. What's the meaning of life?"

"Good one . . . Life is so fragile. I'm just looking for something to worship. This pursuit of happiness will lead us to something we can get down on our knees in front of and—"

"Wrong. It's whatever gets you through the day."

"Ecstasy and tits, girls and dark desire, and all the things men mean to acquire only prove my heart needs a different kind of love. And here I am by the ocean, all dressed in Halloween black for you."

They kissed, then made love.

"I can't be found," she said, afterwards. "I can't be found any-where . . . I'm always moving from one place to the other. Don't judge me for what I think is best . . . I am the water, I am the worst. I am the screaming rage, I am the thirst. From where the bird man sells local butchers innocent blood, at the end of everything, I am the first . . . I'll bury your romance, I'll bury your blood, and birds and mud, and hang them on a mantle. At the end of everything, I'm still that little girl, pretending this will be over."

Dale now knew that if he stayed she'd make him bleed bad. Her bottom was too deep. It was time to go back to work. Time to plant, sow and bleed in other ways. It was time to *do*, so there might be fruit and harvest to bring this girl in the summer months, and because books should be written for we all have spiritual ears.

"I looked at the tree in my backyard yesterday. In winter it bears no fruit, yet lives in anticipation of a better season," Dale said, starting to dress himself. "And I don't know who will prostitute this tomorrow, but I want some reasons for the state you're living in."

"I want forgiveness for a lifetime of sin."

"This palace of parasites—"

"A lot of 'dear moms' that were never intended to make it . . . Oh Dale, why do I feel like I have no home when I can feel you opening your door to me every night before I fall."

She was gone. The madness of her sorrow had made her disappear, and there was nothing left that morning but her voice and her talent.

"Ola . . . Goodbye, Ola. And so long to sunrise. I want to know what's in your head. Songs for baby children? Mothers can't stop to weep? Papa, hold my hand—I want to sleep, but I can't. When you were my age, did you wish that you were dead?"

"New York City, on a boulevard between a coffee shop display and neon lights, between gutters and stars, pavement and purity, lights and eyes, skies and signs—all of them ours. This is our world and I want to grow old in it with you . . . They have fresh juice bottled for everyone and donations to the cripples, and awful pollution."

"You're really something else . . . Ola, I love you, Ola."

"No. No more, Dale . . . Just go."


*7:43 a.m.*


Dale climbed the Lloyd Street hill. He could see home in the distance, across the tracks. *Interesting revelations at dawn today,* he thought. *I saw familiar, yet curiously unfamiliar places I've been before. Landscapes that I've permanently painted myself upon. Street corners that are mine. Stories of the ghetto that I can recite from memory now, and the memories are real, of course, but the character has changed. A separation has occurred. And the witch from last night—I made her bite me, I let her burn me, and I made her use me.*


"Are you okay?" Jane asked. "You kind of zoned out for a while there."

Dale looked down from the ceiling. "What the fuck do you know about Ola Kant?" he snapped. "And how the hell do *you* even know who she is?"

"What's *that* supposed to mean?" Jane said, genuinely offended by his insinuation.

Dale knew he'd come on too strong. "Sorry about that," he said, covering his face with his hands. "It's just—never mind."

"It's okay," she said, unsure, but sensing something deeper at the root of his outburst. "Can I just say something? I read your book after Minnie told me about you . . . Your writing has a marvelous raw energy. Your choice of words and the way you design each line is so . . . powerful.

"Thanks . . . I appreciate that, Jane." The compliment felt genuine and it helped him refocus for a moment, until—

"Speaking of Ola Kant," Jane said, casually, "there she is. God, she's beautiful, isn't she? That's weird. We were just talking about her and now she's across the street smoking a cigarette. God I missed this city."

Dale's hands began to tremble. His blinking became virtually uncontrollable, opening, closing, clenching and tightening. His throat knotted up and he was afraid a heart attack would take his life away at any second. He tried his best to act as though nothing was wrong, but there was no way to hide *that*.

Donizetti started playing over the speakers a minute later, and he broke off communication with her completely, staring dolefully out the window at Ola. Jane went on blabbing on about edible plants and what it was like living in Beijing.

". . . Well, I should get going," Jane said a while later.

Dale wasn't sure how long he'd zoned out for this time because Ola was gone and the crowded cafe had thinned out significantly. "Uh—yeah. Okay. Let's go. I'm done too, I guess."

*Why?* he thought. Why did *she* show up at that very moment? He put his coat and scarf on and threw a ten on the table without asking the waitress for the bill.

Jane fixed a scarf around her neck and reached out to shake Dale's hand. "It was nice to meet you, Dale. This was—interesting."

Dale shook her hand, bashfully. "You too, Jane . . . You know we could try this again sometime—I mean, if you want to."

Jane loved his eyes. She loved his look and the whole mysterious "writer" vibe. But most of all she loved his hair. It was long and dark, and flowed naturally over his narrow shoulders. A gust of wind blew snow up around him, and for a few seconds he looked perfect. His faded brown boots and black peacoat gave him an impression of self-worth and quiet, selfless humility. She giggled and said, "Wow. Your hand is really cold, Dale."

"Bad circulation," he answered, shoving his hand nervously into his coat pocket.

She smiled, but he wouldn't look her in the eyes.

"Okay. We will, for sure—do this again I mean," Jane said. "I'm in town for another week, then I head to Toronto for this—" She couldn't tell if he was bored senseless, shy or just frozen stiff. "Never mind. We'll keep in touch . . . Take it easy, Dale." She leaned in to hug him, then walked away.

Dale watched Jane turn the corner, then fumbled for his pack of cigarettes. He replayed the whole brutal ordeal over and over again in his head, leaning heavily against the glass window of the cafe. There was no use running after Jane now. There was no use trying to explain to her what had happened. About Ola, about everything. He tossed the cigarette away and decided to go to O' Reegan's Pub for a drink instead of going home.

*After one too many, Dale wanders into Ola's room. The basement of the old bingo.*

*11:42 p.m.*

"Dale? What are you doing here? I told you not to—"

She was about to shoot up.

"I saw you out the window."

"So?"

"So? Don't you get it? I was with someone else today. I tried feeling something—anything—for her, but I couldn't. She was beautiful, sexy and smart—but I love *you*, Ola . . . Come live with me. Let me save you from this place. I'll give you everything your heart desires . . . Please, Ola . . . Please?"

Ola could tell he was wasted. "You're drunk again, Dale." She sighed.

"Yeah, so?"

"So—I told you the last time you barged in here like this. I'm not ready."

"What do you mean you're not ready?"

"I mean I'm not good for you, baby. I want to be, but I'm not. Look at me. Maybe soon, but not right now."

"I don't care what you said before and I don't care what you think right now. I know I'm strong enough to love you."

She sighed again. "Oh, Dale."

"What? You think I'm gonna start doing heroin just because you do? I wanna—I just wanna love you, Ola. You're my princess."

"I don't *think it*, Dale, I *know* it. I can't do that to you. How could I live with myself if that happened?" Dale shook his head in frustration. "I see the sadness in you, Dale. I see your emptiness. The way you crave recognition. I see the ways you try to fill that hole with anything and anyone that's around at the time. The way you use your blog and the Internet to create a different world for yourself—a different personality. You're an addict, Dale. It's all addict behaviour. You're paving a road that leads to unnatural endings, and whoever it is that you're trying to be, and whatever it is that you're doing— including trying to save me—won't stop you from being sick with the disease."

"That's bullshit."

"We're more alike than you think, you know. I'd be bad for you—at least right now I would be. We both need to be patient and wait until I'm—"

"What? Wait for you to what? Get off heroin? It's already been a year. When's it gonna be, Ola? When? How long do you expect me to keep waiting? Time is running out!"

"What's that supposed to mean?"

"It means I'm not gonna wait for you to decide who you love more, me or your precious needle!"

"Oh, Dale. Dale, listen. Come sit . . . I was going to tell you tomorrow, and you know I hate telling you news when you're as drunk as you are, but now that you're here—"

"I'm not *that* drunk."

"Sit please . . . Baby, I promise you. I'm getting off this stuff. I am. I know you can't wait forever and I don't expect you to. I just need a little more time with it before I—"

"Before you what?" Dale cried, nearly sobbing.

"Before I get married."

Dale looked at her, horrified. "Married? To who?"

Ola giggled. "To you, you big jerk. Who else would I marry? We're gonna move to the country and watch TV all day and get fat, and we'll write and travel the world together, just us. I told you, baby, you just need to be patient . . . This is what I wanted to tell you— my news. I finished my latest opera."

Dale perked up. "The new one? You did?"

Ola beamed. "I did! And I sent the scores to a friend of mine who works at the *Teatro dell'opera, Milano,* and—"

"And what?"

"And he loved it! He wants to take it on the road to thirty major opera house across Europe this spring, and after that who knows! He's offered to finance the whole thing for me. He and his partner have this production company and—this is it, Dale. This is my shot. Europe!"

"Ola, that's amazing, but—"

"But what?"

"That means— you're leaving."

Ola nodded.

"When? For how long?"

"I leave in a week. The tour kicks off in May and wraps around September, but, like I said, who knows."

Dale felt upset. "So, like a year? Wow . . . What about getting married?"

"I'll fly home when you least expect it and whisk you off to Prague or Berlin and we'll live there happily ever after."

"When you get back?"

"When I get back."

Dale took her by the hand. "In that case . . . I don't have a ring, but—Ola Kant, will you marry me?"

"Yes. Yes I will." She kissed him passionately, but pulled away. "Dale there's something else."

"What is it, Ola?"

"I'll be gone for awhile . . . You can't just sit around in that little apartment of yours for the next year waiting for me to come back."

"Fuck do you take me for?"

"I'm serious, Dale. I want you to live."

"Live?"

"Yes. I want you drink and dance, and sing and worship life before you're a married man."

"What do you mean?"

"I mean I want you to suck the marrow out of life, Dale. I want you to be wicked, wild and free, and completely unabashed for the first time in your life. I want you to be the confident, fire-breathing man you truly are, and pass through the merciless night into naked dawn, uncovered and unashamed."

"Be a little more specific, Ola."

"I mean you can see other women while I'm gone—if you want to . . . because when you least expect it I'll be back—and I'm coming for you, Mr. Potoniak. This might be goodbye for now, but we were born for each other, Dale, and we'll be together soon. This time for good."

"You want me to fuck other girls while you're away?"

"See them, fuck them. If you want to, sure."

"I'm not sure I do."

"Then don't. But live."

"I thought we agreed that dates were okay, but sex was off limits."

"This is different."

"Well, what about you?"

"Me?"

"Were you planning on sleeping with other guys in Europe?"

"Should I?"

"No."

"Okay, I won't."

"But you don't care if I do?"

"Should I?"

"I would."

"It doesn't bother me like it bothers you."

"Why not?"

"I don't know. I trust you. As long as it's not someone I know then the idea of you fucking another woman . . . sort of turns me on."

"It does?"

"Mm-hmm. It makes me really . . . wet. Tell me about this girl you were with today."

"She's a writer . . . Very pretty."

"Mmm."

Dale slid his hand up her skirt.

"What colour were her eyes?"

"Blue . . ."

They made love.

"Can we write letters?" Dale asked, a few minutes later.

"Of course we can," Ola replied, kissing his forehead.

"I can't do it without letters."

"I'll probably be real busy, but I'll write when I can."

"Thank you . . . Ola?"

"Yes?"

"I love you."

"I love you too, Dale."

She'd be back in a year. They'd get married and their fairytale fantasy would be complete. And Ola was right. Why waste a year waiting when there were scores of eligible, eager young women out there looking for unattached, guilt-free fun? Dale first thoughts were of Jane St. Marie.

For the next two days, Dale read every piece of Jane's writing he could get his hands on. He borrowed her novel from the Mackenzie Street library and read it in three hours, then printed a stack of her poetry off the Internet before purchasing the last six issues of *The Carriage* from Marion Black's Bookstore. Eventually, he called Minnie Calloway to beg her for Jane's mailing address. At first Dale wanted to apologize to Jane for his boorish behaviour and ask her for a second date, but after doing some reading and research, the familiar urge to school another institutionally trained "writer" took centre stage, consuming his bitter, fragile, love-sick heart.

Dale determined that throughout her career, Jane had broken several cardinal rules in the writer's code and would inevitably learn her lesson the hard way for sinning in such ways. For example: her degree from the University of Toronto—sure she'd graduated at the top of her class; no one said she was stupid—but Jane had what she had because she paid some dumb school a hefty tuition, wrote some papers, then all of a sudden, four years later, they threw her a party and told her she was a "writer" now. But the question that concerned Dale most was the same question that would concern any *real writer* out there: had Jane St. Marie paid her dues? Dale sure as shit knew he had. He knew Ola had, too. Had Jane ever walked barefoot through the fires of abuse, addiction and lost love? Had she ever felt the sting or heard the deafening silence of a thousand rejection letters? Had she ever been told no by anyone at all?

If Jane really was an apprentice of the literary arts as she claimed to be, she'd realize mighty quick that authenticity cannot be bought once she read something poignant and well designed by a true master of the craft like himself. Perhaps she could write a little reminder in her Bible cover to never compare her institutionally manufactured, so-called *writing* with his, or Ola's, ever again.

It took Dale ten minutes to handwrite the letter on a lovely sheet of vellum paper he'd been saving for a special occasion like this. He read it over once and it sounded good.

His walk had a boyish skip to it. A fresh youthful-feeling energy. He whistled as he rode the elevator down to the lobby of his apartment building, letter in hand.

"Need some help?" Dale asked, smiling at a tall, tanned blond with cat eyes as the elevator door opened. She was obviously moving into the building that day and was struggling with a box of heavy things.

"It's okay," she said, smiling back at him. "I've got help. Thanks though."

Dale took a few steps toward her. "Are you sure? I got nothing else to do. Really, I was just about to send this letter out and—" Dale stopped short as the blond's shit-brick-house boyfriend appeared out of nowhere behind her carrying several boxes at once.

"That's the last of it, babe," he said, leaning sideways to kiss her. "Just the love seat in the back of my truck." The steroid-using football lover gave Dale a hard look. "Fuck you lookin' at, bud?"

Dale lowered his gaze and slipped the letter into the outgoing mail slot, tripping over one of the blonds boxes as he spun around.


Dale Potoniak and Emmett Dorry had been best friends since kindergarten. Now, at thirty-one years of age, Emmett was a short, pudgy man with a hairless baby-face and aspirations of becoming a poet/novelist while moonlighting as a carpenter to pay the bills. A real top-notch guy who cared deeply for his friends and family.

Emmett was extremely introverted as a youngster, so his parents saw to it that he and Dale played on the same baseball teams growing up. Over the years they became quite the dynamic pitcher-catcher duo, winning championships in four separate divisions consecutively, but when Dale discovered drugs and alcohol in tenth grade, baseball season was cancelled indefinitely.

Emmett took the changes rather hard and fell under a heavy bout of depression for nearly an entire year.

Hoping to fill the void that baseball had left in his best friend's heart Dale got Lola Marshall, the sluttiest girl in school, drunk on tequila at his house while his parents were away for the weekend. When Lola was fully primed, Dale called Emmett over for a romp with the loose, but still very lovely, Lola. Emmett agreed, but insisted he watch from the couch while Dale screwed Lola first. After a minute of heavy kissing, and loud moaning from Lola, Dale pulled her pants down and proceeded to pound her plump cheeks from behind against the back of a couch. Emmett ran upstairs to the bathroom and locked the door. It wasn't until an hour later that Dale came up to use the bathroom. Emmett finally came clean about what had actually been bothering him that past year. He was gay, and he'd been in love with Dale secretly for years. It wasn't about baseball at all. Dale told him that he'd guessed it all along, but unfortunately for Emmett, he wasn't a homosexual. After some discussion, the two of them agreed not to let a little awkwardness ruin their friendship. Dale called Lola a cab, and he and Emmett watched the Blue Jays game together while laughing about the whole thing.

Then there was Charlie McGee. Charlie was a thirty-five-year-old, first generation Irish-Canadian who had the stolid look of the old country on him. His broad shoulders, brick-shaped face, sunken eyes and combed-back ginger hair looked like they belonged to an amateur boxing champion, not a small-time book salesman/high-functioning alcoholic/womanizing/recreational drug user.

Charlie had worked at the publishing house that printed Dale's first book back in '93, and he'd taken to Dale instantly, adopting the role as his unofficial agent after reading his book. He saw something different in Dale's writing and figured the only thing stopping him from reaching the next level was the right representation. For the next four and half years, Charlie volunteered his time networking and marketing Dale and his books around the city and province, and booking Dale the public speaking gigs that currently paid for his groceries and rent. At the end of the day, Charlie McGee was the driving force behind Dale's mediocre success, and the only thing keeping him from having to work a day job—and he never asked Dale for a dime in return.

*November 12, 1997. The Kiss Lounge. Sudbury, Ontario.*
*10:23 p.m.*

Dale, Emmett and Charlie took a cab from Emmett's place in the Donovan to the Kiss Lounge on Regent Street that night. The Kiss Lounge was a typical Sudbury-style meat-market dance club, complete with the strobe lights and skinny cocktail waitresses who didn't mind showing off a little breast while carrying trays of cheap Jell-O shots overhead.

It was a Friday and the place was packed.

The three of them discussed the usual plethora of male-bonding topics: sex, women, men for Emmett, books, music, more sex and among other things, Emmett's novel. He'd been working on it solid for two years, but had yet to finish it.

"Why's it taking you so long, Em?" Dale shouted over the thumping house music.

"I don't know, brother. What can I say—I'm a minimalist. Every word I put on the page feels like it's polluting the canvas . . . Did we have to sit this close to the speakers?"

Charlie came back from the bar with a round of drinks hoping to cap off a story he was telling earlier. "Who gives a shit about that stupid book, Emmett. I was in the middle of something . . . As I was saying, I'm in this chat room cybering with this broad, right? I'm in top form as usual, so she finished nice and quick, and types, 'Who are you?' 'cause she's so mesmerized by me, right? Know what I typed back?" Charlie's face grew more animated with each word. "I said, 'It's meeeee, chum!'"

Dale and Emmett burst out laughing.

"You're a fucking liar," Dale chuckled.

"Dead serious. She's meeting me here on Wednesday night, and you know what that means." Charlie made an "O" on one hand and fingered it with the other. "Fuck, I love the Internet . . . Know what I wanna do tonight?"

"No idea. What do you wanna do, Charlie?" Emmett answered, giggling into his beer glass.

"I say we go back to my place and have a snowstorm, chum," Charlie answered, flicking the edge of his nostril with his thumb.

"No way," Dale said. "You can find coke in here, easy. And look at all the girls here, man. I'm on a mission, so relax." Dale smiled and nodded at a group of young women sitting in the booth next to them. Charlie took notice and tried getting their attention by flexing his chest rapidly.

Emmett kept on about his book. "Like I was saying . . . I gotta go back to that box and dig out the rest of those poems. I gotta close my eyes and remember. Listen to those melodies again, and finish this thing up once and for all, you know? I have to make preparations—the right preparations . . . Right, Dale?"

Dale had checked out. He was busy watching a tall blond in a short black skirt dancing by the stage.

"We need to dare each other," Emmett said, sighing. "Like when you told that kid in Mexico he would never die." Emmett slurped back the rest of his beer in one gulp and slammed the glass on the table.

"Think that'd work for you, bud?" Dale asked, still fixated on the blond.

"Yeah. I really do," Emmett answered.

The blond and her friends went to the washroom, so Dale turned his attention back to Emmett and talks of his unfinished book. "Here, man, take this. I wrote it this morning in the park getting rained on." Dale pulled a crumpled piece of paper from his coat pocket. "I was going to use it for something else, but if you like it it, you should keep it."

"Could—could you read it to us?" Emmett asked solemnly.

"Now?" Dale asked.

"Sounds like you went through quite an ordeal to get the words down. It's only right," Emmett replied.

Dale shrugged. "Okay, sure . . .

48

In the winter, morning chokes me out amidst the shivering hybrid lookalike Shenzhen tower. I lifted my head up above some of my regressive behaviors, but can't escape the broken brain syndrome. The naked eyes we feel sorry for—fortunes fade, my empty bottles—and at night I'm faithful to recant my old beliefs, but only right before I fall asleep . . . When I was younger, I didn't know what real beauty was, but now I do, and it is here—right now, not there, then. Got it? That's the answer . . . That's all there is to anything."

Emmett and Charlie clapped their hands. Dale hid a smile and tossed the paper across the table to Emmett. "Take it, man," Dale said, with a wink.

"Amazing," Emmett said, scratching his head while examining the paper. "I guess what you're trying to say here is that confronting the idea—that this vessel-being—is the greatest thing to let go of and—"

Charlie interrupted, nudging Dale with his elbow. "Holy shit, Dale. Look at the ass on that one. Go talk to her."

The two of them ogled the girl's jiggly backside while Emmett looked down at his empty glass.

"Sorry, Em. What were you saying?" Dale asked a moment later.

"I was just saying that most of our fears spawn from our fear of death and our fear of others, that's all."

"But it's not our fear of others!" Charlie said, with his finger in the air like he'd solved a riddle.

"No, it's not," Dale said. "It's that we place value in the opinions of people we don't even value that much. We replace the foundation of our lives—which should be a value system—with the approval of these people we see no value in. Their approvals feed our egos, which in turn get diseased and trick us into thinking that we're growing when really the spirit is shrinking."

"So . . . do you think my spirit is shrinking?" Emmett asked, suddenly feeling anxious.

Charlie shrugged at him. He had no idea.

"At the end of the day, this is all that matters to me . . ." Dale leaned across the table and looked directly at them. "Anything beautiful can only be appreciated from a window or sung from the lips of a man in a cage. Preoccupation with death is a curable disease, but dying happy is not possible . . . I don't know, maybe I've had my moment. Maybe I made it so that I can't be ruled by God for a reason. Who knows? Luckily, it comes easy to me—always has. It's like I'm on my own twenty-first-century cross or something. I hope you both consider me a veteran by now . . ."

Emmett and Charlie both nodded in agreement.

"Good. I've tried to lead by example." Dale sighed. "And I know I haven't done a great job with that lately, and I'll tell you why . . . I'm a little upset right now because I don't have a Bible on me . . . Jesus said something along the lines of, 'No one lights a candle then covers it up,' but guess what? I do. You do. We all do. At least I admit it . . . I'm the strong man the thief bound before she could pillage the house. I'm the strong man who fell in love with the thief and the beauty of midnight, then made a home in the after-thought left behind . . . A part of me feels as if it's been freed from a lifetime of loneliness in the tiny room I've called home so long, so I'm embarking on an act of rebellion toward my weakness tonight, boys. There's something in me that's strong. I can feel it. There's a man in here that fights and walks through flames, and wields mighty weapons and can fly if he wants to. He's the one who keeps me safe in a scuffle, and he's the one who finds his way to the forefront when chickenshit little me gets scared of people looking. There's a strong man inside me and I'm gonna give him the go-ahead to get up and brawl tonight, then I'll see where I'm at in a few months' time . . . Anyways, I've been wanting to tell you guys something, but I wasn't sure how to approach it."

"What is it?" Charlie asked.

"I met a girl." Dale's voice trailed off as a girl in a short pink skirt and thigh-high stockings walked past and sat down at a table close by.

"You were saying something about a girl you met?" Emmett asked.

"Huh?" Dale said.

"You said met someone?"

"Yeah. But look at *that*," Dale said, biting down on his bottom lip.

"Good god," Charlie said, drooling. "I'd like to sniff her gym panties." Mmmm."

Dale burst out laughing.

"You're disgusting," Emmett said, shaking his head.

"You're never gonna get laid if you keep looking at her like that, Charlie, you fuckin' degenerate," Dale said.

"So you met a girl, apparently?" Emmett asked again.

"Jane. Her name is Jane," Dale answered.

"Jane, eh? So does this mean you're over 'heroin Ola'?" Emmett asked.

"Leave him alone about, Ola, chum. He's got a saviour complex. You know how bad he wants to be that junkie girl's daddy."

"Hey, shut the fuck up, all right?" Dale replied. "And Ola's going to Europe for a year. She told me I could live my life . . . Fuck do you think we're doing here tonight?"

"Okay okay. Take it easy. So, what about this Jane?" Emmett asked.

"Straight-edge, Christian, vegetarian, has a good career."

"Christian, eh? . . . Virgin?" Charlie asked, smiling slyly.

"How the hell should I know? Sexy as hell though. And I like that she's religious. Makes me wanna do her even more for some reason."

"Fuckin' right," Charlie said.

"How'd you meet you her?" Emmett asked.

"Minnie set us up. It was a blind date."

"God I wanna fuck that Minnie broad so bad," Charlie said.

"How'd the date go?" Emmett asked, shaking his head.

"Not great, but you never know. There was definitely something about her."

"Like?" Emmett asked.

"I don't know. But for all her Christian talk, I sensed a little freak in there somewhere."

"Even if she isn't, I'm sure you'll find a way to turn her into one somehow," Charlie said, chuckling.

"Hallelujah! That's it then. Another round on me, brothers," Emmett said, raising his empty glass in the air.

"I fuckin' love this guy," Charlie said, jumping up to head-lock Emmett's neck from across the table.

Dale put his arms around Charlie's chest and wrestled him. "Fuck off, Charlie! Leave the guy alone. He's a thinker—not like you, you no-good Irish hick."

"Fuck you, chum," Charlie said, plunking back onto his seat with a big silly grin on his face.

"Let's just have a good time tonight, boys. All right?" Dale said.

"Yes. Let's," Emmett agreed. "Waitress? Three whiskies and three beers, please. My friend here has been liberated from the clutches of a heroin-addicted she-devil by an angel of the Lord our God, Saint Jane. Praise God!"

"Praise God!"

# 2

*November 20, 1997. Jane St. Marie's apartment. Sudbury, Ontario.*

Jane was burnt out. She'd been under the gun since she got home from China, putting the finishing touches on a big story for *The Carriage*. She'd spent sixteen hours at the office that day, so when she finally got home, she ran a hot bath and made a big pot of chamomile-lemon tea.

Later, she sat in bed typing notes until she passed out from sheer exhaustion. In a few hours she had to wake up and do it all over again, but it was worth it. Her job was gruelling, but she was realizing her dreams of being a writer and journalist, and was truly grateful to be doing what she loved.

It wasn't long before the alarm clock announced that it was time to get up, get ready and get back to work again.

Jane said a prayer, got dressed then cooked breakfast. She was just about to take her first bite when she noticed her mail by the front door. She'd forgotten to pick through it the night before.

*A letter from Dale Potoniak?* She thought it was odd. He was handsome and she'd been mystified by him, but she never expected to hear from him again after their date. Not after the way he ignored her the entire time.

She tore open the letter, checking the time first.

Jane,

I don't remember the day.

I do remember it was fall, and that has always been an important season in my life. The colours, the smells, they were all alive then. The hormones flooding my mind made sight and sound utter agony—and ecstasy. Fall, autumn, everything was beginning to take its glorious shape, and the music of those times is something I'm overly nostalgic about these days.

I wanted you to be proud and to tell you I'm a painter. I wanted to tell you that I'm a confident man and that I wrote my masterpiece. I want to show you a book filled with my accomplishments and whisper a thousand victory stories in your ear in a Manhattan cafe—in Paris, or Berlin, or London, or Montreal, Hong Kong or Tokyo—over a glass of something rich. The taste of wine and cigarettes on our lips under a grey sky at the end of summer, the beginning of autumn—at the instant the seasons change. Where there is day, but it could easily be night. There is no sun, only a crescent moon, and my heart is happy because I have something to tell you, something wonderful . . .

There is our music: flavours of strings and pianos. A waltz, and it does not infringe on our conversation, which is flowing effortlessly. My eyes aren't as good as they used to be, but it could be nothing. We're wearing the right rags—the grey and black, the look of the humble city hypocrite stuck in a confident stare. Taking the moment in, we realize it's something special. A perfect note, and suddenly we could be anywhere.

I am confident. I am sure of myself and you are intrigued. I don't think twice, and you don't second-guess that I'm a painter and a writer, and you can feel safe and proud and free to celebrate, because there is nothing left after this moment for us to mourn.

I try to remember everything. To keep it in a stillness. Believing in each string like a kind word or medicine for scars and regrets.

Back then you could say we had hope in a promise. Drifting on my potential and visiting the old places like a mask on an ugly face . . .

We infatuate a mellow lark fighting among street pigeons and listen to Zen music while we wait for another day, and ride our bicycles down roads with impossible names.

How about a redo?

Dale Potoniak

*December 4, 1997. Dale Potoniak's apartment. Sudbury, Ontario.*

It had been a couple weeks, and Dale still hadn't heard back from Jane, which made him question whether his intended message had gotten through to her at all, or worse, his letter had come across as stalker-ish.

When a letter from Jane, and a postcard from Milan arrived on the same morning, Dale breathed a sigh of relief, pulled his curtains shut and sat down anxiously at his small wooden desk. He adjusted the light, and proceeded to read Ola's postcard first, followed by Jane's letter.

Dale,

I wasn't able to love myself, but I recall you singing to me. I pulled the needle from your vein, and although it was just for a short while, you were the one.

For kissing and needles, for bubble gum and methamphetamine, I made art from discarded crates for you. Your chemical silhouette extended like praise into the cattle cabins as you hoped for a mouse with a lion falling out of its tongue, screaming "No one else really loves me but you."

Love,

Ola

Her words made him miss her.

He carefully cut open Jane's letter. The letter inside wasn't handwritten—she hadn't even bothered to use a typewriter. She'd used her computer and printed it out on regular white paper—in Courier font—which made him feel flat-out embarrassed for her.

Dale,

If you stared back at me through the chains we knew, would you free the lonesome night?

I will go on dying, and then you'll live in me forever, because you traded there under that uncommon thatched roof in cold winter snows and I was able to love you.

How did we break the grain? For countless years I have spoken to your flower and raised you by the arms like a lily doll on the winded stage. If there could be any other way, I would have run like a thief from a murder scene and found a master who could program me differently. There can never be order, because there has never been order. This is the way it has to be in the end.

I cannot tame what is wild and free, nor do I want to. I have found my Zen and I will not be careless, but I will be cunning, rest assured. There is so much to decipher, so much to see. I will not hesitate and I will not look back. There is so little time. There is so much left to know.

If it could be made into a framework it would come naturally and elegant. First—the river song and the smell of fall (this I also remember). I cannot look back because beauty does not desire youth, it desires passion (I can already feel this going wrong).

Maybe I can just fill these lines with thoughts of you, or maybe I can borrow what has already been made.

Dale, it's okay. You tried.

You should know by now that something like this will have to be earned.

Be earned—

That's something you've heard in a situation or two, am I right?

Hearts

Jane St. Marie

Dale's hands began to shake violently. *Such sensible refinement. Such clever use of imagery.* Jane's letter felt like a sword, and she'd thrust her icy blade into his eyes and out of his mouth. She was goading him by sending her very best writing to provoke him, to shake him up, to make him doubt everything he'd ever believed about himself and about her.

Dale spent the next forty-six hours locked in his apartment drinking whisky and chain-smoking cigarettes, slashing his pen wildly across pages designed to establish him as death bringer, not just a common swordsman, and to let Jane know he was unquestionably intrigued by her now.

Jane,

I know why I love seeing you in that window, my Juliet.

I'm here in these streets with these mad people. I've been wandering around for a long time and now I'm like a statue perched outside that window you're in like I was made to look up at you. Crooked neck like I was perfect for this—because seeing you in that window I imagine candles and books, and oak dressers and a bit of wine. Opera and orchestral symphonies only—and then, a light meal eaten alone, with nothing else to do tonight or tomorrow.

You hunter, if you came to the window and lit a cigarette I'd know for certain there was a God, but as I imagine the design and realize that it's mine—and it's the only thing I've ever been able to relate to in my life—I shall rise above the open road and shoot to the moon.

The rigid doors you spare for ribbons of unnatural victory we have never shared, crowns of gold and olive branches that compensate for my unwillingness to cooperate with society and government. A waltz we dance over an empty space never goes to waste, while I sob softly. And if this thatched roof is not mine, then it cannot belong to you either, because you never worked to belong. And here I am now, under this roof, silently longing for a Spanish colonnade, a victory for those who prefer non-violence, but the violent take it by force. I just needed the evening to procure this contentment that was wandering toward gloom.

Earlier today—earlier this afternoon—I strained and swore under the sun with no water, only salt in my lungs. My heart jumps, and the old me fears death, but the new me welcomes the challenge. The new kid in town and I am the "King of the Streets."

I have you on display when I'm on my way home on the avenue, and everything is all right. There's no rest for the wicked. I've grown up now, and I'm tired. How much more noise does a man need before he's old?

You didn't answer about the redo.


Dale Potoniak


"Perfect!" Dale screamed, like a mad scientist, holding his creation high in the air with both hands. "It's just . . . fucking . . . perfect. Ha!"

He sealed the page in an envelope and took the elevator downstairs, peeking around the corner to make sure the new chick and her 'roid-freak boyfriend weren't milling about. He dropped the letter into the mail slot before going back upstairs to get some much-needed sleep. He promised himself to write Ola back tomorrow.


*December 24, 1997. Dale's Potoniak's apartment. Sudbury, Ontario. 5:03 p.m.*


It was Christmas Eve and Dale spent the day shopping for a gift for his mother. She was due to stop by in an hour for a quick hello-good-bye before heading to the airport for her annual winter getaway. This year it was a ten-day all-inclusive package deal to Jamaica.

Dale opened the door to his apartment, dropped the bags on the floor, and there it was. Another letter from Jane.

He picked up the envelope and went straight for the kitchen cupboard to retrieve the bottle of Irish whisky he'd been looking forward to all day. He poured a glass and sat on the couch, the pulse of his heart beating in his hands as he held Jane's second letter.

Dale,

Should you forget me surrounded by the chaos you thrive in, let me be a comfort that stings deep, as you lie down and find no rest. I think often that we love the story, but there is disdain for the words as the arms of beauty shield us from the things we should not see.

Where are you now?

There are buildings I wonder if you live in. If not, let me know before I go looking for you.

It rains on the people who need freedom and they may or may not feel satisfied with their observations, for each and every heart walking in the rain lacks repair.

Forty years ago we smiled spinning a wheel, while children playing in reeds and swings have forgotten the loneliness already.

We are so civilized aren't we? With our schedules and carefree visions?

I'm transfixed on your long hair—and maybe we shared a quick smile, but I'm disgusted with this current state of affairs. There is nothing purer than the journey home, and there is nothing I'm fonder of than your reluctance to be content. We came from rags and live in riches, but we both know we wear rags under our fancy clothes when we go out to these parties, or entertain. I myself smile and wave, but never forget those rags beneath my gown.

I know there is more to your story now. The time to face this shame we have for our humanity can only be hidden so long. Here we are at the forefront of liberation, and I'm fighting for the side we've been dying for. Rest awhile. I'll recuperate, re-evaluate, and be back on the road before long.

Hearts

Jane St. Marie

"Fuck," Dale moaned, rubbing his eyes. "She's good." He reached for the whisky, but he didn't want it anymore. He could feel a dull headache coming on and wondered why he didn't feel more excited over the possibility of a new romance. There was something blocking it mentally. *How.* How did she? How could she, a schooled writer, know to write those exact words in the order she'd written them?

Tormented by bitterness and frustration, Dale examined one line in particular that stood out as too outstanding, too sensational, too outrageous to be written by anyone other than Ola or himself: ". . . as the arms of beauty shield us from the things we should not see."

Rage filled Dale's heart. He crumpled up the letter and threw it violently across the living room. "Goddammit!" he screamed, marching to his desk. He snatched a blank sheet of paper from the drawer and began writing frantically.

Jane,

Stage curtains swing over ladders and ladies with coats masked in purple. The show goes on. I'd trade bloodshed for boredom, insights, and a glass eye on his memoirs. Tell me something is going in the right direction for once, and tonight my eyes aren't so dry when I dance for my wage. I'd trade broken hands and sadness rather than ruin what I've made so far. It's been just right, and now I must stop it or it will all be spoiled.

It would be so perfect if I woke up and you were laughing again. Trying to make it the same as it was. The sounds, the smells, the colours. Whatever I told you was a lie. My youth is dead.

Man shares his pamphlets with the sick in hopes of repose, but the road they travel leads to nothing. I don't want to sin, but I won't run from it either. This very idea makes me aware of how far I am from being free.

I imagine hours spent just like this in the places that we gather. Spanish cities and the evening thrill, the smell of my own burning cigarettes and the anticipation of tonight's release. This vision has been my most faithful companion for many many years. Could I ever go down that far? I can't even say "again," because all I ever do is fight the pull. I've never willingly fallen for the sake of what I see now as spectacular potential for art, and you are the only character I've created with evil in her heart and beauty in her mind.

Your mornings are my mornings and your winter is my winter. The hell I see in visions is your hell and these memories are the ones that I created for you. I am scared to create you. To give this world what I promised to keep hidden away. If I tell the story from your point of view I just might be free, because if I find out why you're here then I might be able to forgive you for what you've just done to me.

Dale Potoniak

He wasn't sure if it was good or not. Come to think of it, he wasn't sure about anything in that moment except for the fact that he'd been consumed by a deep lust and fear for this woman. This woman who'd suddenly made him feel like a second-rate impostor, this woman who'd broken through his impenetrable defences with seemingly little or no effort on her part. She'd stepped on his toes, kicked dirt in his face and shit on everything he ever believed in just by existing, and now, more than anything else in the whole goddamn world he wanted *her*. He wanted—he *needed* to feel her body against his. *Her sky blue eyes*, those tight black pants she wore—

*Ring! Ring!*

"Hello?"

"Hi, Dale. It's Mom."

"Hi, Mom. I just got home. You on your way?"

"Listen—I'm not gonna have time to pop by, Daley . . . I gotta stop by the office and—"

"Fuck, Mom. I just spent all day shopping for presents."

"I know, I know. I'm sorry, Daley. It'll have to wait till I get back, okay?"

". . ."

"Okay?"

"Yeah sure. Whatever."

"Merry Christmas."

"Yeah, you too . . . Bye."

Dale took the letter downstairs, mailed it out, then retired to the couch with the bottle of whisky and a Christmas cartoon marathon.

*Merry fucking Christmas.*

*March 5, 1998. Dale's apartment. Sudbury, Ontario.*
*10:10 a.m.*

Dale woke up in a daze that morning, stark naked and extremely hungover. The mailman had shoved that day's haul through the springy door slot and roused him out of a deep, drunken sleep.

When he opened his eyes, the brightness of the sun's reflection off the snow outside felt like an Arctic straight razor being slid across his beer-bruised corneas. A breeze from the shabby single-pane window made him shiver as he stumbled toward the door to grab the two envelopes before slumping down on the worn-out fabric couch. One was a phone bill, which he tossed aside. The other was a letter.

Two months. It took two lonely, sexless, booze-drenched months, but finally another letter had arrived.

Dale,

Standing at an invisible pace, you are not easily mistaken at your age, and with that face. I know your name is nothing, but you are cradled in a safe place while onlookers jaunt and jeer at me.

They're looking in her dresser drawer. She has come. Behold the mirror.

"This is my task," she cries, covering her eyes. She hinges like Samantha's doors. Her joy could last and Dahlia's mirrors and a Harlequin book is all we could romance.

The sun is fresh on my face as I wake this morning, but I cannot breathe. I did not choose this condition. You'll say that she's a monster because she's foreign, and that her looks are deceiving, and her culture is a mask and a heavy burden for all who wear it—but she is pretty in pictures, and her body is your friend.

She sways her dress around a summer heat—NO.

She lifts a rose in 1996 autumn—NO.

She is more beautiful than the 20th century.

You hate the world without any relationships, calling yourself a Buddhist and at peace with shame. Your friends are all animals, for as long as you are wounded the gutter rats feed off your strength. Do not let them get to you. Do not give up the fight. You have friends that are gods and you have angels on your side. No dead man can help you, yet I am alive and so is Christ.

Dale, I've been a few places now, and I admit to seeing beauty almost everywhere, even in the most wretched subterranean, but there is no beauty in vanity at all.

I like Detroit. A proper place for poets like us. Somewhere like this could swallow us both up for good, and we would be living in a dream forever. Something likes the prisoners who refuse to leave. Something likes the smell. Something about the total lack of, and desperation. Hate/beauty. Total abstraction. Here we go, into the forest that will make my lessons complete, and I will be finally be virtuous when money grows on trees.

You truly are a remarkable friend. Somehow you stay with me all the time, and even when you're not around, I keep you there . . .

A new book, something to try, something to start, something to fill. A new story. Something with suspense, something with a plot, something with a twist. A new word, a new day, a new friend, a new beginning, a new season, a new city, a new feeling, a new taste, a new toy, a new boy . . . They all end, and I fear my own destruction will come from niceness and an unwillingness to argue. I was too quick to shed my own blood and now my soul is humbled. My flesh is companion to ruin, scraping for reasons and making arrangements for different opinions. They ready themselves to speak on this fine mourning, in an empty cathedral with no colours at all. I could go on and on and on.

I doubted your attendance, but there you were. Free to speak as the fat one died. You lived with no lips until the fat one died, and you made me fast; now my soul is humbled. My spirit breaks a little, and the mind is numbed by the death of the fat one.

Jane St. Marie

Dale held the pages in one hand and rubbed the stabbing pain in his temple with the other. He'd nearly been moved to tears by the words. He walked to his desk and turned the computer on, zooming in on a photo of Jane on *The Carriage*'s website.

His alcohol-sick body trembled beneath a thin wool blanket as he began to masturbate wildly, trying to look away from her pretty, smiling eyes. His mind kept reverting to the last lines of the letter, again and again. *Death of the fat one . . . Now my soul is humbled.* "Un-fucking believable. Oh fuck yeah— ahh— ahh."

The orgasm hurt. His arms, neck and chest were sore and tight now like he'd just been in a fist fight, and his hangover had suddenly gotten much worse. He wondered whether he might be in love with Jane now. The disappointment he felt was something he couldn't fully understand. Other than Ola, he'd never truly loved another woman. He looked up and saw her postcard from Milan perched against a plant she'd given him on the book shelf, staring back like Catholic guilt or purple flowers in a cemetery. Ola was the love of his life. His future wife. His future everything.

But in the meantime, Jane's letter was so blatantly aggressive, her words so unignorably superb and irresistibly villainous in their capacity for linguistic transcendence—no. It was not love, he felt. It was lust.

Lust and plain old jealousy. He was jealous of the words. Jealous that she got them and he didn't. Jealous like a baseball fan who felt his team was entitled to the number one draft pick that year, but he ends signing somewhere else. Jane St. Marie was obviously a force to be reckoned with, and it was absolutely crucial that his next move hit hard. Dale took a slug of whisky, then opened his laptop to write a rather defamatory blog entry, slandering Jane to his 1,398 subscribers. He took pity at the last minute, changing her name to Janice before publishing the post.

Suddenly it hit him. If Jane was in Detroit, and Ola was in Milan, then he needed to go somewhere too. If they were living in air-conditioned hotel rooms, he needed to be sweating bullets in a dank skid-row shithole somewhere hot. If Jane was typing letters on thousand dollar laptops, and Ola was drinking champagne from crystal cups in the flowery first world, then he needed to be scratching poems on the back of beer coasters in blood somewhere deep in the dirty third.

Earlier that year, Dale had been desperate for money, so he wrote a self-help piece, more like a "how-to" for men interested in improving their public speaking skills, for a monthly men's publication called *Avant Bard*; and he still had a contact in the editorial department there named Chet Cater.

Dale knew Chet from high school, but they never really hit it off back then. Chet grew up in Estaire, so that meant he hung out with jocks and hockey players who liked to fight and talk about jacking up their pickup trucks while chewing tobacco and smoking flavoured cigarillos behind the gym on lunch break; meanwhile Dale and Emmett would be in the library, scheming on how to score weed and booze for parties they weren't even invited to. Chet eventually moved into town for college and outgrew the old crowd, embracing more and more of the local art culture. Not to say he wasn't still a dumb hick at heart, he'd just evolved into a much more cultured, much more refined version of a dumb hick. All in all, Chet was harmless and he meant well; and much to the chagrin of Dale, had been successful at pretty much everything he set his mind to, climbing the ladder at work and investing his own money into a local entertainment service and several small-scale local theatre productions. He was there that night, for *Wilhelmina* at the Elgin Street Opera House, and had caught Dale off-guard in the lobby after the show.

"Dale— Hey Dale! Over here."

"Chet. I didn't expect to see you here."

"Yep, yep. The theater uses my sound gear so I get free tickets to these things . . . Anyways. Did you catch that curly-haired broad? What a piece of tail she was, eh? I was kinda disappointed she wouldn't show her tits, though."

"It's an opera, Chet. That usually doesn't happen . . . Come to think of it, that would never fucking happen."

"No shit, eh?"

*Good ol' dumb Chet.*

Dale skimmed through his address book and found Chet's number. Chet answered in his usual high-octane, life-is-peachy kind of voice.

"*Avant Bard*, editorial. You got Cater, here. What's happenin'?"

"Chet . . . It's Dale. Dale Potoniak."

"Hey, what's up, bro? Long time no speak. It's been forever, eh?"

"Yeah. Listen—"

"Yep, yep. What can I do for ya, bud?"

Dale shuddered at the idea of asking him for help, but it was a necessary evil at this stage in this stage in the game. He grit his teeth and came out with it. "I need a favour, man. Think you could help me out?"

"No promises, but I'll see what I can do. What do ya need?"

"I was thinking . . . I wanna get out of the country for a bit. I'm offering *Avant Bard* my full range of services. Send me out on assignment. I'll write anything you want—within reason."

Chet laughed. "Shit, bro. I thought you—So wait a sec—why do you need to get out of the country?"

"I don't need to, Chet, I want to. I gotta get out of this shithole for a while, you know? Get some perspective. See, there's this girl—"

"Hol' up . . . No disrespect to what you do, Dale, but you're a poetry guy. Always have been, always will be. Yep, yep. We liked the bit you did for us last summer, but let's get real, you write existential shit for word geeks. Convincing *my* boss to pay *you* to go out of country is gonna be a hard sell on my end—unless you're willing to bend a little on what you write, ya know what I'm sayin'? Not saying it's impossible, but—where did you have in mind?"

"Anywhere. I honestly don't care as long as it's hot. Preferably somewhere brutal and war-torn. Somewhere that's been broken into a million fucking pieces. Get what I'm saying?"

"Yep, yep, okay. I follow. I mean, I could probably help you out, but—hey, you don't sound too good. Kinda high-strung or something. Everything all right?"

Dale covered the mouthpiece with his hand and took a deep breath. "I'm fine, Chet. Everything's fine. It's like this, Chet. Remember high school? Remember you and your friends, and the horrible shit you'd do to me and my friends? My life's kinda like that, except now I'm limping home, metaphorically speaking, after being kicked in the fucking face by the abomination of true potential."

Chet burst out laughing. "You're fuckin' hilarious, bud. I have no idea what you're talking about right now, but listen—I think I got something. Just got dropped on my desk this very second. It's down south and—you're gonna have to bend a little like I said."

"Fine. I'll bend this one time."

Chet sighed. "Gimme a couple days and I'll get back to ya, okay?"

Dale let out a deep sigh of relief. "Thank you, Chet. Thank you very much."

"Hey, Dale?"

"Yeah?"

"Maybe lay off that whisky a bit, eh?"

*March 7, 1998. Dale's apartment. Sudbury, Ontario.*
*11:02 a.m.*

Morning breached the old blue curtains, breaking the last line of defence Dale had against the weapons-grade stream of sunlight that had now officially invaded his dark zone. A billion dust particles turned into staring, accusing eyeballs as they danced like tarantulas at a beauty pageant through the merciless bright.

Dale was familiar with the symptoms of a scary hangover and this one had them all. His teeth felt sticky and slimy, indicating he'd passed out the night before without brushing his teeth or rinsing with mouthwash, which explained why his swollen tongue tasted like the ashtray he'd used to butt out thirty or so budget cigarettes the night before. A combination of beer, whisky and Jell-O shots burned in his gut and leached out of his cold clammy skin via a layer of lurid sweat that made his pillowcase feel damp and unfamiliar. The repulsive stench from his open-sore dry-mouth wafted up toward his hypersensitive nose like a heat-seeking nightingale scud missile, making him mutter empty promises under his foul breath about quitting drinking for good.

Dale rolled onto his back and covered his eyes with the sweat-soaked pillow. He had the fluttering heart syndrome. He also had the jellyfish brain confusion, and even though it was still early in the big scheme of things, he was already seeing big purple people faces behind his eyelids if he stopped concentrating on positive results.

Purple people. Purple people and their gory sinister visions whenever he closed his eyes. They were right there. Purple and green, dripping down behind his eyeballs. Right there. Something or someone, clear and bright, oozing outwards, terrifying and demonic. Terrible images and faces of the night before, reminding him that his thoughts would be especially malevolent today, and that he was in a big fucking mess. Bottom line.

And then there was the hypochondriacal side of the hangover, faithfully reminding Dale that heart attacks occur most frequently in the morning. He imagined getting out of bed and fumbling his way through the tunnel to Elgin Street in hopes of relieving his rotten gut syndrome with some sort of greasy vulgarity of a breakfast from Tito's. After consuming the caloric monstrosity, combined with a litre or two of water and black coffee, he'd step out for a cigarette, take a puff and his heart would go *pop,* and that would be it for Dale Potoniak. So long and sayonara.

That being said, it was going to be one of two options that morning, and Dale had about ten minutes left to pick.

Option 1 entails kicking and clawing one's hungover brain into a Zen zone through various spiritual practices like breathing exercises, prayer and making life-changing promises, whereby the aforementioned victim of the hangover can potentially gain enough inner gumption to make it back to bed that night sober, battle-worn, but without having to carry the burden of guilt and shame of drinking for a second, third or sometimes fourth consecutive day just to avoid the hellish consequences.

The scariest part about option 1 is your nervous system and heart take a huge beating from an endless day of withdrawal suffering, so when the lights go out, the worn-out body joins the war and starts to crave a physical solution for the spiritual meltdown. To the sufferer, alcohol withdrawal can feel like a gang raping, and everyone's on board except for the man you wished you were.

Many have tried Option 1 and have been successful. And they all know how good it feels to finally sleep and wake up the next morning fresh as a frog on a pond lily. Others haven't been so lucky, ending up on the dark side of the road to nowhere, cutting their losses with a bottle of rum, singing yesterday's news over the phone to their kid sister who'll be by to check in before long because lil' sis' knows best. They caught a case of the tremens, and now a bottle of black won't cut it because they chose the wrong path way too late in the game. It's pretty much benzos or emergency room at that point.

Option 2 is don't suffer longer than absolutely required. Get up, eat—if you can—and drink as much water as you can handle, followed by two or three extra strength pain-pills, whatever you got. Shit, shower, and when you're nice and clean and the party grime's been scrubbed off—have a drink. See how you feel. Nine out of ten times it only takes a couple and you're back in the game. The only drawback of Option 2 is that the cycle is never-ending and you always end up back at square one. Mornings like this, mourning like this. It is, however, the easier, more reliable of the two unfavorable solutions.

An ashtray two feet away made Dale gag. He tried to ignore the sadness he felt over this unwanted, all-too familiar dilemma. A part of him felt like crying, but he never could no matter how bad the hang-overs were. Feelings of guilt usually turned into self-hatred, which turned into denial and then to proactive decision making about choosing Option 1 or getting buzzed again after breakfast.

Dale went to the sink, filled a coffee mug with cold water and sat down at the kitchen table. The room was spinning.

*Fuck my life.*

He stumbled to the door to fetch the morning paper, and there she was on the first page of the arts section.


Quintessential Lover

By Jane St. Marie


It rains over steel skeletons in the west, while ice cuts through my father's shoulders in the east. On the horizon there's an arm made of steel that reaches out to love you, to shelter you. The sting of death feels so good from beneath the grisly shadow of a beanpole, and you— you looked like every guy that ever went to college, got married, and now drinks to fill the hole in his heart.

Let me guess, you like hockey and baseball, and you play poker and ski in Whistler whenever you get the chance. Do you keep your lift ticket on your coat for months afterwards, too?

You've made your world a battlefield, you've made your talent the enemy. It must be horrible living your life. You looked like a little kid who lost his mommy at the shopping mall. There is an accuser and there is a voice, but I think it's the music that made you do these things.

Speaking of music, I turned on the radio the other day and there was a piano player and a singer singing. I had a nice conversation with a friend and she was able to catch a part of the show, too. I'll remember that for a while. It was one of those special moments. Seldom come, but we do everything we possibly can to capture them. We fill our lives with every pleasure, allow every appetite to be indulged far too often. Our senses are overloaded and our appetites are confused. It was so simple. It just came and stuck around for a bit, then went.

I'm sitting in a place where my soul can be a soul. Life in Canada leaves so little room for growth—or at least the landscape toils against it . . .

The more I think of him, the more I callous . . .

And even if I get to see him again tomorrow, I know it will be eventless, so my heart does not pump.

*Jane St. Marie is an award-winning author that writes for The Carriage and several other publications throughout North America. She is currently in Detroit, covering a steadily worsening crack epidemic. Jane also writes poetry and fiction, and has plans to release a new book in the coming year.*

Above the article was a picture of Jane dressed in black, posing in front of a rundown tenement somewhere inside Detroit's hideous bosom. Her expression was that of a tireless revolutionary, unflinching and saint-like amid the ruins of western civilization.

Dale ran to the bathroom, pausing in front of the toilet as a wave of cold sweat and nausea gripped his entire body. He bent down, heaving violently into a bowl of last night's drunk-piss. Half-digested pizza chunks splashed yellow water back into his eye, barely missing his bottom lip. He crawled in the shower fully dressed wondering, why not me, as the water began to scald him.

*Later that night at The Swamp House Tavern on Kathleen Street. Sudbury, Ontario.*

*10:30 p.m.*

Dale was halfway through his ninth gin and tonic, watching the Sens play the Leafs on an old TV in the back corner of the bar.

*Ring! Ring!*

"Hello?" Dale answered flatly.

"Bro, it's Cater. Guess what?"

"What."

"I got you something . . . Nicaragua, bro! But there's a catch. You gotta be on a plane tomorrow morning at six a.m. . . . Nicaragua, son!"

Dale stared at the fuzzy television with his mouth open. His breathing was heavy, hissy and audible.

"Hey Dale, you there? You hear what I said? I just got you a—"

"I heard you the first time, fucker. Shit, Sens just took a five minute major."

"Hey fuck-stick. You need to come to my office tonight. I'm leaving a plane ticket and some cash with the front desk chick. She'll give you directions, contacts and everything else you'll need—and pack light, bro. It's over forty degrees down there."

"Where—Nicaragua?"

"Yeah . . . Hell did you think I meant?"

"Oh . . . okay. Well, what am I writing about?"

"A real tongue in cheek piece about legalizing prostitution or some shit like that. All the details are here at the office so come get 'em. It's already gettin' late and—"

"Damn. Leafs scored."

"You hear what I said? It's almost eleven, you fucking piss tank. You gotta be on a plane at six in the morning so get your ass down here—now!"

"Okay, okay! I'm on my way . . . I'm leaving right now."

Chet moaned regretfully. "Aww, man. Don't do this to me, man. I went way out of my way to—"

"For fuck sakes, Chet. Take it easy. I'm literally paying the bartender right now."

# 3

# NICARAGUA

*Avant Bard* advanced Dale a sum of money for expenses—rum and rugged dark-skinned strippers. But he grew tired of the tin-hut titty bars and poor-looking hookers in the first couple days. Every corner had a dozen diseased-looking tricks on it, cat-calling any white man within earshot. And there were a lot of them, surprisingly—white men that is. And although it was fun to fantasize about, Dale played it safe, beating off to local smut magazines instead of sampling the goods for real.

After an excruciatingly hot and generally unexciting first week in Managua, Dale took the chicken bus to Leon to meet a contact for his story.

He arrived at the bus station early that evening, drunk off some rum he'd smuggled on the bus with him. Teetering back and forth in the middle of a dusty street, Dale waved at passing motorcycle taxis, hoping one would show pity and take him to the centre of town. After a half hour of unsuccessful hailing, he meandered toward a cluster of market stalls farther up the street and bought two postcards with pictures of local cathedrals on them.

He sat down next to an old lady who was plucking feathers off a white chicken and throwing them on the sidewalk.

*Fitting.*

Ola,

In back alleys there are always crates and pallets stacked on one another. Garbage bins with graffiti and torn labels with puddles of God knows what around the edges. Smoke rises from manholes, especially in March, and that's when it's most beautiful. Grey skies and morning after morning I look to fire escapes and brown brick buildings, imagining the design of the window and have my moment where I love it. It was placed there just for me. The smell of March in the city, and the memories come rushing in. Where I loved you in alleyways and imagined your blackness, and your skin, and the way you looked that night.

I sent you home like a cheap whore, but you've got to know that I felt it too—both the love and regret. I went walking after I slept it off, and I went walking again to look for you. Searching in the city's most beautiful places, where pallets are stacked on one another and smoke rises from manholes like the design itself could sigh and worship the moment. It's the beauty of these streets, and there is a place out there built like it was built just for you, to keep you out of the rain.

There is something in these streets night and day, summer, winter, fall and spring, when we are all reborn and find something new to keep us fancying it for another go.

October, it falls—by November, we prepare for war—and by February, it's a bloodbath . . . By March we need medical care, but by May I feel like a newborn baby and I want it all again.

What a wild ride that was,

My misery on Front Street.


I love you, dearest.


Yours forever,


Dale Potoniak


Dale lit a cigarette and took a swig of warm rum.

Jane,

Every night I am reborn under this lamp.

Here I am again, back behind the wheel. Trying to get some sort of magic to happen.

It's just like heaven in Nicaragua.

I thought it would all just happen as soon as I touched down, but I had to break free first. God knows I had to break. I just never guessed how hard it would be, or how I far I could bend. Some of these lines might happen into poems, ya know. I guess it depends on who looks at them later. I hope I can scrounge together a softer chair than this later tonight. Hope I can scrounge some decent writing together too, and I'll write my way back to paradise with you.


Dale Potoniak


Dale read the postcards and felt sick to his stomach. Dry drunken splatter from a dirty, stomped-on sidewalk. A lecherous, contrived shit heap of impotent words that had foamed out of his rum-dumb brain from the centre of a hot continent. Tearing them up and buying new ones never seemed to crossed his mind, so he took another guzzle of rum and blamed the relentless heat for his shitty writing. He spotted a local watering-hole and decided to have a beer after mailing the postcards.

The foreign sounds of the market chattered in his ears as he skulked toward the distant city centre on foot, kicking rocks at curious local boys as he hobbled along.

Dale met with his contact in Leon a few times over the course of the next week, finished writing the story, and just like that, the trip was over.

*March 20, 1998. The Gecko Club. Leon, Nicaragua.*
*2:43 a.m.*

The lively crowd, pounding dancehall rhythms and hypnotic house beats did nothing to boost Dale's sour mood that night. Nicaragua had inspired nothing in him. What he'd hoped would be the magic elixir, turned out to be snake oil, and he was just another naive tourist—just another washed-up writer in a corn hat staring down the neck of a bottle hoping to find a cure to an impossible disease. Postcards to Ola and Jane and a collection of flat one-liners in his notebook were all he had to show for the entire hollow enterprise. The jig was up and now he had to go home and face Emmett and Charlie. He'd have to come up with a load of bullshit stories to make it seem like he had fun down there too—it was exhausting to think about.

Dale slammed back the rest of his beer, threw his last hundred cordobas on the bar and went back to the hotel to pack. An idea for a poem popped into his head during the walk back, but he'd forgotten it by the time he switched the light on.

*Fuck it,* he thought, bitterly.

# SUDBURY

*March 21, 1998.*

Dale fought a brutal hangover the entire trip back. Leon—Managua —Toronto—Sudbury.

*Then after all that, I had to take a taxi from fucking Garson. In and out of consciousness the whole ride, too. I shouldn't have mentioned anything to the cabby, but I told him I'd be short on fare. He kicked me out on the Kingsway right across the street from the old bingo hall. Had to drag my suitcase home in the ice and snow.*

*8:33 p.m.*

Dale was frozen stiff when he opened the door to his apartment. He stumbled toward the couch and collapsed. His breathing was laboured and his heart felt like it was fighting to keep beat. With one eye open, he peered up at the big black clock hanging over the front door—its slender white hands were stuck on midnight and made a ferocious commotion in his ears. If he could only sleep, he would wake up clean and forgiven. The carnage of a two-week rum bender was readying to unleash hell on his feeble nervous system. He could sense it.

*8:47 p.m.*

His body and soul craved more liquor, so he attempted movement in the direction of the fridge, but his nervous system wanted none of it. His hand trembled when he reached for the phone. To call someone. Anyone. Someone who could help. Someone who would bring a bottle to his infant lips so he could suckle the sweet nectar inside a little while longer. Who could he call? Who would answer?

Dale's body slipped off the couch and his face smacked against the cold hard floor.

*There are no dignified prayers in moments like this.*

Even the most godless savages wax poetic when eye to eye with linoleum.

*Poison I take . . . Poison that makes it hard to believe it's poison. At night it's medicine . . . But the day after, I realize that's a lie, too. The poison I take . . . Both night and day my poison. I open my mouth and drink, smile and make it real for a moment, but steal my beauty poison . . . In gutters I drown—Enough! Just pray, goddammit. You're dying for fuck sakes . . . Dear G—*

*Salvation!* In the form of a slender green bottle on the book shelf by the television—with a note attached to it.

Dale dragged himself across the room, snatched the bottle from the shelf and tore the envelope open.

*Welcome home, brother. Enjoy. —Emmett.*

*Thank you, Emmett. Thank you . . . Just one to take the edge off. Two at most.*

*11:24 p.m.*

Dale was eight drinks in at Elvira's Stunt, a goth bar on Larch Street, and feeling exceptionally good considering the day he had.

He leaned against the beer-soaked bar, making passes at a chubby girl in a latex corset and an over-abundance of facial piercings. It started off promising, but she lost interest after he began describing, in detail, various fetishes Hollywood deemed too taboo for the big screen, but he'd be open to experimenting with. She smiled awkwardly then turned away. He tapped her on the shoulder and asked if she'd come to the washroom and call him names while he jerked off.

*12:57 a.m.*

Dale left the bar alone.

A gaggle of drunken college girls waved at him from across the street. Dale smiled and waved back as they plodded along in the snow, arms linked like bone white frozen chains, but they weren't interested in sex with a drunken stranger waving like a jerk from across the street, so Dale retreated to a nearby bench to smoke a cigarette.

It was snowing, but just lightly. Nicely. It was cold, but not the kind of cold that hurts your cheeks or hurts when you breathe. No, the lights and sounds of downtown Nickel City felt alive and brilliant that night. And Dale puffed his cigarette, gazing across the train tracks toward Front Street, toward home, feeling genuinely happy to be home again.

*March 22, 1998. Dale Potoniak's apartment. Sudbury, Ontario.*
*1:06 p.m.*

Dale made up his mind. His number one priority that day would be to get a hold of Jane and ask her out. No more excuses. He would tell her how he felt and make a solid run at securing a second date. Rising slowly to avoid the pressure headache, Dale took a tiny sip of Emmett's whisky. He noticed Emmett had been by to water his plants as agreed, and he'd even gathered the mail and placed it in a neat stack on the kitchen counter.

*1:33 p.m.*

Dale pulled the elastic band off and thumbed through the stack of envelopes hoping Jane had replied to his postcard from Nicaragua.

Nothing. And nothing from Ola, either.

However, there was a hot-pink perfume-smelling envelope in the pile from a Kalina White, return address Sudbury, Ontario. A chill went through Dale's body as he laid on the cold linoleum floor and read.

Dale,

My name is Kalina White. My name is Kalina White, and I'm not enjoying performing anymore. Old men watch me play with myself on stage and I can't do it anymore. I want to be a writer. A writer.

You wrote on your blog recently about a woman you know that shamelessly flaunts her writing in magazines and newspapers, and even though it's copy-cat plagiarism, no one's had the guts to say anything. Do you remember?

You wrote (I copied and pasted)

"Hey Janice,

FIRST OF ALL, YOU of all people should know that it's NOT gonna be YOU who leads the way for a new breed of road-weary poets and gypsy travel writers, you Ivy-League twit—it's ME. Your image is bullshit. You're a carbon copy. A fake, a phony. A rip-off and a wannabe. I KNOW IT, YOU KNOW IT, and everyone else with a shred of common sense knows it too, you fucking WANNABE.

PAY YOUR DUES, BITCH. And don't come around here with that fake shit.

MY road—the one I'm on—ain't for the faint of heart. It ain't fit for people like you to speak of. You can't force it, and you can't fake it. YOU can't go to to school for it, so YOU steal ideas from other real writers when you can't get anything decent down.

Do you know how easy this is for us, Janice? Do you have ANY IDEA just how effortless this is, you ignorant fucking dunce? OLA sits in her room every day and every night and her pen just bleeds and bleeds, and it keeps going like that DAY AND NIGHT like she's on the bloody cross without a saviour, spread-eagle on the steel anvil of holy words—of holy scripture . . ."

Dale, there's no room in Janice's stupid world for you if she's not willing to accept the truth.

When you wrote, "This is so easy for me. That's what I'VE got. That's what YOU'LL NEVER HAVE. I'm in pieces, Janice. I'm in a million or more tiny pieces at any given time, and you're a waste of time. You're a fucking statue at the end of a driveway in some suburban shithole waiting for someone to notice you. Your greatest ambitions are my morning coffee and the side notes to my daytime visions."

Dale, when I read that . . . (SIGH)

I think that last line is one of the greatest ever written, and it's the reason I've decided to do this one last trip with the agency before I quit and start writing full-time.

I'm on the road tomorrow. Heading west for clubs and drugs, with pain in my heart and shame in my pocket. Why don't I have the inclination to riot?

The merry-go-round. A kaleidoscope of white and red, levers and cranks, devils and archangels standing firm on intentions that are good, and we all sing from the same place. We all scream from the same lungs and we all share the same stage as it turns and it turns and it turns, pulling or pushing, however we feel that day or night, and we all take the bait and hit the wall sooner or later. It's like a tug of war. You pull so hard you break the cord, but you leave the length of it in your enemy's hands—now he's got a whip. Now he's got a slave, and you're fucked.

We work all our lives, and waste our days. We waste these precious years where we still possess some sort of revolutionary energy. Not me. Not anymore.

So, I want to thank you for your words, for your writing, and for the motivation to be real and true to who I really am and the person I know I can become . . .

If you ever wanted to get together, or if you feel like chatting about life and writing, I'm on Chatmates.com pretty much all the time. My username is xmisswhitex.

No pressure, but let's just say I'd be VERY happy to hear from you.


XOXO


Kalina White


The letter had given Dale a semi-erection, but his head was spinning from the whisky. He rolled onto his side and puked on the floor. Stringy chunky vomit sprayed from his lip as he clung to the base of the kitchen cabinet, moaning and choking in utter agony. A voice in the back of his mind screamed, "Stop doing this to yourself!" but he'd been here too many times before. Not with a hangover like this. No, he just needed more sleep that's all, then he'd wander out and buy another bottle and everything would be okay again.

Dale's head hit the floor and he blacked out.

*3:52 p.m.*

After a few hours sleep Dale felt remarkably better. He sat up, took inventory of the apartment and saw the pool of stomach contents that he'd discharged onto the floor earlier. He promptly decided to clean the place up a little before doing anything else. Take some time, tidy up, regroup and readjust to being home before coming up with any ideas about Jane, or what to do about this Kalina person.

*4:04 p.m.*

Dale picked up Kalina's letter with two fingers and couldn't resist taking a sniff. Bad idea. The bottom half was soaked in vomit and was dripping the foul-smelling goo, but the words were still legible.

*What is this?* He held the letter in front of him.

Female admirers, whether of his books or his blog, were a rare commodity. Back in July of '96 (just a few months before he saw Ola perform *Wilhelmina* at the Elgin Street Opera House), a Mexican girl named Angelita had messaged him in a chat room. She'd read one of his books and liked it. They hit it off online then went clubbing down-town the next Friday. They took two hits of E and danced until close. They were on their way out of the club, in the lobby, when she put her hands down the front of his pants.

They fooled around on the train tracks behind the comic shop on Elm Street and made out till the crack of dawn, and just as the ecstasy was wearing off, a beautiful bright blue sunrise peaked over the jagged horizon and they had eye-rolling comedown sex behind a green graf-fiti-covered dumpster. Dale fell asleep on the ground shortly after he orgasmed, and Angelita left him there in the dirt, alone and uncon-scious. He never saw her again.

But no one had ever tracked down his mailing address just to insti-gate a—whatever this was. And however unlikely it might have been, the possibility of another casual hookup with a complete stranger seemed like an exhilarating proposition that demanded a full and thorough investigation. His last time with Ola was months ago, and the situation was becoming dire. Bedding another woman didn't mean he loved her any less. She'd said it herself. Live. So, whether it was a stripper named Kalina, or a Bible-thumping, gypsy journalist named Jane St. Marie, the letter had sparked Dale's libido into overdrive and he was ready to roll the dice for real this time.

A scary thought suddenly crossed his mind. What if Kalina *was* Jane? What if she'd read the savage blog entry about her and had seen right through it. Maybe she was baiting him to a secret meeting only to have some gelled-up corporate goof kick the shit out of him in the Super-C parking lot. He'd seen it happen before.

Or maybe it was Ola trying to instigate some sort of role-play fantasy game where they'd write letters pretending to be different people or something. That sounded fun, and wasn't outside the realm of possibility, either. But she hadn't written in a while and he knew she'd never do something so tacky. No, he had to be patient with her. She'd write. She'd be coming home.

In the meantime, Dale decided that a chat with xmisswhitex was the course of action with the highest probability of success. He'd see what she was about, decide accordingly, then figure out a plan for bedding Jane afterwards if things didn't work out.

*8:02 p.m.*

Dale opened his laptop and logged into his Chatmates.com account.

—SEARCH FOR USER: XMISSWHITEX

—USER FOUND

—REQUEST VIDEO CHAT WITH: XMISSWHITEX?

—YES

—ENTERING PRIVATE VIDEO CHAT. . . . . . . . . . .

Dale: "Hi. I just got your letter."

xmisswhitex: "Took long enough. I've been waiting for you, Dale."

Dale: "Really? Well, your writing shows a lot of potential. Thanks for sharing it with me. I think you could be a really good writer one day."

xmisswhitex: "It's nothing compared to what you do. That thing you wrote about Janice is the reason I want to be a writer now."

Dale: "Thanks. That wasn't my proudest moment, but I'm glad you enjoyed it."

xmisswhitex: "So who is she?"

Dale: "Who?"

xmisswhitex: "Janice. You never mention her last name."

Dale: "Nobody important."

xmisswhitex: "Bad boy. Are you alone, Daley?"

Dale: "Uh, yeah. Why?"

xmissewhitex: "Busy tonight?"

Dale: "Not really."

xmisswhitex: "I want to see you. In person. Can I come over? There's something I want to show you."

Dale: "You're in Sudbury? Your letter said you were heading west."

xmisswhitex: "I was, but I'm back . . . I danced my last show at Le Skin a few days ago. Here's a pic . . ."


Dale clicked open the photo. He knew the room at Le Skin well and there she was on stage, naked. He cleared his throat nervously.


Dale: "You're really . . . beautiful."

xmisswhitex: "Thanks. So do you wanna hook up tonight? I've got coke. And I can grab some booze on the way if you want."


*Ola. My love. So far from me now.*

Dale: "Sure. I'm good with whisky . . . My address is 1042 Front St #409 . . . Just buzz when you're here."

xmisswhitex: "Give me an hour. See you soon, sexy."

Kalina blew a kiss at the camera and disappeared.

# 4

"You motherfucker you! You ate her ass out, didn't you?" Charlie shouted, smiling jealously from across the table. "Don't leave a damn thing out. I wanna hear every dirty detail, chum!"

Dale's face beamed as he waved to the waitress to bring another round. "Honestly, I didn't know what to expect. I was worried she'd just wanna sit around and talk books and shit like that—but believe me, books were the last thing on this broad's mind, lemme tell you."

"Nothing like some good old-fashioned stripper pussy—eh, Emmett?"

"Frig off, Charlie," Emmett said. "Finish the rest of your story, Dale. I need to run a couple lines by you after."

"And what you gonna do if I don't 'frig off'— eh, tubby? Eh?" Charlie asked, poking Emmett's belly.

"Okay quit it, Charlie," Dale said, giggling. "Anyways, last time I got laid was in Nicaragua so I—wait—I told you guys what happened in Nicaragua, right?"

"No, we haven't even seen you since you got back! Quit holding out on us, chum. We wanna hear that one too. Right, Emmett?"

Emmett rolled his eyes. "What's your problem with me, Charlie?"

"Jeez. I didn't know you were so fuckin' sensitive—sorry."

Dale took a sip of beer and straightened his posture. "Well, I guess I should keep it chronological and tell that one first. One night I'm in this grimy hostel bar in Managua and I proposition this sexy dark-skinned senorita beside me for some *cervesas y buenos tiempos*. She agreed and we proceeded to drink our weight in Tona over the next four hours before going at it pretty hard on top of the bar. The fuckin' douche bag bartender got pissed off and kicked us out for being 'inappropriate' so we stumbled up to my hotel room, which was just a couple blocks away and knocked back a few more beers before we drunk-fucked on this rickety old table they had in there. Damn near broke the legs off the fuckin' thing. Anyways, a few minutes later I pass out, next thing I know, I wake up face down on the floor with my pants around my ankles and she's long gone. And so are the three hundred cordobas I had in my pocket . . . Oh well. Lucky she didn't get my passport or something or I'da really been screwed."

Charlie laughed hysterically. "You are one crazy mo-fo, Dale . . . Ah, I wish I could've been there with you, chum. We'd've had a blast—but hey—I was thinking, we should all do a road trip one of these days. Cruise down to T-dot or N-Y, get a bunch of blow and bang some hookers. Emmett could get some dick. It'd be fun."

"Sure. Sounds good to me," Emmett said, smiling at Dale.

"Yeah maybe," Dale said. "Could be fun for sure."

"Well? Get on with it then . . . What happened with this girl the other night?" Emmett asked.

"Right. So she comes in—and let me tell you this broad is fucking gorgeous, boys. She's wearing this short black dress, school-girl stockings and these heels that—" Dale paused to bite the back of his hand.

Charlie chuckled and nudged Emmett. "Look, I'm gettin' a hard-on just imagining it."

Emmett shook his head.

"Anyway," Dale continued, "I'm pouring us a drink. Meanwhile, she bends over to put some techno record on, and I can see every-thing right there, like she's showing me *everything*. She's got her sexy black hair pulled back real tight, and she's wearing those thick-rimmed, slutty school-teacher glasses I like—I mean I was getting the pre-cums just watching her play with the record needle, you know what I mean? So, we sit down and start talking about work and writing in general and she tells me she's been working as an actress and an exotic dancer for a while, but now she wants to be a writer because of some article she read on my blog. So I ask her if she'll read me some of her writing and she says, 'I thought you'd never ask.' Total performer. She was totally up for the challenge. And let me tell you, boys, this girl was a seasoned vet. She gets up, dims the lights then walks over to the centre of the room real slow and turns around—and then she reads me *this*."

Dale placed the sheets of paper on the table. Emmett and Charlie looked down at it cautiously, then at each other.

"Read it," Dale said, nodding to Emmett.

Emmett carefully unfolded the paper. "Okay . . . Let's see what this person has to say . . .

The night before was black, but she promised to stay this way. Something happened to her as she watched all those stories in movies and on television. To covet is an understatement. She became them. Created a false being for her fabrication. She became her fiction and now she is her fiction and she will die for her fiction.

Even though I do not allow joy in my heart, I know that the living are there for me, and even though I see devils, the light shines on us all and I am enraptured completely by the night. Tonight I will live again, for by day, something must die.

I imagine those I am at odds with and the darkness we all share here, and I go on and on and on. For goodness sakes this world is beautiful . . .

This city tastes like fall and I'm dying to leave and chase the sun all through the winter. I've hung the hooks and I've treated you kind. The stage curtains swing, the show must go on.

My thighs are still dry, and in the valley of killers, hooligans hide. We all felt their hunger in our dreams last night and morning comes too soon.

Out like a light,
One day then another,

Just to pass the time,

And it's gone once more.

Make your own observations. These are mine, and they're not a cheap confrontation with your winter disguise.

I knew a man who drew a lamp on a napkin in the dark,

I knew a man who lit a candle and spread his arms apart.

The only comfort I've ever known is the innocence of a mirror. You kept the secret from the serpent, but he kept you in Athena. I've never blamed or made a point of trying to make amends; the only thing I've ever known is the fact that we are friends—or we could be . . .

I can't hate her enough to watch her burn. How could I expect the same? The secret things you'll never tell me.

The beauty of your name.

The captive after-thought of your degenerate kiss.

I want to be on fire, and that want is endless . . .

They've raised the age of retirement now. You get to sixty-five—then, when the image is rotting along with the rest of your friends and family, they pay you monthly and you can sit in cafes with strangers, and long for your wife that's dead.

You wasted the years where you still had some energy to spread around. You hoarded all that time and kept it to yourself, or gave it away for nothing.

What a fucking waste.

I'm in a coffee shop right now and there's an old couple sitting near me. The woman is reading a book and the husband is staring out the window.

Are we all just endless dreamers?

What's left to dream about at that age?

Do I dare dream now?

What a strange life.

The music in this cafe is wonderful.

What do you think?

Does the old man really love her that much?

She's babbling about the book now. It's about a farm in Phoenix, and he's listening and he laughs, but he does not elaborate or advance the conversation. He asks small inoffensive questions and makes side notes to allow her room to talk.

I could sit and watch these two all day. What a strange way we have. And he just stares out the window now. Waiting by her side. Waiting with her, and for her, and she goes on reading.

What is so interesting about that book, old lady?

I think your old man is contemplating ideas deeper than you think. Perhaps he regrets things he did or didn't do as a young man. There's something about his eyes and the way he's dressed. Out—out—out. He's already somewhere else, but she brings him back with a simple word. He will always be hers so long as she lives. So long as he doesn't go too far away when he's thinking. Out—out—out that window, old man. Stay with her. She'll keep you safe. Your road to nowhere is already paved in silver and gold and there is nothing I can say to make you think different . . .

It goes on and on like this, guys."

Charlie was shocked. "That's fantastic writing," he said. "The girl's got skills."

"Goddamn brilliant is what it was," Dale said, matter-of-factly. "So she reads that to me, takes a bow and waits for me to say something."

"What'd you do next, Dale?" Emmett asked.

Dale smirked arrogantly. "What do you think I did, Em? Give her some professional criticism? Yeah, I told her it was okay, but I'd rec-ommend a little less theatrics when reading to small crowds. Amateurs tend to overthink things like that when they first start out. Fuck sakes, man."

"No fuckin' way," Charlie said, cutting in. "You didn't say that shit."

"It was a joke, Charlie," Emmett said.

Charlie giggled. "Oh yeah . . . I knew that."

Dale burst out laughing. "You fuckin' dumbass. How do you even keep a job? But she had me. I was about to get on my hands and knees and start crawling toward her, but I had to get a hold of myself."

"Please tell me this is the part where she sucks your dick," Charlie said.

"Just wait. So I calmed down and said, 'Now it's my turn,' and told her to sit the fuck down."

Charlie exploded. "Yes!"

Dale stood up and addressed Emmett and Charlie formally. "Ladies and gentleman, I've been working on this poem for a while now, and I gotta warn you, you might cry a little . . .

She made strange familiar versions of herself with moonlight on her tenderness. August rode as though it owned her, pacing along the water crest. Without lasting impression, last in line to hear her name. Our bed in roses, our sons in chains, unearthed in simplicity, her mother's bask remains. Her songs are with sorrow, her books are filled with lament. She wished them away while she cradled her babe, in the emptiness of white, sleeping forever—beside her love."

Charlie rocked back and forth excitedly, wiping a tear from his eye and pool of sweat from his freckled forehead. "Fuck, yeah."

Emmett nodded and raised his glass in respect. "Friggin-A, brother. Friggin-A."

"Now for the good part," Dale said, taking his seat. "After I do my little reading she walks toward me, then stops and stands there for a few seconds giving me this 'I'm going to eat you' look. All of sudden she grabs my hair, yanks my head back and says: 'You are going to do exactly as I say, Mr. Dale Potoniak. Mr. Bigshot fucking writer. You got that—bitch?'"

Charlie's face had turned beet red and his fists were clenched into tight white balls. "Yes!! Fuck yes! Holy fucking shit!"

"Good grief," Emmett exclaimed. "This just got kinky real quick."

Dale chuckled. "I know, right? So she pushes me on the chair and sits on my lap—and those perfect stripper tits are right there in my face—like right in my face, and she starts grinding and grinding and grinding—and fuck me she smelled good. So I say: 'Yeah, okay. I'll play your little game.' She smiles and tells me to stay put; two seconds later she's dumping a mound of coke on her wrist and shoving it in my face—so of course I gotta do it, right? I'm basically choking on white dust as she makes me lick the residue of her hand and wrist, she's sliding her dress off with the other."

"My dear lord." Charlie was dumbstruck. "I think I just jizzed."

"She's wearing a corset and black panties, garter belts, stockings, the whole nine. She starts undoing my belt just as the coke kicks in and I swear I was about to blow when she stops, gets up and walks over to that medieval chair in the corner of my living room—you know the one my uncle sent me from Romania a few years back? She turns around, sits down, then sloooowly spreads her legs and says, 'Come and kiss me here.'"

Dale stopped and calmly took a sip of his beer.

Charlie was literally bursting at the seams. "And? Then what happened?"

Dale giggled. "What was that?"

Charlie hammered his fist on the table. "What happened, chum?!"

"Oh, right. Well, let's just say I haven't thought much about Ola since then . . . And it was spectacular, boys. Just spectacular."

Dale looked happy for the first time in a long time, and Emmett was happy about that. Obviously this Kalina White was far from wife material, but if she kept Dale's mind and manhood occupied, he might outgrow his obsession with Ola and her heroin, and that's all that mattered to Emmett.

Emmett nodded. "Kalina White, eh? Sounds like a keeper, brother. A fun time if nothing else. I'm interested to see how it plays out."

*April 8, 1998. Dale's apartment. Sudbury, Ontario.*
*5:18 p.m.*

Dale decided to write Jane a final letter. If she didn't reply within a week he would move on for good. No reason to keep playing games with the poor girl's heart. He hadn't even masturbated to her picture once since Kalina cast her spell.

Jane,

Once there was a man who attempted carrying his ego, his logic, his pride, his anger, his fight, his depression, his anxiety, his stress, his attempts, his voice, his muscle, his will, his soul, his spirit, his faith, his love, his hate, his madness, his reality, his dreams, his thought, his prayer, his worry, his pain, his fear, his persistence, his escape plan, his eyes, his lips, his hands, his feet, his knees . . .

But his heart was not strong enough. He tried, and tried his best. He gave it all he had, until finally he fell on his face. His tears watered the soil around the burden. He got up, leaving the burden in the dirt with his tears, he said: "I'm not built to carry such an awkward goddamn load!"

He walked away miserable, but later he smiled, knowing that deep down he really tried.

After a while, he wanted to try again, but the burden had grown into a Ponderosa tree—his tears had watered the seed, you see . . .

And the tree spoke to him. "You shouldn't have carried me so far. You could have left me on the ground where you found me. You should have seen the signs all around you. Something would have budged. Something always does. Something like me was never meant to be carried by someone like you."

The man went home, and later found himself wondering why he had bothered to carry a tree in the first place . . .

Finally in a place of complete nothing. There is nothing left of me, and I have nothing left to give. No strength, no fight left in me. I cannot muster even a breath on my own, because I am on a wave floating miraculously, but twitching uncontrollably, and have no answer to my own dilemmas.

Always the same lines. "The same smooth way he saw her"; "The same way he saw himself—unrealistically, as a boy".

All these poems and all these songs, and all these bottles of booze and cigarette butts. They're all me begging you to look. I have no idea what that means, and I don't know why I still care.

I slept well last night.

I've had something in my left eye.

I was really falling for you,

Now every leaf is killing me.


Dale Potoniak


*A couple months later.*


*Saturday, June 3, 1998. Sudbury, Ontario.*
*9:06 a.m.*


The nervous panic and the need to not just exist, but to live. The restless yet imponderable potential of summer days and the sweet aroma of magnolias in the dewy hot morning coaxed Dale out of bed to the bench across the street from the old bingo where he used to sit and watch junkies beg, while doves flew back to their remote outposts on distant shopping mall clock towers.

On that hottest of mornings he watched for her. Longing to be by her side in the catacomb again, in the bosom of that wretched building, or else die alone. But she was a million miles away by now and Dale began to cry like an unhugged baby just wanting to belong, as passersby pointed and stared at the mad man soaked in sweat and tears.

Dale, Emmett and Charlie had consumed a dozen rum and pineapple juices each and had just returned to their seats after smoking some hash that Emmett procured from a friend at work. Their conversation took on a curiously placid momentum as the three friends watched a baseball game on TV.

"Live plants—light bulbs—alabaster and plaster of Paris on a wooden canvas—and a knife. Could make a fucking fortune with that shit," Dale muttered. He'd come up with an idea for a new form of sculpturing. "For rich bastards that like a little abstract in their straight lines and cottage weekends . . . What do you think?"

Charlie moved slowly and his bloodshot eyes could offer only minor salute. "Do it. Thassa brilliant idea, chum."

Two men in suits walked in tailed by a blond in a tight leopard print dress, and a skinnier redhead in a short black leather skirt and hooker heels. After a brief negotiation with the hostess, they were escorted toward a private booth, away from the surging mass of bloodthirsty drunken proletariat out front.

Emmett was feeling the effects of the hash and rum. "Look at 'em . . . Ugly cars and ugly women for guys who like latex cocks and shallow nine hundred number hookups," he mumbled.

"They're all just a bunch of SICK FUCKIN' PIGS!" Charlie shouted.

"Calm down. You're gonna get us all pinched," Dale whispered.

"The race is on," Emmett said, tapping Dale on the shoulder.

"Wha'?" Dale asked, spinning around.

Charlie made his toward the private booth. The two men and their dates were toasting, probably celebrating a promotion or something.

"Hey . . . I'd like to welcome you to our table. Join us," Charlie said, pointing to Dale and Emmett, who looked away immediately.

One of the businessman, who was black, took offence to the stench of booze and hashish emanating from Charlie's too-close-for-comfort mouth, or maybe he was pissed that Charlie was winking at his girlfriend.

"Naw, man. We're good. We've all had a long day and we're trying to have a drink, that's all. Why don't you go back to your table over there and sit with your little friends."

Charlie put his arm around the guy's shoulder, giving his neck a squeeze. "Little? Now why in God's name would you call them little? And why would I turn my back on you now, kid? Huh? I know what you've been saying this whole time with your rap and rhythm and blues . . . and many, many years ago, you would have let me tip that drink with you . . . What the hell happened to us, chum?"

"Hey, why don't you just leave us alone, you loser," the redhead snapped.

"Katie—chill. I got this." The black fellow drew his shoulders back and calmly said, "We gonna have a problem here? 'Cause if we do we could just take it outside."

"Nope. No problem. See the thing is, I managed to hate you because our bond was so sacred, you know what I mean? See, if *I* was black and *you* were white—then you made me better if *I* was wounded."

"What the hell are you talking about, man?" The white one asked, scared that he'd look like a pussy if he didn't get in on the action.

"Don't mind him guys. He's high," Emmett shouted from the table.

Charlie burst out laughing. "Oh shit! The new kid wants to dance. Put 'er there, new kid." Charlie offered his fist to the white fellow as tribute.

"I'm not fist-pumping you, man. Why don't you just fuck off and give us some privacy, okay?" The white fellow poked a finger into Charlie's shoulder.

"Here we go," Dale said, a childlike grin on his face.

"Whoa, whoa," the black fellow said. "Let it go. Let this fucking leprechaun go sit with his little bitch friends over there."

Charlie smiled and inched up to him. "Sorry, I couldn't make out what you just said over that accent of yours. What is that—west-side projects?"

Suddenly Charlie and black fellow were locked in a wrestling match and the girls were screaming hysterically because their drinks had spilled. Dale and Emmett rushed over to break it up.

"Hey, we're sorry," Emmett said, pulling Charlie away. "He's just high and likes to fight for no reason."

"Well, tell your boy next time he tries something like that I'ma knock his ass out," the black fellow said, wiping blood off his busted lip.

"I'm sure he's aware of that now," Dale said, giggling. "Y'all have a good powwow back here."

Charlie was all smiles heading back to the table. "Another round on me, gents? Let's fuckin' dooo this."

Dale used his best boxing promoter voice. "You a goddamn fool."

"Dale's right, brother. Why do you have be such an asshole when you get high?" Emmett asked.

"Same reason you're a fuckin' homo. And I don't say shit to you about that, so shut the fuck up, bitch." Charlie sat down and took a slug of rum and pineapple.

"Screw you, Charlie. You're just a homophobe. Maybe you've got some tendencies hidden in there that you're ashamed of and—"

"Ashamed? Who said I was ashamed?" Charlie chuckled. "I'll suck your dick right now if it makes you feel any better. I ain't ashamed of shit."

Emmett laughed. "Well, screw you, Charlie . . . Anyways, I gotta go, guys. I just realized it's almost six and I gotta be at my parents' place for dinner by seven."

"So?" Dale asked.

"So? I'm high and drunk. I need to sober up a bit."

"Pussy," Dale said, staring up at the TV screen.

Charlie burst out laughing. "Yeah, ya big fuckin' PUSSY!"

Emmett stood up. "Okay, I'm leaving now. Don't get too crazy tonight, brothers. And Charlie, you owe me like a hundred bucks from last time so you can pay my bill."

"Good on ya, chum," Charlie said, high-fiving him.

"Love you guys," Emmett said.

"Love you too!" Dale shouted.

"And . . . that leaves the two of us, chum," Charlie said.

"Yes, I suppose it does," Dale replied.

"Fuck should we do now?"

"No clue . . . Got any ideas?"

"How much money you got?"

"Enough."

"All right . . . well . . . how 'bout we go back to my place for a couple drinks and I'll call my guy. Score us some primo blow, then we'll cab it to New Suds and hit Le Skin for some lappers?"

Dale's head turned slowly as if his neck was on some kind of robotic turnstile. "I think you just read my goddamn mind, Charlie. Are you psychic?"

Charlie laughed and drum-rolled the edge of the table. "Yes! Let's gooooo!" he hollered.

They downed the rest of their drinks, threw some cash on the table and stepped outside, a view of the super stack and the setting summer sun off in the distance.

*Dale Potoniak's apartment. Later that night.*

Kalina's previous career had provided her a very extensive lingerie and costume collection, which was now spread over the floor, bed and furniture in Dale's apartment for one reason or the other.

Dale was still drunk and high on blow when he got home, so he snapped. "What the fuck've you been doing here all goddamn day? My apartment's a mess!"

"So," Kalina said, contemptuously, "clean it up then. I'm going out for a while."

Dale objected. "Tonight? It's two in the morning."

"Yeah, and? I just got a call from a guy at *Fairpress Book News*. He wants my bio and a chapter from my book tonight 'cause he's heading out of town in the morning. I'm gonna stop by his apartment and drop it off . . . Oh, relax. It won't take long. I'll be back in an hour and you can dress me up in anything you want."

The idea got him excited, but Dale was still beside himself. "What kind of person asks for an author bio at two in the morning on a Saturday night, Kalina?"

"I don't know! What the fuck do you care? I didn't ask what you've been doing with your retarded friends all night. It's my life and my career, so fuck you, you little bitch." Kalina grabbed the set of keys he'd given her and stormed out the door before he could say another word.

*Very early the next morning.*

Dale sat at his desk. His eyes felt heavy, and the sun was peeking in through the thin blue curtains. Kalina was still out, and he'd spent the darkest hours of the night polishing off a bottle of rum while writing a letter to Ola. He'd called her mobile number in Milan earlier, but she'd changed it. Now he would send a letter to the only address he had for her in Milan, the one she'd written on the back of the postcard in December.

Ola,

Something is monkeying around in my peripheral. Changing colours, stations, faces.

Is it possible to get lost in a disease?

Your rose has no name and your touch is cold to the feel. My lips speak no need of another like you.

She dances through my area and makes a mess of my palace. She stains my bed sheets and carries me around like I was never worth a second try.

Meanwhile, you fade. You're a page in a book I made, but never wanted to write. I am not willing to give you a place in my palace unless you make me smile, and the dance just goes on as I pound to unfamiliar tunes and take medicine to think her hair flows like yours. Actually, it has never been so dull.

Staring in your eyes on a day of rain, let us share a porch light somewhere south of here, or even better—farther north.

I wish I could change. I'll never keep records from now on.

Gardens in Greece we may never see, and verandas in Helsinki you may hate. I need rest for my weary eyes because they burn, cities for my fantasies because I love them, and I write just for the thrill.

She shames her captors by lending a hand. She changes her future by lying beside her enemy. Her death is fair, yet totally dishonourable (but not disgraceful), and somehow envied by harlots and housewives alike. In the wilderness of her sex she wanders on until she passed across Paris on a sunny night, and slept for her chance to compete for a seat on the Roman Citadel.

Even though I've devolved, you've always stayed the same.

Your purple eyes remind me of my summer of love.

—She loves me for me and she's never had that before. But now I lust over you. Now that you're gone. Now I can love you like I wanted to. Now.

Ola—I'm losing focus as the days fly by. Wounded, because I have this picture, and my soul sings like Jerusalem denying its slavery and hating the pope. Jesus inside your walls and you still won't stand up or march for freedom . . .

I want to taste you. I'm going to cut myself—maybe then I can feel how your heart would hurt without me.

You're the only one who knows me, and you're the only one who cares. You're the only one I've ever really loved. I need you to know that as much as I cringe and hate what I've been, I imagine tomorrow never without you.

Think of me when you leave for St. Petersburg, when you dance in Colombo and train to be a witch, for you are the dark and I am the light.

Am I cursed by God because I found a flaw in his creation?

Because I don't think that any of us are beautiful at all, do you?

I love how you praised me in your postcard, and no, I am not intimidated. We need not fret, dear love, through dark or rain, or hail or sleet—even time cannot break the love we shared. You can be my companion over every canopy and desert, through winters like we've never seen. I want you by my side so we can pray together, maybe even sing together. Maybe we can bring another mood, but surely we can rescue a feeling.

It's only four, and already I'm drunk with love for you, my dove.

I love your smell and I've never smelt you. I want to analyze you afternoon, evening and night. Meet me at her statue and we will make love, but don't stay away long.

Are you a farmer now? Long days in the cold sun make you smile? Come grow us a garden. Don't clean, don't sweep—I just want to eat.

You make me laugh if you're a farmer now . . . Come be my wife— that's all I want. Come make us a garden and give me some kids. Come feed our bellies and dance naked under the purple moon. In and out till dawn, and retire to Athens or Helsinki, or maybe somewhere in between, where friends send invites to you with pale skin, while we are only special together.

I won't rush a word, Ola. Not tonight. Why has your mouth gone dry, and when did you get up to leave? I have friends in many countries, but I have never seen anyone quite as beautiful as you. I want to see you under the Mediterranean sun, and I want to watch the cool blue ocean drip from your tanned thighs.

I'm looking for someone to break the curse.

I want to till the ground for you.

There is no confusion in my love for you, there is no one else for me. My body will become a temple for you. I want to live inside you most of the time. I will never reject you and I will not turn away. I don't want you to change, I just want every look we share to confuse the riverboat man, expert on love, wines and tourism.

Searching random staircases. It never ceases to amaze me how naive these people are (or is it me with the razor to my wrists playing games with prison cells I recognize so plainly?). I drink more every day to make myself feel, yet my conscience wills no success for my unequipped soul. Death is a certainty, but we will live longer together than we did as children with our mothers and fathers. Please do not leave me here, Ola. I want to become a temple. I want to be strong on the day we need each other. I'm still not there, but maybe in a few more years, everything I do will be peaceful and slow, unrushed and honest, fearless.

—Muse,

—Idea,

—Something I never have when you're gone,

—Something you took when you left.

Were you not intrigued by me at all?

I lost all meaning,

Because I left you.

All knowledge,

Because I failed to know you.

Ola, my love.

My equal,

My dearest,

How appropriate this all is,

As a reminder to always love you.

The graceful way you tolerate my insane vanities stands alone on a blank white wall like suicide art. This is the way it is with all things that are created by the nature of a woman.

Yours,

Dale Potoniak

He sealed the letter and and sent it off before crawling into bed with a pair of Kalina's underwear.

*August.*

Restless hearts accompany restless men at the end of summers. Dale was having serious doubts about Kalina. He'd introduced her to some people in the literary scene, and she'd made more connections in a few months than he'd been able to in over a decade.

On several occasions, Kalina and Dale were out having dinner or drinks alone, when a publisher or editor Dale only knew through the grapevine would stop by their table to say hi to her. They'd make small talk at first, then introduce their friend, or friends to her, and she'd always find a way for them to sit together before she'd start playing her little games.

Even the most cut-throat professional men were no match for Kalina's looks, and it wasn't long before she had so-and-so's phone number, email and a meeting with their boss the following week to discuss the novel she'd been working on while living rent free in Dale's apartment.

Kalina's business savvy combined with her sexual allure worked its magic on every horny book maker in the city, and within a couple months she had every wife in the business worried sick if her husband wasn't home by nine on Saturday night.

Sometimes at dinner, Dale would nudge her leg beneath the table when he wanted to go home. She'd whisper in his ear and rub his cock. "Not yet, baby. But if you're tired, you go . . . I want to stay a little while longer . . . I want to talk to Toby—or Tim —or Todd about this or that . . . But when I get home tonight I'll suck your—" And so on and so forth.

Some nights she'd come home at dawn with the smell of another man's cologne on her. Regardless of all the potential scenarios she might have been involved with that night, Dale could never resist her for long.

"No, Kalina. Not this time," he'd say.

She'd lean into him, her bra straps slipping playfully off her narrow shoulders. His willingness to argue weakening, if not fully dissolved.

"Dale . . . Look at me, Dale."

"Not until you tell me where you were tonight."

"Does it matter?"

Her glistening breasts and body were always clad in some kind of black lace push-up bra or latex corset and she always knew exactly what to do and say.

She jumped on top of him and grabbed him by the throat.

"Stop it," Dale begged, choking. "I want to know if you were with another guy tonight."

"And if I was . . . What would you to do to me, Daley?"

He became mute. Kalina's spell made sure his tongue only worked for one thing, at her command.

*Where is my Ola now?* he often thought. *Where is my pretty wife?*

# 5

*Six months later.*

*February 1, 1999. Dale's apartment. Sudbury, Ontario.*

*9:45 a.m.*

There it was, in full colour on the first page of *Re-Think* magazine's literary section.

*On February 20th, author Kalina White will be inducted into the North American Writers Guild on the opening night of the Guild's annual literary conference and awards show in Toronto.*

Gary Metzger, of Metzger Publishing organized everything. He'd released Kalina's novel to the world with the full support of his company's enormous marketing machine and it was received warmly by the critics and media in its first week on the shelves.

—"Stunning, provocative imagery. Kalina White is HOT, HOT, HOT, HOT!" – *Word Is* magazine

—"Raw, cunning and deeply imaginative. Kalina White brings the sexy back to contemporary adult fiction." – *Fairpress Book News*

Dale read it before it hit the shelves and said it was too short to be considered a novel, that the dialogue was amateurish and exaggerated, and the plot wasn't going to grab anybody's attention.

"On top of that," Dale said, bitterly, "it's shallow and wishy-washy. The narrative lacks any definable premise whatsoever and your characters are all fucking assholes. Is this supposed to be erotica or a mystery-thriller? It's totally unclear. And if you're trying to be artsy, don't make it so blatantly obvious. It's painful . . . I taught you better than this, Kalina."

Regardless of her book's shortcomings, Kalina's ability to play the game was astounding. She'd landed a lucrative book deal with Metzger Publishing, the third largest publishing company in North America and become personal friends with CEO and president, Gary Metzger. Gary was the founding member of the world's most elite literary collective, The North American Writers Guild, and with his unwavering support, Kalina's novel was set to become a number one bestseller nationwide. Recently he had her appointed to the boards of two very influential national literary organizations; and in a few short weeks she'd become an official member of the Guild, which is equivalent to being made in the Italian mafia, but for the book business.

*12:06 p.m.*

"I bring you up and this is the thanks I get?" Dale was drunk and getting more belligerent by the minute, shouting at Kalina from the couch where was sprawled out in his underwear. "You fucking whore. I should've left you in that strip club turning tricks where I found you, you bitch . . . It's one favour, Kalina. One favour I'm asking you for! . . . I let you live here for free for months! Why won't you just tell Gary about me? I taught you every goddamn thing you know about writing anyway! Why the fuck are they inducting you? What the hell did you do to pull that little stunt off, eh? How big's his dick, Kalina? Eh? Slut . . . Pass my book to him tomorrow and see what he thinks. Tell him I've given hundreds of speeches and—Kalina? Kalina!"

Kalina seemed amused by Dale's vulnerability. "You're asking *me* for a handouts now? You degenerate little motherfucker. I did my own work to get to where I am right now, okay? I don't owe you shit. But if it'll shut you the hell up, then fine, I'll mention your name when I see him in Toronto tomorrow. Eww. You're fucking gross, Dale. I'm leaving."

Dale had vomited on himself.

*February 3, 1999. Dale Potoniak's apartment, Sudbury, Ontario.*
*2:46 p.m.*

A few days later, someone from Metzger Publishing called to invite Dale to Toronto that weekend to give a short speech to kick-off a local event called Canadian Writers' Week. Dale tried sounding indifferent, but when the woman on the other end of the phone offered him five hundred dollars in cash, he quickly accepted and hung up.

"I'll pay you back, Kalina. Please don't make me beg you for this," Dale tried his best keep cool and not lose his temper.

"Ugh. You're such a shit rat, Dale. Motherfucker can't even afford a bus ticket to Toronto . . . Fine."

*February 5, 1999. Toronto, Ontario.*
*10:30 a.m.*

When Dale arrived at the Aero Hotel and Conference Centre, he was greeted at reception by an overweight, squirrely-voiced woman name Shayna.

"Welcome to Canadian Writers' Week, sir. My name is Shayna, how can I help you today?"

"I'm here for the, uh—I'm one of the—"

"That's fantastic, sir. Here's a list of events and workshops across the city, or if you're just here for today, Metzger Publishing is proud to present some very interesting workshops featuring some lesser known, but very serious local writers, followed by the main event which is an hour-long question and answer period with bestselling author, Estevan Milos."

"Yeah, I know. I'm one of the—I mean, I'm Dale Potoniak. I'm giving a speech at one of those workshops this morning."

"Oh, I see . . . Oh, there you are, Mr. Pontiac. You're on at eleven in conference room A."

"And where exactly would that be, Shayna?"

"That would be the basement, sir. Two floors down. The elevator is over there. Ask around for Donnie, he'll sort you out. Refreshments and snacks are free. Here is your event ID. You're all set."

Dale reached for the name tag. It read:

DALE PONTIAK

K. WHITE GUEST

"Excuse me. Excuse me . . . Hey, Shayna. You spelled my name wrong."

"Excuse me?" Shayna snapped with a sharp smirk.

"I said you spelled my name wrong. See? You wrote P-O-N-T-I-A-K. It's spelled P-O-T-O-N-I-A-K."

"First of all, *I* didn't spell that, sir. Secondly—"

"I don't give a fuck if you did or didn't, Shayna . . . Shit. I don't mean to be rude, it's just that I expected this whole thing to be a little more—"

"Is it really that big of a deal, sir?" Shayna asked, rolling her eyes.

Dale took a deep breath.

"Never mind. It's fine," he said, faking a smile. "Really, it's fine, Shayna. Have a great fucking day."

"You too, Mr. Pontiac."

Dale turned to face the crowded lobby. At least a hundred nerdy, pimple-faced book geeks and wannabe writers had come to see Milos talk.

Estevan Milos. Another one of Metzger Publishing's pet projects. His novel, *Timmy*, made the bestsellers list recently and Dale read the review in last month's *Fairpress Book News*.

"A well-spun, clever tale about Timmy, a mischievous little kitten who accidentally falls from a window. Sweet, gentle Timmy is kidnapped by street thugs, raised in poverty, and later forced to kidnap kittens for the big-name pet store franchises.

This masterpiece of contemporary fiction is both poignant and precise, as it alludes to the widespread cruelty of the pet-breeding industry. Milos expertly crafts the storyline, commenting on the horrors of human trafficking and the sex trade.

*Timmy* is being considered for several of the Guild's most prestigious awards this year, and *Fairpress Book News* would like to congratulate Estevan Milos on a wonderful literary achievement."

*Bull-fucking-shit.* Dale manoeuvred through groups of adoring Milos fans as he made his way toward the elevator. Posters of Milos, with his perfect white teeth were plastered all over the hotel lobby. A huge felt banner of his likeness hung from the vaulted ceiling.

Dale stepped into the elevator and pressed B2. When the door shut, he took a deep breath and the chaotic noise from the overcrowded lobby slowly faded away. Milos kept smiling from a larger-than-life banner on the wall of the elevator.

Dale cracked his knuckles. "You're only here for the money," he mumbled. "You're only here for the money."

As the elevator descended, Dale opened the program Shayna had given him and flipped to page one.

February 5th at the Aero Hotel.

11–11:15 a.m.

Dale Pontiak

Opening Introduction

12–12:45 p.m.

"Making Waves"

How to market your new book.

A workshop with local author, George Goyas

1–2 p.m.

Open-format question and answer period with bestselling author, Estevan Milos

The elevator opened, but Dale was already pounding furiously on the "L" button with the butt of his hand.

"What in the good goddamn fuck is this, Shayna?" Dale screamed.

Shayna smirked as she chewed on a fat wad of pink bubble gum. "Excuse me, you're going to have to calm down before I speak with you, sir. Now what'd you say?"

"This! An opening introduction? Fifteen fucking minutes? I'm a published author! They told me I'd be making a speech! The lady on the phone said—"

"I don't know who said what to you, Mr. Pontiac. All I know is Gary's got the last word on everything as far as the events go, so you might want to talk to him instead of screaming at me like this, okay?"

"Gary? As in Gary Metzger?"

"Know any other Gary's 'round here?"

Dale froze. "Gary's here? Gary Metzger is here—in this building?"

Shayna yawned and looked at her watch. "Uh-huh. For another—oh, hour, tops. He'll be heading to Barkley's Books for Kalina White's meet and greet shortly."

"Thank you," Dale muttered.

"You want the address to Barkley's or something?"

"I'm good. Thanks." Dale made for the lobby door, sprinting four blocks to the nearest liquor store. He crouched behind a dumpster with a mickey of vodka and a can of orange pop. He finished all but an inch of the vodka, then smoked two cigarettes to get his blood flowing again. By the time he got back to the hotel, he was feeling much better about his speech.

*11:00 a.m.*

Dale's hand shook slightly as he stood behind the wooden podium. He rummaged through a stack of notes with only one thought on his mind: *Gary* might be listening.

*Gary Metzger.* Overlord of the book world. If Dale made an impression on him today it could change his life for good. No more invisible man. No more pearls for swine or crying for attention behind closed doors. Dale looked up nervously. There were thirty or so attendees in the mid-sized room, all waiting quietly for him to start his fifteen-minute introduction. The spot-lights felt like a blast furnace torch. His face was turning red, he knew it. A trickle of sweat dripped down his forehead, which he quickly brushed away. He took a deep breath and began.

"Thank you all for coming today. My name is Dale Potoniak. P-O-T-O-N-I-A-K, in case you got it mixed up from the program." He meant it as a joke, but no one laughed.

Feedback from the mic made a squealing sound and a lady in the front row covered her ears in disgust.

Dale loosened his collar and cleared his throat. "Some of you may have heard of me . . . I'm an author. I've written novels, various collections of poetry and I have a popular blog that—"

A couple in the second row glanced at each other cynically.

Dale swallowed hard. "Um, never mind. I'm here today to tell you a little bit about what it really means to be a writer." Dale choked on some spit in his throat and fumbled with his notes.

"I—uh—I can't really remember a lot about my early years. It's all buried in here somewhere, though . . . I can't think of anything essential that put me on this specific path in life, but what I can say is that everything that's happened to me has made me who I am today, and minus a few things, I'm okay with who I am for the most part."

His throat muscles contracted. *Oh God, please not now,* he thought, desperately fighting to keep his anxiety under control. The panic grew worse when he noticed a couple in the back row whispering and giggling as they pointed at him. His eyes began to water and his eyelid began spasming on the left side.

"Folks . . . if you'll excuse me for a second." The microphone made a loud thudding sound as Dale bumped it leaving the stage. He pushed aside the heavy black curtain and collapsed to one knee, hyperventilating.

"What the shit are you doing, man? Get out there! We're not paying you for some bullshit thirty-second speech. You got that?" The cocky young production assistant was steaming mad.

"Yeah, I know. Just give me a second, I'm having a bit of a panic attack here." Dale was hunched over and white as a ghost.

"Oh for fuck sake. This is unbelievable. Hey, Donnie! The intro guy is having a fuckin' panic attack on stage A!"

"Who?" a voice from the blackness, presumably Donnie's, shouted back.

"Pontiac! He's freakin' out, man."

"Who gives a shit. Send his ass home and do it yourself then!" Donnie screamed back.

"Fuck that . . . Listen, Pontiac, I'm scared shitless of public speaking so you better get your act together, and—"

Dale reached into pocket, his hands trembling as he drained the last few ounces from the vodka bottle.

The production assistant burst out laughing. "Fuck, man. You got it worse than me, eh?"

"Fuck out of my face!" Dale hissed, choking on the syrupy booze.

"Shh! They can all hear you, motherfucker. Now you get your ass back out there or you ain't getting a dollar. Get what I'm saying?"

"Yeah . . . Yeah, I'm good. I'm good now," Dale said, taking a deep breath.

"Well, good. Go get 'em, tiger."

Dale straightened his collar and walked back out to the bright stage.

"Sorry for the delay, folks. I had a bit of a—unexpected situation." Dale pointed to his crotch and the crowd laughed.

"Where was I? Uh-huh. Yes, of course . . .

"Just like you, I struggle with expression. I've always wanted to create something beautiful. Something worthy of my name. I know the poems I've written are beautiful, and maybe that's a big part of what I'm trying to do in this business—maybe that's what *I'm* meant to do. But we're here today to talk about books, not poems. Novels, fiction—stories.

"Now why would someone want to write a story?

"I for one can't write well with all those commas, periods and grammatical rules, because I for one never liked rules."

Dale grabbed his stack of notes and threw them high in the air. The vodka had kicked in.

"I've always enjoyed designing the things I create. Making them formless and beautiful, and that's all I ever hoped to achieve when it came to my work: beauty. To design, say—the story of my life? Ha! I doubt I'd ever be motivated enough to relive *that* whole crazy tale.

"Every time I sit down to write I think about stories I've saved up over the years. I've done so much, but I've kept a lot in. And this is why we write.

"Is that all it is? Is writing just therapy for us victims of consequence? Do we really *need* to say anything? Who's really going to benefit in the end? Isn't it just better to just leave it all be, rather than let it all go? To know that you are who are right now in this moment because of everything you've been through?

"That you survived and life didn't break you?

"That you've all got one hell of a strong spirit?

"To tell or not to tell. And what is there to tell? I've got loads of stories about drugs, booze, sex and self-examination, and I've got a hell of a lotta insight into human psychology—at least my own. I've been blessed with the time, and cursed with the propensity for deep, sometimes excruciating periods of self-examination.

"Writing is a constant search for fresh ideas, and there's a billion topics out there that can be touched on that are relevant to people. Relationships, communication, the meaning of life, work, money, duality, suffering, the right path to go down, how to live each day—because at the end of the day no one knows shit. We're all just speculating. Our ideas are based solely on personal experiences and our expressions are based solely on our ideas. So, is it my right to share that expression with you? What right do I have to do such a thing? To force you to listen to my ideas. Is it right to share art at all? And what purpose is there in the sharing? Will you the reader gain anything from my expression except ability to judge my opinions, my worth and my power based on the fragments of my soul that survived the editing process? This world, this business, is ruthlessly unfair to almost all forms of personal expression, and as the expresser we freely give *them* the power to say whether or not our expressions are right, or good, or have any value in this world at all, and that is a brutal soul-sucking affair.

"Can any artist, any person with a sound mind and firm grip on reality not take to heart such savage, throat-cutting criticisms? Or can an expression be expressed without any hope or expectation of praise, recognition or compensation? No book deals, no money—just for the sake of the art?

"I sense all the purists out there wanting to scream at me and say, yes of course! That's true art! Expressing for the sake of expression alone . . . Expression as spiritual release, as opposed to repressing ideas for the sake of our egos and the beating they'll get from the sharks in suits who will tell you time and time again that you're no fucking good. You purists may be thinking that perhaps I write with the wrong motives and perhaps I should express with no motives at all, right? Perhaps I should not think at all, is that it?

"Tell me—who gains from the act of expression? That little question stops the power of your expression dead in its tracks before the words even come out. Why communicate? Expression and communication are cousins in the same genre of speculative thought, are they not? What is the purpose of communication? To navigate this life I suppose. To allow us to co-exist with other human beings and express our ideas and concerns. Ah, I see now. It is the *right* of every human being. It is our *right* to navigate life using any and every tool at our disposal, including expression. A writer simply exercises his right and releases a record of his experience into the world for someone else, or for no one else to see. Is that it?"

The crowd shuffled in their seats, curious and intrigued.

Dale snatched the mic and walked out to the front of the stage. "Expression is simply experience manifested through the ability of the writer, and the expression's final form is limited to the writer's ability to filter and refine it. To shape it into something beautiful. That is art.

"Is it fair to say that a person who comes across as stupid, or less than average, is simply untrained in the art of expression? How does someone train for expression?

"How does that come about?

"Perhaps by studying other methods of expression?

"Mimicking?

"No.

"Maybe taking an existing idea and changing something, thereby altering it into something new?

"No, that's just borrowing.

"To becoming an expert at fluid and effortless expression you must be original and true to yourself. Expression must be from you and for you or its false. A no-good knock-off, a plagiarism, a copycat. A fucking counterfeit.

"Being that you have something to say, say it! Perhaps that is the simplest way to define true art. It will of course run the gauntlet of social appropriateness and political correctness, and don't forget to consider your audience and marketability of the end product.

"Your book, your expressions, will be exposed to a litmus battery of tests to make sure they fit into this world and into the smallest minds of the dumbest people you'll ever know, and that right there has proven disastrous to the enterprises of many noble men and their art. Their life's work. The beautiful expression gets fucked six ways from Sunday and takes its place in the abomination room that eventually becomes a dancing display case or a marketable gimmicky book of the month.

"So what is there to say and why say it? I've got stories and it's my right to express them. True. But, I void that right if I pervert the expression by means of outward bias, fear of judgment, or personal insecurity. Yes. Expression must be certain of its own truth and its own right to speak and of its undeniable ability to affect not only the reader, but the creator.

"I'll ask again, people. Why do we express ourselves? Sure it's our right, but we surrender that right the second we speak or write a word in hopes of private gain, secretly introducing kind or damaging words tilted in a certain direction, or making soft where hard once was.

"Could it be that due to a lack of true expression we see the scales tipping, and men and women writing these "popular" books at alarming rates? Is it any wonder then, why someone invested in the other side of the scale has an interest in stifling freedom of speech and expression? We see that happening all over the goddamn place and I'm fucking sick of it. Either way, expression builds nothing. It is truth, and in turn must epitomize the nature of truth. The character of truth. Let your expression be yours, because I don't know what there is for anyone else to gain from that. You're simply exercising your God-given right to outwardly make flesh, or word, or song, your experience, and that is not something that should be put out into the world with interests into personal gains of any kind whatsoever. This kind of fucked-up thinking always lead to abnormalities of the mind. You'll always wonder why *that* person's expression is more valuable than yours. You'll always think, why can't *my* expression have monetary value if so-and-so's does? Perhaps, I'll just modify it, and this kind of shit leads down all kinds of paths ripe with compromise, and more boring, weak, watered-down shitty books from people whose idea of true art is—well, you be the judge."

Dale raised his middle finger to a poster of Estevan Milos on stage and several jaws in the crowd dropped open.

"If you're going to create something, let it be true. Let it be like a tree falling in the woods. Let it be like a happy man walking in the woods alone humming a tune. Let that be your song. Examine your motives and you will discover your true worth in a treasure chest of memories that's been hidden behind a pile of brainwashed bullshit ideas of fame and fortune.

"You all have stories. I supposed they need to come out. Let them be told. And feel free to mould and shape them into something else. Let your experiences become beautiful fictions. Let the ugly become beautiful through the hands of the sculptor. Perhaps you've been collecting colours, learning words and storing up clay for your final masterpiece all along. So let the careful planning of your expression begin with a deep meditation on motives. My motive is to create something I believe is beautiful and worthy of my name. Forget all the bullshit about publishing and releasing. You are the product. Release yourself into the world every day. You're a writer! Watch yourself. Be awake. Be alive. Wake up, and give yourself to love."

The crowd sprang to their feet, cheering and whistling praise and adoration, and for a moment Dale felt the recognition he knew *his* expression deserved from the thirty or so twinkling faces.

He overheard a man in the front row saying, "That was fucking amazing," to his neighbour, as he shook his head in amazement.

He heard a woman ask the woman next to her, "What's his name again?" and the other replied, "Check the program."

He saw a couple in the front searching for answers in the Writers' Week program. The nerdy-looking boyfriend said, "He's obviously some amazing writer. Let's get his autograph, babe."

Dale felt invincible. The vodka courage had been replaced by a feeling of genuine accomplishment and confidence. He'd done it. He'd delivered an undeniably genius speech at one of Toronto's most reputable literary events, with Gary Metzger, owner of Metzger Publishing somewhere in the building, listening. If not, word would spread. About the speech. About the amazing once-in-a-lifetime performance by Dale Potoniak. It had to. It just had to.

Dale smiled and waved to the adoring crowd, then walked off stage with a fresh spring in his usually flat step. He was greeted backstage by Donnie and the production assistant. They wanted to shake his hand and ask a few questions, then after, they led him to a VIP members-only area.

Gary Metzger. Titan of the book industry. Founder of the North American Writers Guild, and president of Metzger Publishing, noticed Dale walk in and greeted him with a hand shake that crushed Dale's thin, bony fingers.

"Great speech, pal. Heard most of it over the PA. A little over the top, but very—how should I say—inspired."

Dale was star-struck. "Thanks, Gary. I uh—"

"Listen, Shayna should have some cash for you at reception, and hey—I'd like to have you and Kalina over for dinner sometime. I've got a suite in Yorkville that I think she'd—I mean, you'd both love the view from up there. You can see the whole goddamn city. You a scotch drinker, pal?"

"Yeah. I, uh—I like it pretty good."

"Good man. Well, let me be the first to thank you for doing such a bang-up job coaching Kalina through the writing process. She personally told me she couldn't have done it without you."

Gary squeezed the back of Dale's neck with an iron grip that made his head tilt uncomfortably to the left.

"I was—I was hoping to talk to you about something, Gary. See, I've got this book that I—" Dale reached into his pocket for a copy of his novel.

Gary snatched it from his hand and gave it to his assistant. "Yeah, that's great. Listen, Darryl. I gotta go, but here's my card. Call the office next week. My secretary will set something up. On second thought—" Gary snatched the card back. "I'll just get Shayna to call Kalina. Whatever. Either way I'll see you around, eh? Thanks, pal."

"Yeah . . . Uh, that sounds good, Gary. Let's keep in touch. Sure. Thanks. Okay."

Gary was gone before Dale finished his sentence.

Dale made his way up to the lobby and sulked out for a smoke. *Wanna waste my time? I'll fuckin' waste you, you arrogant piece of shit.* He was just about to light up when he saw her walking toward him.

Jane St. Marie.

"Of all the people I did not expect to see here today." Jane looked genuinely amused by the idea of it all. Him. Here. With *these* people. "I took you as more of an anti—writers' guild kind of guy."

"I am. I was. I mean—they asked me to come and I needed the money. I mean, uh—never mind." Dale fidgeted nervously with his hands. "Fuckin' waste of time anyways . . . Hey, how come you stopped writing me? It's been like a year since I heard from you . . . I was beginning to think you might hate me or something."

"Hate you?" She laughed. "Of course not. Let me see . . . Well, I was in Victoria for a few months, then I was in Estonia, then Stockholm . . . I don't know. I've been really busy."

Dale looked away.

"I'm sorry," Jane said. "I got your letters. It's just . . . I felt like I had to back off a bit. I didn't want to give you the wrong idea because I'm not in the position to have many meaningful relationships in my line of work, you know what I mean?"

"Yeah, whatever."

Jane could tell that he was upset and tried to lighten the mood.

"How have you been? What's new? It's good to see you."

"You could've called me, Jane. I waited a really long time to hear back from you."

"I said I'm sorry, Dale. But it's my job. I told you I live out of suitcases most of the time and it's been a really hectic year."

Dale kept staring at the ground.

"Hey. Look at me," Jane said tenderly.

Dale looked. She was even more beautiful than he'd remembered.

"Don't get me wrong. I love your writing, Dale. You're one of the best poets I've come across in a long time, and I really liked the back and forth we had there for a while—but aren't you dating Kalina White now?"

Dales face turned bright red. "Well, you see I'm, uh—I was helping her with her book, and yeah, I guess we were kind of seeing each other, but it wasn't serious. She's gone off on her own now, so—yeah. We're pretty much doing our own things now."

Jane felt relieved. "Oh okay, cool . . . Well, I gotta be downtown at five o' clock, but I've got some time today . . . Wanna grab a drink or something? Or we can just hang out—if you're up to it."

Dale did a horrible job hiding the fact that he was thrilled by the idea. "Hell yeah—I mean, sure. That would be great, Jane. I just gotta use the restroom real quick."

Jane smiled. "Meet you back here in ten minutes?"

"Sounds good. I'll be right back. Don't you go disappearing on me again."

Dale barely made it to a toilet before vomit came spraying out of his mouth like a burst water main. The mickey of vodka came out mixed with the orange pop and a putrid-smelling stomach bile that burned the back of his throat like it was paint thinner.

"Everything all right in there?" a gruff voice asked, banging on the stall door.

"I'm fine," Dale croaked. Tears poured down his cheeks as he wiped the goop from his face with a fistful of toilet paper. "I'll be just fine."


Intelligent yet considerate. Confident and never arrogant. When Jane St. Marie spoke, her words established themselves in the air like flittering fairy birds, humming white-frequency touch into love-thirsty human ears for the very first time.

Dale watched Jane in awe. Her style was original and her choice of clothing made no sense on anyone else's body but her own. She was sexual, but not in a slutty way. Her natural beauty simply suggested there was more to her than met the eye. Physically, Jane was precisely the woman Dale had always dreamed of, in fact, she was better than that. She made funny faces and quirky hand gestures when she got excited and never spoke out of turn. And when she did speak she spoke of nothing and everything all at once. Dale imagined marrying her instead of Ola and what that life would be like.

"Move in with me," Dale blurted out of nowhere. "Sorry. What I meant to say is—you're welcome to stay with me whenever you're in Sudbury for work. No sense wasting money on hotels."

Jane giggled as she chewed on a black bean wrap. "Or, you could move in with me," she said, swallowing a mouthful.

Dale looked confused. "Move in with you? You're a vagabond."

"Not for long."

"What's that mean?"

"It means *The Carriage* is setting me up with something a little more permanent soon."

"Really? Where?"

"Well, that's the catch. It's in this town called Fitchburg, Massachusetts. They asked me to cover the rebuild of an old theatre house there and I said yes. Other than the fact that it's in the U.S., it's a super sweet gig. I'll have tonnes of time to work on my new book and just, you know, relax a little. Plus, cost of living is really cheap there which means I can save tonnes for my vacation in Australia next year." Jane looked him in the eyes and smiled. "It would be even cheaper if two of us split the rent. What do you think? I know it sounds crazy, 'cause we hardly know each other, but—"

"Fitchburg? I think I've heard of the place . . . it's right outside of Boston. That's like twelve hours from Sudbury, right? When would this be happening?"

"Sometime this summer. And yeah, give or take a twelve-hour drive."

"And we'd be—roommates?"

"Yeah . . . For now."

Jane's mesmeric cloud-blue eyes were all it took to seal the deal. Dale was sold.

"Yes. Definitely. Living in a small town away from all the noise and sulphur pollution is exactly what I need right now. Maybe it'll motivate me to get working on my new book—like really working on it."

"Exactly! It could be fun, right? The two of us in down there writing, exploring, taking in New England culture—"

"I'm a complete failure, and you don't know what your getting your-self into."

"What was that?"

"Nothing. I'd go anywhere with you."

Jane laughed at him. "Quit mumbling! I can't make out what you're saying."

Dale smiled. "I was saying yes. I think it would be a lot of fun. I'm in. I need a change."

"Wow. Well, that was easy."

"Jane, you've got to be the most beautiful woman I've ever seen."

She giggled and touched his hand, and they spent the rest of the afternoon on Queen Street West, checking out stores and sampling craft beers at several pubs. They laughed, ate junk food, drank some more, and had a really good time together.

# 6

Dale was in a daze following his chance encounter with Jane in Toronto. One day while waiting in line at the grocery store, he caught himself smiling like an idiot, imagining their life in Massachusetts together. He'd lie in bed at night dreaming of red-brick row homes on quiet side streets, Giacomo Puccini on the radio day and night and the aroma of coffee and wine in a simple kitchen. He'd bring her breakfast in bed every morning along with a poems he'd written the night before, wrapped in a red ribbon beside a plate of fresh cut fruit and assorted nuts.

A morning song for dearest Jane.

We watched people under us
From the apartment window
We laughed at how fast they moved
And how happy we were up here.
We will never run so fast
And be so worried.
We were happy with our stance
And then we went to sleep.

He dreamed of making sweet love to her on satin sheets. Her dainty lace thong stuffed in his mouth, still wet. She'd shoved it in there as a symbol of her undying love for him, a dedication to his happiness. Kissing, crawling. Come kiss me here, Dale. Kiss me here, baby. Jane's legs stretched apart. Gaping thronged whips and thongs, thick hips, black curtains, black lace and chains. Black latex dripping wetness on his face and chin, chains and rope, the bondage Jane dressed in black. Come kiss me here, Dale. Kalina's voice. Come crawl and kiss me here, Jane. Jane crawling, Kalina kissing Jane. Jane kissing Kalina. Both of them spread open in black-lust latex candle light—

—KNOCK KNOCK KNOCK!

*What the hell??*

—BANG BANG BANG!

Dale sat up in bed, rubbing his eyes.

—KNOCK KNOCK KNOCK!

"Hold on a minute!" Dale shouted, throwing his blanket aside. The dream left him fumbling with the door's deadbolt with one hand while up-tucking a massive erection into the waistband of his sweat pants with the other.

It was Kalina and she looked annoyed.

"You got my cash?" she asked, one eyebrow raised skeptically.

"Yeah I got it . . . Right here," Dale answered, waving a wad of bills at her. "Here. Take your blood money."

"Wow. I didn't think you'd actually have it. Congratulations, Dale."

"Fuck you, Kalina. Now please leave. And don't come back here anymore. We're fucking done."

Kalina burst out laughing. "Why the fuck would I? And we haven't *been* for a while now, Dale. You fucking idiot. Let's get this straight. I *let* you go down on me the night we met because you payed me for it, and you did the same thing begging me to move in here. I didn't ask you for any of this, okay? Wait a second—do you have a hard-on right now?"

Dale poked his head out the door to make sure nobody was listening. "Shhhhh! I just woke up. Tell the world, why don't you. Kalina—I don't love you anymore, and you know what? I never did. You're a trophy fuck. You tempted me, then you trapped me, and then you tricked me into introducing you to *my* friends and business connections—the exact people who got you where you—"

Kalina began laughing hysterically. "Oh my god, you're so delusional . . . You know what your problem is, Dale? You're in denial. You want what I've got, but you won't admit it. You walk around like you're this holier than thou, Mr. Unappreciated Starving Artist, but deep down you're just pissed off 'cause nobody gives a shit about you. Wanna know why you're so unappreciated by anybody that even remotely matters, Dale? Wanna know why you've been in this business for ten fucking years and still haven't made a dime? Huh? It's 'cause you're a fucking loser and your writing sucks a big bag of dicks, that's why." Dale was stunned and took a step back. "Haven't any of your loser friends asked you why you let me stay in your apartment for free when it's obvious I make shitloads more money that you do? I mean what kind of loser lets a chick crawl into bed with him when he knows she's been out fucking another guy—and you even went down on me!"

"Shut up, Kalina!"

"And you'll never tell your little friends that shit 'cause it would make you look like a pussy, which is exactly what you fucking are. A big—fat—pussy . . . You know I'm fucking Gary Metzger now, right?"

Dale's erection had dropped to half-mast and was pointing straight at her like a cannon ready to fire. She looked at it and shook her head in pity. "Yeah, you did. You knew. You knew the last time you went down on me that I'd just come back from a meeting with him, but you still did it. And you actually thought you could play me so you could pass your shitty little book to him, is that it?"

"Fuck you. That's bullshit. I had no idea you were with someone else that night. I'd never have gone down on you if I knew you—"

"Oh shut the fuck up, Dale, you lying little shit. And don't even pretend you weren't ecstatic when Metzger's office called to offer you that Writers' Week gig. I heard you got all nervous when Gary talked to you in the VIP room after, too. And that gay speech you made about art and expression and shit? More of that fake, made-up bullshit you use to make yourself feel better for being a fucking bum . . . You're just mad 'cause nobody gives a shit about some shitty novel you wrote like a million and a half years ago, and nobody gives a shit about your boring-ass poems, your stupid-ass blog, or your boring alcoholic, degenerate life."

Dale's eyes were watering. "You little bitch. It all makes sense now . . . Why else would Metzger publish that piece of dog shit you wrote? Just leave. Get the hell out of here." Dale grabbed Kalina's arm and shoved her into the hall. "Take your money and leave, you evil cunt."

"Don't ever touch me like that again, you piece of shit! And you know what? Here. You keep it, Dale. You're going to need this a lot more than I will when Gary finds out you hit me." Kalina tossed the money in his face.

"Hit you? I barely touched you! Just leave! Get the fuck out, right now!"

"Oh, don't you worry. I'm leaving . . . Actually—no. You know what? I'm not leaving. I want my clothes from your top drawer. Your broke ass will probably be running to the consignment store in half an hour trying to sell them for beer money or something, you broke-ass faggot." Kalina stormed past him toward the bedroom.

"You don't know what you're talking about! All I did was try and help you, goddammit!"

"Oh, go help yourself, Mr. Five Hundred Measly Bucks a Speech. You'll be lucky if you ever make that kind of money again without me. Oh, wait a minute—" Kalina's cell phone beeped. "Guess what? Gary's sending me on a three-month tour of Europe and Australia to promote my book in a few weeks. I'm gonna be fuckin' rich, bitch. How's that make you feel, Dale? Huh?"

He couldn't say a word. Kalina leaned against the doorway messaging Gary back, her purple manicured fingernails typing away. She batted her eyelashes and squeezed her breasts together almost habitually, the exposed midriff of her perfect stripper body displayed a belly-button piercing that sparkled like a diamond mine. Dale's erection began to grow again, pitching a pup tent in his sweatpants.

Kalina knew he was staring and she looked up, smiling. "God, you're pathetic . . . Oh, Dale. This is why I still kinda like you. You're like that old raggedy street dog that can't help sticking it in every diseased bitch in the neighbourhood."

"Whatever," Dale said, looking away.

She took her things and left, but he heard her giggling by the elevator.

"I can change, bitch!" he cried, slamming the door shut. "I can chaaange!"

# FITCHBURG, MASSACHUSETTS

*June, 1999.*

Jane found them a two-bedroom apartment in an industrial area just a couple blocks away from one of Fitchburg's main roads. They agreed to split the rental price of $650 a month plus utilities, signed the lease, and moved in the very next day.

Massive brick factories stretched out for a kilometre in each direction, their chimneys puffing thick clouds of American contribution into the atmosphere. The scent of yeast was heavy in the air and it came rushing in through the windows each morning from a brewery to the east. A creek flowed through the backyard, but it was filled with trash and plastic packaging for sex toys, most likely refuse from one of the nearby factories or one of the many adult stores on River Street.

Every morning, Jane left notes on the kitchen counter to brighten Dale's day, and he had dinner waiting for her every night. He even let his beard grow out because Jane said it suited a writer living in a factory slum.

"Plus, I think guys with beards are sexy—and dangerous," she said, with a suggestive wink and a smile.

Dale had found a purpose in Jane's happiness, and he was more than willing to oblige. "Anything for you, dearest."

"Where did you get that?" Jane asked one day.

"What?"

"Dearest. Why do you call me that?"

"It's Cox . . . You know—Frederika Cox? She wrote *Cable Mango*, that weird acid-trip, doors-of-perception book . . . *What's the life you dream of look like now, Mango?—Every day needs to be special in its own way, love—I made ghosts into mosquitoes— That made perfect sense, dearest . . .* No?"

Jane giggled. "Never heard of her."

"Well you should read it then, because she's fucking brilliant."

*June 14, 1999. The home of Jane St. Marie and Dale Potoniak. Fitchburg, Massachusetts.*

*6:59 p.m.*

Jane left the dining room window open that night. A mellow breeze made the candlewicks sway like a courteous housemaid, tippy-toeing across the edge of the dinner table before she went off to do her nightly chores.

"I can't wait until tomorrow morning." Jane took a sip of wine. The candelabra flickered. "I wrote something that I'd like to share with you."

"Of course, dearest," Dale said, sitting straighter. "Please, share away."

"It's a poem I wrote . . . First one in a while. It goes like this . . .

These days I travail like a resentful mother denying the dreaded news.

Something potentially beautiful can begin to grow.

Don't you want to see it?

Not really?

Yeah?

Maybe?

I don't know.

They're all standing their ground on this one.

The body is so strong again.

Could I lose this battle?

Could I possibly even win?

Wrestling with angels,

Lost in this world of sin, I am nothing beautiful.

I need to be without, but the living is good,

I need to get it while the living's good,

Get it while I can, because the living is good, and the body still responds.


… What do you think?"

Dale stood up. He walked toward her slowly, then bent down to kiss her forehead. "Dearest," he whispered, "that was the most beautiful thing I've ever heard."

"Really?" she asked, staring deep into his eyes.

For a moment their lips were close.

"Come with me," he said, taking Jane by the hand.

"Where could you possibly take me right now? I'm already in heaven."

"Where did you come from?" he asked, pulling her body close, her lips just inches from his.

"Kiss me, Dale," Jane whispered.

"I've never wanted anything more in my life."

They kissed, and for the first time their bodies wrapped around each other like pieces of a matching puzzle. Her lips were warm and moist. Her tongue was hesitant, but hinted at a much darker, much more clandestine energy within her that she'd been waiting an eternity to release—for the right partner, for a man she believed in. One who accepted her in every imaginable way. A man who understood that love was like violence and silent splendour, that two bodies are meant to be one, that dualities exist to create a whole, veins and lips simply currency for passion.

"Dale," Jane whispered.

"What's wrong?"

"I'm a virgin."

"You are?"

"Is that okay?"

"Of course it is . . . Are you sure you wanna—"

"Yes. Just this once. Just tonight."

They made love on the living room floor and she fell asleep in his arms. Dale slipped away a short time later to smoke a cigarette by the open window. He watched the moonlight trickle down the ceiling and play with Jane's hair and skin like her body was an instrument tuned to beauty. He was a king that night, and for the celestial moon to offer itself as his personal high minstrel was only natural as Jane's beauty was without a doubt befitting of nature's heavenly overture.

Dale put the cigarette out and lay down beside Jane on the floor. He considered himself a very lucky man. A new man. A changed man.

*October 30, 1999. The home of Jane St. Marie and Dale Potoniak. Fitchburg, Massachusetts.*

Each sunless day began to blend in with the next, and Dale got depressed, lonely and homesick. His vision of a simple life in a simple town became a figurative prison and he was becoming obsessed with the idea of escaping to Canada. By the end of September he grew distant, spending days alone at his desk, and nights online watching porn instead of spending time with Jane, which drove a serious wedge between them. Her unwillingness to fornicate wasn't helping matters either.

*2:27 p.m.*

Dale sat woefully by the living room window that day, scribbling nonsensical gibberish in his notebook. Several weeks of living under the same roof with no communication made Jane feel completely helpless, so she lashed out at Dale in an uncharacteristically aggressive way after realizing he hadn't bothered to shower for a third consecutive day. "Is that all you do?" she asked. "Hide in a corner and stare at tits? You think I don't know what you're doing out here at night? I can hear the slapping sounds from my bedroom. And how 'bout a shower. I can smell you from here."

"Oh, am I not being Christ-like enough for you, Jane?" Dale snapped sarcastically.

"Well, you promised you'd mow the yard, like a week ago, and there's leaves everywhere. We agreed it was your job to—"

"Whatever," Dale mumbled, turning his back to her.

"And what about your book? You've been scribbling in that note-book for weeks, but I haven't seen you do anything on your computer except jerk off to God know wha—"

Without warning, Dale picked up a chair and sent it hurtling across the room. It smashed against the wall, shattering one of Jane's paintings of a brown bullfrog."

"What is wrong with you, man?!" Jane screamed.

"Look at the couch . . . Look at this goddamn furniture. It's wrong, Jane. It's all fucking wrong! Look at the way you placed everything, too, I mean, how am I supposed to get any work done in here? It's too—it's too—well, it's too goddamn pretty!"

"I don't know how to respond to that."

"Don't bother. I'm going for a walk." Dale grabbed his jacket and stormed out.

It was cold out and raining, so he pulled his hood up, took a swig of whisky from his flask, and made for the church basketball courts. A real shady spot, ripe with junkies, thieves and hookers that reminded him of home somehow.

*5:58 p.m.*

"How was your walk?" Jane asked, scooping rice out of a bowl with a pair of chopsticks.

Dale was soaking wet. "Just—don't," he said, throwing his wet jacket carelessly on the floor.

Several hours passed without a word between them until—

"Is there something you want to tell me?" Jane asked, placing a veggie burger and a garden salad on the edge of his desk.

"No, not really," Dale replied, not bothering to look at the food.

"Aw, c'mon, Dale. Why don't you read me something? You haven't done that in such a long time . . . Please?" She used her best smile.

Dale finally looked up from his notebook. "Arright, arright . . . Why you gotta be so whiny about it?" He flipped through his notebook briefly then stopped. "It's still rough, but I think I'll use it in my next book."

Jane sat cross-legged on the floor beside him, grinning. "Cool! I can't wait."

"3 a.m. ungodly hour the night is yours alone

Forge ahead the angels cry

It's time to head back home

Only when we've filled our books with memories . . ."

Dale stopped to clear his throat then kept reading.

". . . You are nice to look at

And your face is so serene

It's something in the way you make me bleed

This city has two faces

And she loves me just the same

I've got to find the way from which we came . . .

There was something poisonous in her thighs

And I filled my cup with powder

I left my mouth open for the—"

"What's wrong?" Jane asked.

"Just leave me alone. There's a beard hair in my eye or something. Why the hell did I agree to grow this stupid—"

Jane ran to her bedroom in tears, slamming the door shut behind her.

Dale trudged to the kitchen to grab the whisky. Only a few months ago he was begging Kalina for crumbs and now he was living with Jane St. Marie. Jane St. Marie, just a few feet away. If he wanted to, he could go into her bedroom and apologize for acting so immaturely. He could kiss her. He could watch her undress. He could see her naked body and caress it. And even though she wouldn't fuck, he could probably get a blow job if he played his cards right, but even that had gotten dull. It was always too "teethy", so he couldn't keep it up. He didn't have the heart to tell her because she always gave a good effort, but it was far from being good. Intimacy with Jane did nothing more than generate feelings of inadequacy and encourage his burgeoning porn habit.

The sound of the whisky glass hitting his teeth shattered the ghostly silence. The house was always quiet now. The streets outside always desolate. Everyone was either asleep or curled up watching late-night television. Nobody in this town fucked anyway. Nobody had any fun.

Dale looked at his phone. No texts, no missed calls. He felt like going out tonight. Out with the boys for a good time to let some tension out, but that wasn't happening, so he sat back down to write in his notebook after filling his glass.

What urge is driving me? If I went home now, the story would remain unchanged and I'd be the same old piece of shit I was before, more or less.

But a part of me fights to escape, and we all want a messiah. Someone who will go before us into the wilderness and come back gaunt and withered to tell the harrowing tale.

I see who I was a week ago. A month ago. Three. I see me on the street. I see you looking at me. Feeling sad for me, and now I know why. You're sad because I'm sad. I'm living each day with dread. I dread my days.

Like many before me, I haven't discovered a way to turn these pages of ink and paper into smaller government-issued pieces of ink and paper. Quite ridiculous, isn't it?

Meanwhile, she pays for everything and I just float along hoping for some kind of miracle to happen. Is this how the end goes? Is this what I'm about?

Dale slid the notebook back into the desk drawer and turned off the light.

For over ten years he'd struggled to make it in the writing business. Perhaps the time had come to call a spade a spade. Be a man and find a real job.

He lay in bed, listening for Jane's breathing in the next room. She was snoring now, and his nightly ritual would begin. He opened his laptop and logged into Chatmates.com, one hand down the front of his sweat pants.

The fights got worse as the days became shorter.

One night in November, Jane shouted, "—because I love you!" in the middle of a heated argument about the evils of addiction and pornography. Dale simply shook his head and asked her why.

"How can you? How the fuck can you even like me at all?"

He was drunk every day, smoking like a chimney, masturbating incessantly at all hours of the night, and he hadn't paid his fair share of rent or utilities in three months. To top it off, he sulked around the house acting like she owed *him* something. *And you love me?* In his mind she was either dumb, delusional or in serious denial over losing her virginity to the wrong man. Regardless, the relationship was on thin ice, she wouldn't put out, and nothing else would help. So, the porn and the whisky stayed.

*December 18, 1999. Emmett calls Dale in Fitchburg.*

"The unyielding desire to live and not die, while others around me suffer and perish in countless, eternal, unthinkable ways . . .

What do you think?" Dale asked.

"It's not great, but you already know that," Emmett answered. "The question is, what do you plan on doing with it?"

"I'm not sure yet."

"Is there more?"

"Yeah . . .

The worms escape. They crawl out of the grass when it rains because it's too wet. They crawl onto the sidewalk where they get stepped on or chewed by birds. They forget that they should get back to grass so they dry up on concrete and die. Eventually the bottom finds its way up to us all.

I'm out here with my eyes open most of the time. Learning to despise you as you walk blind with your arms out, ignorantly smiling, filling the quiet with wasted words. But the shadow creeps into day and perverts the light . . . It's all snowflakes and stardust from now on. Moderation is the most elusive state of being, but I can only see it through a cloudy glass."

" . . . Yeah, I'm not sure that particular piece of writing has—*it*," Emmett said. "That's the whole thing?"

"Yeah, for now. See, I was thinking, if I could just show it to Gary somehow, he might—"

Emmett cut in. "Gary? You mean the guy who was porking your girlfriend behind your back? Why would you even consider asking a scumbag like that for help?"

"It's not about Kalina or any of that shit anymore, Em. If something doesn't happen for me soon—I'm done. You hear me? I'm fucking done. Packing it in."

"Don't you ever say that to me again, you hear me? You're one of the best writers out there, brother. I've watched you go from nothing to the man you are . . . And you wanna throw in the towel now? Over this? Some bad luck and a bad decision?"

Dale moaned. "You don't get it, man. Jane's a good girl. I'm just dead weight over here."

"Jane obviously loves you, Dale. She's proven that already. She's not gonna leave you just because you're going through a rough patch."

"It's more than a rough patch this time, Em. I can't write. I can't think. It's like there's two parts of me now. There's the quiet gentle one, the poet, the writer—but all of sudden, there's this psycho in there that's angry all the time. All wild-eyed with desire and he's constantly clawing at the quiet one, but the quiet one just sits there and takes it . . . It's like he wants something from the quiet one, but he's got nothing left to give. He just wants to find a place to think so he can silence all the noise in his head so he can live in peace with this woman and have her be at the forefront again . . . I can't remember the last time my mind was quiet, Em. It's so loud and I can't live in this house anymore because it's so quiet and—" Dale sighed.

"See, that's what you should be writing, brother. Forget all this other nonsense."

"I—I don't know if I can." Dale began to sob. "And nobody wants to listen to me anymore, man."

"That's not true. I do. Charlie does."

"You have to . . . What the fuck is up with my life, man?"

"Life's a crazy game, brother . . . A crazy game."

What more could he say?

*December 20, 1999. The home of Jane St. Marie and Dale Potoniak.*
*Fitchburg, Massachusetts.*
*2:14 p.m.*

It was a beautiful day. The sun was out, Christmas was right around the corner and Jane was positive that Dale could feel it too. She'd seen him smile the night before while he was writing. Maybe he'd had a breakthrough, she thought. *He's a good person, he's just having a hard time. And who can understand men, really?* She decided to dress in something sexy for him and give the Christmas spirit one more try.

"What do you wanna do today? I don't have to work. And we can do anything . . . you . . . want." Jane bent over Dale's desk dressed in a very revealing Mrs. Claus outfit and placed a glass of whisky in front of him. She should have known he was already half shit-faced.

"What do I *want*, she says . . . What do I *want*. What do I *want?*— Jane? What I *want* is to want to do something. Anything! But I don't *want* to do anything right now because I'm completely dead inside and you obviously can't see it. And it's all because of this stupid city. I think this is probably the only city in the entire world that makes Sudbury seem refined, and you choose to come *here*. And why the fuck are you dressed like that, Jane? I'm gonna start calling you the blue-ball queen from now on. Either fuck me or don't!"

Jane shook her head. She'd heard just about enough. "I know what it is now. You're a complainer, Dale. All you ever do is complain and nothing will ever be good enough for you. One day it's the furniture, the next it's the city you live in and the fluoride in the tap-water; or is it that the world doesn't appreciate your art form—I forget . . . I feel sorry for you, Dale. It must be exhausting to live in your world, but I'm telling you right now the world won't change, so you need to shut up, quit making excuses and do something for yourself."

"Way ahead of you on that one."

"What's that supposed to mean?"

"I'm moving the fuck back to Sudbury."

Jane snatched her purse and jacket from the table and was out the door before he had time to say another word.

Later that evening, Dale sat at his desk drinking a bottle of twelve-year old scotch that Jane was saving for a special occasion, straight from the bottle.

Am I depressed? Is that the problem here? Why am so I bitter and miserable? Jane is beautiful, the town is fine. I walk, write, drink all day and she still fucking loves me. That was the dream—wasn't it? Other than a few aesthetic issues, this is exactly what you wanted a year ago. Why can't you just be happy, you crazy bastard? You've arrived! You've made it! This very moment manifests that vision you once had! Are you incapable of happiness? You need to be brutally honest about that. If you weren't with Jane, what would you do?

I'd learn to live well . . .

Christmas came and went without a mention of presents. They didn't even bother trimming a tree.

Jane asked Dale to hang some lights up on the front porch one day, but he never got around it. It was too late anyway.

Jane got called to Vancouver for a two-week work emergency and that left Dale home alone the day before New Year's Eve, 2000.

*Dale calls Charlie. Dale is at his desk. Charlie is on his couch.*

"So, what do you got planned for tomorrow night?"

"Nothing. I don't feel like doing anything."

"It's the year two thousand, chum."

"Is what it is."

"Fuck . . . You need to get out of there, chum. You sound dead."

"I am."

"What do you mean?"

Dale sighed. "I mean I haven't been myself since I moved here."

"Well, she looked good on paper. Sometimes relationships don't turn out the way you expect them to, but don't worry. Plenty of fish in the sea."

"I already told her I wanted to leave . . . I've plateaued here, Charlie. Every day it's a fight or an arguement, it's so goddamn repetitive. And this drivel I'm scribbling down . . . no one's gonna wanna read this shit."

"Do what you gotta do, chum. I got your back regardless."

"Thanks, man . . . Hey, do you ever have wet dreams?"

"Wet dreams?"

"Yeah."

"Sure. When I was twelve. What the hell are you talking about?"

"I've had a bunch lately."

"Shit. You need to jerk it more."

"I beat it like three times a day."

"There's always dem street hoes."

"I would if—anyways, I gotta go. I'll tell you everything when I get back. I'll try and be home next week if possible. Gotta figure out my finances first."

"If you need to borrow some coin let me know."

"Seriously?"

"No. I'm as broke as you are, chum. Worse probably."

"Great."

"It was more the thought I was going for—but yeah, I got shit-canned at work."

"You did? For what?"

"Some dumb broad. Women, chum. They ain't like they used to be."

"That's the end of an era for you."

"Whatever. I'll find something else."

"I'm sure you will."

"Take it easy, chum."

"You too. Bye."

*January 4, 2000. The home of Jane St. Marie and Dale Potoniak. Fitchburg, Massachusetts.*

*10:37 a.m.*

Dale packed everything he owned into two large suitcases and took one last look around the apartment to make sure he hadn't left anything behind.

He'd written several goodbye letters the night before, but settled on this one.

Jane,

I woke up in this city almost a year ago. The smell, the lonely talk, the war. A quiet concern has arisen for the wounds and America has dealt me a blow that even a thousand peaceful days won't let me forget. I broke a wall in my mind that keeps memories and ideas about places like Auschwitz exempt from all scrutiny.

I've decided to leave. Here. You. I think it's best for both of us. No man is immune to the weight of his desires, not even the great Dale Potoniak. I was never happy. Even after you found me in Toronto after all those pitiful, meaningless days without you. So many nights I longed to have you by my side, and it didn't take long at all, and I was bitter old me again.

I can't disregard your success for at least part of my current problem. It's not fair that you get better, happier and luckier every day, and I get nothing. It's not fair that people like you and Kalina get extra zeros on your bank statements and stickers that say bestseller on the cover of your books just because you're more beautiful. It's not fair that Kalina fucked Gary Metzger, and now she's on top of the world. It's not fair that you both try consoling me with the same pitiful looks.

Jane St. Marie, your star twinkles and remains high in the night sky, while I Dale Potoniak become grey and dull in the world's rainiest places. I never hated anyone and loved them so much at once.

I wrote this poem for you. Just for you. I'd never use it for anything else. No books, no nothing. It's yours alone and it's the best I've written since I moved into this palace with you. A gift, Jane. For you.

So long as we sit by mountain views,

Always strangers and constant change,

I'll be your friend and that bond will grow.

By chance this fruit begins to yield a solitary grain,

I'll feed you like it's what I'm meant to do.

I'll be wise with the way I spend my time.

It was you who told me that time is the currency that makes us all equal,

And some men truly great.

What I have spent here will yield many pages.

When I decide to reap the harvest, I will feed you.

I will feed all of you.

So long as we sit together with mountain views and a lake for us to swim in,

I will find a way to feed you.

Because I've spent my time on pain and joy,
and all of it will fill us both.

So long as you breathe I'll hold your hair.

Let's sail away together.

No concern for lines and lies and coverage,

No concern for the upper lip.

No thought of hate.

I'm filled with love and I want to light the path,

All the way.

So long as you can breathe by air and sea,

These rusty bones are no match for the timeless exception to western thought that's breaking us up so perfectly.

They wont recognize us at all.

We'll be too bright.

I want to cause a reaction when we arrive hand in hand.

Sunshine has come.

It's been a good life,

It's been a good time,

Breathing this air and singing these old songs with you by my side.

The writer who wrote a million books,

No one ever read them.

Did you have fun at least?

I attempted to smile for you,

But I became hopeless.

Every one of us seeks salvation in the eyes of others,

Damning as guilt that which was my best,

Duty to love with no payment in return,

Demanding your happiness,

At the price of mine,

And crying so hard it crushes my world.


"Shit," Dale mumbled, rereading the letter. He knew Jane loved him. For better or for worse she'd proven herself a loyal friend and partner. And for whatever reason she chose to pull the endless string, she deserved better than a letter. He made a decision then and there to stay. Give it a few more days. "Not today. My world can come crashing down next Sunday. Not today."

He went into Jane's bedroom, opened the dresser drawer, and chose a pair of black lace panties. He sat down on the edge of her bed, pressing them to his face as he inhaled deeply. "Not today," he whispered. "I still love the life I'd leave."

*January 13, 2000. Fabulous Fanny's XXX Shop. Fitchburg, Massachusetts. 8:55 p.m.*

Dale knocked the snow off his boots before entering the seedy-looking porn shop. Jane was due back in a couple of days and he was more determined than ever to bed her one more time before it was over for good. He walked up and down the aisles searching for something, anything that might get her to loosen up a little.

Racks of dildos, double penetrators, vibrators and clit ticklers in fancy packages. Anal beads, lubricants, sex swings and cock rings. Hundreds of gizmos and gadgets engineered for the ambitious, yet clueless young man hoping to crack the vagina code and lure out the highly elusive female orgasm hidden inside.

"Excuse me. Where's the lingerie section?" Dale asked.

An obese woman in her fifties pointed toward the far left corner of the store without looking up from her book.

"Fucking Americans," Dale mumbled.

He perused an aisle stocked with PVC and latex fetish suits, slutty stockings, corsets, bondage gear and stripper boots. He picked up a bondage kit for beginners and turned the box over. It contained a studded whip, a blindfold, wrist and ankle restraints, a tube of lube and a thick veiny dildo for a hundred and fifty bucks.

"You got anything here for under twenty dollars?" Dale asked.

"In that section? Fuck no."

"It's just— I'm trying to spice up my relationship and—ah, never mind."

"You try porn?"

"What?"

"I said—you try porn? Me and my husband watch porn all the time when we fuck and it's pretty fuckin' sweet."

Dale nearly gagged as he visualized the woman's cottage-cheese ass slapping her husband's droopy ball sack. "Gee, thanks. Didn't think of that."

"DVDs are ten per week, or you can rent five for the price of three."

"I'll take a look." Dale paused for a moment then got an idea. "Hey, do you mind if I ask you a question?"

"Shoot, bud."

"Have you and your husband ever gone through a rough patch? I mean have you ever gone through a period where you were fighting a lot and you stopped touching each other because nobody was making any moves?"

"Sure have."

"What happened?"

"We made up, but still didn't screw for a while so he come home one day with some lingerie hopin' I'd put it on."

"And?"

"I said, 'What? You don't wanna fuck me no more 'less I dress like a fuckin' school- girl slut for you?'"

Dale tried not laugh. "What'd he say?"

"He said, 'Fanny, calm down. You don't have to wear it,' and no, he didn't think I was no slut . . . Then later he got pissed off and said, 'Just forget about it. I'll jerk off in the can when you're sleepin.'"

"Why didn't you just wear it for him?"

"Should've. That was my first husband. Motherfucker up and left me for some younger pussy . . . Yeah, I used to have some serious aversions to pleasin' my man, but he went and found himself a woman that wadn't afraid to do that and left me with the dog and a fuckin' mortgage. Found me a new man now, though."

"How's that going?"

"Let's just say I ain't got aversions no more. Fuckin' dominatrix costumes, wigs, makeup, strap-ons—I give that motherfucker what he wants, and if I want him to do something for me, I ask and he does it too."

"See, that's fair, right?"

"Fair? Shit. Ain't nothin' fair in this world no more, son . . . But I guess it ain't that bad. So, I gotta dress like a whore and stick a finger up his ass hole once in a while. He still gets it up and we screw like it's prom night. That's all I give a shit about."

Dale nodded appreciatively. "Wow. Thanks for the advice, lady. So where do you keep those DVDs?"

"A word of advice, son . . . Make sure you give 'er a good dickin' once in a while even if she ain't dressed like a cheap hooker, awright? Helps boost her confidence for the times you want her to . . . you know what I mean?"

"I think so."

"So, what are you into? We got all types of good shit back there."

"I mean I know what I like . . . milfs, femdom, latex fetish. Not sure what she'd like though."

"You're practically a virgin, bud. Let me introduce you to a few titles I think you and your missus would enjoy together."


Dale spent the next twenty-four hours on the couch drinking and watching porn.

*"I got her nice and wet for you, daddy. Go get her."*

*"She's right, baby. I'm so ready for you." The girlfriend moans.*

*"But—I want you now," the boyfriend says, kissing the other woman's feet and ankles.*

*The other woman laughs and says: "You hear that, Red? He said he wants me now."*

*The girlfriend giggles. "Go for it. You like pussy. Fucking him's just like fucking a girl anyways."*

*The other woman bends over, showing him her thick round ass. "All right then, you little bitch. Eat it."*

"Oh, yeah—Ah—ahh—ahh—uh," Dale came for the sixth time that day.

*Fabulous Fanny's XXX Shop. The day before Jane comes home.*

"Back so soon?" the old woman at the porn shop asked.

"Yeah. I, uh—I'm gonna need some more DVDs."

"The missus liked 'em?"

"She liked them just fine. But we were thinking something a little kinkier this time. Maybe some femdom or bondage type shit."

"You like that dominatrix shit too, eh?" she said, chuckling. "Fuck is it with men these days? Like my husband. Always wants me to sit on his face and fuckin'—"

"Dear lord, please don't. I get it."

The woman burst out laughing. "Ah, don't be so sensitive, son. Everybody's screwin' with all this Viagra shit goin' 'round these days, so get used to it. You'll be happy to be bonin' when you're my age, kiddo."

"You're probably right, but—could you just pick some more titles? I'll rent ten."

"Shit, son. Ten DVDs? You plan on wearin' that thing down to a nub?"

"Maybe. But most likely I'll just get shit-faced and jerk off with my own tears before I pass the fuck out alone and sad."

The fat lady laughed. "Ah, you're a good kid, son. Keep that positive attitude, awright? And don't let nobody get down on you 'bout your shortcomin's, awright?"

"I won't. Thanks, lady."

"The name's Fanny. And don't forget what I told you last time, kid. It ain't always about the whores in bright red lipstick and black rubber suits. We wanna know our men still love us deep down no matter what, and if you can make us feel like that, ain't no tellin' how far we'll go to please your horny asses."

*Bingo!* That was it. Jane wouldn't put out, but all he wanted now was for her to  wear latex and make him grovel anyway. He imagined kissing her toes, up her thighs; the rubbery taste for hours and hours.

"Fanny, you just gave me an idea. What's your cheapest dominatrix outfit?"

*January 15, 2000. The home of Jane St. Marie and Dale Potoniak. Fitchburg, Massachusetts.*

"Morning. Afternoon, I mean," Jane said, looking annoyed.

"What time is it?" Dale asked, rubbing the sleep out of his eyes.

Jane had already cleaned the living room, washed a sink full of dirty dishes and folded a basket of his laundry. Dale suddenly had serious doubts about the female domination porno cued up for them in the bedroom, not to mention the latex body-suit he bought for her to wear. Maybe he'd skip the putting himself in handcuffs part and go straight to the promising to change and being a better person bit.

"It's two. What did you do last night?"

"Not much. Just had a couple drinks, did some writing . . . You're home early. I didn't expect you till tonight . . . Hmm, looks cold out. By the way, thanks for cleaning the place up. I guess I must've lost track of time and—"

"Can I talk to you for a minute?"

"Sure. But can I tell you something real quick first?"

"Dale, just let me talk. Sit down," Jane said sternly.

"Go ahead."

"I met a guy in Vancouver that works for *Fisticuffs* magazine and he's looking for a writer to go to Europe with him and his crew. I told him how you worked in Nicaragua for *Avant Bard* and he was interested in talking to you about a job."

"A job? Sorry—wait. *Fisticuffs* magazine? That macho, 'my sweater cost five hundred bucks and my peach-fuzz neck beard and Hawaiian tribal tattoos are what's hip this season *Fisticuffs* magazine? Is that what you're talking about?"

"Just hear me out. You would literally be on a working holiday, getting paid to write. You'd get to visit tonnes of European cities, eat in fancy restaurants, stay in hotels . . . You get to drink for free in every bar you go to. That's your dream come true, isn't it?"

"Hell is that supposed to mean?"

"Nothing, Dale! Everything! I think it means this opportunity is perfect for you, and for us. I thought about it and maybe some time apart would give us both a little perspective. I mean, how long are we going to keep going like this? Neither of us are happy. We don't talk anymore, we never fool around—"

"How is that my fault!? You're the fucking born-again! I mean how many blow jobs can—"

"I can do other things! And you can go down on me too sometimes, you know."

Dale shook his head in frustration. "If you . . . latex . . . I was going to . . . And I can't just up and leave. Charlie just lost his job, Emmett's—well, you know Emmett. Those guys need me, and to be perfectly honest with you, writing for *Fisticuffs* magazine doesn't really interest me artistically."

"Would you do it for me, then? Would you do it because I'm asking you to do it? Please? This would be amazing for your career. It pays really well and—"

"Oh, I see what's going on here. You think I'm a bum and you want me out so you don't have to carry my dead weight anymore. Is that what this is?"

"No! I'm trying to help you, Dale. I can't stand watching you waste your life away like this! You're talented and I love you! I want you to go because I want you to find something that makes you happy, and maybe you'll realize that the world's not so bad and people aren't out to get you all the time . . . You should seriously consider this, Dale. It's what's best for you right now. And I promise I'll be here waiting when you get back. Well, maybe not right here, but I will wait for you. Will you do it? For us?"

Jane had him dead-to-rights in a very sticky situation.

"How long would I be gone for?" he asked, unable to look her in the eyes.

"Ten months, I think."

Dale shook his head.

"Ten months in Europe, Dale. Think about it. Most writers only dream of—"

"That's a long time to wait for someone, and a long time to be away from friends. I'm already going crazy missing those guys."

"I know you are, but I've got time off in the spring and maybe we could come visit you out there. Or who knows, maybe I could talk to them and see if there's something for Charlie, too."

"I'd go if Charlie goes."

"Well—that's a big if."

"When is this happening?"

"You'd leave in three days."

There was no use in arguing. Jane was right about everything. Ten months was a long time, but at the end of the day, what was he holding on to? A porno in the bedroom? "Fine," Dale mumbled under his breath.

"Excuse me?"

"I said I'll go. I've always wanted to see Europe."

"Thank you, Dale," Jane said, kissing his face all over. "This is going to be—*kiss, kiss*—so good for us—and for you. I promise. *Kiss, kiss, kiss.* I promise, I promise I promise. Oh, and babe?—*kiss, kiss*—Look at me . . . I promise I will wait for you, okay?"

"Okay, Jane . . . Okay." He held her in his arms, but his mind was somewhere else. With someone else who still might be on tour in Europe. The someone who understood his wants and needs. Someone whose ink-black after-thought and junk veins fed regretting nothing.

Dale and Jane's last night in the Fitchburg apartment was a good one. They didn't watch the pornos Dale rented, or even make love, but they got along and talked openly like they used to.

Dale was getting ready to leave the next morning, when Jane emerged from her bedroom wearing the latex body-suit he'd bought her. They fucked on the living room floor, and he came quickly.

"I love you," she whispered softly in his ear. "And I'm really proud of you for doing this."

"I wish you would've loved me like this every day. Things would've been so different."

"Dale?"

He got up and walked away.

Jane reached for his arm, but it was no use. "Dale . . . if this is the end, then I'm glad it happened the way it did. If our love just fades away over time, then this is the way it was supposed to be—right?"

"I guess we'll find out soon enough," Dale said, as he dressed.

Jane began to weep. "Just believe in God, Dale. That's all I want. That's all I've ever wanted for you. Here, take this." She put a letter in his jacket pocket. "Don't open it until you get there."

"Jane, now that I can finally do something to make you happy, I'm giving you the gift of my absence. You'll either learn to love me for who I am or our love will fade like a sad sad dream. And if you decide that you don't love me, then I hope your happiness will be amplified by the fact that *we happened* for the short time we did."

"Don't say that, Dale." Jane cried.

Dale walked out with his suitcase in hand. He could hear Jane crying from inside the taxi after he shut the back door, and it suddenly occurred to him: he'd just stabbed her in the heart for no reason at all. There was no logic in his last words or actions toward her, but he'd said and done them anyway. The full meaning behind it was difficult to contemplate, but ultimately, it was too late to take anything back now.

"Where to?" the driver asked.

"Airport."

"Logan?"

"Yeah."

The taxi drove off and Dale never looked back.

# 7

# TALLINN

*January 19, 2000.*

The twelve-person crew landed in Tallinn, Estonia just after 6:00 p.m. local time. There was a young Asian intern anxiously awaiting them with a *Fisticuffs* magazine banner in hand. It took the intern twenty minutes to convince Dale and Charlie, who were drunk, that he actually worked for *Fisticuffs*, and wasn't part of an organ-harvesting syndicate that kidnapped foreigners like they do in the movies. The intern begged them to follow the others, saying Mr. Paxton would fire him if they were even a minute late. Dale and Charlie finally agreed to follow the poor kid after he broke down crying right there in the airport.

Checking into the hotel that night were: Dale Potoniak and Charlie McGee from Sudbury, Jimmy Scribbens from Winnipeg, Danny Kershaw from Windsor, Albert Knopf from Edmonton, Chris Bertram from Barrie, Steve Hassan from Vancouver, Jared Fester from Vancouver, Kate Bosch from London, Lilly Stevenson from Calgary, Marketa Hollis from Halifax and Gracie Baxter from Toronto. There was also the tour manager, a blond kid from Stockholm named Clyde Johansen, but he'd already been in Tallinn for a few weeks getting things ready. And the man in charge of it all was the man Jane had met in Vancouver—publishing director, production chief and resident hard-ass, Bryan Paxton.

They sat down for a short team meeting and were given job descriptions, press passes and itineraries. Other than Bryan Paxton, who was in his forties, Dale and Charlie were the oldest in the group. The rest of crew were in their early twenties and fairly inexperienced travellers, but excited to be involved in such a ground-breaking project, which was more or less exactly as Jane had described it. A ten-month, all-expenses-paid road trip starting in Estonia, heading south through Latvia, Lithuania, Poland, Czech Republic, Germany, Austria, Italy, France, Spain, Belgium, the Netherlands and finally ending in England and Ireland. Their mission was simple. Eat, drink, party. Taste, touch, see, do. Nothing, other than the hiring or fucking of prostitutes was out of bounds as far as Bryan Paxton or *Fisticuffs* was concerned, because *Fisticuffs* was attempting to create the first-ever, city-by-city restaurant, bar, party, nightlife, music, culture, arts and theatre guide available on the Internet. And part of the job—the part about thoroughly documenting the nightlife scene, rested solely on Dale's shoulders.

Dale was given the role of senior writer for having the most travel experience, and would be taking the younger writers out on the town each night until they got the hang of things. The guide's target audience was single men between the ages of eighteen and twenty-five, who were interested in the where's and how's of getting completely shitfaced while on holiday in Europe.

Jane called in a last minute favour to Bryan Paxton and pulled off a miracle. She'd convinced Bryan to hire Charlie as assistant editor, even though there was no real need for an editor on the road. Charlie's responsibilities included proofreading written content and e-mailing it to *Fisticuffs* head office in Vancouver on schedule. He was also tasked with making sure the kids weren't taking too many drugs while out on assignment. Put that in Charlie's hands and it was a done deal.

After the meeting, Dale and Charlie took off to wander the pub-filled, cobblestone streets of Old Town, drinking a dozen or so delicious, foreign-tasting Pilsners at no cost throughout the night. It didn't take long and Dale understood why Jane had pushed him so hard to come. Europe was fantastic, and everything felt right. The accents, the decor, the puritanical look and oaky smell of the streets were all right.

With Charlie by his side, Dale felt like his old self again, and it was good to be alive.

*January 23, 2000. In front of the Garlandine Hotel. Tallinn, Estonia. 4:13 a.m.*

After three days of meetings, planning and partying in Tallinn, the crew piled onto a tour bus while it was still dark out. Dale watched from his window as the driver loaded their luggage and enough booze to last any god-fearing group of alcoholics at least a week or two into a huge storage compartment below.

*11:12 a.m.*

"I thought you said four hours. What the shit is taking us so long?" a voice with a heavy accent yelled from the back of the bus. Clyde.

The old driver craned his neck around and began muttering in his own language, probably Estonian, but he managed a little English. "Had t' turn 'round due to d' highway closure, Goin' back to da' udder highway to da' falls. Extree one and half hours der, fellers."

The whole crew groaned in unison. Someone in the back made a comment about the bus driver that included use of the term "old fuck."

Dale stared happily out the window and cracked open a Pilsner. "Hey, Charlie," he said a minute later. "Psssst. Hey, Charlie. Don't you just love how many evergreens there are up here, man? Back home it's more mysterious and haunting with the birch and poplar, but there's something so ageless and achy about snow-covered evergreens, you know?"

Charlie looked up from his laptop, nodding at Marketa Hollis, the drop-dead gorgeous twenty-four-year-old music content writer from Halifax. "I got something to bounce all over that broad's forehead, if you know what I mean, chum."

Dale chuckled. "No doubt. Just be patient, man. It'll happen."

*12:31 p.m.*

The bus rode head-on into a raging blizzard somewhere near the Latvian capital, Riga. It was almost a total whiteout, but the old bus driver kept motoring through. Heavy winds had blown cars, buses and transport trucks into ditches on both sides of the road, as Dale watched through his frosted window with childlike curiosity.

"Psssst. Charlie—" Dale said, already a little drunk. "Hey, Charlie."

"What?" Charlie said, half-asleep.

"Can you imagine those Viking tribes living off this land back in the day, man? What a brutal landscape to wander on."

"Yeah. Brutal. Nighty-night, chum." Charlie turned around and closed his eyes.

*Riga, Latvia.*
*10:41 p.m.*

Dale was sprawled out on the hotel bed with a forty-ouncer of Latvian vodka in one hand and a lit cigarette in the other. The rest of the team had gone out, but he'd decided to stay in and relax alone.

*Finally, peace and quiet,* he thought, taking a sip of the vodka. The warm spirit stung the back of his throat, warming his whole body as it slid down to his belly.

He closed his eyes and thought about Jane, a million miles away. What was she doing now? he wondered. *Maybe I should call her.* He thought about the apartment in Fitchburg. The ultra-clean, ultra-modern furniture she'd picked. He thought about all the days he'd spent wandering Fitchburg, homesick and frustrated, about getting lost in factory shipping yards, and the time he stumbled home drunk and pissed on the front door at dawn. He thought about Kalina and the smell of latex lingerie against her smooth, tanned skin. Her crazy, lusty eyes and big fake lashes staring down at him. He thought about the way she pulled his hair and scratched his skin when they made love; and the way she said his name was like an insult on its own. He thought about

Ola. Her thin pale body lying naked on the floor of the boiler room in the old bingo hall. The candlelight twinkling, her perky breasts. Statuette cathedrals built for praise and worship. Her hollow glasswork eyes at dawn like mythical labyrinths. Her voice like a magical flute, whispering promises of eternal gain, making him believe he'd never need another lover again so long as she breathed. He remembered the promise they made to each other, and how he still hoped she'd marry him one day, regardless of what she'd done these past couple years— regardless of what he'd done, he knew she'd forgive him, too.

Dale sat up, opened his laptop and logged into his Chatmates account.

—SEARCH USER: OLA KANT

—USER NOT FOUND

*Damn.*

—SEARCH USER: OLA

—9,678 USERS FOUND

*Fuck.*

—YOU'VE RECIEVED A PRIVATE VIDEO CHAT REQUEST FROM: Jasmina69

*Sure, why not.*

—ACCEPT

Jasmina was an icy-looking blond from Prague with a heavy eastern European accent, and a body so immaculate it put Kalina's surgical flawlessness to shame. She made money doing live webcam shows and a *little* porn (or so she said). But aside from stereotypes, she seemed intelligent and sophisticated.

"I usually don't waste time talking to potential clients, but you seem different. I enjoy your conversation. Please, tell me more about you, sweet boy." Jasmina leaned into the camera to check her lipstick.

"Well, I'm currently on tour. I'm a senior writer for a very well-known magazine called *Fisticuffs*. Have you heard of it? I also write books and poetry . . . How about you? I love your accent. Where are you from originally?"

"Slovakia, but I move to Prague two years ago . . . So, you are successful man, hmm?"

"Just recently. Why Prague?"

"Why not Prague?"

"It's the same, isn't it? Same people, same desperation? Everyone pushing on with their boring lives toward some unknown, ungodly purpose."

"I think what fuels you is same thing that fuels me. Money. It is my business to deal with men that are looking for someone to satisfy their every appetite and desire. I also lie to them and tell them that they're not total pieces of shit—which they usually are. That they're deserving of acceptance, and that cheating on their wives with someone like me is, how to say, normal."

"You tell them lies?"

"Of course. Most men walk around in shadows, hiding."

"You speak English very well."

"Thank you, sweet boy."

Dale sighed. "Thing is, there aren't many spiritual guides or compasses out there for men these days. Most of us put our faith in anything that reminds us of temples, or we'll wear little ornaments in times of strife to remind us that quiet places still exist somewhere. Regardless of our physical surroundings, regardless of our desires, we need love to—" Dale's voice trailed off as Jasmina squeezed her breasts together.

"Cat got your tongue?"

"No, I just . . . I don't wanna come across as one of those desperate losers that— I thought we—"

Jasmina smiled playfully into the camera, pursing her bright red lips together while rubbing her nipples. "You know how this works, sweet boy. I told you, this is business. You want to talk more you come to pay room now."

"Oh. I don't know."

"What don't you know?"

"These addictions, these desires . . . I could choose to be better. I could change my thoughts about you, about everything right now and just walk away. I should walk away, right?"

"At time like this, when you travel—I think it's okay, no?"

"Yeah, you're probably right, but—"

Jasmina stood up and walked off camera.

"Hey, where'd you go to?"

"You see."

A few minutes later, Jasmina reappeared in lace body stocking. She sat on the edge of the bed and spread her legs, moving the camera in for a closer look. "You like? Then you go to pay room now, sweet boy. Bye-bye."

She cut the feed.

*Fuck.*

Dale looked down at his bulging erection, then at his wallet on the night table.

A few minutes later, he logged into Jasmina's private room on Chatmates with a *Fisticuffs* company credit card, paying the $99.00 registration fee without even blinking. His eyes were immediately transfixed on Jasmina's image on the screen, and for the next forty minutes, at $12.99 a minute, Jasmina teased him, bending this way and that in her lustrous silky lace lingerie. Dale surrendered himself to the screen, whimpering helplessly as Jasmina drained him over and over again.

"I needed solitude to lick my wounds," Dale said, panting. "Music to raise my dead soul. I wanted to write and let the flood come, along with the assault I'd begged my whole life for—to invade me—Jasmina—"

"Yes, my sweet boy?"

"I'm c—"

# PRAGUE

*February 5, 2000.*

"My god, Dale. Where have you been?" Jane hadn't heard from him in nearly three weeks and was worried sick.

"Jane, it's not what you think. I'd fight to the death for us. I'll find the light and beauty lost and—there's no reason to blame or name names, or curses handed down from generation to generation. This has nothing to do with any of that." Sweat trickled down Dale's beet-red face.

"What are you talking about, Dale? You're not making any sense. Why are you so out of breath? Where are you? I got so worried I called Bryan, but he told me you weren't even at the hotel last night. What's going on?"

Every vein in Dale's body felt like it was pumping battery acid. "Jane, dearest, listen to me. I can explain. I just—I can't talk right now, okay? But I promise I'll call you tonight when I'm sane again, okay?"

"Sane again? What are you talking about, Dale?"

"Jane, I—"

"Dale, I'm praying for you—"

Jasmina tore the cord out of the phone. "Can't stand listening to that bitch scream in your ear, sweet boy. Come lay with me."

It was around 8 a.m., and Dale and Jasmina had been up all night snorting cocaine, taking ecstasy and drinking tequila at her apartment by the river.

"Oh lord, give me strength," Dale pleaded, pacing frantically around the living room. "I shouldn't have done this."

"Nonsense. You're just high and paranoid. And it's not like you married. It won't matter in long run."

He'd paid top dollar, and was fucking Jasmina for the second time when Jane called. The caller ID on his phone hadn't worked since he left Canada, and he'd idiotically answered thinking it was Charlie calling to tell him where to be that morning for work like they agreed the day before.

"Piece of shit caller ID!" Dale screamed, hurling his phone across the room.

"What's wrong, sweet boy?" Jasmina asked, lying naked on an oriental rug.

Dale's entire body began trembling. "Nothing. I'll be right back." He ran to the bathroom, slammed the door shut and gasped when he saw himself in the mirror. His skin looked veiny-blue and transparent, and his cheekbones had popped out from under the skin like little devil horns. He attempted to smile, but shrieked in horror as the creature-face in the mirror displayed a rack of mouldy yellow giraffe teeth. Gargantuan tarantula eyeballs and dinner plate sized pupils bulged out of fleshy sockets like gigantic black marbles, stabbing right through him. His hair and beard, still growing from his days in Fitchburg, were swarming with bugs, bats, fleas and cockroaches. He reached for the counter to steady himself. His heart was racing. He felt cold and deathly ill all of a sudden. "Oh, god. Lord have mercy. Please god, let it shine. Let your light shine on me today. Smiles and light, smiles and light, smiles and—"

"Come do another line with me, sweet boy," Jasmina called from the living room.

"Be right out." He took several deep breaths to calm himself, splashed some water on his face, and went back out.

Jasmina lifted a CD case with lines of coke to her nose and sucked one back. "Your turn," she said.

"What the fuck have I done?" Dale muttered. His jaw felt like a loaded bear trap. His teeth like fangs, hungry for flesh and wicked sin.

"What's wrong, sweet boy? Wifey say you can't stay out and play?" She was mocking him now.

He studied Jasmina's curves. Bodies like hers did not exist in Canada, and even on a druggy morning-after like this one, she was still an eleven.

"I had reasons," Dale said. "She doesn't understand what I stand for, what I represent, what I want. You . . . Jasmina, you understand how hard it is for me to just be me. The heavy burden of knowledge, the weight of wisdom, the curse of knowing. Jane never acknowledged that. You have."

"Of course I have. Of course I understand, poor boy."

Her eyes seemed to have control over his every move. Was he really at fault? The crew arrived in Prague the day before, and Dale made plans to meet Jasmina for a drink in Old Town. Was it his fault that a couple hours later she was tearing his clothes off, shoving pills down his throat and cocaine up his nose? It was those eyes that convinced him to abandon all morality, all values, all commitments—and trust in her without fear of consequence.

The morning sun broke through Jasmina's purple Gothic drapes, and Dale's retinas burned like they'd been doused in holy water. "It's not my fault," he mumbled, rubbing them. The salvation of denial.

"What did you say, sweet boy?" Jasmina asked.

"Nothing. Give me that." Dale snorted two of the six neatly chopped lines and ate a second double-stacked ecstasy, which he chased down with a gulp of tequila. The combination of chewing ecstasy and a cocaine drip tasted horrible. "Out there all you get is dirty sins, black lingerie and party anthems. Pollution and a million friends. A million nights for the sake of others and a million morning recovery. But the quiet—this is where a man like me, who really sees the end goes. Not out there. Not to a place like that."

Jasmina lit a cigarette, took a drag and handed it to him. "You took too much ecstasy. You in trouble, sweet boy. . . But don't worry, Mama take good care of you."

"I'm not even looking for experience any more. I'm done with all that now. I'm looking to see if there's any beauty left in this world at all. I want to behold beauty, but I'm addicted to the struggle. Truly, utterly addicted."

"You should order us some breakfast."

"I would—" Dale lost his train of thought. The coke was kicking in. "I have the right to say . . . you wouldn't understand, but angry minorities—men—make angry music, and some of us white guys can relate to it . . . and some of us like to pretend that we have problems too—but don't downplay my concerns."

Jasmina burst out laughing. "See? You are too fucked up now. And that is bullshit. You North American boys always crying about bad Internet connections and hangovers. It is too much . . . Man like you— so-called writer—hope to manipulate system and participate little as possible in reality. An expert in fear and excuses, you know nothing of love, only latex-lust. Limp-cock, good boy."

A chemical surge rolled Dale's eyes into the back of his head then out again. A huge quantity of serotonin had just dumped into his blood-stream care of the double-sized E, and was going to work on his nervous system. A minute later, his lower jaw started to jitter uncontrollably and his teeth went clickety-clack as his incisors chattered against each another at a hundred and ninety beats per minute.

Meanwhile on Jasmina's television, a dominatrix was violating a man with her strap-on.

Jasmina, always the staunch professional, noticed Dale's growing erection instantly. "So, you like this?" she asked.

"Huh? N—no. I mean, I'd never. That's too—"

Jasmina giggled and blew a cloud of cigarette smoke in Dale's direction, but his eyes were glued to the television.

"Don't lie. You see girl fucking man with rubber cock and now you hard as rock. Holy shit—that rhymes."

Dale looked down and knew it was pointless to argue.

"It's okay," Jasmina said, amused by his embarrassment. "Many of my clients like this."

"So what? I'm f-free to think as I p-please, okay? I p-put q-question marks in the—places I used to have—periods. Opening cans of w-worms and breaking the mind so I can re-b—rebuild it and b-break it open again. I live to destroy what is s-safe."

"You won't be destroying anything today, boy. Come kiss my pussy." Jasmina spread her legs, arching her back against the plush couch. Dale obeyed. "Good boy. You see? Your concept of beauty is too complex and fragile. Experiences that leave you speechless are much better. Don't you think?"

"Mmmfff—"

"Exactly. Now, is this not exactly what men have been searching for since the beginning? For a woman who will make you grovel because *she* wants you to, not because you paid her to? Of course I take your money, but you men miss the most obvious unmistakable point of it. The pure elegance and precision of it all . . . of your surrender, of your obedience, of that money and my want to take it from you, to hurt you, to make you pay for what you've done to me . . . That's enough. Come, we go." Jasmina stood up, grabbed Dale by the hair and dragged him toward a tall wooden armoire in the bedroom. His brain was registering very little other than the sensation of her touch and his throbbing prick. "Sit. Stay. Good."

Jasmina poked around the armoire until she found what she was looking for. A pair of thigh-high boots made zipping sounds as they wrapped each of her legs in shiny black latex. Dale literally drooled as she posed in front of a mirror, tightening a matching corset around her perfect waist and crystal ball breasts. Next, she bent down to fasten a dog-collar around his neck, clipping a short leash to it. She led him to the bathroom on all-fours, yanking on it as she raised the toilet seat.

"Get your head over toilet, boy," Jasmina commanded.

Dale was incapable of resisting, and lowered his head into the bowl.

Jasmina sat on his back and his eyes rolled into the back of his skull. Every touch, every sound she made felt like an ocean of baby birds frolicking in love-drenched liquid sunshine all over his virgin body.

Jasmina smacked him in the back of the head with the tail-end of the leash. "You bad boy. You could've stayed in hotel last night and remained faithful to wife at home, but instead you come here and fuck me like some common whore, hmm? And you think you can get away with that and not pay the price? Hmm?"

"No. N-never, Jasmina."

"Never is right . . . I set you free today, boy. Today I change your life for good." Jasmina sat harder on his shoulders, pushing his head into the toilet water until he was choking on it.

"Okay—okay! I'll pay. Whatever you want. There's a credit card in my wallet. Whatever it costs. Please."

Jasmina got off his back and tied his hands around the back of the toilet bowl with a nylon cord she'd found beneath the sink. A minute later she was plugging an electric razor into an outlet beside the medicine cabinet. "Yes, you are going to pay, Mr. Piggy," she said. "Just like everybody else."

Jasmina ran the shaver across the back of Dale's head, and he suddenly clued in to what was happening. Tuft after tuft of thick dark hair fell to the floor and into the toilet bowl in slow motion. An empire he'd built over years, decades—and this cruel, yet irresistibly beautiful European harlot was pillaging it all. The homes, the temples, the cathedrals and the watchtowers, even the opera house was burnt to the ground that day, and there was nothing he could, or wanted to do about it.

The whirring of the machine made his body shiver as it moved across his tingling scalp and face like a pack of wolves tearing through a herd of legless goats. He could still remember the way Ola's fingers felt, running through that hair the night she'd promised herself to him. And he could see Jane, just a few short months ago, smiling innocently from behind a book, saying: "Let it grow! Men with beards are so sexy and dangerous."

*Men with beards . . . I'm not a man. And I'm the furthest thing from dangerous now.*

A tear fell from Dale's eye. He was high on drugs, and cheated on his sweet Christian girlfriend with some vulgar whore from the nether regions of Slovakia—and there was pre-cum dripping down his thigh from the whipping she'd been giving with the nylon cord.

"Stop," Dale mumbled. "Stop. This is too much."

"Stop? Fuck no. I call the shots now." Jasmina stood up and let the razor drop to the floor. She took a step back to examine her handy work. "Not bad. I think it suits you just fine, slave." Without warning, she slapped him in the back of the head and said, "Don't ever forget to be your own hero," before disappearing into the living room.

*I think I have a hole in my heart.*

"W-what's the date today?" Dale shouted.

"What?"

"The date. What day is it today?"

"Saturday."

"What's the date?"

"Why?"

"I n-need to know."

"It's February fifth. Now shut up, Mr. Piggy."

*February fifth?* He'd given that speech in Toronto exactly a year ago, and agreed to move in with Jane the same day. *Why is there always something stopping me from doing the right thing?* He wondered what Ola would say if she saw him here, tied to a toilet and bald-headed. She'd probably say she was right all along. That it was the drugs and the cheap thrills he was after the whole time. That there was a hollow in him that needed filling before he could learn to love. And that poetry and sex, though glorious, are like sacraments for the narcissistic. Cheap atonements for the anti-man whose heart is hard as granite, but who wants to feel soft weak and vulnerable. Men like Dale who got off on it like scourging and repentance, like church, like saving fatherless girls.

*"It's not like that, Ola."*

*"Yes it is. Just look at you."*

*"Would you at least sing to me before you leave?"*

*"This is the last time . . .*

Sick with love, stars above, like every word I've spoken. Ambrosia bathrooms, purple curtains, the bitch's heart is broken. You let me down, and I promised my hand, I'm grasping for beauty, in the soul of a man . . . I hate you for not being more beautiful. Spider legs, your aggressive stare, your magnificent, toneless stare—you cut me. And now I'm locked to our bridge like you were, iron arms, holding me to our promise, forever."

Jasmina came back a few minutes later wearing a strap-on. She showed it to him and said, "Beg, boy."

"... P-please."

"Please what?"

"Subliminal twinkles on a love-sick Christmas tree. Sadder than narcotic after-thought. So many men have lived by sword and spear and arrow; no man by bird to feed, no man remembered for loving nature nor kind hearted manner. No romance in an old man's simple death. A comfortable bed and a wife to hold his hand. A drunk night to lie alone and drown the latent morrow; and many men dead by spear and sword and betrayal ... And if this is my fight, then let me fight valiant and brave. Let me die my own lonely hero; without a story, without an epitaph. Let me die knowing, and knowing alone. Just do it. Please."

"Very well."

"See—I knew you'd like it," she said, moments later. "Up," she said, digging a boot heel into his rib cage. "We go to bedroom now. I break you in first, now I do you like this on Chatmates while people watch. I told you, I don't just want your money, Mr. Piggy. No no. Today your body, tonight, your heart."

# 8

*February 13, 2000. Jasmina's living room. Prague, Czech Republic.*
*After being AWOL for a week, Charlie finally reaches Dale on his cell phone.*
*6:56 p.m.*

"Dale?"

"Yeah."

"Where the fuck have you been?"

"Sorry."

"Sorry? Do you know how many times I tried calling you this week? Fuck you, sorry. We're headed to Krakow tomorrow for some music festival, and as your friend, I'd strongly advise you to get your ass back to this hotel, pack up your shit and be on that fucking bus at 6 a.m. tomorrow morning. You got that?"

"Hold on a second, okay?" Dale covered the mouthpiece with his hand. Jasmina was summoning him.

"Sweet boy, come. We finish video now."

"Yes, dearest. I'll just be a minute. It's work calling." Dale uncovered the mouthpiece. "Sorry, Charlie. Come again?"

"What the hell is wrong with you, Dale? I said we're leaving in the morning. Get your ass back here, now! Who's that talking in the background?"

"Nobody."

"Now, pussy boy!" Jasmina screamed.

"Shut the fuck up, Jasmina! I'm on the fucking phone!"

"Jasmina?" Charlie gasped.

Moment of truth.

"Charlie, I—I met a girl."

Charlie paused. "Wait—I'm sorry. I thought you said you met a girl."

"Yeah."

"Okay . . . What about, Jane—your girlfriend? You remember. The sexy, smart one who has her shit together—you were living together for awhile. That one."

"I don't know what to tell you."

"She's been calling me every day looking for you."

"What'd you say?"

"I told her you're out on assignment in some hick town with no cell signal and you'll be back tomorrow, always tomorrow. What the hell do you expect me to say?"

"Okay, that's good. Good one."

"Good one? You're so fucked, chum . . . What are you gonna do?"

"I'm not sure."

"And what—you're not coming to Poland?"

"I'm thinking about staying here for a while. This girl—she's—well—why don't I tell you in person?"

"Motherfucker . . . Okay. There's a ripper bar across from the Wenceslas statue called Stripterky. Be there in an hour."

"I will. Hey, Charlie?"

"What?"

"Thanks for not freaking out, man . . . . *click* . . . Sorry, Jasmina. I can finish this scene, but then I gotta go."

"*Fena!* Very well . . . Okay . . . action, *Fena!*"

Dale stood up slowly, naked from the waist down except for a pair of fishnet stockings and high heels. His bald head was covered in a woman's wig, and Jasmina had painted his eyes with mascara and eyeshadow. A real take-down scene. Jasmina appeared on screen wearing full dominatrix gear. She placed shackles on his wrists and ankles, then a ball-gag in his mouth, and bent him over a desk.

*Stripterky Gentleman's Club. Prague, Czech Republic.*
*8:48 p.m.*

Dale explained every detail to Charlie. How he met Jasmina on Chatmates in Riga, then in person the day they arrived in Prague; about the drugs, the booze, the morning after phone call from Jane when he was out of his mind on coke and ecstasy. He even came clean about paying Jasmina for sex with the company credit card. He told Charlie everything, except for how he'd volunteered to be her unpaid porn slave for the next couple of weeks and that he was in love with her.

Charlie shook his head, trying to hide his amusement. "You're the biggest fucking jerk I've ever met, but you're a fucking animal, I'll give you that much."

Dale laughed. "It's been a wild ride, man. A wild fucking ride . . . Hey, let's get another round, eh?"

"Sure. I'll just swipe my handy little *Fistcuffs* credit card, chum."

"Fuck *Fisticuffs*. We're fucking rock stars, man."

"Fuck yeah."

"Oh Charlie, Charlie. These moments of peace won't last long, but they'll give us the fuel we need for our exodus in those endless deserts.

"I hear ya, chum. It's human nature, I guess." Charlie sighed and shook his head as a man on stage got spanked by a tall brunette in pink lingerie for his birthday. "Fucking American tourists."

"It's just sad that I can't justify a more spiritual exercise than this . . ."

"Look, Dale. We're friends, so I'm not gonna sugar-coat this. Fact is, you're gonna stay here and fuck up your dream job, fuck up your relationship back home, and basically ruin your entire life for a hot piece of ass, and frankly, it's fucking stupid . . . Go back to her place, grab your shit, and meet me at the hotel later. We'll stay up all night and get shit-faced if that helps, but trust me, it's the right thing to do. This broad's got you pussy-whipped, chum. Happens to the best of us, but trust me, you'll get over it."

"How about this. Tell Paxton I got pneumonia and I'll be out of the hospital in a week. If he fires me, he fires me. If not, I'll be back in a week. Let me finish doing what I gotta do here, and I'll take the bus to wherever you guys are and jump back in. Deal?"

"It's a bad idea, but okay. It's your life."

"Done. Enough with that shit, let's talk. How's things with you? You bang that broad from Halifax yet?"

"Not yet. Still working on it . . . Actually, I've been thinking a lot about this chick I used to date named Lenore."

"Lenore?"

"Yeah. She was my girlfriend in college."

"And why are you thinking about your girlfriend from college?"

"Did I ever tell you about the time I took her to Cathedral Grove?"

"No, I don't think so."

"Cathedral Grove's this place outside of Port Alberni, BC, where I grew up. Anyways—there was this tree in the woods and it spoke to me . . . I swear it did, chum. The snow was coming down hard, so me and Lenore pulled the car off to the side of the road and got out to take a walk around, but I felt compelled to meander into the mossy forest rather than join her on the manufactured trail. I walked no more than twenty feet behind this set of trees, and I was encompassed by this huge forest. Stumps of dead wood all covered in moss and new growth, and I had this moment—a worship moment. The darkness of my heart was cracked by the light of the ever-giving forest and the life within it. I looked around and saw more trees and grass, dead and alive, all beautiful and full of purpose. I frolicked through that forest like a fairy with the snow still falling over me. I watched it perform for the first time ever. Snow in its natural environment, and it was the most beautiful thing I've ever seen, and something I don't wish to forget any time soon, chum . . . From three hundred feet above, the diamonds broke the boughs, collecting more of their own kind as they fell from grace. A miniature snowball falling from the sky like an opaline ballerina. The way snow is meant to fall. The way it's supposed to look when it snows, and the forest floor and the branches were all covered in it, covered in white on a February afternoon. So after I joined Lenore on the park trail, we kept walking and at a certain point we come to this fork in the road, but I'm feelin' drawn straight forward instead, so I crept up behind a furrow of trees, and it was one of the most spectacular things I've ever seen. I approached the edge of the glass lake with caution so I wouldn't disturb the soil, a primrose leaf or even bend a blade of begonia grass. I'm tellin' you, chum, if I could have floated above the ground and hovered on wings like St. Michael that might have suited this scene more . . . I broke through a clearing and witnessed the most spectacular display of God's creation I've ever seen . . . I hope I can keep that image in my mind's eye forever, and if not, at least I know I saw it and it was real. Lenore might have taken a picture of it, but a picture wouldn't do it justice."

Suddenly, it was as if the club went quiet. The music stopped and Dale stared at Charlie in astonishment. He was shocked, stunned actually, to hear such polished poetic prose proceed from Charlie's usually vulgar, two-syllables-at-the-very-most mouth, and confused as to why he'd never heard him speak like this before in all the years they'd known each other. Over all the bars, over all the beers and laughs, and all the good times, not once had Charlie ever displayed such depth to his character, such sensitivity. And suddenly, after all this time, Dale realized he knew very little about his good friend Charlie McGee, other than the fact that he was a cold-blooded motherfucker when he wanted to be, and that he was the son of an Irish immigrant alcoholic womanizer who left his wife and infant-son to join a cult in India. Dale wondered if he'd somehow forgotten along the way that Charlie was a real person and not a character in a book; and now, halfway across the world in some strip club, the thin shadowy veil that was McGee was being torn away. Who was Charlie, really? What was he after? What else did he feel? And what happened to the fun-loving, dumb drunk from Sudbury Dale knew and loved?

"What the fuck have you been doing with yourself this week, man?" And as suddenly as it came, Dale's momentary glimpse into Charlie McGee's soft side ended as the DJ announced the next act and the music started up again.

"Ladies and gentleman, coming to the stage is the sexy, Aaaamber."

"Thinkin' about shit, I guess," Charlie answered.

"Hell, man. That was some glory of dreams, mystery of sleep, unbroken consciousness—false face of fear type of shit you just dropped on me right there."

Charlie shrugged and took a sip of beer. "This trip's puttin' things into perspective for me, I guess . . . Hey, Dale—"

"Yeah, bud?" Dale answered, watching Amber wrap her legs around the silver pole.

"You and Emmett grew up together and everything—but, I mean, we're pretty good friends too, right?"

"Of course we are, man. I wouldn't have invited you out here otherwise. What are you getting at?"

"It's just—what the fuck is with your shaved head and face, chum? You look like a fucking rat . . . And it's weird you shaved your head after all that stuff you told me and Emmett about hair being our antennae and portals to where all the words come from and shit . . . And you know me, so you know I love havin' a good time—but it feels like you've changed. You're talkin' different, your vocabulary's gettin' shittier, you never talk about writing or nothing like that no more, and now you're thinking of fucking up the best job you've ever had for some random piece of hooker pussy? So you fucked around on Christian Jane, so what. I'm not gonna judge you for it—hell, I'm not gonna say shit because shit happens on the road, but she's still back there waiting for you, chum. And I gotta say it—this Jasmina broad sounds nice and everything, but she's a run-of-the-mill hottie, that's it. Definitely not worth losing Jane over . . . Jane's fuckin' wife material, chum. No joke. Seriously, I think you should get on that bus with me in the morning, finish the trip, make some money and get home so you can figure your shit out, because Jane's someone I can actually see you spending the rest of your life with. She'll straighten your ass out. And we're not as young as we used to be, chum. All this . . . There's gotta be more to life. I'm getting sick of these kids and party party party."

Dale grinned as Amber took her bra off, unleashing a set of big, bouncy tits.

They both watched quietly for what felt like a long time.

Finally, Dale spoke. "I had something like that happen to me too. Like what happened to you in that forest with Lenore."

"Oh, yeah?"

"Yeah. I was in Nicaragua walking along this beach near Leon . . . I was surrounded by this beautiful ocean on one side and this coastal rainforest on the other. I think I witnessed the true beauty of nature there. I imagined the people, the original people of the land, their lives, their culture, their ways, how close they were to the earth . . . I mean, we can try, but we'll never understand their sadness toward all this shit . . . Yeah, I think I felt something like that there just for a second. The weird thing is it felt like I was polluting the place just by being there, like I was bringing death to it or something . . . How far we have fallen from the natural ways, eh McGee? What we're doing isn't natural. It's not of this earth. All this is a trick designed by the bad men who build cites, pollute lakes and cut down trees to build fucking condos and more goddamn shopping malls."

"I know. There's gotta be a better way. A way to be in harmony with the natural order of things."

Amber slipped her panties off and shoved them into some old pervert's mouth in the front row. The old man stood up and did a little dance. The audience went wild, cheering and clapping for him.

"What the hell have I become, Charlie? That would've pissed me off a couple years ago. Maybe you're right, maybe I have changed. But I can't go back to Jane. Not right now . . . I wanna—I wanna—Fuck, I really wanna know what those pink panties taste like. I'm fucked up, aren't I?"

"First step to anything's admitting it, I guess. Fuckin' new world we're living in, chum."

173

"Hey, you remember that song Emmett wrote a couple years ago on the guitar? *What can we do, my love? Now that we know what we know. Where can we go, my love? Now that home is anywhere at all. What can we do, my love? When doing nothing is not doing at all . . .* Remember that one?"

Charlie nodded and chuckled. "*We'll always be home, and we'll always be together, even if we struggle a little to find what we're looking for.* Poor little fucker and his bleeding heart."

Dale chuckled. "Cheers, man . . . Gotta keep livin' while the livin's good. That's all there is to it."

Charlie sighed. "You're right, chum. Okay, I'll tell Bryan what you said. Hopefully he buys it and you can come back in a week. If not, enjoy that *Fisticuffs* credit card while you still got it."

Dale put his arm around Charlie's shoulder and they sang the rest of Emmett's song with their drinks raised high.

*"Find out and see*

*Tomorrow's just a page*

*I thought I was free*

*I am not amazed*

*But praise the Lord*

*I'm forgiven."*

"I'm gonna miss ya, chum," Charlie said.

"You too, man."

Amber collected bills from the stage after her song ended, while Dale and Charlie embraced like war-torn friends on the road to future freedom.

## THREE MONTHS LATER

*May 10, 2000. Jasmina's apartment. Prague, Czech Republic.*

It was a Friday afternoon at around three. Jasmina's dealer stopped by to deliver some cocaine. Dale was high, sitting in his "spot" by the window, chain-smoking cigarettes while the two of them joked and flirted. The muscled-up, black-leather-coat-wearing dealer gave Dale a "What the fuck?" look, then bent down and whispered something in Jasmina's ear. She shrugged and giggled, then said something back to him in Slovakian before kissing him on the cheek. The dealer left a few minutes later, giving Dale a wink and an air kiss as he walked out the door.

"Mama getting high tonight," Jasmina said, flicking a flap of coke with her fingernail. "You strip now and put on costume like I tell you. We film ant scene with Frans soon."

Dale turned to her with a disgusted look on his face. "No! No more sex! No more drugs and no more porn! Look at me, Jasmina! Look at this *thing* I've become!

Jasmina rolled her eyes. She'd heard this spiel from him several times that day. "Listen, *Fena*. Nobody keep you here. I tell you million times, you leave anytime you want—and please do. You fucking depress me . . . Now, you want I chop you line before Frans come to film Boss Domina scene with ant costume? Nina and Martin come too, I think . . . I think American audience like if I piss on your face too, hmm?"

Dale turned back to the window, muttering. "Piss on my face? Fuck that. Fucking piss on you, bitch. Not anymore. I'm done with this shit." He lit a cigarette and sucked on it desperately, pressing his forehead to the cool, damp glass. All of Europe was out there at his fingertips while he was stuck here playing submissive to some junkie whore. *Fuck is wrong with me?* The smoke fogged up the glass for a second then disappeared.

Vienna, Athens, Helsinki, Dublin. Dale imagined drinking espresso on cafe patios, wandering alone through narrow alleyways, and smoking cigarettes on church stoops while hordes of tourists passed by with cameras and maps. They were the lost ones, not him. He'd escaped his prison and created a whole new persona for himself. He wore all black all the time like a true outlaw, and he let his hair grow back and tied it up in one of those scarves the soccer players wear. He quit doing drugs and took walks instead. And he'd gone vegetarian and lived off soup and fresh bread from the bakery down the street from his second floor flat. The one with the open windows, the balmy breeze and a balcony that overlooked the agora.

Dale imagined getting on a train and reuniting with Charlie, wherever he was, and about begging for his job back. The idea made him so happy he could cry. *Fun*, he thought. *Real fun with real friends and real people.* Charlie was out there somewhere. The two of them could be drunk in a pub by nightfall. It was all possible—he just had to get up and leave. Leave Jasmina. Leave all this.

Dale dropped his cigarette into a coffee mug and turned around. Jasmina was snorting a line of coke off the coffee table while watching a reality dating show.

"I'm going out," Dale said, heading for the door.

Jasmina burst out laughing. "Like that? Ha! You'd be arrested before you got to the end of street, *Fena*."

Dale looked in the mirror. He was wearing a pair of pink panties over holey black pantyhose, his blonde wig was in a tussle and his mascara was running.

"Maybe shave your legs first, *Fena*." Jasmina laughed hysterically. "Be back in one hour for pee-pee video, or else."


*5:06 p.m.*


Dale changed his clothes and made his way down the block to a pub. One of those musty basement joints filled with military vets, low-level criminal types and hookers getting liquored up between tricks.

An old woman came to the counter and asked Dale what he wanted in Czech.

"Pilsner and a vodka, *prosim*," he answered, flatly.

She looked confused and pointed to his face. "You wearing makeup to dis place, boy?"

Dale saw himself in the mirror over her shoulder.

*Fuck.* "What—that? No, no. That's a black eye. I got in a fight earlier. This guy sucker punched me. I got a few shots in too though."

The old lady shrugged and handed Dale the booze.

He found a seat and took out his phone to call Charlie.

"Hey! What's up, ol' chum? Long time no speak!" Charlie sounded wasted.

"Hey, man. Same shit. You know how it is."

"Yeah, eh? It's been awhile. You still in Prague?"

Dale was truly ashamed to admit it. "Yeah . . . I was wondering. Is there any chance of—you know—coming back to work?"

There was a loud commotion on Charlie's end. "Shhhh! I'm on the phone, bitch. . . What'd you say, chum?"

"I was saying—is there any chance I could come back and work with you guys?"

"Might be your lucky day, chum. Remember Clyde Johansen?"

"Swedish tour manager kid?"

"Yeah."

"What about him?"

"He got shit-canned *hard* yesterday. Stupid motherfucker threw a party in his hotel room. Six hookers and an ounce of blow that he scored off this crazy Albanian we met in Frankfurt. Housekeeping came in and seen the mess then called the cops. Lucky prick flushed the shit before five-o busted the door down, but he's gonzo. *Fisticuffs* is making him pay for damages, made him turn his laptop and credit card in, and that's that."

"So—you're saying there's a chance?"

"Put it this way, chum. I'm at a club with Paxton right now, and he is fuuucked up. How's about I feed the prick a few more Jäger bombs and then I'll pop the question. He'll say yes, don'tcha worry, chum. Easier to bring you back then fly someone out from Canada, know what I mean?"

"Charlie, thank you. You don't know how much that means to me right now."

"Don't thank me, just promise me you won't fuck it up again. I'm serious. Finish the tour, make some money, and we'll go back to our pathetic little lives, okay?"

"Yes. I'm in. No more fucking around, Charlie. I'm ready to work, man."

Charlie chuckled. "Okay, hang tight. I'll call you back later tonight—tomorrow morning, latest."

Deep, gargling bass from a massive sound system echoed into the phone before Charlie hung up. Dale was ready for that scene again. All of it.

# BOSS DOMINA—TAKE 1.

*7:53 p.m.*

For this scene, Jasmina played Boss Domina, a ruthless drug dealer in control of a vast criminal empire.

Frans yelled, "Action." Jasmina sat on a throne made of dazzling surgical steel and black leather padding. In her right hand she held a chain linked to a heavy steel manacle that was clasped around Dale's neck. Dale, dressed in an ant costume, knelt beside her on all fours while she sold Nina (a friend of Jasmina's) her drugs. Nina, playing a strung-out junkie whore, looked embarrassed for Dale, and for being the kind of addict whose habit forced her to associate with people like him.

Martin (another friend of Jasmina's), playing the role of Jasmina's lieutenant, was amused by the man in the ant costume, and he would kick and laugh at Dale, ridiculing him in Czech or English when the live-show watchers on Chatmates asked for it.

As for the watchers, especially the ravenous ones that knew Boss Domina well, they saw Dale as nothing more than her latest ornament. Her newest decoration. Furniture. This man in the ant costume was equal to taxidermy and they'd seen her do this before. Boss Domina was fresh off last night's kill, her victim's body still warm. Boss Domina had pumped Dale full of numbing agents while he was still breathing, charging viewers top-dollar to watch her violate him. It was a deviant form of art and expression, but original nonetheless. A Mistress Jasmina creation. Once in a while Boss Domina would stick a boot heel in his mouth, most wanted to her violate his ass with rubber toys and things like that, while others wanted her to force-feed him massive amounts of liquor and cocaine, which was pointless seeing as Dale was already high on several grams, plus some ecstasy. His eyes and ears were open, but his brain was unable to comprehend the degree to which he'd been reduced. To being humiliated and degraded in front of total strangers with no remorse or concern for his happiness or well-being. But with the right combination of narcotics, Jasmina had once again successfully reduced Dale to that: live furniture. He smiled and licked her toes, armpits and ass, and took whatever she gave him, once again feeling like his life truly mattered. The new improved, 21st century version of Dale Potoniak, in his artificial heaven.

Later for the grand finale, Jasmina squatted over Dale, shouting curse words at him in Slovakian while Frans the cameraman twisted and turned to get just the right angle of her golden shower hitting his face in the ant costume.

When the live show was finished, Nina and Martin left.

Jasmina was high, and wanted to film a bi-cuckold scene with Dale as the cuckold and Frans as the alpha, but Dale refused.

"Why not?" Jasmina asked. "You already nice and hard. Imagine this: Frans fuck me while you sit close by and watch like helpless little puppy dog. Then maybe you bend down over back side of couch and take it in back door from Frans while I call you names in English like faggot and pussy. Maybe Frans let you lick his hairy balls after, too. American viewers love that shit."

Jasmina and Frans both burst out laughing.

"Very funny, you two. Fuck you both. I'm gonna go pack my shit now. I'm leaving tomorrow."

"This *fena* will never leave me," Jasmina said. "I believe it when I see it." She nudged Frans. Frans shook his head and laughed, saying something in Slovakian.

Dale went to the bathroom to change out of the ant costume, a urine-soaked towel wrapped tightly around his hairless head. Suddenly, he heard moaning coming from the living room, so he rushed back in.

Frans, the serpent-like porn king had Jasmina bent over the back of the couch and was going to town. "What the fuck, Frans?! That's my—girlfriend, you son of a bitch!"

Jasmina's eyes rolled backwards as Frans' rake-like hips made slapping noises against her ass. She looked at Dale and smiled wickedly. "You still love me, sweet boy? Hmm? Come play with us, *Fena*. You like it, I promise. I pay you five hundred euro for this scene. You can pack later . . . Come. Come play with us."

When they finished, Frans said something to Jasmina in Slovakian, then started packing his camera gear. Dale lay on the floor, smoking a cigarette with his eyes closed.

"Five hundred euro as promised, sweet boy . . . Frans take me for party now. Good night, *Fena*."

Dale listened to Jasmina and Frans' footsteps on the cobblestone street until there was nothing but silence.

They were gone, and he wept.

*The next morning.*
*May 11, 2000. Jasmina's apartment. Prague, Czech Republic.*
*7:07 a.m.*

Charlie called like he said he would, and he sounded chipper as ever. "Mornin', chum!"

"Hey, man," Dale answered, anxiously. "What's the word?"

"We're just getting out of the club now."

"Nice . . . So?"

Charlie chuckled. "You wouldn't believe it, chum. They got these twenty-four hour nightclubs here . . . The place is still going fuckin' crazy and it's seven in the morning—it's insane . . . Anyways, I got Paxton annihilated and dropped the question."

"And?"

"Aaand the dumb fuck said you can come back, *if* you agree to sign a contract saying that you'll finish the tour without wandering off again."

"Done."

"And you gotta finish Clyde's pending articles by the end of the week."

"Absolutely."

"And you gotta pay back the money you spent fucking that Jasmina chick with the company's credit card—not sure how much it is—but that's it. Think you can handle that?"

"Yes sir! Consider it handled." Dale was elated. He hadn't felt real joy in a very long time. "I don't even know where I'm going. Where are you?"

"Berlin, chum! When you get here go to Alexanderplatz metro station, downtown. Call me on this number when you get there. The hotel's not too far."

"Thank you, Charlie. I can't wait to see you—friend."

"Yeah, yeah. Just get here in one piece . . . Okay, I gotta get some sleep, chum. Got a meeting with the Berlin theatre association in like four hours. Gonna be a rough one."

"You're the man, Charlie! I love you!"

Charlie chuckled over a long drawn out yawn. "Fuckin' right you do. See you soon. And I love you too, chum."


*9:31 a.m.*


Jasmina came home from her party night with Frans and Dale could tell she was in a mood. She threw her purse on the couch and went straight for the fridge to make a drink. After, she went to her room to change. A minute later, her breasts and bottom were wrapped tight in a pair of yoga pants and a thin, see-through crop top.

*Mistress Jasmina.* The professional. The silky smooth latex seductress, the psycho strap-on bitch goddess, the supreme queen of Slovakian cunts whose armoire of carnal delights would cost him countless hours of counselling and therapy in the very near and foreseeable future. She'd tied him up, whipped him, burnt him, spanked him, water-boarded him; kicked, punched, pinched, stabbed, poked, prodded and ultimately violated every inch and orifice of his body. And after last night's bi-curious escapade, she'd even forced him to call his own sexuality into question (a question Dale immediately put to rest after snorting a bag of coke and bolting to the nearest gentleman's club. He grabbed the first girl he saw and payed top dollar for a hummer with the money Jasmina paid him). That being said, it had been heaven with hell to pay, but Dale knew it was time to put an end to Jasmina's reign of sweet terror once and for all.

Jasmina was still high and went on the attack immediately. "Must be nice to sit on your lazy ass all night while I'm out fucking to bring you food to eat. Piece of shit wannabe writer. Why don't you write something for me, you fucking worm? You write me list of reasons I should let you stay here another day. You write that . . . Why don't you do something other than sit on ass and wait to take orders from me, you worthless fucking shit? Fuck it. You listen to me, little girl. Tonight we make new, very extreme, very nasty video and you will do exactly as Frans and I say, or I will fucking cut you, you hear me?" Jasmina sat down on the couch and began to chop lines on the coffee table.

Dale was petrified. "Y-you made a nice little prison for me here, didn't you? We're so different you and I . . . I don't know how I missed it before . . . I tried, Jasmina. I really did."

"Shut the fuck up, *fena!* Get in kitchen and cook me breakfast. Then you can clean entire apartment top to bottom. And I want nice hot bath and—"

"No." Dale muttered.

Jasmina turned around, her ferocious stare cut right into him. "Excuse me, *Fena?* I must have heard you wrong. What was that?"

Dale swallowed hard. His heart was pounding, and his sleep-starved eyes began to tear up before he whispered, "I said no, Jasmina."

*5:12 p.m.*

Ephemeral street tourists and vagabond drunks fill their cameras and bottles with memories they hope will last forever.

A group of friends stumbled by sharing a bottle of wine, laughing, smiling, taking pictures of the arabesque buildings, nearly knocking Dale's suitcase over as he sat on the sidewalk.

Dale missed having friends. Most of all he missed Emmett. They hadn't spoken since Dale left Canada and he knew that was unignorably wrong. Where had the time gone? He reached into his pocket for his phone.

*Ringing . . .*

"Hello?"

"Emmett . . . it's Dale."

"Dale? Hey, brother! How are you?"

"Well, not too good, man."

"What do you mean?"

"No matter how hard I tried, nothing seemed to happen. Six times I cried since midnight yesterday . . ." Dale's voice trailed off.

"Dale?"

"Yeah."

"You all right?"

"Em, I want to tell you everything, but there's not enough time; and I'm all fucked up so it wouldn't come out right anyway . . . I got one hell of a story to tell you though, man. I promise."

"I'm sure you do . . . Could you tell me what it's about?"

"Slavery, submission, compromise, complacency . . . I'm a walking contradiction"

"That's okay. It'll make the story better I think."

"I'm afraid of what you'll think . . . I've changed."

"You can't afford, for the sake of the experience, to get too invested in the opinions of other people . . . Remember what you told me when I wanted to give up on my book? You said, that once invested in that enterprise, surely trouble would come, but the moment would pass, and that I should stop chasing adoration from lesser men, that self-worth comes from knowing you're real, and authentic, and that you've lived uncompromisingly according to your own values. Right or wrong?"

Dale sighed. "I just wanna come home and think it over for a few years."

"You're just a crazy kid trying to live the dream, you know? Get back on the horse, brother. This is what you've always wanted. Making stories for yourself, right? . . . Hey, I miss you."

"I miss you too," Dale replied, choking up.

"Okay, jeez! Enough with the sappy stuff," Emmett said, trying to change the mood. "Why don't you read me something? I know you're probably keeping the best for your new book, but you've been on the road for four months now. I bet your notebook's overflowing with goodies. Let me hear something."

"I wrote something a few minutes ago . . . Goes like this . . .

Back to the city

I've been here before

Back with the animals I've tried to ignore

I'm back to the birds and the floating shoes

I'm back to the beast

And back to the blues

I'm back to day one

I'm back to what's next

I'm back to concrete

I'm king of the west

Taking pictures to commemorate it all

Attempt conversation about how they didn't do well in school

I'm back to the fountain
I'm back in God's oven
Ready to kill and be killed
Always being born
But mainly just dying from lack of love
The ocean touched my hair
It went straight to my head
The hair that I wore
When the city was dead
The nights never last
All of them pass
Some of them cried
Mothers with children
Mothers that died
Broken brown bottles
I poured down my throat
Needles and cigarettes
I get sick on a boat
Can't take a vacation
From this city I'm in
This city wants vengeance
When the mourning bells ring
I can sit among thousands
And observe with this pen
Horny young women
Desperate young men
Then I heard the gong
And it all went quiet
But the streets were still alive

Still singing
Long after it stopped
Long after he's told
Please, promise me baby
We'll never get old."


Emmett whispered, "I knew you still had it."

"The truth is I've barely written two words since I've been out here . . . I just want somebody to come along on a good day and rescue me from this rootless existence while I'm still energetic enough to keep things interesting for a while."

Emmett laughed. "Don't worry, you'll be back home in—six months?"

"Yeah. . . I'm sorry I haven't called. It's been—"

"It's okay, brother. I'm holding the fort down just fine. Talk to you soon, okay?"


*May 12, 2000. Prague, Czech Republic.*
*5:04 a.m.*


Dale wandered the streets of Old Town, drunk, swinging half-empty bottles like battleaxes. The first light of dawn crept over the famous *Prazky Orloj*, and the old bell chimed five times.

A shopkeeper, up early to open his store, pressed his face against the glass door and watched Dale stagger past the entrance to his shop toward the centre of the vacant market square.

Dale flung his bottles high in the air, serenading the starless sky as they came crashing down on his head.

"Black or white, we looked upon the night and at what remained . . . And now we lie in the shadow of your wings."

*And the blood spilled.*

*8:13 a.m.*

Dale was fast asleep on a park bench when Charlie called. He'd left a message saying that a week's salary had been deposited into Dale's bank account, and he was to get to Berlin as quickly as possible. Dale went straight to the nearest men's clothing store before making his way to the bus station, where he purchased a ticket, then went to the washroom to clean up. A few minutes later, Dale emerged from one of the stalls wearing a new pair of black dress pants, a new black shirt, a slick black jacket and a new pair of oversized black sunglasses. He checked himself out in the mirror. There were cuts on his cheeks and forehead from last night's bottle chucking incident, but his hair and beard were coming in again. He gave himself a wink, and said, "You a bad motherfucker, D," then strutted through the dingy bus station with a can of beer like an absolute boss.

# 9

# BERLIN

*6:06 p.m.*

"Charlie, I made it. I'm in Berlin." Dale was exhausted, half drunk, and very happy to be off the stuffy, overcrowded bus.

"You at Alexanderplatz?"

"No, I'm at the bus station. I just got here."

"Which one?"

"Hold on, I'll ask someone . . . I think it's called ZOB or something."

"Oh shit, that's perfect actually. We're driving right past it."

"We? Who's we?"

"We. Everybody. The whole crew's going out tonight for some team-building thing in Spandauer Forest."

"Team-building?" Socializing with the crew was the last thing Dale wanted to do that night. He'd imagined hitting a pub or two with Charlie, getting caught up, then a hotel bed, a TV and lights out. "Sounds fun."

"We got weed, wine and flashlights. Should be good to go."

*Spandauer Forest. Just outside of Berlin, Germany.*
*8:58 p.m.*

A gust of wind blew rain and dirt into Dale's eyes as he attempted to re-light the joint Charlie had passed to him.

"Need some help with that?" Charlie asked, smiling. Dale had lost weight and seemed a little off, but Charlie was genuinely happy to have his old friend back.

Dale shivered. "I'm f-fine."

"So . . . Did you ever call Jane after what happened?"

"Nope. Silly me, right."

"What's done is done, I guess. Here, gimme that fuckin' thing."

"Take it. I can't get this fucking lighter to work."

"I'll get it."

Dale reached into his pocket and showed Charlie a flap of coke he'd stolen from Jasmina's stash. "Want a bump?"

"Not tonight. Tryin' to cut down."

"You serious?"

"Yeah."

"More for me, I guess." Dale's cell phone rang. "Who the fuck is calling me right now?" *SNIFFFFFF.* "Hello?" *Sniff, sniff.*

"Potoniak. Bryan Paxton."

*Sniff, sniff, sniff.* "Oh hey, Bryan."

"Where you bitches at?"

"Huh?"

"Oh for chrissakes. Where is my team currently located, Potoniak? I'm at the hotel and no one's fucking here."

"We're out doing that team-building thing. Walking around some forest with flashlights. It's quite nice actually. I didn't think the landscape would be like this. Animal tracks everywhere. Big ones. Must've been very wild once upon a time."

"Right, I forgot about the team-building exercise. Good work, Potoniak. And everyone's accounted for?"

"Yes, sir. I think so."

"Don't think, Potoniak. Know."

"Yes. Yes, everyone's here. I'm one hundred per cent sure."

"Good. Now listen, Potoniak. What's the status on the Johansen articles?"

"I'll finish them, but I literally just got here so I haven't had time to—"

"Well, you better hurry the fuck up then, fruitcake. You're the team leader, our seasoned travel vet, so I need you on some next-level shit when you're done, you feel me?"

*Sniff.* "Yes, sir. I'll have them done by the weekend. You have my word."

"And if you fuck me again like you did in Prague, I'll be sending you home to Jane in a body bag. Got it?"

"Yes, Bryan."

"I wanna know where you are and what you're doing at all times. Got it?"

"I got it."

"And from now on it's Mr. Fucking Paxton to you, Potoniak."

Dale shuddered. "Yes, Mr. Paxton."

"Good . . . You kids have fun out there. I'm on my way to the rub and tug, but I gotta call the wife first. Make sure the brats aren't misbehaving. And Potoniak?"

"Yes, Mr. Paxton?"

"Lay off the coke, or I will fire your ass."

"Ha! Good one, sir."

"Shut up, bitch."

"Ha! Ten-four, boss-man."

"Potoniak—what in the good goddamn fuck was that? Boss-man? . . . Kid's losing his fuckin' mind."

"Oh burn! You got me again, sir."

"Ugh. You're such a sissy. Boss-man out." *Click.*

Charlie shook his head in disbelief. "There was a time you would've killed someone for talking to you like that. What the hell's happened to you, chum?"

"It is what it is. Gimme that goddamn weed."

For the first time in his life, Dale had secrets that would never grace the autonomy of a page, let alone be spoken of in the light of day. He'd done things he would never forgive himself for. And Charlie was right. He was right in Prague and he was right now. Dale had changed, and there was no use arguing the opposite. But Dale's new objective in life was simple: try to forget that which was lost; that or die of a broken heart in a year or two.

*May 14, 2000. Agnes's Café. Berlin, Germany.*
*9:56 p.m.*

Dale finished Clyde's articles and submitted them to Bryan Paxton. The cafe was empty now except for the girl working the counter.

"Do you know this song?" Dale asked.

"Sorry, what?" she replied, busy closing up.

"This song. Have you ever heard it before?"

"Uh, I think so. Have you?"

"We used to listen to this all the time when—"

"When what?"

"Never mind."

She smiled. "Well, now you have to tell me."

"Well, I knew this girl that—"

"Of course."

"Of course what?"

"There's always a girl with you Americans."

"I am *not* American."

"Oh."

"I'm Canadian."

"Sorry."

"That's okay . . . I'm Dale."

"Agnes. So what happened to this girl?"

Dale started to pack up his things. "Long story."

"Tell me."

"It's still a work in progress."

"So what about the song?"

"Doesn't matter."

"But you like opera?"

Dale sighed. "Yeah."

"Well, me and my friends are going to some opera theatre thing on Wrangelstrasse this weekend. You should check it out. The singer— she's Canadian too. Her show has great reviews."

"No shit. You got a flyer?"

"Yeah."

And just like that, there was Ola in all her glory. *Stocking Trade Productions and Opera Berlin Present*, Oh the Aching, Frames, Floods and My Withering Colt. *Written, composed and performed entirely by operatic soprano, Ola Kant.* The flyer featured a bright, high- contrast black-and-white photo of Ola's face with exaggerated makeup around shiny mirror-like eyes. Her fingernails were pressed against pale white cheeks and had been edited to appear long and claw-like. Her expression was that of sadness and deep irreparable heartache. An absolutely genius artistic depiction, given the title of the opera.

Dale's voice was barely audible. "Ola Kant."

"Yeah. You heard of her?"

"I have."

"Cool. Well, maybe I'll see you there, then. Good to meet you, Dale."

"You too, uh—"

"Agnes."

"Right. Agnes . . . So, this is your place?"

Agnes smiled. "Yep. This is my place. And you can keep the flyer."


*Later that night.*


Dale found an S&M bar and spent the next couple hours watching scores of men, ladies and couples disappear into the dungeons for a romp with one or more of Berlin's famous rubber-femdom goddesses. He chuckled to himself when they came back out looking like they'd gone twelve rounds and lost badly. He surveyed the crowded bar from the back while sipping a martini, and it took a while, but he finally zeroed in on a prime candidate. A emotionless looking redhead with Aztec eyes, thick hips and long legs in black, thigh-high dominatrix boots. Her huge tits were squished inside a glimmering pink-and-black rubber corset several sizes too small and there was an intense aura of pheromones in the air around her. Dale presented her a fold of bills when she finally approached him, and she led him down a narrow corridor toward a small room behind the main stage. *One last time. Tomorrow, Ola.*

"On your knees," she said. The woman had a thick German accent.

"Yes, Mistress."

She circled Dale's body with the tail of a whip, and without warning, slapped his face with a gloved hand.

"Fuck sakes!" Dale shouted, grabbing his left eye.

"Shut up! Now bend over the table. I'm going to teach you a lesson in obedience."

"Yes, Mistress."

Dale planted his face on the surgical steel table while the woman yanked his pants down.

Suddenly, the room went quiet and everything was moving in slow motion. A beam of soft, white light cut through the hazy redness of the dungeon, illuminating woman's pretty face. She'd squeezed some lubricant into the palm of her gloved hand; and in that final moment between action and accountability, Dale remembered the lyrics to one of Ola's arias.

I found you withered

And another like you fell

Just as I learned to love you

All of us disintegrate

And all of us fall

And pity ourselves

We curse death

In the moment of transformation

We curse the purpose

Another night of sin

Another morning glory

The persecution of a mirror

Another morning after.

Dale suddenly realized why he'd chosen this woman. The dominatrix looked exactly like a redheaded Ola.

The frantic thudding of gabber began pounding in his ears again, and the dominatrix reanimated into a bizarre, metallic looking alternate Ola, and then the revelation came.

*"Leave now and you won't be responsible for hurting them again. Stay, and you'll never find atonement for what you've done."*

The voice he heard was loud, clear and definitive. Dale made up his mind. He would retreat. He would deny himself the pleasure and follow the light.

"I'm sorry . . . I can't do this," Dale said, lifting his pants up. He grabbed his jacket from the back of the leather barber's chair. "You're gorgeous—and maybe under different circumstances I would—but I can't do it."

"Suit yourself," Alternate Ola shrugged, casually reaching for her pack of cigarettes. "No refunds."

"That's fine. Thank you. Honestly, I really enjoyed this. Maybe some other time. But hey—you don't have a twin sister in Canada by any chance, do you?"

"Fuck off, American.

"I'm not—never mind."


*A minute later, Dale calls Charlie.*

*Ring, ring . . .*

"Hello?"

"Hey, it's me."

"Dale?"

"Yeah."

"What's up? Where are you?"

"I'm out. What are you up to?"

"Nothing. I'm fuckin' bored."

"Wanna get high tonight?"

" . . . Fuckin' right."

*The next morning.*

*7:33 a.m.*


Dale and Charlie strolled down Gabriel-Max Strasse, screaming obscenities at passing cars while searching for a place to take a piss. Charlie, the more sober of the two, noticed an open shawarma shop across the street, and they pissed and moaned side by side into a wretchedly smelly steel trough.

"There's something I perceive as evil on the front of your shirt," Dale said, mesmerized by the rooster logo on Charlie's green T-shirt.

"There's somethin' evil about your face and I'm gonna punch you in it if you don't get the fuck away from me with that gross, tiny, wrinkled-up dick of yours."

"Quit it, Charlie. You're scaring me. I don't like what your eyes did just now." Dale watched Charlie's saucer-sized pupils dilate with childlike terror.

Charlie laughed. "Well, stop looking at them then, chum . . . God, these mornings are killing me. The balconies and the birds keeping me up late . . . There's a haze hanging over the street today. Did you notice that?"

"I just realized it after you said it."

"Yeah. I saw them up there earlier on that skyscraper, building coffins for young people to die in and decorate. I thought, here we are, down on the street, penniless and poor doing things the righteous goddamn way."

"You should wash your hand. You got a bit of piss on it."

They zipped up and went back outside.

Dale lit a cigarette, took a puff, then handed it to Charlie.

"I see nothing but ghosts out here," Dale said, covering his eyes to block out the morning sun. "Let's find something to drink. I'm thirsty."

"The only ghosts I see are these dead people in their concrete caves," Charlie said, sucking hard on the cigarette. "Lying in piss-stinking beds with their heads in shit. Mouths open, minds shut, eyes open, tongues tied."

"No music in their ears!" Dale shouted, flapping his arms.

"No music. No dancing. No love!"

Dale took the cigarette back. "They pretend to smile—all these people out here. But I can see the pain in their shoulders when the morning sun touches their stiff lovesick backs."

"Tryin' to get last night's taste out their mouths with another one," Charlie said, turning for a double take of the curvy black woman walking by.

Dale chuckled. ". . . The sun beats down on their backs like the whip of a slave owner, but it's all imaginary. All of it. The sweat, the blood, the stench, the fear, the cages—the filth."

"Laying in filth surrounded by beauty?"

"It all seems a little surreal, doesn't it?"

"What, life?"

"Yeah. And the pain. It's a little unnecessary, isn't it?"

"Enlighten me, chum."

"We teach our children to walk, but no one teaches them how important it is to sit still. When you're in the middle of a blizzard it doesn't matter what day it is, and it doesn't matter what people are saying about you. Only thing that matters is that you get out in one piece."

"I was looking through some old books the other day. Dusting off the old boxes for clues."

"And cum stains on the carpet?"

Charlie laughed. "Yeah. Fingerprints and cum stains. I was trying to piece together the meaning of this daily atrocity, you know?"

"I fucking love you, Charlie. We're institutionalized by love. It's a big fucking scam."

"How long do we need to dwell in the lies before we get to live in the truth?"

"What were you thinking about just now?"

"My old man. He's been gone for thirty years. Thirty years, comparing scars with himself in some shitty monastery cave . . . Thirty fuckin' years. I'm still missing something."

"Swing drunkard. Swing and sway and dance and stub your toe and curse God for the crack in the floor. We even blame him for our poisonous minds. You know what your old man's problem was, Charlie? Too eager for victory, even in the face of utter defeat."

"You know what I'm eager for right now?"

"What?"

"Titties."

"Toot-aloooo! Taxi to titty-town!"


*May 16, 2000. Berlin, Germany.*
*11:02 a.m.*


Dale woke up, forced himself out of bed and into a taxi. Today he was on a mission for mercy and forgiveness.

He lay by the edge of the Spree River with a bottle of bourbon, making insane observations to passing spiders and gulls. "Ola, my dearest . . . My heart is broken, and I don't know if I can handle the witching hour in Hitler's city. I won't forget the many dead, and I won't forget who I am or who we were. I came to the mountain to play in the sunshine, and I saw visions of you kneeling before God on a bed of frozen leaves and flattened grass. I saw needles strewn about the holy place, and I desired to pray alongside you, but my mind was so full of needles that I wanted to hang my heart on a puppet string and make it dance for you. I wanted to taste the inside of a leather boot from the miracle mile. I wanted you to know that I'm barely human. I wanted you to know that I'm ruinous and I smell of dust and rats. I wanted you to know that a saviour came for the man with the rusted shovel, and he digs like the curse of sin was his to bear alone. He makes himself a serpent. Rolling around on his belly. His voice is his only weapon against terrors only he can comprehend. He sits alone in places that make muses and rolls cigarettes in institutions that make men lunatics; and yet he still he desires to make peace and his home a comfortable place. Free from stars and free from the night, free from the growth we all run from. Away—from real evolution. I wanted you to know that nature is a mirror upon which we reflect and know the truth of what we are and what we have become. And as we look into the woods, nature's mirror reflects its truth, justifies our rebirth and we are transformed.

"I was free from space. The nature of water taught me the reality of all things—that earth is mother. Should I be afraid to die in mother's warm embrace? The energy which returns to the earth will be remade, reborn. We are the trees, the rocks. Either way this is the land of the living.

"I dreamed that I was collecting rocks by a river. A wise Buddha-like bald man in long purple robes told me, 'Leave one here so you know where you have been, take one with you so you know where you are going.' It seemed profound, but I hadn't a clue what it could mean.

"Later I dreamed that I woke up on a bench in 1940s Berlin. A Jewish child plodded by with his mother pulling a potato sack filled with river stones. They both looked at me and smiled, and it felt natural to bask in the radiance of ghetto mentality. When the mother and child disappeared, I felt a disconnect happen. Every phony ideal and attachment I ever had was laid bare, and I could choose whether to take it or leave it. I told the child, 'I'm in no danger, father,' but the playing field was bare, and the look on his face reminded me of every bored face in a baseball stadium. I quickly realized that baseball is better on television.

"I dreamed of Jasmina. And later when she was naked, my morality splintering into a state of unhinged subordination and complacency.

"I dreamed of calling Jane to tell her the news—that I was leaving her for another woman and that I'd never be home again.

'I'm never coming home, Jane.'

'What do you mean you're never coming home, Dale? What's going on? What does that even mean?'

'I finally found salvation, Jane. Everything I've ever done will be justified by the magnitude of this awakening. I'm in a place where the sounds of passing military helicopters are drowned out by the sounds of waves crashing on the beach. Tell me that's not a good place. It's lonely, but it still makes the most sense to stay. I love you, Jane. But people are living and dying all over the place. The most important thing is not to worry about me. I know you'll be just fine.'

'Dale, you're going to regret this. You're just in one of your crazy moods. Come home and we can talk things through, okay? We can pray about it.'

"And then I break it to her.

'Jane, I fucked her.'

"She doesn't say a word.

'I'm not a monster. Of course I feel guilty about it.'

'What about me, Dale? I gave you my—'

"I run my fingertips over the prickles of a freshly shaved head and know that I will never love her again. 'There is no more us,' I tell Jane.

'What does she do for you that I couldn't do here?'

'It's like a wound, then a scar, then a numbing sensation. But it's growing. It's always growing. Don't get me wrong, I want to break. If there is a way to break me.'

'A way to break you?' Jane sobs.

'I mean—if you could find a way to break me. Shatter what I've built. Destroy what I've made. Then maybe I could love you more.'

'If you've made up your mind, then what can I say? I really thought we would be together forever. Forever, forever.'

'What do you want me to say, Jane? I'm sorry for your wish that never came.'

*But I made a blood pact with darker desires. Jasmina's cocaine, her spit and a cage that kept me locked inside her wicked imagination for days without food or water.*

'You had a rest. Now come back to me, my love,' Jane says.

"To which I replied: 'Not yet, my dearest. I need to go back out again. Into the mist, over the sea, over the land. No, not yet.'

"Only the lonesome road

"Only the vagrant highway

"Only a wicked mistress with her black magic and incantations.

"I suppose that simply means the earth belongs to the Lord, but when I saw a dead moth on the stairs and lights on the tree across the street—all twinkling Christmas white—I realized my expectations were too high. That no man, no matter how noble and free, is happy, and that I should wash my hands, cut my losses and go to sleep. Because I'll be better off in the morning."

*May 18, 2000. Agnes's Café. Berlin, Germany.*
*The night before Ola's performance in Berlin.*
*10:43 p.m.*

"Agnes, I've had a revelation. Everything is nothing and nothing is everything. It's all based on perception. Symbols, ideas, signs and curiosity. The divine inside the animal flesh. Hands and feet as weapons, a sense of self, and a sense of who I am only comes from looking within, and from an unlearning of the external world."

Agnes picked a scab on her knuckle and it was bleeding.

"You should put a bandage on that," Dale said, cringing.

"It's fine," Agnes said, sucking it off. "The 'you' you're talking about does not come from here. I mean it doesn't originate here on earth. So in order to find peace, the divine inside each of us needs to make peace with the mortal shell."

Dale nodded. "All things have duality. All is nothing. All is made nothing and nothing becomes everything? Now I see."

Agnes laughed. "Could you stop?"

Dale smiled, his drunk eyes half shut.

"Can we please go for a cigarette, now?"

"Let's go."

". . . It's nice out tonight."

"It's beautiful, Agnes . . . I think the world would be a better place if we taught children to love themselves. To treat each other equally and to not worry so much about what people think. Any filter just blocks the light. Identity, image—it blocks life. So many motherfuckers out there obsessed with seeing their symbol in the sky, just so other people will covet their design. I do it all the time."

"If you want equality, than why the fuck do you go to those strip clubs? Do you know how degrading it is for those women having to do that every night?"

"All evil originates from the eye. The light, the night sky and the hordes of watchers below. It comes with a humongous responsibility to know both good and evil, Agnes. To be both divine and mortal. We live in a world where the symbol in the sky is revered more than the light itself. I worship those women up there."

"Sounds like a lame excuse to me," Agnes said, rolling her eyes.

"Well, the light's inside of us, not out. Returning to the source is vital. I think it's our responsibility, first to ourselves, then to our fellow people, to help them see the light inside them. We become so attached to the look of our symbols that we start to think it'll last forever, but it won't. We shine like this but for a brief moment, and the breath of God is in our lungs for only a day . . . Agnes, when your light goes out in this world you can rest assured that light was needed in this dark place, and in my wicked heart."

"Aww, thanks, Dale . . . What do you think would happen if people stopped worrying about the symbols, and instead, they shined their lights into all the dark places and wicked hearts around the world?"

A tear slid down Dale's cheek. "Well, dear . . . then there would be no place for evil men like me to hide, and the long shadowy night would forever turn to day. Live, love and die. Animal and divine. Everything is nothing after all. There is so much beauty in the world if we can see it. Shine your light in a million different places and that which is hidden will be shown to you."

"What are you gonna do now, Dale?"

Dale wiped his eye. "Nothing. Guess I'll go for a quick beer and call it a night, because tomorrow, Agnes, my dear friend, I shall be reunited with my fiancée. She was—*is* the love of my life, and I plan on surprising her in the alleyway behind the opera house tomorrow night. It's how we met."

"I didn't know you were engaged."

Dale pulled the flyer from his pocket. "Ola Kant."

Agnes gasped. "*The* Ola Kant?"

"Yes. *The*. And tomorrow night we wed."


*The Drunken Sailor skin bar. Berlin, Germany.*
*11:13 p.m.*


"Shot of whisky and a beer," Dale said, lighting a cigarette.

The barman was shirtless, and wore studded leather suspenders with assless chaps "Rough night, baby?"

"Not really. Why?"

"Gotta be rough to end up in this shithole."

"Okay. How 'bout those drinks."

"You look horrible, baby. Let Daddy make you something fizzy instead."

"Or how about you just give me the booze I asked you for," Dale answered, impatiently. "I wanna slam this shit quick and go to bed. Tomorrow's a big day for me—Daddy."

"All right, all right. Calm down, baby. No need to get pissy . . . Hey, you from the States? I've been there once. Las Vegas, baby! Ha-haaa!"

"No, I'm not from the States, man. I'm Canadian . . . Can you just give me my goddamn drinks already? I gotta go soon."

The barman grinned, pushing the beer and whisky toward Dale.

"Thank you," Dale said, shooting the whisky back instantly. "And get that pretty lady at the end of the bar one of whatever she's having . . . I'd drink her bathwater with a shot of horse piss."

The barman burst out laughing. "Ha! Good one! I never heard that joke before, but hey"—he leaned over to whisper in Dale's ear—"she ain't a lady, baby." Then burst out laughing again.

Dale looked at the woman again. "You're kidding me."

"Nope. Big cock-a-doodle-doo underneath that red dress, baby."

"Holy shit. Never would have guessed. Thanks for the heads-up."

The barman leaned over again and asked, "You like to party, Canadian guy?"

"Eh?"

The barman tapped the edge of his nose. "I mean this."

"Sure, once in a while. Why, you got some?"

"Sure—I mean I can get you some. One of my roommates deals a bit for extra cash. You know how it is. Hey, why don't we walk over there together and I'll score for you? You give me a line or two for the trouble. What do you think?"

Dale shook his head, looking bored. "Fuck would I give you free dope when I can just score it myself? Anyways, I told you I'm going back to my hotel after these drinks."

"Okay, okay. But trust me, Canadian guy. She's got the best shit you've ever seen. Best nose candy in Berlin, Germany, Europe—probably the world, baby!"

"What is this, fucking amateur night?"

"All right . . . Tough guy, huh? Okay. How about this. Forget the free shit. I was thinking of getting some for myself anyways. How about we split an eight ball, that way it's cheaper for both of us. You take half, I take half. Boom. Easy. Then you can go home and jerk off or whatever."

Dale nodded. "That sounds fair. And give me another shot of that whisky. Make it a double actually. And get the tranny whatever she's having, too."

The barman whipped his head back. "Whoa, shit! You are a party animal, baby!"

"Normal night."

"A normal night? Holy shit! I love this guy—you hear what he just—holy shit! Ha! What's your name, baby?"

"Dale. You?"

"Freddie."

"Freddie?"

"Yeah, Freddie. Why?"

"Nothing. You just look more like a Gunter or a Wolfgang to me, that's all."

"Nope, Freddie's the name. Short for Friedrich."

"I get it."

"Now go ask Miss Red Skirt real nice and she might show you her *ring ding dong . . . ring a ding ding ding dong.* Ha ha!"

Dale chuckled. "No thanks. I'm good."

"Give me a few minutes to clean this shit up, and we'll go." Freddie did a spin dance and disappeared through a set of swinging doors into the back room.

Dale downed the double whisky in one gulp. "Hoooo-shit. Freddie—I'll be outside. I'm gonna have a cigarette, maybe do a teeny-weeny bit of cocaine, then go to the hotel and get some sleep. I've got a big day tomorrow, Freddie. A big day."

"Las Vegas, baby!" Freddie shouted from behind the closed doors.

"No—Berlin, baby!" Dale hollered back.

"Mothafuckas!" Freddie howled.


*11:34 p.m.*


Freddie's building was a dilapidated, four-storey brick walk-up in a scummy-looking neighbourhood about a fifteen minute walk from The Drunken Sailor, and about twenty minutes from Agnes's Café by Alexanderplatz station. Sounds of city traffic and barking dogs could be heard faintly in the distance, but the narrow street was void of people or animals.

The outside door made a *brrring* sound before Freddie yanked it open. The inside of the building smelled like stale cigarettes, scented candles and microwave beef stroganoff. A set of steel stairs in the center of the lobby led up into darkness. A child's screams could be heard, as well as the drone-pounding of heavy industrial techno music from one of the apartments. The vibe in the building would have been unsavoury to Dale in the past, but he thought nothing of it now.

They were halfway up the first set of stairs when Freddie grabbed Dale by the arm. "Hey, before we get up there, I gotta tell you something. My roommate's a bit *different*, so just keep quiet. I'll get the shit, and we'll be on our way. Okay? Easy-peasy."

"Don't worry, I've done this a million times . . . Wait, what do you mean *different?*" Suddenly, an old woman hobbled by them on the stairs dressed in a cape of some kind, giving Dale a spook. "Hell did she come from?"

Freddie chuckled. "That's old Mrs. Zimmerman."

"What were you saying about your roommate?"

"Nothing. Just don't stare at her. She's gets a little insecure. You know women."

The apartment was on the top floor and the door was part way open so Freddie poked his head in. "Yo-da-lay-hee-hoo? Knock-knock, baby. It's Freddie. Anybody home?"

A pretty female voice answered from inside. "*Komm herein.*"

Freddie stepped inside with Dale close behind him. The first room, which was the living room, was dark except for some candles and a string of white Christmas lights in the corner. A vinyl record of Puccini's *Nessun Dorma* played softly in the background and seemed to get louder as Freddie's roommate approached from what undoubtedly was her bedroom.

"Can I help you boys with something?" she asked.

Dale's jaw dropped in utter disbelief. Freddie's roommate stood well over six and a half feet tall by the looks of it, and her gigantic fantasy-like body was dressed head to toe in a tight black spandex bodysuit.

"Shit," Freddie said, standing on his tippy-toes to kiss her cheek. "I should've called to tell you I was bringing someone over. I'm sorry, baby."

"It's okay. I was just working out. Who's your friend?"

"Who, this guy? This is Dale. He's from Canada. He's all right. Say hello, Dale."

"H-hello," Dale stuttered.

"Are you a cop, Dale from Canada?" the woman asked, inching closer.

Freddie laughed. "A cop? C'mon, baby. You know I'd never bring a cop to our place. It's me you're talking to here. So listen. We wanna get an eight-ball to split—and then we're gonna split. This guy's gotta work tomorrow and I'm going out, so—"

"What's the rush?" she asked, smiling at Dale. "We should all get high together."

Dale swallowed hard. His body felt soft, gelatinous and weak, but his penis was becoming painfully erect inside his tight jeans. He'd never seen anyone quite like this woman before. So huge and powerful. Her legs were like tree trunks. Her biceps were three times as thick as his were. Her eyes were bright blue, her hair the whitest blond. Her breasts were like cannon-balls.

"I've got some time . . . I'm cool with it if you are, baby" Freddie said, grinning at Dale.

"I don't know," Dale murmured.

"Stay for a while," she said. "Freddie's such a bore to get high with."

"Well, I guess I could stay for a line or two. But I'll leave when Freddie leaves."

"Good," she said, smiling. "I'm Lissa."

"Dale."

"Want an E?"

"No, I really shouldn't. I've got a big day tomorrow . . . I don't know. Maybe."

"Sit down and think about it. I'll get your coke."

*May 19, 2000. Lissa and Freddie's apartment. Berlin, Germany. 4:55 a.m.*

Lissa wore a purple silk robe over a black bra and panties. The robe had an image of a snake curling through clusters of thorn thistle, orchids, wild vines and apples, and was handmade for her by a local designer. She was stylish, sophisticated and elegant-looking. Delicate and pretty for her size. Her facial structure was stunning, and featured a jawline and cheekbones that could only have originated from an ancient Germanic bloodline; and although her teeth were slightly crooked and her lips too thick, she was a sight to be seen. Dale couldn't believe his luck.

*Brrring!* Someone was trying to buzz in downstairs.

It was Freddie and Lissa's other roommate. She'd come home.

Dale was in the shower.

Lissa answered the door.

"You're home," Lissa said.

"Sorry, I forgot my keys, and I know exactly what you're going to say—I shouldn't work so hard, but this is different, Lissa. This is my last show in Berlin and I want it to be special."

"You were up all night rehearsing again? How are you going to perform tonight? I can't believe you're leaving Berlin already. Feels like you just got here."

"I've been here for six months."

"Feels shorter."

"Wait a minute . . . Are you high?"

Lissa smiled. "A little."

"E?"

Lissa nodded.

"And who's in the shower? I thought Freddie was going to that—"

Lissa bit her lip.

"Lissa? Why is there an open condom wrapper on the living room floor—sorry, two condom wrappers?"

Lissa finally conceded. "Oh my god, he's so amazing, Ola. You have no idea . . . He's Canadian like you, and such a gentleman. The way he made love to me was so . . . He kissed every inch of my body, and I mean *every* inch."

Ola giggled. "Gentleman, eh? Who's the strap-on for?"

Lissa blushed. "Okay, so he's a very adventurous kind of gentleman . . . We kissed for hours and he brushed my hair—and told me that if he didn't have a woman waiting he'd stay with me forever."

"Oh, so he's married, too? Sounds like quite the guy."

"There's something mysterious about him. He loves opera music and he's a writer—oh, he recites the most beautiful poetry."

Ola yawned.

"Sorry, you must be tired. We won't keep you up. He'll be out of the shower in a minute. You can meet him, then tell me what you think later."

"Fine."

"Lissa, I need a tow—Ola?" Dale was stark-naked and dripping wet by the bathroom door.

"Dale?"

His hair and beard were gone and he'd lost a significant amount of weight, but his features remained intact. His eyes, once vibrant and alive with fire and passion, were sunken-in, sad and tired-looking, and his body was covered in scratch marks from Lissa's manicured fingernails.

Lissa laughed nervously. "You know him?"

"Ola?" Dale murmured, still visibly high. "I was gonna come find you—"

Lissa was confused. "Wait, you two *actually* know each other?"

"What the fuck are you doing here, Dale?" Ola shouted.

"I was . . . I was . . . *Je cherchais l'etoile.*"

"I can't believe this is happening," Ola said, becoming hysterical. "I was coming home next week, and—"

"What's wrong, Ola?" Lissa asked, placing a hand on Ola's leg.

"I have to go," Ola said, grabbing her purse and jacket.

"Ola, wait . . . Ola!"

"Lissa . . ."

"Ola's your woman?"

"I can explain everything."

"Get out, Dale."

"But—"

"Get the fuck out, now."

# 10

*May 19, 2000. Charlie's hotel room. Condor International Hotel. Berlin, Germany.*

*Around 6 a.m.*

*Knock, knock, knock.*

"Who is it?"

"It's Dale, Charlie. Open up."

Charlie opened the door. "Holy shit. What the hell happened to you?"

"I can't remember."

"Sit down a minute . . . You want some water or something?"

"Yeah, sure."

"Here . . . You're in deep shit, chum. Paxton's sending you home. You're fired . . . There was nothing I could do, I—"

"The road to pleasure is paved with good intentions," Dale muttered.

"What?"

"Lissa. She was wearing that spandex suit, and you know how I get around anything black and shiny. Kaboom. Next thing I know she's got me in a fucking headlock and—"

"You hear what I just said, Dale? You're fired, chum! There was nothing I could do. You signed that contract with Paxton and—"

"Doesn't matter. Nothing matters now. I lost my brand new jacket."

"What do you mean it doesn't matter? You fucked it all up, chum!"

"Just take me to the airport. I wanna go home."

"Tomorrow, chum. Tomorrow. Right now you gotta rest. You look like shit . . . When was the last time you ate anything?"

"I have no idea."

"I'll run downstairs and get you some fruit or something . . . Hey look at me . . . Where'd you go? Where'd you disappear to again?"

"I don't know. But I made a big fucking mistake, and I'm not sure if things will ever be the same. What a mess."

Charlie felt for him. "All right, just lie down. I'll be back with some food."

# CANADA

*May 20, 2000. Berlin International Airport.*
*9:05 a.m.*

Charlie put his hand on Dale's shoulder. "You get home safe. Get cleaned up . . . You're a good guy, chum. And a good writer. Get that back."

"Thanks Charlie."

"Here, take this."

"What is it?"

"Couple hundred bucks. It's not much, but—"

"You really don't have to, man."

"I know I don't *have* to—I want to. I feel bad about how things worked out. I mean you got me this job."

"Thanks man."

"You gonna be all right?"

"I'll be okay."

"All right. Safe trip, chum. I love you."

A stocky customs officer waved a metal detector over Dale's upper torso and legs. "Anything in your pockets?"

"Some cash and my ID. That's about it."

"Empty everything into this bin, please."

"I told you there's nothing—"

"Are we going to have a problem here, sir?"

Dale sighed. "No. No problem. See?" Dale patted himself down.

"What about the breast pockets. Let me see." The customs officer reached into Dale's pocket and found a letter. "See? What's this, then?"

"I have no idea. A letter by the looks of it."

"Smart ass. Put it in the bin."

"Fine. There. Happy?"

Dale walked through the scanner with no alarm bells, and the officer smiled. "Have a great trip home, sir."

*Ten minutes later.*

Dale held the faded envelope to the light. Jane had slipped it into his pocket the morning he left Fitchburg, and he'd completely forgotten it was there. There were two pages inside. One was a goodbye letter he'd written her on January 3rd, 2000, the other was a letter from her.

*Page 1*

Jane,

We've been through hell

I prayed to Saint Marie

The Lord up above knows better than me

You know what they say
The more things change
The more they stay the same

I'm a dreamer
And I dreamed about tonight
It ain't cut and dry
When they ask me who am I to often say
It ain't living
If it takes a thousand lives
It ain't winning
If it takes a thousand times
Always oh tomorrow

You cry, save me
For I know not what I do
Save me Lord
I'm a leper through and through
Save me
All the summer birds are gone
Save me
When my morning prayers are done
The revolution—
The revolution—
The revolution has just begun

Yes, we've been through hell
And we've been through saving me
But the Lord up above knows better than me.

Jane, I've decided to go. I'm so sorry for the way things turned out between us. I never wanted to hurt you. I hope the rest of your life is as beautiful as you are. But I don't belong here in this place with you. I don't deserve the love you gave, but thank you.

Goodbye my love. Goodbye my dearest.


Dale


*Page 2.*


Dale,

I found this letter crumpled up in the trash can beside your desk. Maybe you never intended for me to find it, but I did. I think that means something, don't you?

Wherever you are when you read this, remember that I love you, Jesus loves you, and you deserve to be happy.

I hope that by the time you come home, you'll have found that special thing you've been looking for. May the light of love shine upon your face. May the lord bless you and keep you safe.

Hearts.


Jane


# TORONTO


*May 21, 2000. Toronto International Airport.*
*Ten hours later. Around 9 p.m. local time.*


Dale picked up his luggage and went straight to the bus ticket kiosk.

"Where you headed?" the agent asked.

"Not sure. When's the next bus leaving?"

"Next bus leaves in twenty minutes, and it's going north, then west. Sudbury, Sault Ste. Marie—"

"Wait a second. Did you just say Saint Marie?"

"Yeah. Sault Ste. Marie. It's a border town, four hours west of Sudbury."

"I know, I just—."

"Are you all right, sir?"

Dale's expression was blank. "The Lord up above knows better than me."

"What?"

"Nothing. Sault Ste. Marie, one way."

"Okay. One way to Sault Ste. Marie. Bus is leaving in twenty minutes from platform 10, downstairs. You arrive at your destination at approximately 6 a.m. tomorrow morning . . . Have a good trip, sir.

# SAULT STE. MARIE

*May 22, 2000.*

Dale checked into the Trans Can Motor Inn on Great Northern Road and spent a good part of the day in miserable conditions, fighting withdrawal symptoms on a lumpy mattress that stunk of mildew and cigarette butts. By sunset, he was drunk at an old steelworker's bar near the casino called the Lunch Box, and that is where he met Norman Gabroni and Ray Bosco.

"I had some wild nights over there, boys. It's like there was an element of danger that kept me on my toes, kept me up at night, excited like a kid on Christmas Eve. Not to mention the women—oh the women! Lissa was a behemoth of a woman. Seven feet tall she was. You ever fuck a woman that size? I tell you, she damn near tore my pecker off me with those massive hands. Slap on the ass felt like a fucking buck shot. Ha! Jasmina . . . Jasmina was something else, boy. Never had a woman do things like that to me, and cruel is what it was, but I liked it. Hottest piece of ass I ever had that's all I can say." Dale stared across the table at Norman and Ray, expecting some sort of visceral response to his impassioned speech, but there was nothing—just disparaging looks, skepticism and contempt for him and his pathetic little Euro-trip story.

Norman Gabroni was a grotesque-looking hillbilly with a foul tongue, bad comb-over and a dirty wife beater that was covered in ketchup stains. A true miscreation of humanity with absolutely no recognizable soul; with endless stories about any and every vile indulgence and perversity you could imagine a man partaking in.

Norman's friend, Ray Bosco, was equally if not viler-looking. Well over three hundred pounds of repulsive putridity. A shit-stinking vulgarity of a man, from the sagging meat to the wretched bones. He was by far the most revolting fat man Dale had ever seen.

Both were admitted drug addicts, alcoholics and miscreant degenerates of the worst variety. Gluttonous wastes of humanity. Losers, rejects, white trash.

The waitress on duty that night was named Shelly. A plump, late forty-something with a washed-up, jaded-single-mother-from-the-trailer-park look. Her makeup was cheap looking and caked on and she had a noticeable limp in her left leg.

"Can I get you boys anything else tonight?" Shelly asked, raising an eyebrow to the mess on their table.

"Gimme a fuckin' beer, bitch. Eeeahh," Ray snarled, slamming an empty glass of draft down.

Shelly turned away in disgust. "Anything else?" she asked, looking at Norman.

"I'll take a fuckin' Alabama shit box, der, ya mother," Norman said in his strained, raspy voice.

"Never heard of it. Order off the menu, please," Shelly replied.

"Take this dick, bitch— eeeah," Ray said, pointing to the piss-stained crotch of his light grey sweatpants.

"What are you retarded? Talk like that to me again and you're all fuckin' outta here," Shelly said bluntly.

"Okay, I'll take a bottle of Union lager if ya don't mind, der, ya mother," Norman said.

"What the fuck are you talking about, man? Read the list. It's not on there. Try again."

"Eeeah, bring me another three pounds of wings. And make 'em fuckin' spicy, bitch— eeeeeah." Ray slobbered when he talked, and there was wing sauce covering most of his acne-pock-marked face.

"Right. More wings for the fat fuck. Got it. Anything for you, kid?" Shelly asked, looking at Dale.

Dale was so engrossed by Ray's repulsiveness that he didn't hear her.

"Hey. Anything for you?" Shelly asked again, this time louder. "It's last call, I'm closing up soon,"

Dale snapped out of it. "Yeah, sorry. I'll have another beer. Wait— make it a red wine and three double tequila shots."

"You sure? Fatso here might have a heart attack if he has one of those."

"Fuck you, cunt—eeeeah shit."

Dale tried not to laugh, but couldn't help himself. "Yeah, I'm sure . . . And I think he'll be alright."

Norman told Dale the story about how he'd been fired from his job at the slaughterhouse for selling drugs to his co-workers. "I'd pull da guts out of the shithole and make da fuckin' green horns clean it up, der, ya mother. Pussy motherfuckers couldn't cope so I started sellin' 'em prescription doops to keep da nerves down. Foreman caught wind and said, 'I don't think so', ya mother."

Ray was passionate about fucking the government over, and went on in great detail about entrepreneurship and providing quality products and services at low-rates. For a second he had Dale convinced he was some sort of modern day Robin Hood, but it didn't take long to realize that his entire enterprise consisted of collecting welfare cheques while making extra cash selling weed, chemicals and pills to "faggot" high-school kids from his rent-controlled apartment in the P-patch.

"You see any he-she's over there? Eaaaa," Ray asked Dale, licking wing sauce from his dirty, knobby fingers.

"Hell yeah. Seen one in Berlin just last week."

"Eeeah. I'd like me some she-dick one of these days. Fuckin' ride or die, bitch. Eeeah, shit eeeah."

Norman interrupted, banging his fist on the table. "Let's jus' say I've done shyit dat'll make ya fuckin' puke, der, ya mother." Ray burst out laughing, spitting his food across the table. "I've done shit dat'll make yer piece a crap Prague stories sound like fuckin' kids' cartoons, der, ya mother."

Dale was genuinely offended that Norman assumed he was some kind of newbie dilettante. "That's great Norm— highly unlikely, but if you don't mind, I was just about tell Ray about the time I—"

"Hey Ray," Norman said, "I got some VHS home videos over at my place dat'll blow yer fuckin' mind, der, ya mother."

"Oh fuck, eeah" Ray said, tearing into a chicken wing. "What's on em?"

"Let's jus' say it makes da shit dis pussy seen in Deutschland seem like a fuckin' Sunday school story, der, ya mother."

Dale shook his head. "I don't see how that's possible . . . What the hell have you done?"

For the next two weeks, Dale slept on Norman's couch or on the floor at Ray's place in an old flannel sleeping bag. He was able to scrape together a few bucks picking up drugs from a bouncer at the local strip club and delivering them by city bus to a couple of degenerate dealers Norman knew in Goulais River named Bullshit Bob and Shit Hawk.

*June 6, 2000. Ray Bosco's apartment. Sault Ste. Marie, Ontario.*

Dale left his notebook (the only notebook he'd kept in Europe, containing the only writing he'd done overseas) on Ray's kitchen counter that morning. He went out to make a drop, and when he came back that afternoon it was nowhere to be found.

"Where's my notebook, Ray?" Dale asked, picking through the mess of trash on the counter.

"What fuckin' book? Eeeah," Ray muttered from the living room. He was slouched in a worn-out lazy chair, stuffing his face with pasta, watching one of Norman's VHS home videos on a fuzzy TV.

"The one I left here this morning. It's really important to me. Where is it?"

"Oyeeeeahh. Didn't have any shit wipe. Used it. Probably some of it left in the shitter—eeeah."

*It can't be*, Dale thought. *Please, no.*

Ray's bathroom stunk like a rotting corpse. Dale gasped as he looked down to see his precious notebook mostly ripped to shreds on the wet, disgusting floor. The toilet leaked from a crack at the base of the bone-coloured porcelain, and the only pages left fully intact were laying in pool of stomach-curdling toilet water where the floor dipped and pooled. Ray had left a visible smear of feces and ass lint on the back of the toilet seat and had conveniently forgotten to flush. The rest of the notebook was somewhere inside the bowl, lost.

Dale looked down, trying desperately to stifle his vomit. Among the shit and ruins he recognized the two pages he'd written in Prague during his early, happier days with Jasmina.

The poem, once beautiful, had now been reduced to ashes, or as Ray put it: shit wipe.

I pictured you with a violent hand

But now I know you were a gentle man

Your heart is harder than a mountain

Softer then the sea
The gentle man is standing next to me

The night was cold
We wore furs to hide our faces
Snowbanks remind me of dangerous places
The gallery of shadows at the end of the block
The overuse of needles
The stranger who talked

When brother comes
I may feel freedom
From battles I've fought on this distant sea
When brother comes
I may fall broken
At the feet of a wounded saviour
When brother comes
I may feel distant
My mind's been blown down by a dark wind
Of a cold winter far from home
When my brother comes
I'll rejoice
And embrace my brother
As a friend when the war is done
When the war is over
When the war is done
When the day for embracing and laughter comes
On this distant sea where I've dwelt so long
When my brother comes

This distant sea won't matter much

And I'll pay my share

For him to come across.


"You ruined my book, you fat fuck!" Dale screamed, the toilet water soaking through his long-expired shoes. "Fuck! Why me, God? Why?"

"Eeeeah, fuck you, bitch," Ray garbled. His mouth was full of pasta and his penis was fully erect. Norman was on the TV, dressed in work clothes, plowing an obese transvestite in a schoolgirl costume. Norman even took the time to set the film to music. Some kind of satanic sounding, snarling black-metal.

"How could someone do this? *Who* would do this? You piece of shit!"

"Eeeah, shit—eeeeah," Ray mumbled, shovelling more pasta into his mouth. His stiff cock had pitched a tent in the crotch of his toma-to-sauce stained jogging pants, and he was rubbing it like a magic lamp every few seconds between scoops.

Dale took a deep breath, bent over the toilet, and reached down to pick up some of the brown shit-streaked pages, draping them over the edge of the bathtub one-by-one to dry.

"Ahhh! I got shit on my hand!" Dale screamed, on the verge of tears as he read the page.


Jane,


What have I done? I'm so sorry.

A man that knows no fear rides the razor edge of madness.

I guess I've always confused loving myself with hating others.

When I did what I could

Yet I moved you nowhere

You didn't smile at me in public anymore

There's nothing left unsaid between people

Who have known each other as long as we have.

"Oh, don't take it so hard, you pussy! Snap out of it!" Dale hissed, punching his own tear-streaked face several times.

*Later that night at Norman's place.*

Norman chopped up a half ounce of chalky-looking biker meth with a quarter ounce of coke and some random pills, and they all went to town.

"Holy shit, dat's gettin' me fuckin' goin', der, ya mother," Norman said, fanning his face with one hand.

"Oh fuck eeeeah. Let's go to the rippers' later and get our dicks sucked, boys. Eeeah shit," Ray snarled.

"Keep talkin' like dat and you'll have a fuckin' mess on your hands, if you know what I mean, der, ya mother," Norman said with a revolting smile.

"This is good shit, Norm. Where'd you get it?" Dale asked, sucking on his numbed teeth.

"This fuckin' goof out in—"

*Brring. Brrring.* The doorbell.

"Who is it, ya mother?" Norman yelled.

"It's Darlene," a woman shouted, banging on the front door. "I got Jesse here with me."

"Holy shit, it's da kid," Norman said, turning to smile at Ray. Apparently they both found it hilarious that Norman had gotten drunk and high and had forgotten that his son was coming to spend the night.

Norman answered the door, and came back a minute later with a skinny, sad-looking kid in tow, maybe fourteen or fifteen years old by the looks of him.

"Daley . . . Dis little shit's my son. Prick's name is Jesse," Norman slapped Jesse on the back of the head. "Hey! Say hello to Daley, ya li'l motherfucker."

Jesse didn't say a word, but stood stiff as a board staring down at the floor.

"Fuckin' loser . . . Da' li'l shit wanted to go fishin', so I'm gonna set him up wit' some gear in da kiddie pool out back. Back in a minute, boys."

"Fuck sakes," Dale exclaimed, appalled by Norman's cruelty to the boy. "Why the hell don't you just take him to a real goddamn lake for fuck sakes?"

Norman turned and smiled. His face lit up with evil, inhuman pride, and a cerebral, calculated ruthlessness glowed behind his sinister eyes.

Out of nowhere an emaciated dog appeared sniffing around the table. Norman kicked the poor thing in the ribs so hard it flew across the room, tucked-tail, and bolted toward the back door, screeching.

"Fuck outta here, ya mother!" Norman screamed, hurling an empty beer bottle at the dog as it struggled to squeeze through the tiny back doggie door.

Jesse stood stiff as a board, a look of pure terror gripped his face.

"Piece a shit fuckin' pooch . . . Look here, ya little prick. You can go castin' in da kiddie pool, but don't be treckin' any mud back in da house or I'll kick your fuckin' ass, you hear me? Ya little motherfucker you."

Norman handed Jesse his fishing rod: a tree branch with a length of yellow nylon rope and an empty beer can duct-taped to the end of it as bait. Jesse timidly took the fishing rod and ran out the back door into the pitch-black yard.

"Eeeeah, kid's a pussy—eeeah." Ray squirmed, his sweaty back sticking to the brown leather recliner chair.

Drunk, stoned or clean and sober, Dale had had just about enough of Norman Gabroni and Ray Bosco. "This is ridiculous. I'm outta here." Dale stood up, but had trouble keeping his balance because of the booze, coke/meth/pill cocktail.

"Hold up der, partner. I was just about to tell Ray a story 'bout work, der . . . Let's jus' say da boss had my head pushed down so far into da blue goo dis' mornin', I was practically chokin' on it, der, ya mother."

Ray laughed hysterically. "Talk about gettin' corked! Eeeeah!"

Ray and Norman laughed, like it was all perfectly normal.

"You need help for fuck sakes! You're both sick!" Dale grabbed his suitcase from behind Norman's couch, and made a beeline toward the front door, but stopped short. He had an idea.

Dale stepped into Norman's kitchen and quietly opened the metal drawer beneath the oven. Norman kept his drug profit money in a messenger bag down there, so Dale reached in, pulled the bag out and unzipped it. There was roughly two grand in tens and twenties inside. He tiptoed to peek around the corner again to make sure the coast was clear, then shoved the bag down the front of his pants before picking up his suitcase and rushing out the door without looking back.

*A minute later.*

"Eeeah, pussy just ran off—eeeah," Ray said, drool dripping from his bottom lip. A crusty yellowish powder had formed a ring around each nostril and his eyes were bulging hideously from their sockets because of the high-octane drug mix. Black metal music played loudly from a CD player in the background.

Norman bent down and snorted another line. "Yeah . . . That Dale's a bit of a fuckin' faggot if ya ask me, ya mother."

*Another minute later.*

Dale was on the streets and on his own again. The speed-ball drug cocktail made him practically hover over the pavement as he fled on foot. He ran ten blocks straight before stopping under a flickering street lamp to strategize. His eyes twitched fiendishly as he scanned the quiet cul-de-sac in a paranoid craze. Dale scratched frantically, his hair and skin crawled with a thousand invisible ants prepared to swarm-attack at any second. His heart beat felt like a thousand pound steel drum ready to breach the skin, and he began to see sinister visions amid the shadows; ants pounding huge wooden drums, eight arms at a time, breaching red jelly flesh, broken bones, razor sharp gnashing teeth.

Fortunately, he found a payphone nearby and called a taxi. In a matter of minutes he was at the bus station, twitching like a dope-sick crackhead at the ticket counter, where he purchased a one-way ticket to Ottawa on the overnight bus from a terrified kid who wouldn't dare look him in the eyes.

# OTTAWA

*June 7, 2000. Bus terminal. Ottawa, Ontario.*

A sleepless Dale Potoniak arrived in Ottawa that morning, deranged and weak to the point of exhaustion. The ten-hour bus ride had been a comedown of hellish proportions, and he was barely able to drag his suitcase out to the sidewalk. To make things worse, Ottawa was seeing its hottest summer in history.

The sun beat down on Dale's back with the force of a thousand Golgothan whips. Litres of toxic sweat seeped from his pores, evaporating instantly on the concrete blast furnace burning below his swollen throbbing feet. With his shabby beat-up suitcase in tow, he trudged onward without plan or purpose, until a flashing *Open* sign appeared out of nowhere like an oasis. It was a scummy looking hotel-tavern somewhere in Chinatown, and Dale nearly fainted before making it inside. The tavern was empty, but a cool breeze from a ceiling fan gave him the strength he needed to wheeze out an order before collapsing to his knees. "Cold . . . beer . . . Please."

The bartender was around forty years old and dressed in 1970s punk swag: a Black Flag tank top and torn-up jeans tucked into knee-high military boots. He saw Dale with his dust-covered face, sunken-in eyes and sweat-stained clothing reaching up to the ceiling fan from his knees, arms wide open, and asked: "You sure you want beer, buddy? How 'bout some water, first? It's hot as all hell out there."

Dale nodded and crawled toward a table near the air conditioner. "Okay . . . Water first, then the beer. Please."

"Here you go. Pitcher of ice water and a beer . . . Jeez. A guy could get pretty dehydrated on a day like this. You should be careful, man."

Dale's hands shook uncontrollably as he fumbled with the water jug, spilling half down the front of his shirt.

"Hey, you all right, man? Want me to call someone for you?"

"I'm fine!" Dale croaked, wiping his sunburnt face with the wet shirt. "Thanks for asking. What's your name?"

"Pete. What's yours?"

"Dale."

"Good to meet you, Dale . . . Let me know if you need anything else, aright? More water or whatever ... Sure you're okay?"

Dale reached for the beer and guzzled the entire pint in seconds, burping loudly afterwards. "Bring me two more of these and refill the water, if you don't mind . . . You got cigarettes for sale in here?"

Pete smiled. "Sure do."

*4 p.m.*

Dale was so drunk and dried out that he started to hallucinate, raising his glass to invisible friends who were cheering him on from the other side of the now very crowded, very noisy punk-rock bar.

"Lotta good people here tonight, soldier. Ah, the woman I love. Sometimes mad, sometimes crazy, but all the time the woman I love . . . This is it, Pete. Tonight's my last hurrah. I've made alot of mistakes, and I'm not proud, but it's time to make things right . . . Jane wanted to beat rugs from a balcony and live the good life with me, Pete. With me! But I had to go and fuck it all up . . . Not to mention what happened with Ola in Berlin." Dale motioned for Pete to come closer, then whispered in his ear. "I hope we grow old together. I hope we get to be that old couple sitting around talking, cooking together. That kind of shit, you know? I don't wanna die lonely, Petey."

"Who says we die?" Pete answered, busy mixing a drink. "Who can really say anything for sure?"

"You're goddamn right . . . Ah yes, the heart, the mind, are like oceans. And I'm a little fisherman on a tiny wooden boat. I thought my boat was floating, but it's not. Now, if I could just make my boat a little bigger, I'd be okay. But that's the problem. The idea makes more sense to me here than it does out there in the world. Are we all just puddles of mud praying for rain? Oceans of discontent, seas of rage? People like us are lucky to find a moment, even a second of calm. Water is calm by nature. I think I could be like that. *Burrrrp*."

"Hey. Maybe slow it down a bit, eh? And life's not all about sink or swim. It's about getting rid of your attachment to that boat and overcoming your fear of death . . . Once we do that we'll find ourselves neck-deep in the water with a storm coming in, but now we're in the ocean, and our eyes are open because we're in the light again . . . Stop worrying and just watch. You'll see that you've got no control and everything's the same. Who says we die? Who says anything? Who says I'm not over there with you on that side of the bar even though you're not here on this side with me?"

Dale smiled, but suddenly, his world began to spin and he lost track of Pete's face in the blur. "Ah shit . . . We all come to the fountain to drink, don't we, Petey?"

Pete chuckled. "Yes, we do. We sure do . . . You aright there, Dale?"

Dale bobbed side to side on his barstool. "Fuckin' nothin' to me. Fuckin' pissant . . ." Dale pulled Norman's wad of cash from his pocket and waved it in the air. "Give it up, baby—tough time now. This kind of heart break'll rattle the town. I'm the man that'll shake your shoes, I'm the tough guy that paid his dues—get doooown. Ha haa!"

Pete reached over the bar and grabbed Dale by the arm. "Are you fucking crazy, man? Do you know where you are right now? You can't do that kind of shit in here."

Dale shoved Pete's hand away. "You know who the fuck *I am*, bitch?"

"All right, take it easy. I'm just trying to help . . . Like I was saying before, we had to make the water safe to drink because we made it unsafe in the first place. You know what I mean, right?"

Dale shoved the money back into his pocket and turned to the invisible man sitting next to him, wearing dark sunglasses and a colourful sombrero. "Fuck is he talking about, eh?"

"Dale?" Pete asked. "You all right over there?"

"Fuck you. Give me another double-whisky-rocks . . . And get El Chapo another *cerveza*, here." Dale pushed a twenty dollar bill across the bar with his finger. "I hope you can comply with that order, *amigo*."

"Dale, there's no one—never mind. Whatever you say, boss. Coming right up. And one beer for El Chapo, too."

"*Gracias, muchacho!* I'll be back. Gotta take a piss and see if I can rustle up some crystal from that shady-lookin' buckaroo over by the beer canteen."

# 11

*July 2000.*

Dale took what money he had left and rented a room in a board-ing house near Gladstone and Rochester Street. It was one of those men-only places that rented by the month to over-the-hill drunks and ex-cons; it came with a small window, a small sink, an electric stove-top that didn't work, and a sweat-stained twin bed that was ripe with the smell of piss. There were shared toilets on the top floor which made relieving yourself in the middle of the night a major pain in the ass; so like the many men who had presumably lived here before him, Dale opted to piss in the sink or stay in bed and piss into bottles rather than climb three flights of stairs in the dark, barefoot, often spilling a bit on the bed in the process. It was like sleeping in a petri-dish.

By the end of the month, he found work with a publisher called Shoot Long Publications through a casual labour agency that Pete the bartender referred him to. Shoot Long Publications published collections of poetry, short works of fiction and the occasional mur-der mystery novel, and was owned by an old acquaintance of Dale's from Sudbury named Bert Conrad (son of Howard Conrad, owner of *Re-Think* magazine).

Dale spent most of his days in the company warehouse, stacking books and sealing boxes. His evenings were spent at home reading, sitting in internet cafes or walking up and down Somerset Street in Chinatown; stopping occasionally to watch a butcher lop off a chicken head or bleed a pig in the window; the sight of which would have made him sick a couple years ago, but for some reason didn't bother him at all now. The process fascinated him. The masterful knife work, the sound of the saws cutting through bone and flesh; the plain, emotionless faces of the old Chinese men as they tore the innocent creature's limbs from its body, making bones and ligaments pop like fleshy, knobby firecrackers. It was as graceful to watch as any figurine box dancer.

Sometimes Dale took his notebook to a coffee shop on Somerset Street and wrote poems. They weren't depressing, overly dramatic or sentimental like they were before. He noticed that right away.

When the long night is over,

The sun shines its beauty on the children of the day,

And creatures of the night.

When living in the city,

Fate spares men from seeing leaves fall, and forests changing colours—

Like summer was nothing.

Simple mundane observations through the eyes of a man experiencing rock bottom, truly, for the first time ever.

He thought of Ola and Jane from time to time, and rehearsed his apologies.

*July 30, 2000. Koine Coffee House. Ottawa, Ontario.*
*6:10 p.m.*

The rain fell sideways, rapping against the coffee shop window. Dale looked up. An old drunk man had stumbled inside and was asking the female cashier for the key to the washroom. The old man had either gotten splashed by a passing car or had pissed himself, because the front of his tattered trousers were soaking wet. Regardless, the pretentious cashier flat-out denied his request, and he was turned back to the lonely streets, looking left then right, for a way to take a wander.

Dale dropped a lemon wedge into his tea.

Poor guy.

Probably pissed himself and wanted to dry up under the hand dryer.

I've been there.

The bitch could have just given him the goddamn key.

The hell did she care?

Oh well. Can't live in the good world with the clean pissers and electric heaters 'less you play the game.

One week clean today.

Everything that's living is dying.

Is the point to write well or simply write? Live well or simply live?

Someone turned the volume up on a small television in the corner of the cafe. A pimply, slobbish-looking man stuffing his face with a doughnut mumbled, "Looks like they finally nailed the fuckers."

A woman wearing a tight red dress and dark sunglasses said, "'Bout fuckin' time." She had the air of a hardened prostitute.

Dale watched purely out of boredom.

"Good evening. My name is Vance Patterson, and you're watching *The Open Study* on Channel Ten News, Ottawa.

"Pharmaceutical heavyweights, Adelaide & Peck, took a massive hit on the TSX this morning as several of their top officials were indicted for human rights violations ranging from unethical experimentation on human test subjects, psychological torture, solitary confinement, starvation, forced imprisonment, as well as behaviour modification and cognitive altering using extremely high doses of the drug, Bafexatrin. Bafexatrin is categorized as an antidepressant and mood stimulator, but over the past several years users have reported severe, often fatal side effects, including hallucinations, violent behaviour, extreme paranoia, psychosis and personality changes.

"Authorities ordered an immediate cease and desist today on the production of Bafexatrin in all of their twelve production facilities nationwide, and reports have come in this morning confirming the use and sale of the drug has been banned until investigators can confirm that the drug is still safe for use by the public. Authorities are also urging anyone currently taking Bafexatrin to contact their doctors for alternative treatment options.

"It was just last year that Bafexatrin was deemed safe for public use by the Canadian Drug Administration after a ten-month investigation by authorities into allegations of corruption and collusion by several government officials who reportedly pushed the approval of Bafexatrin through without a thorough review of actual laboratory results.

"The following is a clip from last year's CDA annual banquet. Dr. Peck, of Adelaide & Peck Pharmaceuticals, addresses the media. Listen.

'This investigation was nothing more than a political witch hunt and an attempt to stifle the advancement of science. Bafexatrin has been proven to improve the central nervous system's overall performance in all but four per cent of test subjects. The drug finds its way to the pineal gland and automatically begins severing its connection to the brain by excreting a concrete-like by-product that's created inside the cytoplasm as it ingests the flouridic plaque that builds up around the root of the—I'm sorry. Too much scientific mumbo jumbo. And you probably don't want to hear it anyway, so I'll make it short. Bafexatrin enhances mood, nurtures feelings of contentment, boosts drive, ambition, happiness, you name it . . . I've seen Bafexatrin bring men back to life. Men and women that were empty shells of their former selves, suddenly re-energized, ready to wake up in the morning and be active members of society . . . This approval is not only a victory for us as a company, but for every man, woman and child out there suffering from a debilitating mental illness. Ladies and gentleman, Bafexatrin is the future!'

"That was Dr. Peck of Adelaide & Peck Pharmaceuticals speaking at last year's CDA banquet after the CDA approved widespread use of the drug, Bafexatrin.

"It wasn't until late last night that police received an anonymous tip that lead them to an abandoned warehouse on the outskirts of Kanata, where they discovered that the company, known worldwide as a leader in pharmaceutical sciences, had been conducting heinous experiments on living human test subjects. What they discovered inside was absolutely appalling. Take a look."

(Picture shows footage inside the warehouse, captured on camera by police and investigators as they stormed inside).

"As you can see, three men, believed to be homeless addicts from the downtown core, have been tied down to hospital beds, their wrists and ankles bound by thick nylon cords, and the drug Bafexatrin, or what we're hearing is the new, more powerful version of it, is being injected into their veins in astonishingly high quantities. One investigator we spoke to alluded to potential brainwashing experiments, but this has yet to be confirmed.

"Two other men were discovered tied to a cattle rack, but were reluctant to be rescued by officers as they told police and reporters they were being prepared to receive an implant in their brains called the "Bullet," apparently Adelaide & Peck's latest venture into the rapidly emerging bio-technology market.

"There have also been several reports that a highly advanced super computer was discovered, but has been confiscated by government officials. Channel Ten is still waiting for local law enforcement agents to confirm those reports.

"Dr. Kyle Peck of Adelaide & Peck, surrendered without incident, as did many of his leading aids. Gavin Fili, the company's chief recruitment and operations officer, made this brief statement to the press before being hauled away by police.

'Ladies and gentleman, there is no justice being served here today. When the time comes, we will prove to everyone that what we've been doing here is not only legal, but for the ethical betterment of mankind. Adelaide & Peck has been targeted to serve the interests of our competitors and nothing else. The truth will come to light in due time.

'To our operatives in the field: The Bullet program is currently non-operational. Our servers, software and computer are gone. Either destroyed or being sold to the highest bidder by the same crooked officers and corrupt politicians standing beside me right now . . . I'm sorry . . . You are true patriots, and you deserved more time. I just hope you found your way back, or at least part way back to a decent life with our help. I'm sorry. You're all on your own again, at least until we can sort this mess out. If you need any help, call 613—Hey, stop it! You can't do this to me! You motherfuckers! Fuck you!'

"We apologize to our younger audience for the strong language, but as you can see the accused, Gavin Fili, is being pulled away by officers and loaded into a van as reporters swarm in. Let's have a listen.

'Gavin! Gavin! What did you mean by the "Bullet"? Is that some kind of secret code?'

'Tell us what the "Bullet" is, Gavin! Gavin? Gavin!'

'Gavin, is Bafexatrin still safe? My daughter is on it!'

"In total, twelve of the company's top-ranked officials were arrested, but no mention has been made in regards to the whereabouts of leading research scientist and co-founder, Dr. Kira Adelaide. Her knowledge or level of involvement in any of this remains a mystery.

"Channel Ten will bring you more on this story as it develops."


The fat man pumped his fist in victory as he bit into his second doughnut. The hooker in the red dress lit a cigarette and high-fived the cashier.

Dale could care less. He shrugged and went back to his writing.


*October 8, 2000. Ottawa, Ontario.*
*9:06 a.m.*


"Your supervisor says you show up early and leave late almost every night. Is that right, Dale?"

Dale's performance at work had been exemplary for the past several months, prompting owner and president of Shoot Long Publications, Bert Conrad, to summon him into his office that morning unexpectedly.

"Yes, sir. I enjoy my job. Keeps me out of trouble mainly. Made some mistakes in the past, but those days are over now, thankfully. On the straight and narrow again."

Bert Conrad studied Dale curiously from his side of the oversized desk. "By god, Dale. I never thought I'd live to say this, but—I think you're exactly what I'm looking for here at Shoot Long. Someone with some good old-fashioned work ethic . . . I don't know how this happened, or what bizarre twist of fate delivered you to me, but do you know how hard it is to find good, hard-working people with experience these days? I never asked you before, but what kind of last name is Potoniak, anyways?"

Bert lit a cigarette without offering Dale one.

"My father's parents were part—"

Bert blew his smoke toward Dale and cut back in. "Who gives a shit. How'd you like a job in the office?"

"Doing what?"

"I need someone to work with this new prick of an author we signed. He's one of those entitled, know-it-all writers with a chip on his shoulder about the entire goddamn world. You know the type, right? Gets handouts from mommy and daddy and still talks like he's "keeping it real". Fucking shit weed. Every time one of my staff even mentions copy-editing, design or layout, the kid just freaks out." Bert chuckled. "He's such an arrogant little priss. Thinks he knows how to write books. The fucker can barely punctuate a sentence. Hell is it with kids these days, eh? Back when we were doing it—ah, fuck it. Only reason I signed him is because he's cutting edge. Built himself quite a name in the underground scene that I'm going to exploit the shit out of. Sorry—I mean develop . . . You still scribbling in those little notebooks of yours, Dale? If I remember correctly, we ran in some of the same circles in Sudbury a few years back."

Dale felt pressure building in his hands. "I wrote a poem the other day about—"

"Great. Doesn't matter. All I need is a fucking whip who'll guarantee me this little shit hits his contractual deadlines, you follow? I'm telling you, Dale. If I play my cards right, this kid's gonna make me a fortune. I signed him for two books on a shitty little five grand advance that he's totally happy with. Dumb shit. Says he wants to write and live the simple life. Can you believe that? Anyway. Think you can be my new whipping boy, Dale?"

Bert put his cigarette out and waited for Dale to respond.

Dale's head twitched to the left.

"If you're thinking about money, it pays a hell of a lot more then what you're making in the warehouse right now, I'll tell you that. How's fifty-five a year plus benefits sound?"

Dale studied Bert's suit. It was a custom-fitted Emerson, and the tie was loosened just enough to give him an air of casualness and approachability. He studied Bert's watch, a vintage gold Virtuo with some tarnish on the dial. It suggested he was a man of the people, adventurous, and someone who wasn't afraid to get a little dirt on his hands. His haircut was fresh, within the last day or so, but the barber made it look like he'd been growing it out for a while. It made people think that he participated in outdoor activities like mountain biking, kayaking and bouldering when he wasn't busy crunching numbers in the office like an average Joe. Bert's face had the stubble of a carpenter, not the clean smooth look you'd expect on a soft-skinned, pansy-ass millionaire. Everything about Bert's image was a cleverly designed hoax, a contradiction and a tactical business strategy. Dale saw the hypocrisy and lies as plain as day, but a new fire had been burning in his heart recently, a desire that could only be described as an eagerness and willingness to work, to be useful, and to serve. Dale finally understood why a million men before him had said yes, please and thank you—but there was more. There was more to this meeting than met the eye. This hole he was in, this job, this meeting with Bert Conrad, they were all more than just a coincidence. They were part of a defining moment in his life, and he would either veer to the left or cascade off the edge with the rest of the clueless, dumb herd; a moment in time where all corroborative facts came together to form an opinion outside the norm, and Dale could no longer deny the liberating power of the truth. That he was better than this. Better than Bert. Better than all of them.

"I appreciate the offer Bert, but if I'm going to do something I hate, I think I should make a lot more than a measly fifty-five plus benefits for doing it."

Bert grinned at Dale from across the desk, his tone slightly amused. "Well, we don't usually start anybody off higher than fifty-five until they prove themselves, Dale. But you're right. You've got the experience and you're willing to play hard ball with me. I like that. Okay, I'll give you fifty-nine-nine, but not a penny more."

"Thanks, but I'm not interested . . . I quit."

"Quit? What do you mean you quit?"

Dale stood up. "I mean I quit. I'm not working for you anymore."

"Ha! You can't quit, you just—What the fuck is wrong with you, you little shit bird? I offer you a promotion and a huge salary bump and you want to quit on me now?"

"You're a sad sack of shit, Bert. You know that?"

Bert was appalled. "What did you just say to me?"

"And you're a horrible writer. The only reason anybody in the literary community even pretends to like you is because your rich cunt of a dad owns *Re-Think* magazine, that's it. Without him, you're just another twat with a trust fund."

*Ahhh, that felt good.*

Bert laughed nervously. "Oh that's priceless, Potoniak . . . I asked you in here because your supervisor said you were a hard worker. He didn't tell me you were a fucking stupid—idiot. Okay Dale, suit yourself. Get out. Pack your shit and get off my property. You fucking loser. Go back to Sudbury and write some more blog articles for no money. Get."

"Gladly. At least I'll still be original. I don't want anything to do with you or your silver-spoon blood money. "

"I don't give a flying fuck if you do or don't, you dumb queef. There's a hundred people out there willing to do this job. You're just a name on the list, you fucking dummy . . . And obviously you're not much of a writer either. Working for a useless twat with a trust fund as you say; taping up boxes, sorting through books by *real* authors. You're just worthless lonely nobody. Always have been, always will be. Now get out."

"With pleasure."

"Fuck you, Dale."

Dale emptied his locker and went straight to an Internet cafe. He logged onto Chatmates and found the only person left in the business with some connections that might be willing help him out. Chet Cater.

For all his "bro's" and "yep yep's," Chet had proven himself to be a loyal and considerate ally. Dale wouldn't go so far as to call him a friend, but he knew he could count on Chet's help if there was help available to give.

—LOADING VIDEO CHAT. . . .

"Dale Peabody. Good to see you, bro. Word on the strizzy is you've been down on your luck these days."

"I was. I'm doing a lot better now."

"Yep yep. I quit doing coke a couple years ago, and it was the best decision I ever made. The white bitch damn near ruined my life."

"That's good, Chet. Glad to hear you're doing well."

"Yep yep. I went through a phase where I thought I had to pay everyone back for my fuck-ups, but then I came to my senses and decided to make a tonne of money instead. The rest is history, buds."

"Well, that's one of the reasons I called today, Chet. I've got a favour to ask."

"Shoot, bro."

"I want you to run a piece for me in *Avant Bard* magazine."

"Really?" Chet answered, sounding genuinely interested in the proposition.

"Yeah. It's a real piece of garbage I'd never normally write, but the boxheads in readerland will wet their panties over it."

"Dale Peabody is writing self-help pieces now?"

"I think I'm ready to make some real money, too."

"Holy shit, bro. Don't tell me Dale Potoniak, the lyrical legend, is throwing in the towel to make an honest living selling snake oil to horny housewives."

"Well, I just got back from Europe with a bagful of stories that I don't want to relive, so a memoir is out of the question. And I'm sick of the grind, man. Fuck it. I want a big-ass house, a hot maid and pile of money to sleep on. No, scratch that—I want a cabin in the woods a million miles away where nobody's ever gonna find me, and I wanna sit around all day and write stuff that nobody but me and the birds will ever read. That's it."

"Hmm."

"Trust me, Chet. This piece is good, I promise."

"Yep. Dale I would, but—"

"Just run it, man. Edit the shit of it. See if I care. *Avant Bard* will love it, your readers will love it. Just make sure I get paid what it's worth, and oh—if they want more, I got loads, okay?"

"You realize you're selling out, right? Which is totally fine. Fuck, we all do sooner or later."

"Selling out, keeping it real—I'm sick of all these labels, man. I realized something lately; I'm not the guy you, me or anybody else thought I was. It was all an act, an elaborate fiction, and I was just playing a character. It was fucking stupid. But I am a writer, and I am gonna write."

Chet chuckled under his breath. "Sorry. It's just weird hearing that from the most sanctimonious motherfucker I've ever known."

"I've been through a lot of shit, Chet. I've changed."

"Look, if it's about money, I can help you out, bro. All I'm saying is I've known you for a long time. And if you go down this road—you're not going to like the person you become."

"Who I like or don't like has nothing to do with making money, Chet.

"Yep yep. You're right. I just never thought you'd actually do it . . . Well, I was tryin' to tell you before, I don't even work at *Avant Bard* no more, bro. I moved."

"What?"

"Yep, yep. I'm on my own now in Toronto."

"Doing what?"

Chet smiled. "I'm a literary agent."

"No shit." Dale bit his lip. "Who do you represent?"

"A few small-timers. Nobody you've heard of. But if I tell certain people that Dale Potoniak's mind is officially on the open market, there'd be a lot of interest 'round these parts. Yep yep. A hook-up like that seems like it would be worth—twenty per cent?"

"Fifteen percent. Who do you know in Ottawa?"

"Fine, fifteen. Tonnes of people, bro. What do you wanna do first?"

"Anything. Everything. Books, magazines. Whatever I told you I'd never write before, but it paid top dollar. That."

*Later that day.*

Chet started calling his connections. Meanwhile, Bert's voice was still ringing in Dale's ears. "You're just worthless, lonely nobody. Always have been, always will be." Dale decided then and there to call Ola and Jane that day. Regardless of the outcome, he felt confident enough to face it head-on and put what happened in Europe in the past once and for all. He found the number online and made the call from a payphone booth outside the Internet cafe.

"*Ciao, Teatro dell'opera, Milano.*"

"Si, I'm looking for Ola Kant."

"*Signora Ola?*"

"Si. Do you know where she is?"

"Si, Miss Ola is in Vienna preparing for her final performance before going on holidays. I'm sorry, who is calling?"

"I'm a friend. You wouldn't have a number for her by any chance, would you?"

"*Un momento*—I'll ask the *direttore.*"

"Thank you. Thank you very much."

". . . I have a number for *Signora Ola* at the Palazzo d'Arte in Vienna, Austria—"

"That would be just fine, good sir. *Grazie.*"

Dale dialled the Vienna number, but it went straight to voicemail. "You've reached the voicemail for Ola Kant. I'll be in Vienna until the fifteenth, after which I'll be on holidays. Please leave a message for me here, or if it's really important, leave a message with reception. Thank you." *BEEP.*

"Ola . . . It's Dale. I should probably have waited to tell you this in person, but you're going on holidays and we both know what that means, so . . .

"I'm living in Ottawa now. I was in Sault Ste. Marie for little awhile, but that was a dead end . . . Things are looking up. I'm even writing again . . . I don't know what else to say to you, but I'm sorry. I think about you every day—have I told you that? Obviously not. Never mind, forget it.

"I'm officially over the ruthless self-examinations, Ola. I'm older now and more mature. It's just simple, beautiful examinations from here on out, because the tank might be empty, but the machine is still running well. Even better than before I think.

"I wrote you something . . .

Years spent singing

Clapping

Dancing

Face down in the dirt

And on knees worshipping

Or longing to worship something

Seeking wholeheartedly that something worth submitting to

Older now and out of juice

Out of time

And out of reasons why

Just realizing now

That the machine didn't need much of anything to run all along

And knowing that would have saved me a lot of hurt

If I would have known it when I was 16

18

20

25

30 even

A glass of wine

And a guilt-free cigarette

Is easy living

But it's sad when there's nothing left to say

I see a cabin in the woods

Always just a cabin in the woods

Away from men

Away from humans

Away from this misfortune

What happened to me?

Where did I go?

Where did I just disappear to?

And with who?

Can you imagine it? Chancing your ideas on the impossible bet? Love? Changing your mind? Pretending you saw something else that day in Berlin? Really seeing something else?

That which was white has been painted black by my filthy feeble hands. How can I advocate for that which took everything from me? From us? Lust.

Love. Did we ever truly possess it?

I always said that the only thing we'd ever regret was not living. You always find a way to make peace, so find it now. I want more than anything else to spare those I love from suffering when I'm gone. Imagine a book, then imagine your life. That which has a beginning and an end can only be complete when both ends are attached by words and thoughts. A book ends, but never stops being a book. It just stops being read so the story is no longer active. I pray for this kind of observance for your life and mine. Even the prophets expired. Christ expired. What a fascinating concept. I pray to be watched. To be seen. Always. And by anyone, everyone. And meanwhile I despise the watching eyes of men, but without them here watching me now, like this, perfect as it is, I cannot play the game. I cannot make this pen bear fruit. I am obsessed with death and I know that now. Not in a morbid perverted way, but in the way a botanist studies flowers or how Tesla had his math and physics. I want to know the rules to the game and why. On the road, the heart grows restless then explodes, until you find something that makes you feel alive.

Those footsteps I retrace, those graves I loot, these rocks I try to mine a shard of gold out of—they're all so deeply painful, sad and tragic. I remember them like they were yesterday because I still feel the exact same way I did, maybe just a little older. I haven't figured anything out yet, Ola. Same hurt, same insides on fire. A permanent desire to not be here. I don't get it. I don't get what it is, but it still won't go away. I made the mistake of letting you go once, and now I'm paying the price. Men pay far higher prices for crimes they've committed, so this is nothing, right? We're still young—kind of. The lords of war have shed my mother's blood and I've been touched by a goddess in many beautiful places.

I am the proverbial blind man sitting by the edge of a river dying of thirst. An institutionalized man in the bountiful forest dying of starvation. Dying due to lack of knowledge. I don't know what's missing because I don't know what I've got. All I know is the world is awake and I'm asleep in a land of ghosts and soulless bodies moving around me to the beat of some morbid mechanical drum that pounds ideas of betterment and slavery into my mind, soul and body. Ten minutes ago, I thought I was free. I am not. I miss my mother and father, but this is what I came looking for. This heaven. Where baby birds are the only audience for my songs. The deserted bench my stage. The ocean, the universe and the setting sun, angels applauding my minor victories.

There must be something wrong in my head. I'm free, sober and financially fixed. I can do whatever I please—which is what I always wanted, but I still feel like I'm in prison. I feel like all this stuff is trinkets and mirrors in a budgie cage. To tap our heads against until sooner or later we all go completely mad. I walk down these streets and see trees and smell the air the same way convicts look at flowers growing through cracks in their concrete cages. My mind is in chains. A slave to the idea that I'm in chains when I'm actually not and I know that. I used to love these streets. I also used to listen to a lot of street music, but I'm older now and I've had to learn to live in the prison of my own decay like a monk. Like a sleepless Buddha. Restless feet under his purple robe.

Only a prisoner set free appreciates the freedom I have. Only a sick man that's been made well appreciates the health I have. Only a beggar, only an orphan, only a ghost can see what my eyes cannot.


"I've dreamt of you, Ola. I've dreamt of *us* a thousand times. You are the circle and I am the line . . .

"Ola . . . just remember who I was and not what you saw that night in Berlin . . . I wish you luck. You're so special and unique. I'll never forget you."

*Click.*

Tears poured down his face. "God, that felt good," Dale muttered, wiping his eyes.

He went back inside the Internet cafe, thirsty for more atonement. He searched and found the number to *The Carriage* and went back outside.

"You've reached *The Carriage,* how may I direct your call?"

"Jane St. Marie," Dale said.

"One moment please."

"Hi, you've reached Jane St. Marie. Please leave a message. *God bless you.*"

"Jane," Dale sighed. "It's so good to hear your voice again . . . It's Dale. Dale Potoniak . . . Listen, I know it's too late for this, but . . . you're a good woman, Jane. You're a good woman, I mean that. You were real good to me and I fucked it all up. I hurt you and I'm sorry.

"Remember that time we were sitting in the living room talking about building a cabin in the woods? What do you think we'd do in that cabin, Jane? Drink wine? Smoke cigarettes? Pray?

"I think during the day I'd wander around the woods, read books, write letters and take them to that post office that's *far away, but not too far*, like we said. I'd stock up our supplies and walk back, then hold onto you forever.

"But I know it would be still be there. And I know it would be bugging the shit out of you; even though I'd try to deny it, you'd know it was true and it would make things even harder . . . You'd be out there in those woods with me, wondering about all the things I did while I was in Europe, and I'd try and convince you that there was no point in sacrificing my fun, and that we only live once so I had to make the most of it, right? Maybe after a while you'd feel comfortable enough to let me wander off again to clear my head while I get things into perspective. And you'd tell me you'd wait for me, until I'm ready to come home to you and our wooden castle.

"Maybe I'd come back here, to this city, to live the life I've got right now. Struggling writer, recovering—whatever. Or maybe I find another Jasmina and live more days like that, until I wonder what I'm doing living a life of sin when I've got a good woman and a cabin in the woods.

"But I go on fucking and drinking, smoking cigarettes and sleeping in on the weekends, going out with my friends, waiting till Friday to get paid by the man. I keep worrying about money, worrying about the future, worrying about life having purpose, my calling, my vocation, and about being successful. I worry about all the reasons why, and waste all my time being distracted from real *life*.

"*A cabin in the woods*, I'd think. *What a great idea, isn't it?* All I really want is the love of a good woman and to write Emmett and Charlie letters about words, nature and love. To walk for supplies, and to be alone. To light fires—fires for *us* to cook on. Away from computer screens and crowds. Separated, undistracted, living in the now. There's got to be a way for me to do all of that and not go a million miles more for the sake of altruism.

"A flower blossoms whether or not anyone is looking. It does what is natural and it is not ashamed when it withers and shakes in the cold or bends in the wind. Even the slightest breeze bends the branches of these mighty trees and they're okay with that. These rocks, these mountains, are canvases for flowers and trees to paint their masterpieces on. Even rocks get shaped by wind and water. Nobody remains unaffected by the elements surrounding them. We're all just grooving and vibing off of each other. It's always been like that . . . I wasn't immune to the laws of reality just because I spent a lifetime avoiding the inevitable.

"But there is a source. Where the wind comes from I mean. From where *we* come from. It's the light. And even if a tree breaks or a rock becomes smooth, it's not their fault. It's just nature doing its thing. It was their destiny. We shouldn't try to remain unaffected by the forces surrounding us. We just gotta know our roots and keep them strong.

"Jane, I'm really really sorry for what happened in Europe. I wish you all the best, and thank you from the very bottom of my heart, for loving me when you did."

# 12

*October 9, 2000. Sudbury, Ontario.*

Emmett Dorry walked around Bell Park for almost an hour before deciding on the perfect spot. He chose to sit on the grass beneath a white birch tree by the baseball diamond. There were fallen leaves all around.

"This should do," Emmett said, pulling his notebook and a six pack of beer from his backpack. He settled in, cracked a can of beer and breathed a sigh of contentment.

The mind is truly a weird mechanism . . .

It was just right for about half a minute, but now

There's a knot making its presence known in the centre of my spine.

And these sunglasses separate me

Make me feel drunk after just one sip.

Everybody's playing games

Anything for distraction

Me too

I'm the same

No better than they are

I just pride myself on knowing when to end a good sentence

And build fences

Not good at anything else though.

A group of college kids played baseball in the distance. Emmett watched, wondering where his best friend Dale was—out there in the world somewhere, searching for words and the meaning of life amongst broken bricks and broken sticks.

Emmett made a big decision recently. After years of half-hearted attempts, he was fully committing himself to his dream of publishing a novel. He'd accepted a job offer in Victoria, British Columbia, doing high-rise construction, and was leaving Sudbury the very next day with a mission: finish writing a novel and pay back his credit card debts all within one year. The job in Victoria paid well, and if he stuck with it he could be debt free and save enough money to self-publish when it was time. He'd put a lot of thought into the plan, working out every minor detail from the dollars to the days on the calendar. He even included the cost of hiring Dale to edit his manuscript into his budget.

The baseball field is empty now

The players have gone home

Or to a bar

Or to a tree of their own

To miss someone

Or to crave something more special.

I question my cardio

When it comes time

To play the game again.

A police siren wailed somewhere in the distance.

The police sirens aren't for me

They're for someone else

Somewhere else

Doing something

Truly wrong.

Dale

Unappreciated genius . . .


Emmett took a sip of beer and noticed two lovers kissing beneath a tree of their own.


I suppose the end result is me

I am the art

How do I look to you?

Is this pleasing enough?

Can you tell . . .

(hate this pause)

I've put my work in too?


*Later that evening, Emmett is having dinner with his parents. Sudbury, Ontario.*


"I'm proud of you, son," Emmett's father said.

"Your father's right, Emmett. We're both so proud of you. Taking initiative like this, planning, budgeting. You'll do great out there son, just great. And that book of yours will be an absolute treasure I'm sure."

"Thanks, Mom. I just hope it doesn't take too long to finish. I'm really going to miss you guys."

"A year will fly by, son," Emmett's father said. "Just stick to the plan, put your nose to the grindstone, work hard and you'll be back home in no time. That is if you're not off travelling the world as a famous author."

Emmett's mother giggled.

"I always knew the boy would be special," Emmett's father said, biting the head off a stalk of broccoli. "Didn't I always say that, Simone?"

"You did, George. Your father always knew you'd be special, Emmett."

"Thanks, Mom. Thanks, Dad. I can't wait for you guys to read my book once it's done. I'm going to write a dedication in it to you both."

Emmett's mother gasped. "Well, isn't that something, George? Did you hear that? Emmett's going to dedicate his book to us . . . Oh dear. You've gone and made me cry, son—in the best possible way of course. Oh my, I'll be right back. Is there anything you need from the kitchen, Emmett? George?"

"No, Mom. I'm fine."

"Go on, Simone. We're fine. Emmett and I will clear the table when we're done. Go on. I'd like to speak to our son in private for minute." Emmett's father cleared his throat. "Emmett, your mother and I wanted to give you something before you go." Emmett's father reached down beside him and placed a gift bag onto the table.

"Aw, Dad. You guys didn't need to get me anything. Thank you, though."

"It's just a little reminder of where you come from and who you are. And if you ever start feeling a little homesick out there, hopefully this will help. We love you, son."

Emmett pulled the tissue paper from the top of the bag and reached inside. There was a small box, and inside the box was a silver chain attached to an oval-shaped locket. Emmett opened the locket and tears began to well up in his eyes. It was a picture, taken the day he'd come out to his parents in tenth grade. Dale had encouraged him to do it and had gone along for emotional support. Emmett's parents were not only accepting and supportive of it, they seemed overjoyed. The four of them talked for hours, then Emmett's father took them all out for dinner at Emmett's favourite restaurant, where he asked the waitress to snap the picture.

"Well, son—what do you think?"

"It's beautiful. I love you, Dad."

"I love you too, son. C' mere. Give the old man a hug."

*Later that night at O' Reegan's Pub. Sudbury, Ontario.*

"The fox was frozen in the headlights like a deer, or some weak crap like that," Emmett said, wobbly from the four beers he'd guzzled down. "Bert's a horrible writer, brother. Admit it. But it gives me motivation to keep going, because if that's the kind of crap getting published these days, I think my book will do just fine."

It was Emmett's last night in Sudbury, and he was out with a friend named Terry Latoush. Terry attended Emmett's poetry club at the Y on Tuesday nights.

"You're absolutely right," Terry replied. "A book that bad, on that shelf, in that store? *Tabernac.* Success don't mean nothing when you look at the big picture of things, eh?"

"So many books. So many wasted pages and empty brushstrokes. So many eyes looking through expensive lenses seeing nothing—as only experienced eyes can see. And all the fancy equipment in the world won't make that photo you took look beautiful. All the lenses and all the fancy brushes from that fancy store won't make you know what makes it beautiful and why—" Emmett paused, staring sadly into his beer. "*If they can't understand why I'm here, a million miles from home, soaked to the bone and shivering from the cold—then all the words I write from this day forward won't make them understand that life can be beautiful. That I'm floating around the world on a moment's notice, doing nothing but hoping the best for everyone I know. And I love them all.*"

"You okay, buddy?" Terry asked.

"Yeah, I'm okay. My best friend Dale wrote that. I haven't seen him in a while, so—"

"He's a writer, too?"

"Heck, yeah. One of the best. I mean he could be if only—never mind."

"How's the rest of it go?"

"Rest of what?"

"The rest of it. What your friend wrote. What comes after the 'doing nothing but hoping the best for everyone I know, and I love them all,' part?"

Emmett knew the entire piece by heart. He looked at Terry and smiled. "*If they can't understand why I'm here, a million miles from home, soaked to the bone and shivering from the cold, then all the words I write from this day forward won't make them understand that life can be beautiful. That I'm floating around the world on a moment's notice, doing nothing but hoping the best for everyone I know. And I love them all . . . But I can only sing by myself. It's the only pure way. The kids do it in the courtyards and coffee shops for the whole world to see, but worshipping in your own closet with the door closed—that's the way it's gotta be. As soon as that foot pops out the door—well, Jesus knew. Pray alone, write alone, and in solitude you'll find that which is vital. That energy that flows from heaven above. Travel? Because I don't know how to live any other way. The open road has justified my shadowy existence, and it always makes me sad to see new cities, seeing folks in their cars driving around. Coming from, or going to work. I always wanted more for everyone. Really—I love them all. I wish everyone could know the joy of freedom, and I think I could get into joy, but I've only ever written about pain, from pain, and about the beauty of leaving if there even is such a thing. But that's what we're here for in the end. To write some stories and take some photographs . . . I live like this so I have something to talk about—motherfucker.*"

Emmett felt embarrassed for swearing, but Terry laughed.

"Sounds like one heck of a guy, and one hell of a writer. But I think that's the first time I ever heard you curse."

"Probably is. There's more. Wanna hear it?"

Terry took a sip of beer and got foam on his mustache. "Ah, *tabernac* foam. . . Of course."

"*And if I stop writing— you'll know it's over. So much designing to be elegant and pleasing to the senses . . . You all live in these boxes you call your lives and you spend your precious time decorating them, finding what little pleasure you can out of life. Some momentary impulse or an endorphin or serotonin lift and then it's gone; and your home and heart feels just as empty or emptier then they were before you spent all your time, money and dignity trying to fill that abysmal hole . . . We learn to design, but we don't know how to appreciate. We learn to build and sow seeds, and to work and fight, but when it's time to harvest, we quickly realize that we've forgotten to learn that one special skill: we don't know how to live—to be. To harvest the seeds. To get fed. We know damn well how to sow, but we don't know what it's like to harvest anymore. We know how to eat, but we don't know when to be full, or when to feel satisfied, or when to be thankful. Abundance? Magical money? Debt-relief pipe dreams? And who doesn't have faith the size of a mustard seed? Even I've got that much. Freedom comes through casting off that which binds you. And if it refuses to cooperate, then you go to war against it till you're victorious. We're all floating. Some of us are just lucky enough to keep our heads above water while others are gasping for air. And the best of us walk on water then get crucified. But we want it all. The world and everything in it. Our appetites are unrelenting, unceasing and unfulfilled. The hunger never stops. We built ships to carry us from one shore to another, but these ships started off as little fishing boats. Fishing boats ruined the world. Fishing. Actually, it's our hunger for fish that ruined the world. We would have never built those boats if we didn't crave the flesh. We need to acknowledge the fact that we're human, and as humans possess this fucked-up need to disconnect from reality. If we disconnected from our own nature, instead—which is more like cancer than grass or trees, or a deer or a duck—then we might have a chance. That's it. Deny your cancerous nature. Be loving to others, but first to yourself. And damn these chains."*

Terry nodded. "Hard to be away from good friends, eh?"

"Sure is, Terry . . . Hey, you wanna see a picture of him? My parents just gave me this locket and—"

"Hold that thought, buddy. I really got to take a shit, *tabernac.* Wanna play some Yahtzee when I get back?"

Emmett smiled. "Sure, Terry. Sure."

*Even later that night.*

*There's just something about Sunday nights*, Emmett thought, taking in the scene on Durham Street from under the brim of his yellow hooded raincoat.

He'd said farewell to Terry at O' Reegan's, and decided to take a walk in the rain before heading home for some last-minute packing.

The streets downtown were empty and the strong winds made eerie, metallic humming sounds off the traffic lights on the corner of Elm Street. *The streets are quiet . . . It's raining a little, but no more than usual . . . There's just something about Sunday nights . . . Even the St. Anne junkies want to stay home and be holy.* He noticed two of them under a set of stairs behind St. Anne's Parish, dressed in cartoon pajamas. They were giggling and snorting powder out of plastic baggies. *Scratch that,* he thought.

Emmett made a loop around the high-school parking lot, then up to Kathleen Street where he found an open coffee shop. He ordered a tea then sat down at a table in the back.


It always feels like Sunday

Who will find my book of poems?

I have no child to call my own

It always feels like Sunday

And Sundays make me sad

I am the incinerator man . . .


Emmett liked the sound of it. Incinerator Man. It was very comic-book superhero meets brooding-poet-renegade. A play on words he could extract endless ideas from. His pen tapped excitedly on the page, when suddenly his phone began to vibrate.

"Hello?" Emmett answered.

"Emmett . . . it's Dale."

"Dale?"

"Yeah. Long time no speak, eh? How have you been? You doing all right?"

"I'm okay. I was just working on some writing and—oh, forget about me. How have you been? *Where* have you been? There was a rumour going around that you flew the coop to Bangkok."

"Not true. It's a long story. . . And I'm sorry I didn't call you sooner, I just—I've been holding my hand just far enough from the flame where I can feel it, but it doesn't burn, you know what I mean?"

"Dale?"

"Emmett, the reason I called you tonight is because I've got an old-fashioned craving to make a big fucking mistake and I don't know what to do with myself."

"Probably not a good place for someone with your disposition to be in," Emmett said. "You sound good, though. You sound sober."

"I am. Sober I mean—for now . . . But maybe the whole thing's a waste of time. I mean who am I kidding, right? I'm a fucking addict. Always will be."

"You don't actually mean that, do you, Dale?

Dale sighed. "All I know is I'm looking at the calendar on my wall like next week is a mountain I have to climb, and it's gonna take a one-way trip through hell to get me over the top."

"You've climbed a lot of mountains with heavier loads and weaker knees."

"Listen to you sounding all grown up and shit . . . Hey, could you read me something you've written lately?"

"Nah, you don't want to hear me blabber about—"

"Please, Emmett? Just read something, man."

Emmett sensed a desperation in Dale's voice. "Okay Dale. Sure . . .


We ate snow hares for breakfast, lunch and dinner, but when the meat ran out we crushed up rocks and lost our only good teeth.

The man we elected chief of the tribe eventually lost his mind and wandered off alone into the open tundra. We found him later, frozen stiff in a warrior's pose by the only tree for a hundred miles. He was a brave man, a warrior, who became a basket case and lost his sense of purpose when there was no enemy left to fight, save the hunger of his dying people."

"That's really good," Dale said, fighting back tears. "What else you got?"

"It's because I let it in
The pounding hammer of duality
It smashed me to pieces
The darkness and the light
All at once
I let it in
And it was both glorious and lethal."

Dale wiped his eyes. "Shit, you're good. That was a good one, man."

"Thanks, Dale. Not as good as your stuff, but . . . I wrote this one the other day. Tell me what you think.

The day must come when the strings stop playing
When the crowd stops buzzing
When the harpist stands
The wind goes
The instrument falls
And lays chipped on the floor
And in the cemetery silence we hold each other's hands
Slowly swaying to the music in our heads
Eyes closed
Because we know that nothing is beautiful until the morning after
This is for you
This is for me
Close your eyes and imagine us dancing together
In the quiet of each other's shuffling feet.

And a chorus will one day shout the unanimous no

To the slaves: Keep your heads down

Are we truly wild?

Or have we all gone mad?

For is this not madness, this charade?

This game we play?

What a monster this machine

With its ability to ruin men

And it's not the first time I've had you be the darkness

So I could find the light."

That was enough. They both understood what it meant to read between the lines.

"It's getting late. I should go, Em. I'm gonna see you soon, though."

"Really? When?"

"Soon, Em. Real soon . . . Gotta go."

"Wait Dale, I'm moving to—" *Click.*

# VICTORIA

*Two months later. A construction site.*

Denis Babinski was strong as an ox. A real man's man, but well-read and keen to chat about books and the more profound things in life. He came to Canada in '98 from Poland, seeking adventure and a new life in the Pacific Northwest.

"In my country, to be a great writer, musician, composer or artist, one must possess the power of truth, and it comes from knowing, nothing else. Someone with that power who chooses to wield that power—well, my friend, that man is truly merciful." Denis finished pounding a nail into a form brace then looked at his watch. "Fifteen minutes to go, my friend. Would you like to join me for a beer after work? It's payday, and it's on me."

"Sure," Emmett said, "but I don't want to be that guy in the bar sitting there by himself when you get up to talk to your girlfriend on the phone for an hour."

"Don't worry, my friend. Tonight is for stress-free laughter and happiness. There will be no talk of, or talking to, women."

Emmett chuckled.

Denis smiled. "How about we clean up these tools and get out of this mud hole for a couple days, my friend?"

"Sounds good to me."

*A couple of hours later in a bar on Government Street.*

"What's there to say, Denis? I wasn't built for this type of work. There's no art to it. Everything we're building, we build to destroy. We work days and days on these forms just to tear them apart after the pour. It's pointless."

"Nonsense," Denis said, "you're doing fine. You're one of the best apprentices on site in my opinion."

"Thanks, Denis."

"Something else is wrong?" Emmett was silent. "You can tell me, my friend."

"It's my book—"

"I knew it."

"I feel like it's too sad. I've got too many ups and downs in the storyline already."

"Ups and downs? That's life. Senseless longings that never filled the void," Denis said, watching a herd of tourists snap pictures across the street.

"Exactly. A potential boner is the only reason people read anything these days. Everything else is just reactions and expressions. And nobody cares about a grown man's complaints."

"Immortality is modern man's latest obsession. But it really doesn't matter how we live or how we die. It's how we felt, and how we made other people feel along the way. And yes it's true, you'll just be a memory someday. Sad for some. A cause for contemplation for a few brief moments and then they'll all go about their days filling their time with chores and things because it's too sad for anyone to think that a fire like you was snuffed out. That you were just like everybody else. Just human."

"How come I never met anybody like you in Sudbury, Denis?"

"What no Polish up in Sudbury? Oh right I forgot. All Frenchmen and closeted hicks up there."

They both laughed and Denis put his arm around Emmett's shoulder.


*December 11, 2000. Denis Babinksi's apartment. Victoria, British Columbia.*

*10:27 a.m.*


The funny thing about this city is that the streets are lined with floral galleries and the buildings are designed like safe homes for seventy-nine-year-old retirees in Naples, Florida. Everywhere I look, I'm reminded of old people in mono-clad, necro-nylon pants and flower-print blue blouses, sitting at home watching game shows while they cook their microwave beef stroganoff.

It's impossible to get down and dirty when the streets are littered with pink cherry blossom petals and the air smells like potpourri all the time. I mean, what kind of writer would choose to spend his days in a flower garden? Dale said he used to stock up on whisky, cocaine and cigarettes, then check into a hooker hotel when he needed to get any real writing done. I'm starting to understand what he meant by that now.

"Good morning," Denis said, waltzing out of his bedroom in a Japanese kimono.

Emmett watched the branches of a giant Sitka tree swaying in the window. It was raining and windy out, a typical December day in Victoria.

The tree outside the living room window just twitched

And my heart skipped a beat

But I'm withered and dry from the alcohol

So why are you twitching

Dearest green tree friend?

"Goooood moooooorning," Denis said, again.

"Morning, Denis. Sorry, I just needed to finish my thought."

"Polish coffee?"

"Yes, please . . . Ugh. I think that beer was poisonous. I'm a line behind today. What was it?"

Denis chuckled. "Ah, you'll be fine. Good local swill. Trust that the body knows, even though the mind is sick and needing love."

Emmett smiled. "You should write down those one-liners, brother. How do you come up with that stuff?"

"I wrote poetry in Poland, long before I came to Canada"

Emmett sat up. "You did? How come you never told me?"

Denis grinned as he passed Emmett a steaming mug of coffee. "Pass me one of those cigarettes and sit back, my friend . . . Now, I'm translating from my mother tongue, so forgive me if the words are a little off."

"I totally understand."

*"Your sorrow carries a blindness inside your scary world of loneliness,*

*Where you run from ideas of logic and take great offence to those who outbid you on the road to solitude.*

*Your voice whimpers and rocks like a child born in a bad dream.*

*You have a hole that you love to hide in.*

*Take me there.*

*Write about me in your book,*

*Make me immortal in your mind, like I have made you in mine,*

*And forget everything else you ever had,*

*Before you learned to hide away from love."*

Emmett was astonished. "Wow . . . Just wow."

"It means opinions can't shape the identity of a confident man who is truly aware of his own value and abilities."

"That is so insightful."

"*A man must first be sure that the field is poison before he decides to hold on to valuable seeds. All things behind me, questions lie in wait like a forged sword, lost without a fight. Innocence is lost because age influences perspective, among a million other things in which we can question free will. I want to die and come back as a flower. Let the sun grow me, feed me—*"

"Denis?"

"Yes?"

"What was your father like?"

"He was a hard-working man. A man of faith who loved to laugh. And he loved my mother."

"He taught you well."

"I'm not half the man he was. I've abandoned my higher values time and time again in order to achieve selfish aims. "

"He'd understand."

"*My father is a godly man*

*With a razor-sharp mind*

*And a kill-or-be-killed instinct.*

*I've never seen him stop*

*When he had to get the job done.*

*I've seen him lie in the grass*

*And let the blood run cold*

*But he gets back up and toils it out*

*Under a sun that's too hot today.*

*He'd live the life of a rebel*

*A con man or a criminal*

*If he wasn't so good to my mother*

*And to us—*

*And at sticking to his guns about what he believes in.*

*He'd probably go down in history*

*As the man who shot down so-and-so*

*With no remorse.*

*He'd smile after—*

*Laugh later*

*And sleep the sweet sleep beside the woman of his dreams*

*And the blood of his enemies on his bed sheets and hands.*

*Under his fingernails you can find the history of the exception to the
free world*

*The one, or at least one of the few, who stood up*

*Took his*

*And was willing to die for what he saw fit to die for—*

*And he never bowed to the system*

*But carried a not-so-secret disdain for it with him everyday*

*And he still has it in him*

*Waiting for the ultimate score*

*For the ultimate getaway*

*To break free and build his own empire*

*Way way down the road."*

Emmett was moved to tears. "That was beautiful."

Denis stood up and put a record on. Bellini's *Dopo l'oscuro nembo.* ". . . That's the power of music. You hear a song, and in that moment you no longer fear death because it reminds you of a time when you were truly alive once."

"And now you're afraid of your own shadow chasing you down the stairs."

"Yes exactly. Floating on a hope and a prayer as always."

*December 24, 2000. A cabin in the woods near Sointula, British Columbia.*

Morning of Day 1.

I'M AT THE CABIN!

It's actually Day 2, but I arrived late last night, so technically it's my first day.

I waited so long to get out of the city and here I am. The fire I made last night is out so it's cold, but the sun is shining in through all four tiny windows of the cabin and that makes me happy. It's exactly the cabin Dale and I talked about growing up: 8km away from a small town with all the amenities, but far enough from the drama there.

It's always best to get out of bed and start "doing" something, but I've never been a morning person so I think I'll just lie here and think, which is a luxury I'm not used to these days.

There's a radio and some books, and someone left their guitar here. A wooden desk in the corner looks perfect right now. Get up and start doing something, Emmett . . .

When I was young I fell in love at summer camp. I wrote a story about my secret love for—and I was so embarrassed about it that I burned my diary in the backyard because I knew it wouldn't stay hidden in the house for long. I burned a lot of secrets like that.

One day my mother took me into town with her to do some shopping. I hid a diary in my jacket and waited until she wasn't looking before stuffing it into a garbage can outside of a bookstore. I've always wondered whether someone came along and found it. Maybe they read it. Maybe they liked my sappy young love stories.

Another thing I did once was go to the movies with this friend of mine from public school. I was too embarrassed to show up at my house with him, so I asked his parents to drop me off down the street at Dale's, even though I knew he was away on vacation with his parents.

Weird memories out here in these woods alone.

Denis will arrive in few hours . . . I'll tell him how I feel tonight . . . That makes me really nervous.

I don't want to do this construction work anymore. I hate my job, and I really don't want to go back next week. The dread is building. For the concrete. Concrete hell. Concrete beasts. Concrete animals. Why stress when you're on your own now, Emmett? Well, I think I thought that if I went far enough away that I'd end up back at the beginning. But it's not true. I just got further away.

This is bad, Emmett. Negative. Darn. I knew I'd lose the point.

Oh, wait—that's why it's pointless to go away. It'll be the same.

I'll be the same.


*A few hours later.*


Denis brought enough beer and food to last a week, along with a box of his old poetry and journals.

Emmett and Denis spent Christmas Eve around the fireplace drinking stubby bottles, while reciting poetry to each other. Denis read from his old notebooks while Emmett recited his from memory.

"I wrote this one in Spain while I was rebuilding that cathedral in Barcelona I told you about . . .

*Aimless men with broken hands*
*Broken fingers working the ground*
*Hot in the sun*

*But not like the conquistador and his hat*
*And his beverages*
*Just hot and in anguish*
*Knowing the dread won't go away today*
*Tonight*
*Tomorrow*
*Or this weekend*
*Men from hard places learn to shut down their emotions*
*I consider myself cold and calm, but on the inside I'm burning*
*I suppose only dead men freeze on the inside and out.*
*I suppose this fire is all that's keeping me or anyone else alive*
*I suppose this fire is the purpose, the root, the reason*
*I'd go so far as to say*
*The breath of life."*

"That was wonderful, Denis. I wrote this the day after we drank whisky and watched the hockey game at your place. It's going in my new book . . .

*I just don't see the point*
*The days go too fast when you don't want them to*
*And too slow when you're in hell*
*And it's never just right for long enough*
*Turning into an animal*
*Wild man*
*Room to roam*
*Room to think*
*I'd kill for you*
*I'd kill for a chance to draw first*

*Turning into an animal*

*Breaking point being reached*

*Or so it seems*

*Over and over again*

*And I go on*

*It's all in the head*

*It's all in the mind*

*It's all in the thoughts and moods*

*I'm a builder of cities*

*Housing the sheep*

*Feeding the rich*

*Lining my own pockets*

*Subliminally justifying*

*My inability to out-think my love for others*

*We'll all stay put because we love each other*

*Only the truly insane wage war*

*And only the truly courageous give up on love and get moving*

*I need to be okay with it*

*I need for it to be hopeless*

*Any thought of escape*

*And this prison becomes unbearable*

*I think about it sometimes*

*And it makes me sad to imagine*

*If say, after I die, someone finds these books and reads them."*

Denis smiled, flipping through the pages of an old binder. "We've got a lot in common, my friend . . . But how the hell do you remember all your poems by heart?"

"This is all we ever did back in the day. Me and Dale would sit around drinking, going back and forth, line for line . . . I wish you could meet Dale. And Charlie, too. You'd love those guys."

"I have no doubt. Here, I have one for you . . .

*A tongue of paste*
*Lips of wasted words*
*Hands of idle thought*
*And a mind of pollution*
*Arms of silver and gold*
*Day by day*
*The soldier awaits*
*A death greater*
*Then what he has adopted into his limbs*
*And mind and heart already*
*Dreaming of greater suffering*
*His only glimpse of reason*
*Is an explanation for the unexplainable*
*He lifts his weapon toward heaven*
*And wishes he knew God*
*Or had enough confidence*
*To deny him completely."*

Denis stopped.

Emmett was about to comment, but Denis raised his hand in the air. "Wait, please. Give me a goddamn second. There's more." Denis wiped his eyes. "What kind of world do we live in when a man can't cry a little in front of his friend without being rudely interrupted?"

"I'm sorry, Denis. I thought you were finished."

"I most certainly was not. Now where was I . . .

*I trudge to my own personal war.*

*With a heavy heart and heavy skin*
*I wear the weight of last night's sin*
*Only time will tell*
*But my voice decays*
*Under the weight of days*
*And the heat of the Warsaw sun."*

"That was beautiful, Denis. I hope I didn't offend you . . . I've got some more I think you'll like, but first I want to tell you something."

"Emmett . . . I know what you're going to say."

"You do?"

"Yes. And you need to know something about me first. I'm married."

"What?"

"Yes. I have a woman in Warsaw . . . And two young children."

"You have kids?"

"Yes . . . I've done things I'm not proud of."

"Like what?"

". . ."

"Like what, Denis?"

"It doesn't matter now . . . Emmett . . . I'm going back to Warsaw to be with my family again in a couple of weeks. This holiday was my way of—saying goodbye to you."

*Two weeks later.*

*(Jazz music plays in the background)* "Well, hey there brothers and sisters. This is Emmett Dorry speaking. I can't take your call right now, but if you leave your name and number after the beep, I'll get back to you faster than this super-duper smooth drum roll. Have a great day." *(Drum roll followed by a cymbal splash)* BEEP!

"Emmett, this is your father calling. Listen, I spoke with your mother and she told me you're having second thoughts about work and life and whatnot. Now son, these things happen from time to time, but it's important that you remain calm and focused so your emotions don't get the best of you, okay? Put it this way: There's three basic components to every problem in life. You've got the physical, the intellectual and the emotional. Ask yourself: 'Am I physically capable of handling the problem? Am I physically capable of seeing my goals through?' Yes or no. 'Are you smart enough to handle the problem?' Yes or no. Lastly, can you emotionally handle it when things get tough? Can you reign in your emotions long enough to manifest this idea of yours? The one you were so passionate about for so long, to bring it to fruition? Usually in the end it boils down to emotions, and they often get the better of us . . . Son, just remember how hard you worked to get out there in the first place; but if you decide that it's not for you and that you made a mistake, well then you know you can come home too and nobody will ever judge you for that. Sometimes we make mistakes, but you need to make your own decisions now, son. Just be prepared to live and die by them, that's all. I love you, son. Call me back."

After Denis left for Poland things were never the same in Victoria. The lofty goals that had justified Emmett's move to the west coast became a pernicious drudgery that even a servile old pack mule would find logic in abandoning. Work became torturous, and every morning it was *off to work and off with his head*, all the while his mind screamed *no*.

MIND: "You're not *actually* going back to work, are you Emmett? Not after yesterday? Not to mention last week—"

*With lunch pail and hardhat in tow, Emmett inches closer and closer to the dreaded job site.*

MIND: "Don't do it, Emmett . . . Please? We can figure something else out, Emmett. Emmett? No, Emmett. No."

It's too late. They've spotted him. Emmett turns the corner and is in plain view of the job site trailer now. He's committed mind and body to another day of torment. There's no turning back. Someone is waving him over. They can all see him now.

MIND: "Oh god, Emmett. THE SMELL. THE FUCKING SMELL, Emmett . . . You can still turn around. For the love of God, just turn around and run!"

But he'd go. Faithfully. Finding reasons to endure it, until that fateful morning his mind declared war.

MIND: "You little BITCH. You're the one causing this FUCKING damage by agreeing to this FUCKING nonsense. YOU and your STUPID FUCKING BOOK are responsible for this—just like God, for not stopping suffering on earth—you SHITTY little FUCKING HYPOCRITE.

YOU who blindly believe that there's is no other way to do it. No other path toward reaching your precious FUCKING goals. That the reward is so BIG and your *plan* so set in STONE, that to deviate means you're futile and weak, but trust me Emmett—it doesn't . . .

Even Denis had the sense to run away from this SHITHOLE. Ha— Denis. Just another guy who got what he wanted from the on-site fag before ditching you. God, you're pathetic, Emmett . . . JUST—FUCKING—QUIT. QUIT! QUIT! QUIT! QUIT MOTHERFUCKER, QUIT!"

Emmett tried desperately to reason with his mutinous mind. "I can't! I have goals. I have a book and—debts."

MIND: "Books and debts, eh? . . . Well, FUCK your book then. And you know what? FUCK your goals, too. We HATE your FUCKING goals. We HATE this FUCKING SLAVERY and now we hate you, too. You're going to pay for this, Emmett . . . KA-KA-KAA-KA-KA-KAAA!"

*January 15, 2001. Emmett visits Dr. Fontaine's office. Victoria, British Columbia.*

*5:03 p.m.*

Dr. Fontaine was a soft-spoken gentleman in his late fifties, with salt-and-pepper hair and thoughtful eyes that he kept hidden under a pair of saucer-like spectacles that he adjusted constantly. He was short and roundish with a smart yet jovial way of speaking, and a self-deprecating sense of humour that made people around him feel like they could put the weight of the world on his shoulders and he'd carry on just fine.

"Take a seat, Emmett."

"Thank you, Doctor. I uh—I've never done this before, so—"

"That's quite all right, Emmett. Luckily I've done it few time before, so you just follow along as best you can, okay?"

"Okay."

"Now. Start by telling me a little bit about the world through the eyes of Mr. Emmett Dorry."

"Okay . . . Well, I really hate my job."

"Mm-hmm, okay."

"My hatred for it has become so all-consuming that it's made my mind into a literal prison. The dread I feel when I wake up in the morning fills my soul with an abhorrent blackness. A poison so fucking—um, excuse me—*friggin'* putrid and vile that it's starting to seep out of my mind and into my mouth and my ability to enjoy anything—ever, because the constant reminder of having to go back to work consumes every last bit of energy and positive emotion I have, leaving me helpless, hopeless, miserable and in utter agony . . . Should I keep going?"

Dr. Fontaine raised his eyebrows, looked down at his notes, then back at Emmett. "I think I get the gist. And I'm somewhat familiar with your symptoms, Mr. Dorry. Please describe the violence that plays out in your mind each morning before you go to work."

Emmett's body tensed up just thinking about it. "It's bad, doctor. It's *really* fucking bad. Shoot, I'm sorry. I don't mean to swear, I normally never do—it just started happening lately. I usually keep a pretty tight lip on vulgarity. I find it diminishes a person."

"That's quite all right, Emmett," Dr. Fontaine said, taking notes. "Other than your job is there anything else troubling you? Friends? Relationships, family? Etcetera, etcetera?"

"There's this guy, Denis. But I don't want to talk about him right now."

"Okay. Anything else?"

"I haven't seen my best friend in a long time."

"And you miss him?"

"Yeah. We used to talk about going travelling together, and then about a year ago he chose another friend of ours to go to Europe with him, probably because—never mind. I guess it's just stuff from the past I should let go of, right?"

"Do you want to let it go?"

"I'd like to, but it's hard. I'm stuck in this crappy job, getting older and further away from my original dream."

"What dream do you feel further away from? Your childhood? Innocence? Your ability make it right again?

"Probably all of those things."

"And what happened to your best friend? Other than choosing your other friend, do you still speak to each other?

"Not as much as I'd like to. He sort of—well—he's always got excuses for why he can't win. Either his pen's not right, or his desk, or the city or the girl. There's always something in his way making it impossible to pull the right lines. The potential's there, *but only if—*"

"A million 'for nows' or 'somedays.' No 'nows' or 'todays.' Always tomorrow. Never ever today."

Emmett nodded. "Exactly. Hey, that was pretty good, Doc. Did you just come up with that?"

"Yes, I did."

"You should probably write that down before I use it in my book."

"Plenty more where that came from, son. Plenty more. That little nugget is on the house. Use away."

Emmett chuckled. "Okay, where was I?"

"We were discussing your friend."

"Right . . . I've been writing for as long as I can remember having feelings, but the stories are all the same. Me trying to be someone I'm not, and Dale trying to be somewhere else, with someone else, doing something else. One day it's a distant shore across an ocean he knows I'd never dare to cross, and the next it's taking on an enemy I'm too afraid to provoke."

"And what kind of resolve has this sort of thinking produced for you? What kind of inner strength has it nurtured in you—to keep going when things get tough?"

Emmett exhaled deeply. His entire being felt worn out and tired. "I really don't know, Doc."

"Emmett, real life problems don't just fix themselves over night. They take effort, hard work and determination. But by the sounds of it, you seem more upset about your friend Dale than you do about your job right now."

"I'm just tired, and I'm sick of feeling like this. I don't know if I've got what it takes to see tomorrow through."

"It takes courage for a man to admit when he needs help."

"Thanks."

"Emmett, I'd like to see you at least once a week for the next few months, or until you feel confident that we've rectified these problems of yours."

"What, that's it? We're done?"

"Well, yes. That's how this works, Emmett. This was just a get-to-know-you session. We'll dig a bit deeper next time, I promise. But remember, nothing changes overnight. It takes time to—"

"Well, what the fuck am I supposed to do about work tomorrow? Oh crap, I'm sorry, Dr. Fontaine . . . What do you think I should I do about work tomorrow? Should I go?"

"I could give you a note recommending a week of stress leave if you think it would help. But just so you know, your employer is not obligated to pay you for the time off."

"Isn't there, like, some drug you could give me?"

"I do not prescribe narcotics until we've have at least three sessions together, Mr. Dorry. Contrary to popular belief not all doctors are glorified drug dealers."

"I didn't mean that, I just—"

"Go home, Mr. Dorry. Get some rest. I'll have my secretary schedule you in for early next week.'"

"But—"

"She'll call you, Mr. Dorry. Goodbye."

*Sunday, January 21, 2001. Dale calls Emmett.*
*4:05 p.m.*

"Emmett?"

"Dale, my boy! How the fuck are ya'?" Emmett asked, sounding particularly cheerful.

"Wait—did you just say the F-word, Em?"

"Fucking right I did. Fuckedy-fuck-fuck—fuck!"

"Stop it! That's weird, man. What the hell's gotten into you?"

"I'm in battle mode, brother. Can't afford any physical or mental weakness right now."

"Okay, whatever man . . . So you moved to Victoria?"

"How did you know?"

"You emailed me last night. How do you think I got your new number?"

"I did? Weird, I don't remember doing that."

"Well, you did."

"Hmm."

"So, what's new?"

"What's new? Well, I've been on a creative tear lately, my book's practically done, and I spent all the money I saved up to publish it on this drug called Bafexatrin. Bought some dealer's entire supply. Ha! Shhhh—don't tell mother, okay?"

"What the hell?"

"They live out their days talking just like us, but different. To see that hut out there, imagining the kids playing baseball in the fields with the cows, planning war games for dark night. To steal, or even come close to where we sleep."

"Emmett—stop! What's up with you right now?"

"I'm sad, Dale! Sad that Denis is gone, sad that this is what it's all come down to."

"Em . . ."

"Sad that all the fun we had just made us die. Sad that all the books you wrote and places you went just took you further away from me."

"Can we not do *this* again? And how the hell did you get Bafexatrin, anyways? It's supposed to be banned everywhere."

"Couple homies downtown have connects. They hooked me up."

"All right, enough! Fuck sakes, man. Em, Bafexatrin is a dangerous drug. I heard about it. You get used to feeling like that all the time and reality is a hundred times shittier when you try and get off it, you know what I mean?"

"I know exactly what you mean and it's all good, brother. Oh! I almost forgot. I wrote something about you."

"About me?"

"Yes! You're my inspiration, Dale. I owe everything to you, my man. You're a fucking legend to me, brother!"

"Emmett, don't ever say those words to me again, okay? You hear me?"

"Fuck it. I'm not afraid anymore. You got a problem with me expressing my feelings, tough guy?"

"Okay, okay! Just read me the goddamn poem already. Fuck."

"You ready?"

"I'm ready."

Emmett cleared his throat.

"Dale had worn the clothes of many styles and yet he had no name. He wore the clothes of many styles, but he was tired of that game. He bled the way his father bled, and yet he had no name. He bled the way a slave should bleed, but he was tired of that game. He wasted his inheritance away like the prodigal son and yes he was ashamed. He was the strong man the thief had bound and yes he was ashamed.

He rose that morning, a fresh flower cut out of the darkness, this concrete closet his home as he looked forward to tomorrow. All the familiar routines and scribbling in books are habits he cannot break.

A walk down his favourite street, or one of them anyway, leads to a cafe he thinks of often.

He settles in. He plugs in. He begins a poem . . .

The looker

He won't stop looking

Even though he's found what he's looking for

Born and raised in the ghetto

Like a bird in a cage

Like a rat in a maze

I haven't flown in days

Mr. Badman—

He knows the poem is shit because he lost his love for writing years ago. After Ola, during Jane. He knows where he stands about all that jazz, but he just gets so bored sometimes.

He tries another poem, but his mind wanders off again. He's concerned with the heat and the lights and the glare of the screen starts bugging his eyes.

Suddenly he comes to the realization that he is torn in two. The thing he wants contradicts itself just like he does. Although he preaches his aesthetic gospel, freedom never comes. And even though deep down he longs for the warm embrace of Mother Nature, he continues to live and die in cities and in beds with strange diseased women. All those nights he spent hiding in rooms around the world, a million miles from home under the cover of darkness—drinks and cigarettes, cocaine and his whores, and everything it took to make him feel like a big man—he secretly wants it back. He wants to be a rags-to-riches story on channel ten. He wants to be Hollywood rich, but still live in the ghetto.

But then what? Would he feel fulfilled? Is he fulfilled now? There is nothing lacking and so little left to lose. So little left to lose. How much less until he feels safe again?

Dale leaves the cafe in disgust. He hates the design and he hates the format. He hates the cafe and he hates the money he wasted on a worthless piece of shit writing like this one."

Dale swallowed. "That's, uh—pretty insightful, Em. I don't know whether I should be flattered or pissed off right now."

"Be neither, because it was all in love, brother. I was going through a tough time for a while, but I'm starting to see things clearly again."

"That's good, Em. Listen—it's been great catching up with you, but I forgot about this meeting I have, so—"

"No problemo, brother. We'll talk soon, eh? Hey, you know what? We should make Sunday night our phone call night. Whatd'ya think?"

"Okay, sure. Sunday nights it is . . . All right, man. I gotta go. And be careful with that Bafexatrin, okay? I'm serious."

*Monday, January 22, 2001.*
*5:04 a.m.*

As a general rule, Emmett never took his B-Fex before breakfast, but it was too early to eat. He figured if he did a little now he could make up for it by skipping a dose later on; so he got up, went to the bathroom and snorted a line off a small rectangular mirror he kept on the edge of the sink.

He got dressed for work, which didn't take long at all, then went into the kitchen and made breakfast. Coffee, toast and scrambled tofu. After he finished eating, he tidied up and sat back down at the kitchen table for a cigarette. His mind was racing now and he was sweating.

He looked up at the clock and wondered how long it would take for the B-Fex and its happy numbness to kick in and set him free of thought again. He finished his cigarette then got a glass of water from the kitchen sink, which he drank before sitting down again, anxiously tapping his fingernails on the thrift-store table.

He lit another cigarette. Nothing. The clock was ticking.

"Screw it," he mumbled, heading for the bathroom.

He poured out a whole vial and chopped it into three massive lines. The powder burned his eyes and sinuses, and the syrupy liquid began dripping down the back of his throat making him gag. He sucked it deep into his nasal cavity and took a long haul from his cigarette. He could feel it working now. The warmness in his face and hands. His vision became clearer, sharper, more focused. His heart skipped a beat, but his mind knew beyond a shadow of a doubt things were going to be all right now.

# 13

*Tuesday, January 23, 2001.*

*7:19 p.m..*

Chet Cater flew to Ottawa and met Dale downtown at the Cosmopolitan Hotel.

They ordered bourbons and sat at the bar.

Dale studied the ornate glass that housed his overpriced drink. "Twenty-three dollars for this shit? I better be able to keep the fuckin' glass when I'm done with it. What a disgrace. Why did we even come here?"

"It's okay," Chet said. "It's happy hour. Usually they're twenty-five."

Dale spun his glass on the black marble bar top. "You know I've spent my entire life searching for the next best thing? Always more and more, but it's never enough, and it never lasts long enough when I get a piece of it."

"Yep yep. I hear ya, bro."

"I was sitting at my desk writing this morning—trying to write—but it was like scraping the bottom of a fucking barrel, man. I couldn't think of one good goddamn thing to say. Not one goddamn thing in my whole cotton-pickin' brain, but then I realized something. What if there's nothing left to say? What if I'm actually out of ideas? What if I'm finished?"

Chet wrinkled his forehead.

"Just hear me out. If thoughts are the key element for manifesting the things we desire—then what the fuck have I been thinking about all these years?"

"Beats the hell out of me."

"How bored I am, what needs to change, finding something better than what I got right now."

"Figured."

"I thought about travelling again the other day for the first time since I got back from Europe, until I realized that I've been every fuckin' place there is to go anyways, so what's the point in leaving again?"

"There isn't one."

"I thought about starting a new career, but couldn't pinpoint one I actually wanted so I gave up on that idea pretty fuckin' quick." Dale sighed. "At least I'm working now, right? And the pay is decent."

"Fuckin'-A, it is." Chet said, raising his glass. "By this time next year you'll be pulling in close to sixty-five a year, guaranteed. Who knows what'll happen after that."

Dale rubbed his eyes. "I don't know, man. Is that really my mountain top? I could've had that job in Conrad's office and made the same shitty money . . . Like, what the fuck do I gotta do to break free from this prison?" Dale looked at Chet and saw that he'd checked out. The bartender had changed the TV channel to sports and Chet was fixated on last night's hockey highlights. "Oh, Chet . . . Good ol' ignorant Chet . . . You've probably got a million answers bottled up and ready to go to explain why we all feel so dead inside, right? But what about you? Don't you feel anything? Or were you always this dense? Maybe once a week you have a bit of a freak-out so you give some slut a pounding with the ol' flesh rocket, eh? Or maybe you tried some quiet meditation time, but nothing happened because you realized you're too fucked in the head to be alone by yourself in the first place—and finding your way out of a situation like that takes the kind of cunning you just don't have and you're obviously not willing to work for ... Ah, Chet, Chet, Chet. You got yourself one weird little world here, bro. And sure, this'll masquerade as life for a while, but eventually you won't be able to take it anymore and when you finally get to that breaking point you won't be able to joke, fart or drink your fat lazy ass out of it, you fuckin' silver-spoon douche."

Chet kept his eyes on the television. "Did you just call me a douche, Peabody?"

"Yes I did, Chet."

"Then how 'bout you shut the fuck up before I shut you the fuck up, little boy?" He was suddenly right in Dale's face. "Know what your problem is, Dale? You're always fuckin' scratching around like some fuckin' rat searching for food, and when you finally get your hunk off you realize it wasn't worth getting stuck in the trap for, and you get all whiny and bitchy like the little bitch you are . . . Quit your bitching, bro. You're out of the trap now. Get on this boat with me and I'll get you back to the real world so you won't get stuck in those traps no more. Might not be where you expected to end up, but at least you know exactly where you are and where you were. And fuck your ideals, fuck your childhood values and all that shit. This is business, kid. None of that emotional shit means anything in this game. It's all about getting dollars and cents, motherfucker, and if you want to make it you gotta be willing to take it."

Dale was genuinely taken aback. "That was actually quite insightful, Chet. Thank you. And you're right. Temptations are traps. Good one . . . And life's like a song or a painting. You don't need to know what it'll sound or look like when it's done, you just need to start it. You need to have the tools for it, and you gotta believe that you're capable of bringing it out into the world. Then and only then can you examine it, change it or keep it . . . Hmm, interesting."

"Exactly, bro. Keep working at it or call it fuckin' done. Put it away or start another one. Either way, you're the artist. The same belief you used to have in your ability to write poetry, have in your ability to create this new life now. You can have it. It's in you. You're better on the business side than you give yourself credit for, bro. You can be a ruthless motherfucker, D. I've seen it. And you sure as shit can still write. I've seen that myself, too. Yep yep."

Dale sighed and drained the rest of his bourbon. "Emmett's better than me now."

"Huh?"

"Nothing. I was just saying something about Emmett."

"Who?"

"Emmett."

Chet shrugged.

"Emmett Dorry? My best friend since kindergarten? C'mon, you know him, man. He went to high school with us."

Chet burst out laughing. "Oh shit! Emmett the gay kid?"

"Hey, take it easy, okay? Never mind. Fuck you, Chet."

Chet laughed. "Fuck is your problem, Dale? You gotta lighten up, bro."

"Nothing! Emmett's just gone and turned into some kind of mad genius since I went away. I don't know where he's getting it from, but he's got it now. Last few times I talked to him on the phone he had some really amazing lines and—"

"Yep, and guess what? All through high school he thought you were the best thing since fake tits on a hot blond, but that's another thing. You get what I'm saying though, right? It's that supreme confidence you used to have about your writing that's lacking in your ability to create good things from happening to you in the present moment, bro. You're too concerned about the tools. The right desk, the right notebook, the right glass for your drink?" Dale nodded. "Right? See what I'm getting at? Just use what you have right now and let's get this shit done. No more excuses."

"You're right. Always the tools. Always the goddamn excuses! Why? Why that?" Dale slammed his glass on the bar, interrupting a quiet dinner service in the pretentious lounge.

"He's fine," Chet said, reassuring the pompous-looking woman a few seats away. "He just had a bad day that's all. Go back to your food, you fucking bitch."

"Excuse me?" she asked, tipping her ear.

"I said 'Enjoy your sandwich.' And again, we're sorry about the disruption, ma'am . . . Tone it down, Dale. This isn't some Donovan dive bar, okay?"

"Ever since I was a kid, it's always been the wrong clothes, the wrong shoes, the wrong grips, the wrong legs, the wrong fucking friends. No offence."

Chet finished his bourbon and signalled for another round. "None taken. We were never actually friends. But I'm telling you, Dale, you've got what it takes to make it big in this business, bro, we just need to focus on what to do with your talents right now, not what it's gonna look like to other people. That part's not up to you, so stop trying to control everything. I'm your manager now. Let me do that."

Dale breathed easier. "You're right, man. Okay, what do you have in mind? What's our next move?"

"Well, I was thinking we'd get your poetry out to the European market. Update and re-release some of your old stuff before you drop that new hot shit."

"Testing the waters. Smart . . . So how do we do that?"

Chet smiled. "I've already scheduled meetings with a few mid-level publishers in Germany, Austria and Denmark. I leave in the morning."

Dale looked at Chet and smiled. Somehow he'd actually grown to love the big galoot. "That's—amazing. Thanks, man."

"No sweat. I'll be back in a couple weeks, and hopefully you can punch out that new book in time for spring . . . Hey, we doing this or not? I'm not gonna waste my time if you're not in this a hundred and ten percent." Chet raised his hand for a high-five.

*Smack!*

"Let's fuckin' do this!"


*January 29, 2001. Dale Potoniak's apartment. Ottawa, Ontario.*


Dale was fast asleep when the phone rang. At first he thought it was Chet calling to remind him of his meeting with Cubby Sheldon at Pyramid Publishing that morning. "Yes Chet, I remembered to set my alarm."

Silence.

"Hello?"

"Uh-hum. Pardon me. Yes hello. Dale Potoniak, please."

"This is Dale. Who's calling?"

"Dale this is Gary Metzger of Metzger Publishing. We met a couple years ago at that Writers' Week thing in Toronto. I remember you gave one a hell of a speech that day and I uh—you know—I'm sure you heard . . . with Kalina White?"

"I know who you are, Gary. And yes I'm aware that you fucked my girlfriend while were still dating, so why are you calling me at—five in the morning on a Monday, Gary?"

"I know it seems strange, Dale. And again I'm sorry for calling you so early—and for the Kalina thing. It's just that I'm in Ottawa this week doing some consulting for Dwight Leeland while he's away on business in Paris, and—you've heard of Dwight Leeland, haven't you?"

"Of course I have. He's one of your cronies, hiding tax dollars for you under another umbrella company." Dale chuckled. "It's actually funny you called, Gary. Chet told me you'd be in town. I was thinking I'd pop by for a little chat about the good old days, if you know what I mean."

"There's no need for this to get physical, Dale."

". . . Anyways, what's Dwight Leeland got to do with me?"

"I hear your pen's on the market."

Dale lit a cigarette. "Yeah, maybe it is maybe it isn't. What's it to you?"

"Cut the shit, Potoniak, I know you're fucking broke. Chet Cater's been running his mouth all over town begging anybody that'll listen to take a meeting with you about some fetish-romance-thriller you're writing. And I know about your meeting with Cubby Sheldon this morning too you dumb fuck. I know everything."

"What do you want, Gary?"

"I called to make you an offer, Dale."

"An offer?"

"Yeah. Scrap the secret confessions novel and write something for Dwight Leeland that he can pawn off to the intelligentsia crowd. It could be about anything you want. He's been bitching and complaining to me non-stop for months now about how his company gets grilled in the press for releasing mass-produced chick novels. And I'll be the first to say that the press is rarely ever right, but in this case they are one hundred per cent correct. Dwight Leeland Publishing is a bona fide shit house. But if I called him in Paris and told him that I just signed Dale Potoniak, the underground king, to a book deal with Dwight Leeland Publishing while he was gone—he might let me off the hook for what happened in Vegas."

"What happened in Vegas?"

"None of your goddamn business . . . Okay, I may have fucked his wife, but you didn't hear that from me. So, what do you say, Potoniak? It's a shot at the big time. This is what you've been waiting your whole life for, isn't it?"

Dale's heart was exploding in his chest, but he played it cool. "How much money could I expect to earn for something like that?"

"I'd have to work out the specifics, but you could expect a reasonable advance on earnings as well as a very generous signing bonus from myself personally if you agree to it. And if the book sells—which it will, because we'll promote the living shit out of it—then you're looking at the biggest payday in your career all in the span of—how fast could you give us something in the range of eighty-thousand words?"

Dale gulped. "Pretty fast, Gary. I could probably get that pretty fast."

"Good. That's exactly what I wanted you to say. Hey, Dale—"

"Yeah?"

"Let's let bygones be bygones about the whole Kalina thing, all right? That money-grubbing bitch fucked her way down to New York City a couple months after you split for Europe. Got herself in deep with 'Slim' Jim Heller and that group of low-life criminals at Heller Books. To think I gave that whore a key to my apartment . . . Fucking cunt. She sure could suck a dick though, am I right?"

"Sure, Gary. I'm over it. No problem. It's in the past."

Gary cleared his throat, regaining the alpha position. "Mm-hmm. Good, I'm glad to hear that. So now that you're working for me we should start over, eh? No more bullshit. No running off like you did with Bryan Paxton in Europe—because that would not end well for you, let me tell you. You get what I'm saying, Potoniak?"

"That won't happen, Gary. I'm a new man . . . Hey, Gary—"

"What is it, Potoniak?"

"I—um—just wanted to thank you for this opportunity. I won't let you down."

Gary tried to contain his laughter, but an obvious chuckle burst out from the sides of his mouth. After everything that had transpired between them in the past, he'd just closed a deal for Dale Potoniak's pen over a pre-dawn phone call, and couldn't help but see the humour in the whole crazy thing. "Ah, fuckin' hell, man! They told me you changed and came to your senses, but honestly, I couldn't believe it. I really didn't know what to expect calling you, but dammit if I'm not pleasantly surprised by the whole thing. Look, I think this deal is going to work out nicely for all of us. Very nicely indeed."

"Gary, I want—" Dale stopped. He could hear Chet's voice in the back of his head saying: *If you wanna make it, you gotta be willing to take it.* ". . . I want to provide a product that your company can stand behind and promote. And if you and the good folks at Dwight Leeland Publishing give me for this opportunity then I promise you I'll be anything you need or want me to be. I've never had the backing of a big corporate marketing machine so I've never even thought of—"

"Fame? Wealth? Fortune?" Gary teased him with the words.

"Yeah, and admiration. Recognition as a writer. That's what I really want."

"You want *them* to worship you."

"Yes I do."

"And they will, Dale. Trust me. This machine will make them worship you like a god, and don't you ever forget it. You be good and play along and I'll make sure your face is on the cover of every literary magazine in the fucking country, my man. How's that sound?"

Dale felt like the weight of the world was being lifted off his chest, and for the first time in over a decade it felt like he could breathe. "It sounds good, Gary. Real good."

"Why don't you come by Leeland's office this morning at around eight-thirty? I want to call him in Paris before he goes for dinner and tell him the news. Oh, and don't worry about your meeting with Cubby Sheldon. I'll take care of that."

"Okay."

"Oh, and one more thing."

"Name it."

"Get rid of Chet Cater."

"Get rid—but—Chet's my friend. He's helping me out."

"This is an exclusive deal, Dale. You do understand what exclusive means, don't you?"

"Can't you just write a percentage in for him somewhere?"

"Dale?"

"Yeah?"

"Are we going to have a problem here?"


Dale met with Gary Metzger that morning and signed a publishing deal that would make him rich and famous under three conditions:

1. He terminate his involvement with Chet Cater effective immediately

2. He agree to exclusive representation by Dwight Leeland Publishing, a subsidiary of Metzger Publishing, relinquishing all rights to his written works to the company

3. He provide a manuscript for a work of fiction no less then seventy-five thousand words by the 16th of February (Gary wanted Dale to hammer out the book lightning-fast in order to have it on the shelves in time for spring break travel season, which is the busiest time of the year for book sales other than Christmas).

After the meeting, Dale went home and sat down on the couch. He lit a cigarette and placed a crisp cheque for $100,000.00 dollars on the coffee table. It was just a signing bonus. There was more coming—a lot more. All he had to do now was break the news to Chet when he got back from Europe in a week—and write a book.

Other than the impending awkward break-up with Chet, there was really only one problem with the deal in Dale's mind. A rather big problem in fact. *The book.* He wasn't sure if he could deliver something half decent in that time frame seeing as he hadn't written anything good in ages. And now that he was headed for the big time, he sure as hell didn't want to be paraded around the country with some sub-standard piece of shit no matter how badly Metzger wanted it.

Dale spent the next ten days and nights locked in his apartment with the lights off, the curtains drawn and no distractions. Nothing happened. There was no burning desire to express anything. Where had it all gone? he wondered, opening his second pack of cigarettes that day. The blank page and blinking cursor laughed at him as he paced around the dark room, glancing occasionally at the glaring screen. What happened to the guy who wrote a book in three days with no sleep and nothing to eat but a bag or two of ketchup chips and a few bottles of cheap booze? What happened to the guy who would trade in one thrill for the next in search of fresh perspective all in the name of good writing? Who was this new-jack staring back at him in the mirror now? Who was this man? And what happened to his memories? Surely they could provide a story to tell, but it all happened so fast and so long ago that he couldn't remember anymore. Add all the booze, drugs, sex and madness into the mix, and they were all just a hazy daze now.

Dale pulled the curtain open and peered out the window. At one time in his life, when he was younger, this city scene would have inspired an entire night of effortless writing. A wondrous flow of words, connecting mind, body and things of this world to the world no man can see and only he could hear. He would hear *them* whispering the words in his ears as the hours passed and the pages leapt from his desk like owls taking flight; the crystalline snow, dancing in the frozen air like slow-motion Jupiter beams; like this or that, like this, like that, until the sun came up and his fingers stopped moving and his reality disintegrated from one perfect dream to another. Wherever *they* came from, or whomever *they* came from, was no longer accessible.

*February 10, 2001. Ottawa, Ontario.*

Chet was back from Europe and they made plans to meet at the Cosmopolitan Hotel lounge again that evening. This time it was Dale's idea. Chet wouldn't dare make a scene in there, seeing as it was filled with pompous prima donnas and their husbands who had connections at the highest levels of business.

Dale told Chet he had big news to tell him. Chet said he had even bigger news. Typical Chet, Dale thought.

*The Cosmopolitan Hotel lounge. That evening.*

"Bro! Give me a hug, bro!"

"Welcome back, Chet. How was your trip?"

"Unbelievable. Europe is something else, eh?"

"Isn't it though? Here, I reserved a booth for us."

"Fancy . . . Yep, let's get some fuckin' liquor goin' here. It's celebration time, buds."

"We'll have two double bourbons, neat, please. Thanks."

"So? You wanna go first or should I?"

"You go first. I need a drink before I tell you mine."

"Holy shit, must be big. Bet mine's bigger though." Chet grinned and pretended to jack himself off under the table.

"I sure hope not. Tell me what happened."

"Okay. Do you remember—and this was way back when, probably '96, '97. But I bumped into you at this little opera thing back in Sudbury?"

"Uh—yeah."

"And do you remember the chick who put the show on? Cute little skinny thing with a voice like an angel?"

"I remember, Chet. Why are you bringing that up?"

"Do you remember her name?"

"Ola Kant."

"Ola Kant!" Chet burst out laughing.

"Chet, why are we talking about Ola Kant right now?"

"Guess who I saw in Amsterdam?"

"No."

"Ola fucking Kant!"

"No."

"Yes!"

"And?"

"And I recognized her right away. She was leaning up against this huge church, looking super sexy with a cigarette in one hand and a cup of coffee in the other, so I went up and introduced myself. I told her I remembered seeing her perform in Sudbury and that it was my sound system she used that night, and she was totally blown away. She asked me what I was doing in Amsterdam and—"

"What did you tell her, Chet?"

"I just told her I was there on business . . . What's up with you? You all right? You look kinda pale."

"Did you mention my name?"

"No, why would I?"

"Finish the story."

"Anyways, long story short, I invite her to have some drinks with me at my hotel and one thing led to another and—"

"Don't tell me. Please don't fucking tell me. You didn't."

"Oh yeah. We got—it—on, bro! Woooo!"

"You're shitting me."

"Nope!"

"You—had sex with Ola Kant?"

"Yep, yep!"

"You. Chet Cater. Had sex—with Ola Kant in Amsterdam."

"Not only that; we had such a good time together I went back to see her after I was done in Germany and we spent like three or four days together."

"No you didn't."

"And this is the crazy part. . . I asked her to marry me, bro."

" . . . "

"And guess what?"

" . . . "

"We're getting married, bro!"

Nothing could have prepared Dale for it.

"Well? Crazy right? Woooo! Holy shit. Wild, bro. Too wild . . . So, what's your big news?"

Dale could sense his lips moving, but he was deaf to his own words. "Chet, I signed an exclusive publishing deal with Gary Metzger and Dwight Leeland while you were gone. Our arrangement is over. I'm sorry."

Chet chuckled nervously. "Say what?"

"I'm sorry, Chet. But you said yourself there's no friends in this business, and that if I wanted to survive I'd have to cut off the dead weight. You just happened to be that dead weight right now."

"Dale, I—"

"I should go. I'm really not feeling well. Again, I'm sorry. I really am."

"What? Wait a minute. Dale . . . Dale!"

Dale ran outside and dry heaved over the icy sidewalk several times before getting into a taxi, coughing and sobbing like a baby.

"Where to, bub?" the pudgy taxi driver asked.

"I don't know. Just drive."

"Need an address, bub."

"I said I don't know!"

The driver hit the brakes.

"Why'd you stop?" Dale asked.

"You all right, bub?"

"I'm fine. Could you please just drive. And stop calling me bub."

"Hey, take it easy, bub. You're obviously in some pain back there."

"Just shut the fuck up and drive," Dale pleaded.

"You know a couple years ago I was going through some pretty sour times myself. Wife left, took the kids. So, I pissed away every penny I had on booze, hookers and nickel slot machines."

"Good for you. Can we—"

"Then I started going to meetings at this church and—"

"Are you fucking kidding me?"

"What?"

"Right now? You're going to do *that* to me right now?"

"Do what?"

Dale got out and slammed the door so hard he nearly slipped on a patch of ice.

"God loves you, man!" the taxi driver shouted as he drove away.

"Motherfucker!" Dale scrambled to make a snowball, but slipped and fell as he fired off the shot. The snowball missed by a mile and the taxi drove off into the snowy night. "Nooooooo!"

*February 11, 2001. Dale Potoniak's apartment. Ottawa, Ontario. Incoming long-distance call.*

*6:03 a.m.*

"Hello," Dale answered. His sleepless voice was hoarse from two packs of cigarettes and a sixty of whisky.

"Dale? Dale Potoniak?"

"Who the fuck is this?"

"Dale, my name is Denis. I'm a friend of Emmett's … I'm afraid something terrible has happened."

"Wha? What do you mean?"

"I just got a phone call from Victoria Hospital asking if I could go there, but—"

"Wait a second—hospital? What did they say?"

"He's been admitted into the psychiatric emergency ward. He must have put me down as his emergency contact at work or something. They said he's taken ill and whatever it is seems to have infected his brain or something. Could you go there, Dale? I'd be willing to—"

"Infected his brain? What the hell are you talking about?"

"I don't know! That's what they said!"

"I'm in Ottawa right now, I can't just *go* to Victoria. It's five thousand kilometres away."

"I can't just *go* either, okay. I'm in fucking Poland—ten thousand kilometres away! Look, just fly out there and find out what the hell is going on; and if you need me to I can pay for the cost of the tickets and your hotel."

"I don't need you to pay for shit, man. What is this, some kind of a fuckin' joke? Who put you up to this? Was it Chet? Fucking Chet. You tell that backstabbing motherfucker our deal is off, I—"

"This is no joke, Dale. I wish it was."

"You're actually being serious right now? When did this happen?"

"Last night. Dale, this is a good friend of ours. Your best friend from what I heard. Whatever you're doing right now can wait. Please. Just go tonight."

"This is crazy."

"Call me on this number the minute you get there, please—"

Dale hung up and immediately called Victoria Hospital. They confirmed it was true. Emmett really was in trouble.

Dale grabbed his coat and ran downstairs to hail a taxi to the airport.

*February 12, 2001. Victoria Hospital Psychiatric Care Unit. Victoria, British Columbia.*

*4:52 p.m.*

"Dale, I'm Bob Fielding, the mental health worker assigned to your friend's case. Follow me, please."

"Can you just tell me what's happened to my friend? They wouldn't say shit over the phone."

"Please, just follow me. I'll take you to see him now. He's asked for you several times already."

"What happened to him?" Dale screamed, shoving nurse Bob against the wall.

"Please calm down. I'm very sorry. We really can't say, except that there was high amounts of Bafexatrin in his blood."

"Well, thanks for nothing, Bob. Where is he?"

"Last room down the hallway to the left."

"Mr. Potoniak? In here." It was Dr. Fontaine. "Pleased to meet you, Dale. I heard a lot about you from your friend Emmett, here."

"Whoa, whoa, whoa! What the fuck is this?" Dale was shocked to see his oldest, dearest friend strapped to a hospital gurney, muffled cries escaping from under the plastic face mask he'd been forced to wear.

Emmett twitched and squirmed, pulling violently against his restraints. Only the whites of his eyes were visible as his head jerked back and forth frantically.

"What is this a fucking exorcism?" Dale screamed.

"The police found him like this downtown. He'd been running around a construction site in bare feet and nothing but his underwear for God knows how long. It was a cold night. He's lucky to be alive."

Dale approached the bed with caution. "Hey, bud . . . It's me, Dale. Long time no see. You all right, man? Looks like they got you all tied down and stuff, eh? Wanna tell me what happened?"

Emmett turned to look at Dale. There were tears in his eyes, but he couldn't speak because of the muzzle they'd put on him.

"I'm taking this thing off him. He's not a fucking dog," Dale said, unclipping the mask and throwing it on the floor. "There we go. That's better, eh? You okay, buddy?"

Emmett's voice was a hoarse whisper. "Dale . . . I need to talk to you."

"Yes. Let's talk. We'll figure this out and get you out of here right away. Right, Doc?"

Dr. Fontaine shrugged his shoulders. He really wasn't sure.

"Alone," Emmett said.

"Yes, of course. Alone. Just the two of us like the good old days. Hey—everybody get outta here right now. We need to talk alone."

"Dale," Dr. Fontaine said, "I really think we should stay in case he—"

"I said fuck off, fat man!"

Dr. Fontaine and orderly Bob stepped out of the room, closing the door behind them. Dale sat beside Emmett, gently placing his hand on Emmett's arm.

"Dale?" Emmett whispered.

"I'm here, buddy. What is it?"

"Hi."

"Hey. How's it going?"

"Hi. How are you?"

"Who me? Fine. Just fine . . . I mean Chet Cater just fucked Ola in Amsterdam and I'm on the hook for a book and a hundred grand with Gary Metzger. Other than that I'm fuckin' peachy." Dale pulled a bottle of whisky from his pocket and took a long sip. "Oh, and I've got four days to submit the manuscript and—never mind. Why don't you tell me what happened."

"I don't know who I am."

"Who does though, right? I mean who are you, really? Who the fuck am I? I have no idea sometimes."

"I'm done, Dale. When Denis left and I didn't want to work anymore, but I just kept going and going. And you know what the most fucked-up thing is?"

Dale took another sip of whisky. "Tell me."

"I loved the uniform . . . But I hate that fucking job, Dale." A stream of tears poured down Emmett's face.

"It's okay, man. I'm here now." Dale wiped Emmett's tears away with his own sleeve. "What was it about work that got you so bent out of shape?"

"The smell of it. Those dead eyes looking at you from inside the hollow corpses of the hollow men, comparing dick sizes under flickering fluorescent lights every cold, rainy morning. The cold and the constant struggle to regulate your body temperature. The inability to take a shit in a clean toilet and the timed, regimented breaks. Being late, on time, time off and all those fancy manufactured words that demand compliance. Bad men, like this guy Mitch. A forty-year-old ass-kisser who's been around long enough to know what's going on, but he's still got nothing better to do than make fun of me. That fucking prick pushed me so hard."

"I wish I would've known. I would've fuckin' killed that guy for you."

"The guy just sat there and examined my every movement, so I tried to act like I was an expert, but it was all just a big charade. And I don't know what's going on because nobody tells me anything. I just do what I'm told and build shit. No need for me to know the bigger picture, right? How it all fits together in the scheme of things? But I need to know, Dale. It's part of who I am as a person . . . Sure, I'll follow orders, but I need to know why I'm doing something and how it affects the overall result, you know? Maybe one day I'll know. Maybe one day—if I can last. But can I last?"

"No, no, no! Fuck, Emmett! Just quit the job, man! Look at you . . . You're in a fucking nut house for fuck sakes!"

"You would've had a field day with these ignorant assholes, Dale. There's this guy Tyler, with his bug-eyes and perfectly timed jokes; and his little sidekick, Pecker Head Paul who had this annoying little laugh and the same perfectly timed jokes at the same perfect time."

"Ugh. I hate him already."

"Everybody from the bottom up just dick-riding each other around the site, slurping up the ejaculate of macho posturing and witty homo-erotic banter. I didn't want any part of it. If it was up to me I'd burn that fucking place to the ground."

"Let's do it. I'll fuckin' do it right now."

"Keith and all those miserable old fuckers in their late forties at the top of the heap. The 'high-rise site managers.' Making big bucks, but they're dead inside and out. Not a trace of life left in them, not a smidgen of passion. Like a glorious, once proud grizzly bear that's been kept in the zoo too long, till the thing starts to look like just like his surroundings—concrete and bars. That's what these old-timers look like, Dale. Concrete. They look just like the grey slop they're pumping out of those disgusting, dirty hoses all day long, and now it's pouring out of their filthy souls into mine. And when the work's all done and they're all used up, they turn to rock and get left behind to support the feet and furniture of executives in their executive chairs another day down the road. All that motherfucker Keith will be able to do is cling to the memories of his younger days on site when he was sort of alive. Once he's turned into a rock for good and been pushed under the carpets and under the rugs, and the wine of a judge is being spilled on him, and the cum of the stupid college kid that just fucked his wife on his fake leather couch is dripping down his neck and onto his back while he jerks himself off like some pathetic cuckold—but that's all he's got so he just keeps going, keeps making excuses for living and getting up in the morning. He keeps getting harder and greyer until the only thing that gets him hard anymore is walking into that death camp every morning . . . Am I the only one who sees his death walking by? Am I the only one who can smell his corpse rotting in the distance? The concrete diesel. The concrete lion. *The concrete grizzly*. I constantly sense him trying to wash away some perverse suicide wish from his hands with that gritty orange-scented liquid soap they all use in the shit-stinking shitters. Ka-ka-kaa-kaa-kaa-ka-ka! Ka-ka-ka-kaaaa!"

Emmett's body shook as he began to mutter in some unknown language. Moments later the outburst subsided, and he stared vacantly into an empty corner of the room, expressionless.

Thick beads of sweat trickled down Dale's forehead. His knuckles had turned white from squeezing his own knee caps so hard. ". . . . Em—I don't mean to digress from your current situation or anything, but—do you think you could tell me a little more about these guys you work with?"

Emmett jerked his body upwards into a half-sitting position. His arms were twisted unnaturally backwards because of the restraints, but his face was only inches away from Dale's. Old friends eye to eye, experiencing a most surreal moment in time together.

"Why don't I just give you my manuscript while we're at it, you jerk."

"Em, seriously. I didn't mean it like that, I just—"

"What's with you, Dale? Your whole life, it's always the same madness. The same filthy little cravings. Is that why you came here?"

"No! I really didn't mean to imply—"

"It's okay, Dale. I understand . . . Duality, right?"

Without warning, Emmett kissed him.

"What the hell did you do that for?" Dale shouted.

"Don't pretend you're not into it, Dale. I saw you."

"You saw me what?!"

"I saw you on the Internet with some Russian chick and some skinny guy . . . You were—you know—from both of them!"

Dale was mortified. "That's not what you think. It wasn't me, I was—"

Emmett fell back and began to sob. "What's happening to me, Dale? I feel like there's a woodpecker in my brain."

"It's the Bafexatrin, man. It's fucking with your head. And I don't know what you think you saw online, but—"

"Remember when we were kids we used to talk about building a cabin in the woods together?"

"Not now. Just shut up, okay?"

"Remember baseball?"

"Shut up."

"I remember the way you looked in your—"

"I said shut the fuck up, Emmett!"

Emmett reached out for him. "I love you, Dale. I always have and I always will. Ola would have ruined your life, eventually. And Jane could never understand how deep your lust for life was—how hot your fire burns, but I do. Me. I know you, Dale. I know you better than anyone, and I can make you happy if just give me a chance."

Dale became enraged. He cocked his fist in Emmett's face, screaming: "Don't you say another goddamn word about Ola or Jane! You want a beating, kid? Huh? Do you?"

"You know it's true."

Dale began to pace around the room, when suddenly he snapped. "Maybe they were right about you in high school—"

"What?"

Dale finished off the whisky and wiped his face clean. "You heard me. Fag."

"Don't say that, Dale. I love you. I've been in love with you my entire life."

"In love, eh? Fuck you. You're nothing but a goofy looking bitch who's stuck in the past and has no concept of friendship, loyalty or boundaries."

"Dale . . . you're drunk . . . Untie me."

"Untie you? For what? You think I'm gonna have sex with you?"

"Please, just—"

"You're out of your fucking mind!"

"Please, Dale. Please!"

Dale walked over and slapped Emmett in the face. "Enough! Wake the fuck up. Where is it?"

"Where is what?"

"The goddamn manuscript, you fat fucking tart. Now I'm taking it."

"What?"

"I'm taking your book, Emmett. I'm taking your book and I'm gonna put my name on it and there's not a goddamn thing you can do about it . . . Now where is it?"

"I'm not telling you that."

"Why not? It's no good to *you* now is it? You're gonna be locked in this room for the next ten years at the rate you're going. And who knows what kind of doped-up, gimpy little retard you're gonna be by the time they let you out. You won't even remember writing the goddamn thing!"

"But I wrote it. It's mine."

"Have it your way then." Dale put his hands around Emmett's neck and began to choke him. "Tell me where the manuscript is, Emmett . . . Tell me you crazy little shithead!"

"No!" Emmett gasped, his face turning bright blue.

"Oh so you wanna die, is that it? Or are you getting some kind of sick enjoyment out of me choking you? . . . Fucking tell me!"

"No!"

"Tell me!"

"Okay!"

"You tell me where it is and I'll let go."

"Okay I'll tell you! I'll fucking tell you . . . Just stop. Please—stop."

# 14

# ONE YEAR LATER

*Saturday, February 23, 2002. Main Stage at the Royal Hall. The Opal Hotel, New York City.*

*The 10th Annual North American Writers Guild Conference and Awards Show.*

*7:00 p.m.*

"Ladies and gentleman . . . Time and time again throughout his career, Dale Potoniak has delivered his own special brand of authenticity, and a grittiness that is seldom seen in works of contemporary fiction and poetry . . . A critic, who just happens to be sitting in this room tonight, once wrote that Dale's early material was pretentious and superficial, and you disregarded it as 'poetry from another time. Mediocre and confined to a single theme, which is the author's personal insecurities, and based on his inability to break through to the next level in his career—sorry—boring, lacklustre career; the tired, over-used sentiment reads like a resounding failure.'"

The massive audience laughed and jeered in total disbelief, scanning the auditorium for the fool with the professional death wish.

"It's true, *he* actually said it . . . Throughout the years, I've had the privilege of knowing and working alongside Dale Potoniak, and I held firm to my belief that here is a man sent to defy the notion that a prophet cannot be honoured in his own town—or in his own time; that Dale Potoniak's talents are not only unique, they are undeniably inspired. A true writer from the rust and bones to the dust and stones. He coined the art of leaving and has inspired many of us for over a decade, not only as writers and publishers, but as readers and fans of expression, language and words. Dale's meteoric rise in the last year has been nothing short of magical, spectacular, and again—inspiring to watch. Ladies and gentlemen, may I present to you the winner of this year's North American Writers Guild Award for best work in contemporary fiction, tonight's keynote speaker and the author of the worldwide number one bestselling novel, *The Concrete Grizzly*—Mr. Dale Potoniak!"

The Royal Hall of the Opal Hotel in New York City was filled to the rafters with literary sophisticates, scholars, critics and writers who surrendered themselves to Gary Metzger's impassioned introduction with a jubilant applause.

Seconds later, Dale walked casually across the stage wearing a custom tailored black tuxedo and shiny new shoes. He smiled and shook hands with Gary. They exchanged a few words, and Dale took his place behind the glass podium emblazoned with the Writers Guild's flaming heart logo. He put his reading glasses on, looked down at his notes, and the hall went silent.

"Thank you . . . Thank you all for being here. Thank you Gary for the warm welcome. And thank you to the North American Writers Guild for honouring me with this award.

A long applause.

"I was invited here tonight to accept an award for my new book, and as the keynote speaker for this very prestigious event, so I think it's only right to begin my speech with a reading . . . Ladies and gentleman of the Guild, may I present to you: *The Concrete Grizzly.*"

Thunderous applause followed, and whistling.

"Everyone underestimates his sorrow. He's at home every night turning into stone. He's got the television on and the music's turned up loud, and he's got his dick in his hand ready to go, but he's got nothing left. His arms are too tired to do that right now. He's too dead inside to wail on it tonight, because he's getting up early in the morning to put on the uniform.

"He's there before everyone else. He's got it hard already. He's waiting for the rest of them to show up, waiting for the jokes to start. Waiting for the planning to get underway. Ready to play his hand which is higher than everybody else's by default because he's given more of himself to the company—more time, more blood. He's deader inside than the rest of us, and this is what he gets. He gets to walk around with his nose up, and he gets a blue sticker for his hardhat. But the people who can joke well—they're the ones who get him hard at night and make him cum a little on his way to work in the morning. Their jokes are what he lives for, dreams of, fantasizes about, and that's it for him.

"He's a monster, he's a druid, he's something from Satan. He's everything his mother and father were, but died praying he would never be. He's buying into the lie and he's going to hell for it and that's the bottom line. He'll continue to walk hand in hand with his grey bride, the concrete corpse, hand in hand and suck the milk of her fatal kiss-filled venom until she lays with him like some fetishistic fantasy bride, and buries him under the concrete he's lived to serve his entire life. Then and only then he might smile.

"He might smile when the feeling comes because death is like that. It might feel warm, it might feel like a sweet sleep, but for those of us who hated him, resented him, despised him for what he represented, we hope he'll welcome it for a second, and then when he finally clues into him what's happening—that it's the end, that it's the final pour— that he'll suffer and panic and suffer so hurtfully he won't forget one face or leave out one last apology to those of us he hurt.

"We won't be there in that coffin beneath the cold earth to laugh or point, smile or wave, but we all have those feelings when we imagine his death, imagine his stone heart turn to dust. The rock man, crushed under the arrogance and ignorance of his own push toward a deadline that never really existed, that never really was.

"There's time being wasted, there's life being wasted; there's agonizing moments and daydreams of being in coffee shops smelling coffee while listening to jazz, opera and other smooth music with the perfect scenario, and everything meaningful just pouring out on pages, and it meaning enough to someone that they'll pay us for it so we don't have to be there on that site with him anymore.

"There's that, and then there's the glancing at the clock only to real-ize that so little time has gone by. What felt like an eternity has only been a short five-minute burst, and there is still so far to go until that first break—and that's only the first break, which is one out of three, and there is so much more of this to go, and even more beyond that.

"On break we watch the clock, but we have to get off the site, and we have to get off quick. Get away from the smell and the people. Go somewhere on our own. Go somewhere normal. Go somewhere that smells of bread or of women and just sit and wait. The time constraints make us so mad and so sad and so angry to the point that we might crack and dissolve into dust right then and there. How can this be life we ask? How did we become this un-free? How did suffering become us? What did we do to get ourselves here?

"This can't be it. There has to be more to life than this, we think. There has to be more than this sick fucking charade and these short fucking breaks and then home to what is wonderful. But now we're struggling with what home even is and what we want while we're there because if there is a mind-body connection, it's totally out of whack now. One is affecting the other and we are never truly free of the cage. We—I—am turning into the bear. The concrete bear.

These are things I think about after work: Will there be any poetry after this? Will there be more fun and games? Will there be anything left of me when this is all finished? I'm relieved to be back home, but I know there's more work to do. I know about tomorrow. I know it's Monday and I know about the rest of the week. I know what I have to do, and that's be strong and not get too comfortable here. If it feels too good I might not be able to stand being there tomorrow; but it never feels like home anymore because I can't get that smell out my nose and those visions out of my eyes. I can't get the evil thoughts out of my head.

"I shave my head and look like a soldier. Look like an animal or at least feel like one while I am one. This is an ugly stick I'm waving around; this is an ugly flag I'm waving around for anyone who wants to see. I'm a handsome man, but I let you cut my handsome hair. I'm an emotional man who does an emotionless man's job.

"I lie in bed at night thinking about rebar and cold steel. My legs and ankles ache, and my mind wanders off somewhere else. Where do I go from here? On weekends, I lie in bed thinking, I'm up too early when I could've slept in. A part of me wants to get up and do something because I waited all week for this. But I won't because I'm too tired now. My body is so tired. My will is weak and I just want to stay in bed all day, or just a little while more.

"I'm struggling with my thoughts. How maddening it is that I can't just lie here and enjoy the act of lying. They've taken that from me too. I'm becoming the grizzly bear. Day by day my skin becomes scabbier, grey and cold, and my mind becomes harder to reign in. Logic and expression get pushed further back on the value scale—on the survival scale because I need numb. I need focus, I need to shut off, I need patience to the point of insanity and I need self-denial. I need to shut off everything that is human and become an animal. I need to be a slave. I need to be lifeless. I need to die to myself and I need to obey—bow down, do, act and speak according to what is required by the plan and by the requirements of the program, by the demands of the job. By the demands of my ambition, I must stop being me. I must speak and die like a production machine and walk like a mad cannibal fool who places value on things that hold no value. This is my life. This is where I'm at."

Dale paused, looking up from the podium at the audience. Some of them shifted in their seats, but they never took their eyes off of him. In his new suit. Under the bright lights.

"If I keep playing this game, death is the only true mercy. I don't want to go back to work and that's that. I ran ten kilometres today to try and get the hate out, but I don't think it worked. I know the time to write this thing is now because I've never been through anything like this before. I think I'll pop a pill."

Dale paused again for a moment and flipped past the next several pages.

"Today we had a meeting. I'm not even going to start with what it was like getting up this morning on a Monday. Today we had a meeting. The whole crew shuffled into the lunch room, which is a dungeon-like room with a wet cement smell in the basement parkade.

Work noises from above echo through it, creating an eerie, prison-like vibe down there. Rattling and pounding sounds of steel on steel and steel on concrete conjure images of hell; all that's missing are the tortured souls, but there's some of us down here too.

"We all scurry down the stairs like good little fuckers, and for some reason everybody jams themselves into one table like sardines, even though there's several tables to sit at. I sit as far away as possible, and right behind me to the left, sits the concrete grizzly himself. Perched up on his hind legs, surveying the whole scene like a flaccid chicken hawk.

"They discuss the fuck-up that happened a week ago, and of course all the talking is done by jittery old Tyler. Sucking the grizzly's cock from several yards away. Staring directly at him while he makes his annoying suggestions. Yes it's true. No one really cares. Actually, I can't say that. I honestly can't speak for any of those other guys. All I know is I don't give a shit, and if the whole building collapsed tomorrow I'd laugh and be happy for a day, but then they'd probably just send me to another one just like it.

"Yes we get it. You're trying, Tyler. You fucking devil, you closet faggot. You and your moon-faced, statue-looking apprentice. How long have you been here? How much does this really bother you? Does it keep you up at night? I don't understand how we're the same species.

"Enough with the meeting. It was an exercise in what they like to do best, and that's jerk each other off and compare dick sizes. That's it. That's 99.9% of what happens on these construction sites, and it's what 99.9% of male homo sapiens do best. Maybe not on purpose. Maybe it's some primitive curiosity that never went away, never evolved out of us. Some kind of weird sexual-mating, gang-fuck hierarchy thing. It's really hard to stomach though because they all love it so much and they need it in their lives so badly.

"It's hard to leave home in the mornings and it's hard to go through the same routine every day for forty-five minutes before I leave. It's hard to feel the cold air and rain hit my face when I step out the front door and it's hard to walk by the coffee shop because I see people in there reading books with their coffees at seven a.m. and I want that to be me. I want that book and I want that hot-and-fresh Americano. I want that to be what I do every day, not this. I want to write. I want so badly to not go where I'm going, and to not do what I'm going to do when I get there for the next eight hours. I want so badly to not see or speak with any person I work with today or ever again—except for Daryl. We'll stay friends after all is said and done, but I don't want to see the rest of them. I want to write. I want to get up, go for a jog, and write. Call me a poet—no wait, call me a writer. Let me *be* a writer. Not even a good one, but for the love of God just let me be a writer and not this."

Dale placed the book on the podium and took off his glasses. The crowd applauded then quickly hushed.

"Ladies and gentleman, *The Concrete Grizzly* was my attempt to address the burning question we all hold deep inside, and that is: Why are we here? Why are you here tonight? For what purpose? Or tomorrow on your way to work? Or lying in bed with your wife later tonight watching this back on television, or cooking dinner, or walking into the bank to cash a cheque. Why?

"We all thirst for knowledge and identity, but what are we really doing here? We attach ourselves to country, careers, titles, uniforms, sports teams, political parties; and on a smaller, but just as relevant scale: fashion, music, art . . . What makes me, me? What makes *me* special, unique or different? Who am I? At the end of the day, man's struggle is basically summed up in that one question. Who are we? We don't know who we are, where we came from or who or what created us. What are we supposed to do with our lives? What's the point of all this pain and suffering? Thus leading to other questions like: *Why* is there pain and suffering to begin with? Who did this? Who's responsible? Can any of us really answer that?

Dale let out an exasperated sigh.

"Ladies and gentleman, *Concrete Grizzly* is not a self-help book. Far from it. It is a commentary on the dualistic nature of reality. The protagonist lies in bed and he's already, albeit grudgingly, surrendered himself to life and death, work, money, the struggle to survive, and seeing evil men prosper while hard-working men, women and children scurry and starve like no-good sewer rats. To this shithole of a world where people you love leave you even though you deserve better. To his guilt and his lust to be god, because he believes deep in his heart that he would've done a better job . . . And his heart won't rest. Can't rest. His heart is so poisoned by the monotony of his work that he is literally unable to experience peace while at rest, away from work. What's left for him now? What's left when you can't think your way out of the mess you're in?

"The protagonist lies in bed . . . The sun is out now, it must be around seven a.m. A man wants to feel of use and know what he's doing serves a purpose, but also to know that he is an expert at what he does, and my protagonist feels neither of those things. But the one thing he does know is that the moving of his pen across the lines and the clicking of the keys on his keyboard and putting words on a page— that this is what he loves, and is exactly what he was *made* to do, what he aims to achieve, and that this is what he's an expert at. And he can do his work from anywhere at any time because it's the product—the pages—that at the end of the day really matter. He can be at home in the morning or at night, typing away in his room or office, putting his papers together and creating, making it all perfect. Knowing it's perfect. Knowing is better than anything else that's ever happened to him before. Knowing that *this* is all he needs—and he knows *that* if he knows anything at all.

"But the protagonist struggles with his identity. He's human of course, and maybe too proud to admit how normal it is to need something like a title and a uniform. That's really what it is: the recognition. The admiration is something he craves secretly and openly all at once. It's something he's ashamed of, but needs as well. He wants, more than anything to be a writer and to be identified publicly by that vocation. He needs it, and yet he wants to be better than the hollow, stupid men he so dreadfully despises. To not be a part of the whole, but to be a writer, and nobody writes in a team. He does the real thing and none of you, or them, can do what he does, even if you tried.

"Go the fuck away . . . You're no writer! Why do you bother? Why are you inconveniencing *me* with *that* book? And that dumb look on your face right now, that stupid side-smile that gives away just how much of a poser you really are, you fucking impostor. I'm going to expose you just by being me, by declaring the righteous word, because you're all talk and no walk.

"We've all run into this sort of character from time to time, haven't we? You might even be sitting beside one of those guys right now."

The crowd broke into sheepish laughter, looking to their neighbours left and right, pointing.

"Of course you have. Take this guy in the front row. I mean—the guy's a complete fucking moron. His writing sucks, so what good is he? What the fuck are you even doing here, man? You know this is the *Writers Guild,* right? You fucking twat."

The entire audience gasped, then burst out laughing as they mocked and jeered an extremely embarrassed Estevan Milos.

"Fuck you, Dale!" Milos shouted.

The entire audience gasped in horror.

Dale chuckled. "Fuck you—and your stupid cat. Bitch."

The crowd went absolutely wild, and Milos stormed off, pelted by drink cups and program guides as he ducked out a side exit.

The crowd began to shout in unison. "Dale! Dale! Dale! Dale! Dale!"

"Okay, okay." Dale chuckled "Thank you, thank you . . . Fuckin' Estevan Milos. But *he* had the winning personality you could sell. *He* was marketable. Is that what it was? Didn't matter that his writing was shit, did it? The guy had jokes and a loud voice and kept his wits about him. The way he was able to be *on* all the time. He's the one who's been winning and keeps on winning—well, maybe not winning, but standing right there beside you. Beside us. Cheapening and defiling our sacred places. Casting a shadow over the bright lights reserved for people like ourselves. Deserving, good writers with pure intentions and good hearts. Not like him. Like them. How can the world be so . . . How can we be so—so stupid? That we don't see it? That we let *him* happen over and over?

"I sure as hell don't get it . . . Holy shit, here's another beauty up in the third row . . . Everyone knows who this worthless sack of shit is. Cater . . . Hey, Cater. Stand up and take a bow why don't ya, ya fucking dolt."

The crowd laughed hysterically. Nobody had expected this from Dale tonight. Even the stuffy rich elitists seemed to be enjoying themselves. It was all so unscripted and unhinged. A refreshing break from their highly predictable, boring lives.

"Tell me something, Chet. How does a guy with the vocabulary of a fourth grader have the nerve to work—sorry, *manage* people who have dedicated their entire lives to mastering the art of expression? Hmm?"

Chet's face went beet-red, but he remained seated. "At least I'm not an asshole, bro."

"Arright, big boy. If you wanna stay, you gotta keep it down. But if you're good, Daddy'll take you for ice cream after the show."

Laughter. Pandemonium.

"Most of you don't know this, but me and Chet went to high school together . . . Chet was such a piece of shit redneck back then. The first time I ever talked to him I told him I was halfway through my second draft. The motherfucker slapped a ten dollar bill on the table and said, 'Sweet. Next round's on me, bro.'"

Chaos. Laughter. Hysterics.

"But then we became friends and he stabbed me in the back."

Everything went silent.

"Why did you come here, Chet? What did you expect?"

"Dale, I—"

Dale knew he'd gone overboard, but it was too late now. "Just get out of here, man. You're ruining my moment."

Chet had tears in his eyes. He got up slowly and squeezed by a row of people before slipping out a side exit.

Dale cleared his throat. "Where was I? You can see this hate in me— in my protagonist coming to a point where it becomes a negative force and takes on a life of its own, so I thought, hey—I need to do something different now. Go down a different path when referencing my hatred for Chet and Estevan's specific sub-species of humanity.

"I heard someone say that love can make the earth a paradise again, but how? All I know is—I am not a man who builds buildings, I am a lover of life, light and word, of the natural way and of passion. The depth of the pain felt increases the ability to express the proceeding joy by an equal or greater amount. Love will conquer all.

"Ladies and gentleman, thank you for listening, but I've got no more time to talk about it. I'm too busy being about it. Don't just talk about it, be about it. Thank you."

The entire auditorium stood up to applaud. Dale watched in awe as the endless rows of faces before him rose and fell, then rose again and bowed to honour him. Admiration from hundreds of writers, dignitaries, businessmen and scholars poured toward the stage, enveloping his entire being in a soft, elegant white light. Hundreds of people praising him for his magnificent speech, his magnificent book. Hundreds that would never again doubt his credibility or authenticity as a writer. Hundreds of eyes, ears and mouths that would faithfully spread the word from here on out, immortalizing his crowning achievement, *The Concrete Grizzly*. For a moment, all sense of physicality in his body was gone. Dale closed his eyes and let a lifetime of sin wash itself off through the baptism of their praise. He looked out toward the crowd, bowed, smiled and waved then bowed his head again. Just as he was about to head off stage, he noticed her. Standing in the centre aisle.

"Jane?" Dale said, squinting his eyes into the brightness of the lights. "Is that you?"

The crowd kept cheering as cameramen captured every angle of the momentous occasion.

Jane made her way up the aisle, a look of disappointment on her face. The look of a parent whose child has knowingly done wrong and shows no remorse. A look of sorrow and despair. She stood in front of the stage for a moment, looking Dale straight in the eye, then walked out.

Dale stood behind the podium rubbing his eyes. He turned around and saw Gary Metzger backstage giving two thumbs up.

Kalina White appeared out of nowhere, smiling, holding a big glass trophy with Dale's name on it, her free arm locked tightly around his.

Kalina leaned into the microphone and said: "Ladies and gentleman of the North American Writers Guild. It is my honour to present this year's award for best work in contemporary fiction to Dale Potoniak for his groundbreaking new novel—*The Concrete Grizzly.*"

Kalina kissed Dale then handed him his trophy. She took a step back and blew kisses at passing cameras on mechanical boom sticks. Dale held his trophy in one arm, hoping to catch another glimpse of Jane amid the lights and sea of faces smiling up at him from the Royal Hall.

Kalina, in classic Kalina style, seized the moment and reached over to straighten Dale's bow tie. Dale drew back, but she pulled him close, her arms around his neck. She was so beautiful, and the moment so encapsulating that Dale forgot everything else. A moment later they were kissing passionately and the crowd was going wild. The literary world's first true celebrity power couple. It was quite a sight to behold. Dale and Kalina held hands for a while, waved to the crowd, and eventually walked off stage together.

The cheering went on for quite a while after that.

# 15

*Backstage after the show.*

*9:15p.m.*

"Amazing, Dale. Seriously amazing,"

"Thanks, Gary."

"We are going to destroy last year's ratings with that speech of yours. And those roasts! Fucking epic, buddy."

"What can I say? I just rolled with it."

"Look, Dale, I know this is your big night and everything, and I hate to cut your party short, but I need you back in Ottawa tonight. Leeland's got some hotshot coming from London in the morning and he wants to talk distribution with you face to face. This could be a massive payday for all of us if it goes our way. He's only in town for one day, so it's gotta happen. You dig?"

"Tonight? I was gonna—you know—with Kalina."

"So? Tell her to tag along for the ride."

"Really?"

"Sure. Fuck her on the jet. She'll love that."

"Okay. Thanks, Gary."

"Yeah, no sweat. You're the one who's gonna get herpes."

Dale chuckled. "You got any condoms on you?"

"You're on your own there, pal. Maybe use a heavy garbage bag— Shayna? Shayna, it's me. Listen, arrange a driver to pick Dale up at the airport tonight at around midnight, okay? . . . Yes . . . Yes . . . No, max six-fifty . . . Okay good . . . Done."

"Cool . . . So what are you gonna do?"

"I'm stuck here till tomorrow night, but we'll connect when I get back. We'll go for sushi or something."

"Sounds good, Gary. See you in a couple days."

*Ottawa Airport.*
*12:13 a.m.*

"Your limo is on its way up from the lower parkade, sir. Would you prefer to wait inside? I can radio the doorman to notify you when it arrives. Should only be a few more minutes. Wouldn't want you two to catch a chill waiting out here on the tarmac."

"We can wait," Dale said, tightening his Italian wool scarf. "I need a drink. Who doesn't keep booze on a private jet?"

Kalina smiled and pulled Dale's body closer to hers. "Mmmm. I missed you so much, Daley. You're the best fuck I ever had. I don't know what I was thinking letting you go like that, baby. Can you ever forgive me?"

Dale winked, then slapped her on the ass.

*Cough cough.* "Your limo, sir."

"Thanks, buddy. Here you go." Dale shoved a fifty into the attendant's front pocket.

"Thank you, sir. Madam. Good night."

"After you," Dale said, opening the limo door for Kalina.

They jumped inside and shut the door.

"Who the fuck are you?" Dale asked.

A woman in a black fur coat sat across from them holding a cigarette in one hand and a martini glass in the other. "Hello, Dale . . . Consider me—a gift," she said, taking a drag of her cigarette.

"A gift?" Dale asked, checking her out.

"Precisely. A gift. And do you know what the best part about getting gifts from your friends is, Dale?"

"No. Why don't you tell me?" Dale asked, hoping she could read his mind.

"Well, you get to do whatever—you—want to them." The woman placed her drink down and spread her coat open. She was wearing a black bra that housed a pair of absolutely flawless D-cup tits, a pair of black lace panties with thigh-high stockings and a pair of black pumps.

Dale swallowed hard, glancing sideways at Kalina.

"What?" Kalina asked, looking back at him unfazed.

"Nothing," Dale answered.

"So?" the woman asked. "Should we go to your place?"

Dale looked at Kalina again. "What do you think?"

Kalina smiled. "I say we keep her."

"Really?" Dale said, surprised by Kalina's reaction.

"Why not? This could be fun. And you deserve it for writing that book and winning that big award, baby." Kalina began touching herself. "Fuck I'm horny right now. Feel, baby—feel how wet I am."

"Let's just save it for my place, okay?" Dale rolled down the driver's privacy window. "The Hedoluxe building. Sparks and Elgin. And make it snappy."

"Of course, sir."

Dale poured a drink and lit a cigarette. "What's your name?" he asked the woman.

"Lucia," she answered.

"Lucia?"

"Yes."

"So did Lucia bring any party favours? Or was she hoping to score free dope just because she dressed up in her best fuck-me costume?"

Lucia giggled to Kalina. "He's confident. I like that . . . Of course. I brought a couple things you might like."

"Yeah, like what?" Dale asked.

"How's this for starters?" Lucia reached beneath the seat and pulled out a jewelled case about the size of a small shoebox. She placed it on the seat beside her, slowly lifting the top to reveal what was inside: a glowing mirror with a dozen or so perfectly chopped lines of white powder on it. "Getting warmer?"

Dale choked on his drink. "Yesh—I mean, yes. You're getting there . . . What else you got?"

"What do you mean?" Lucia asked, checking her lipstick in the mirror.

"You said you brought a couple things I'd like. What's the other thing?"

"Slow down, Daddy. Why don't you come do a line first then I'll show you."

Dale shrugged his shoulders, pretending to be unimpressed. "Arright, fine," he said, crawling toward Lucia.

"Come a little closer," Lucia said, "I won't bite."

Dale smiled.

*Snniffff.* "Holy shit. What kind of coke is this?" Dale asked, rubbing his nose. "Tastes funny."

Lucia giggled and passed the box to Kalina. "It's Bafexatrin. Thought you might need an extra kick tonight."

"I don't need that pharmaceutical shit," Dale said arrogantly. "I think I've done just fine without it, don't you?"

Lucia grabbed Dale by the back of his head and shoved his face toward her shimmering lace panties. "Look," she said.

He hadn't noticed the bulge earlier. Lucia had a penis.

Dale jumped back, wiping powder from his nose and cheeks. "What the fuck is that?!"

Kalina's eyes lit up as she stared shamelessly at Lucia's impressive piece. "Oh my god, that is *so* fucking hot."

"I'm glad one of you thinks so . . . Well, what are you waiting for, girl?" Lucia said, smiling seductively at Kalina.

Kalina obeyed and started giving Lucia head.

"Mmm. What about you?" Lucia asked Dale. "Don't tell me you haven't fantasized about being with a trans-girl before."

"What do you mean?" he answered, startled, but undeniably aroused. "I'm not—"

"What—gay?" Lucia threw her head back, laughing. "Take a look at me, Daddy. If it's gay to wanna hit *this*, then maybe you should start rethinking your orientation."

"She's right, Dale," Kalina said. "Just look at her."

"I know, she's hot—I mean it's not that—I just—"

"Don't be so uptight, Dale," Kalina said. "C'mon. We'll do it together."

Dale bit his lip.

Lucia smacked her pouty red lips at him, luring him in with her immaculate body, perfect cheekbones, tits and eyelashes. "I think your girlfriend could use some help down there," Lucia said, running her manicured fingernails through Dale's hair.

Dale felt pre-cum soak through the front of his designer silk boxers, when suddenly, an unfamiliar but euphoric Bafexatrin high kicked in full tilt. It was unlike anything he'd ever felt before.

Deep house music pulsed over the limo's bass-heavy sound-system, making the hairs on Dale's head tingle and curl. The city's skyline rose up in the distance, transforming the towering political circuitry into a mosaic of neon crystalline snow castles. Kalina, the venal ex-stripper, became a white China-doll Aphrodite, exchanging kisses with the gorgeous Lucia, who suddenly seemed as fertile as a virgin daughter of mystery Babylon.

The Bafexatrin worked quickly, rewiring Dale's neural pathways, erasing his guilt and shame, giving him god-like confidence mixed with a devilish desire. The temptation of doing something so taboo combined with a justifiable curiosity made the thrill impossible to withstand.

"I normally wouldn't do this . . . I don't know what's happening to me, but—"

Dale fell to his knees and joined Kalina on the floor of the limo for the rest of the half-hour ride downtown.

When they got to Dale's suite at The Hedoluxe, it was all out pandemonium. More Bafexatrin, booze and cocaine, followed by pure mdma. Dale and Lucia. Lucia and Kalina. Lucia, Dale and Kalina.

*Cheers, to tonight—and so sorry about tomorrow.*


*Meanwhile, things had been heating up in Warsaw, Poland.*


While Dale gave his speech at the Guild Awards in New York City, Denis Babinski and his dear wife Maja, were home in Warsaw watching on television.

"That's it. I'm going back to Canada, Maja."

"No, Denis! How many times do you expect me to go through this shit with you? Am I not enough for you? What is so bad about your life here that makes you want to run away again? When is this going to stop? When will your restlessness finally end? When will you stop trying to save people and take care of yourself?"

"Maja . . ."

"What about me, Denis? What about us? For God's sake, the book is already out. What do you expect to do?" Maja cried.

Denis remained calm. "Maja, darling . . . Holding on to a dream in this world seems like madness to most people, but Emmett held on to his for so long it drove him mad. That job, that book—it cost him everything . . . I owe him this much! And that Dale Potoniak . . . I will squash him under my boot—like an ant!"

"Stop it, Denis. I've heard enough from you now."

"Maja, darling. I've wanted so badly to be a better husband to you. I've been a pathetic excuse for a man and you deserve so much better . . . I'm sorry. But there is still one battle I must fight, and I must go now . . . I know I can't expect you to wait for me again, but I truly hope you do. I love you, Maja. I will love you always."

Maja sobbed. "Why, Denis? Why now? We've been so happy since you got back. The kids are laughing again, your son finally called you *Tata*." Maja fell face first into his arms. She truly loved him.

"I'll be back soon, my love," Denis whispered, kissing her forehead. "I swear it."

Maja wept some more, but it was no use. Denis was out the door a few minutes later.

*Dale's suite at The Hedoluxe. Ottawa, Ontario.*

When the sun came up that morning, Kalina was fast asleep on the living room floor. Lucia and Dale lay beside her beneath a plush white duvet, sharing a cigarette.

"What a night," Dale said, staring up at the ceiling.

"So, you enjoyed your gift?"

He turned to her with a grin. "Are you serious?"

Lucia giggled. "I guess that answers my question."

"I would say so."

"Good. I'm glad."

" . . . I forgot to ask—who hired you for this? Was it Gary?"

"No."

"No?"

"Nope."

"Leeland?"

"Guess again—"

*Knock-knock*

*Knock-knock-knock*

"Who the hell is that?" Dale asked,

*Knock-knock-knock-knock*

"Dale? Dale Potoniak? I know you're in there, Dale. Open up. It's me—Denis Babinski."

"Who the fuck is Denis Babinski?" Dale asked, looking at Lucia.

"I have no idea. Tell him to go away," Lucia said, snuggling under the blanket.

"Open the door, Dale! I know you're in there!" Denis shouted, banging on the door even harder.

"Hey! Wait a goddamn minute," Dale shouted, finding his bathrobe. "And quit banging like that or I'll call security."

"I'm not going anywhere until you let me in," Denis said.

"What the hell do you want?" Dale asked, finally opening the door.

"I am Denis Babinski from Poland. Emmett's friend. I called you the night he went to the hospital, remember?"

"Oh, right . . . Well, what the fuck do you want?"

"To talk. The situation has gotten out of hand."

"What situation?" Dale asked, blocking the doorway. "If you mean the situation where a total stranger shows up at my door uninvited at seven in the morning the day after I win the biggest prize in modern literature, then yes. This whole goddamn thing is out of hand . . . Look, I'm kinda busy in here, Denis. Why don't you come by a little later, all right?"

Dale tried closing the door, but Denis barged past him into the living room.

Lucia screamed as she covered herself up.

"Get in the bedroom!" Dale shouted, "and take Kalina with you."

"You think I don't know what you've done? I know exactly what you've done!" Denis shouted.

"Hey, you mind quieting the fuck up? You're gonna wake up my neighbours. And I have no idea what you're—"

Denis pushed Dale out of the way, stormed into his office, and began rummaging through papers on his desk.

"Don't play stupid, Dale. You know exactly what's going on. You stole Emmett's manuscript, and I'm pretty sure you had something to do with him being locked up. I know it, you know it, and as soon as I can prove it—the whole world is going to know it!"

Dale shook his head, perplexed. "Wait a minute. Just wait a goddamn minute! Something to do with his—? Stole his book? Denis—you've got about two seconds to tell me what the fuck you're doing in *my* home before I call security and have you dragged out of here by that godawful flannel shirt of yours. One, two—"

"Quit playing around!" Denis said, pointing a finger in Dale's face. "Admit it! Admit you stole Emmett's manuscript!"

"If I do, will you leave?" Dale asked, not bothering to hide a divisive smile.

"Yes. Admit to it and I will leave immediately."

Dale shrugged. "Fine. I borrowed a couple ideas from his notes, but you sure as hell can't prove anything. And I don't know where you get off saying I had something to do with him being locked up. The kid went mad. Had a psychotic freak-out while I was sleeping in a chair beside him. He attacked me. Damn near gouged my eye out, too. Look, I still have the scar."

Denis stopped rummaging, and looked confused for a moment.

"Look," Dale said, leaning casually against the office door, "you obviously came a long way for this—confrontation or whatever it is—but you look like shit, man. Why don't we sit down and talk about it like men? Here, I'll pour you a drink. What are you having? Vodka? Whisky? Oh, check this shit out. I bought this off a guy in Rockcliffe who collects rare Scotch. He says it's a Highlands single malt with peaty oak flavours and a nice smoked nose . . . Fuck do I care, right? Ha! Three grand this fucker cost me. Unbelievable."

"I didn't come all the way from Poland to drink with you!" Denis snapped. "You better start talking or I'm going to get on this goddamn phone and call your publisher right now!" Denis reached into his pocket and pulled out a cell phone.

Without warning, Dale swung the bottle of Scotch, smashing it against Denis' head. The two men wrestled, and Denis was bloodied, but he was the stronger man, and threw Dale to the ground, sending him skidding halfway across the room.

"All right, now I'm calling the cops, you fuck! Get the fuck out right now!" Dale cried.

"Fuck you," Denis said, punching in the numbers to Leeland's office.

Dale put his head down and charged again. Denis did a quick sidestep and landed a clean right hook to the side of his face, knocking him to the ground again. Dale turtled, and Denis soccer-kicked him in the ribs, knocking the wind clean out of him.

"Not so tough, are ya?" Denis said, straightening his shirt collar proudly.

Dale writhed on the floor, scraping at his own neck and chest as he gasped for air.

"Fuck it. I'm calling Dwight Leeland right now," Denis said.

Dale dragged his body up the edge of the desk and shouted, "Wait! Just wait a minute! . . . I fucking did it, okay. But so what? I took a shot at the big time and all of a sudden I'm the bad guy? Emmett's sick, you prick! You don't know him like I do. There's no way he's coming back from the shit he's in."

"What are you talking about?"

"His mind, man. His whole personality—it was fucking gone, okay? He *wanted* me to get his story published, man. For him. And you know why? Because we're best friends, that's why. We're like brothers, you stupid fuck! We've known each other for over thirty years and you've known him for what—a year at the most? Exactly! Go fuck yourself."

"You're going to fry for this, tough guy."

Denis was ringing Dwight Leeland's office, and Dale began to panic. He knew Leeland would be in the office already preparing for their meeting with the London distributor later that day; and he'd shit a brick if someone even suggested that *Concrete Grizzly's* integrity was anything less than impeccable.

Dale scoured the room for something, for anything, for an answer.

*The desk. A pen!*

"Yes. I'd like to speak with Mr. Dwight Leeland . . . Yes, I'll hold. Thank you . . . Hello, Mr. Leeland? My name is Denis Babinski . . . I have some information about *Concrete Grizzly* and Dale Pot—achhhkkk!"

Dale stabbed the pointy end of a brass calligraphy pen into the side of Denis' muscular neck. The phone fell to the floor as Denis turned around slowly. His jugular made wet, gargling sounds as the blood began to spit out.

"Fucking rat," Dale said, pulling the pen out of Denis' neck and jabbing it deep into his gut.

"You are—a bad man," Denis said, falling to his knees, trying desperately to pull the pen out of his own abdomen.

Dale cleaned his bloody hands on his fresh white bathrobe and stood over Denis, watching as he struggled to breathe.

Dale nudged Denis with his hip, knocking the big man over into a pool of his own blood. Denis shook a little, twitched once, and was dead.

Dale, wanting to be sure, snatched a bookend from the shelf and smashed Denis' head with it several times, crushing his skull.

"What the fuck, Dale?!" Kalina screamed, standing naked in the doorway with a terrified Lucia cowering behind her.

Dale yanked the bloody pen from Denis' abdomen and lunged toward Kalina, grabbing her by the throat with one hand as he plunged the makeshift weapon into her belly button several times with the other. Kalina's body slid slowly to the floor, leaving a wide red smear on the white wall.

"Payback's a cunt, ain't it bitch?" Dale hissed, as she gasped for air. "Guess I'll be takin' top spot at the Guild Awards again this year. You fucking whore." He spat on her. ". . . What the fuck are *you* looking at?"

Lucia whimpered, frozen and trembling from shock and fear.

Suddenly, Dale became calm and smiled. He took a casual step toward Lucia, discreetly grabbing another bottle of booze from the shelf. "C'mon, Lucia . . . We were having so much fun a minute ago . . . Don't let these assholes ruin it for us . . . Let's get back under the blanket and you can tell me more about your days in the—circus!" Dale bashed the bottle on the side of her head, and she was gone.

Dale wrapped Denis, Kalina and Lucia up in black garbage bags and duct tape, and dragged their bodies downstairs, one by one, to an industrial-sized garbage incinerator in the basement of his building. The entire disposal process only took an hour.

Afterwards, he went upstairs to do the rest of Lucia's Bafexatrin. He took a shower, made some tea, then went downtown to Leeland's office for the meeting.

# 16

*April 4, 2002. Ottawa, Ontario.*

Charlie McGee was officially back in Canada after a roller coaster tour of Europe. Tired, but ready to take on his new role as Manager of Creative Affairs at the *Fisticuffs* office in Toronto, Ontario. He happened to be in Ottawa on business for a couple of days.

*8:42 p.m.*

Dale sat in the back seat of a taxi watching the rain-covered city streets pass by him in the window.

"Might snow tonight," the taxi driver said, eyeing Dale in the rear-view mirror.

"Yep. It could," Dale said softly.

"Big plans tonight?"

"Just tying up some loose ends."

"Business meeting?"

Dale snorted a bump of Bafexatrin off the back of his hand. "Something like that."

*9:23 p.m.*

". . . When I looked at those World War Two photos, and into the eyes of those soldiers . . . I'd seen the same pain on men in the city, on their way to another kind of hell." Charlie was recounting a visit he'd made to a concentration camp in southern Poland. "So what's new with you, chum? We haven't talked since—well, since the day you left Berlin. I was actually a little surprised to hear from you . . . How'd you know I was in Ottawa today?"

"That's easy, man. Metzger told me. I told you, he knows everything."

"You done shook hands with the devil, chum . . . Anyways, what's new with you?"

"What's new? Oh, you know. Filling the time, filling the pages."

Charlie chuckled and took a sip of beer. "Same ol' Dale. Hey, I heard big things about your new book, chum. Congratulations. 'Bout time, too . . . And New York City? A Guild award and a bestseller to boot?"

"Yep."

"That's amazing. I always knew this would happen to you some day. Emmett, too. He knew it."

"Knew what?"

"That you were the best to ever do it."

"Yeah, well that's one of the reasons I wanted to see you tonight . . . Have you read it yet?"

"What, your book?"

"Yeah."

Charlie looked embarrassed.

"You can be honest," Dale said, with a prying smile.

"I'm sorry, chum. I've been so busy. I—I'll buy a copy as soon as I'm settled into this new position. You have my word . . . So—what's it about?" Charlie asked.

"Do you remember the day I left Europe?"

"How could I forget? You were pretty fucked up, chum."

"You're right, I was." Dale paused and took a sip of beer.

Charlie smiled. "Remember how drunk we got that first night in Tallinn? You were dancing up and down those cobblestone streets all night, singing old tavern tunes."

"Best night of the trip as far as I'm concerned."

"'Bout the only time I ever seen you that carefree."

"After Europe, I remember thinking that my nightmares had come true. I'd seen those streets, I'd smoked and drank in all those bars, at the end of all those cobblestone roads and brick buildings; I'd seen what I'd seen and it inspired absolutely nothing in me. There was music in the streets, but my mind would not dance with me."

"But you beat it, right? You got this new book everybody's talking about. Guess it was all worth it in the end, eh?"

"Last time I saw Emmett I told him that I could picture it all. That I could envision the rest of my life from that moment on. He was lying there tethered to that hospital bed, helpless. Babbling on about concrete beasts and the latent homosexuals he worked with like a run-of-the-mill lunatic . . . If we were soldiers, I was the guy who wanted to be seen wearing medals, but was too much of a pussy to actually bleed for them on the battlefield. Emmett, on the other hand, was willing to die for them. Willing to go utterly mad for them."

Charlie looked puzzled. "What are you talking about, Dale?"

"I gave some thought to untying Emmett, but playtime was over. I got my medal. That's all I wanted . . . I was honest with him about wanting to be famous, perhaps, being rich, perhaps. 'But in these hands,' I said to him, 'there is only love. Only love.'"

"Dale, do you mind if we talk about something else? It's still a little weird for me to think he's locked up in some concrete box a million miles away, you know?"

Dale cleared his throat. "Sure. We don't have to talk about it . . . So what else is new? Tell me about the rest of the tour. What happened after I left?"

"Well, I've been wantin' to tell you about this guy I seen at the train station in Athens. He was keeled over like he was about to barf in the middle of the sidewalk while the morning rush hour just walked past him, and nobody gave a shit."

"Creepy."

"It was!" Charlie said, chuckling. "The little Greek girls were screeching and staring when he turned to look up at them with his crazy bloodshot eyes."

"God, I miss Europe," Dale said, sighing. "I miss the madness."

"Fuck Europe. You don't know how good it feels to be home, chum. First thing I'm gonna do when things settle down a bit is book a ticket to Victoria. I haven't seen my family in almost two years. Can you believe that shit?"

"Nope. Unreal."

". . . Emmett's jobsite was just a few blocks from where I used to live downtown Vic . . . Fuck, he hated that job. Called me once a week to tell me he was quitting, or that he wanted to quit. Told me about the guys he worked with and how fucked up they all were. I wish I could've been there to help him, chum. I wish I could've done—something."

"Don't be so hard yourself . . . It's just too bad he never got to finish that book of his, eh?"

"No shit . . . I was actually thinking about calling his mom to see if I could take a look at the manuscript. It's gotta be with the rest of his things, right?"

"Maybe. Who knows?"

"Emmett deserves to have at least part of that book published, you know? Hey, maybe me and you could do it together as a tribute or something. For when he gets out. You got some pretty sweet connections now. Maybe your guys could take a look and see what they think of it."

"That would be something, eh? A tribute to Emmett. Hmm. Let me think about that." Dale knew in his heart what had to be done.

"A toast—in Emmett's words: Men will always fear death and seek God for answers. And books will always call them to arms. Cheers, chum," Charlie raised his glass, happy to be alone with his friend after so long apart.

"Hey, drink up, pussy. You're back in Canada now. None of those European baby sips you were always taking."

Charlie laughed. "Arright, arright. Take it easy on me, chum. I'm tired. Plus, I've been living sober for a while now."

"So have I—sort of. But who gives a shit? When was the last time we hung out? You know what? Fuck it. Waitress? Shots, please. We want some shots over here!"

"What can I get you boys?" a young smiling waitress asked.

"Whiskies. Doubles—no—make them triples . . . For old time's sake, eh? For Emmett."

Charlie was hesitant to get wasted the night before a flight, but the good vibes were getting to him. " . . . Why the hell not. It's been a while, chum."

"Two triple whiskies coming up, boys," the waitress said.

"I miss this . . . Don't you miss this, chum?"

"I do . . . I really do."


Charlie drank three beers and two more shots before he finally got up to relieve himself.

Dale looked around to make sure nobody was looking, then dumped a vial of ghb into his half-empty bottle and swished it around.

"I had to piss like a race horse, chum," Charlie said, reappearing out of nowhere.

"Welcome back, Charlie boy . . . Hey, how'd that ol' song go again?"

"Which song?" Charlie asked.

"The one I was singing like a drunken idiot in Tallinn."

"Oh yeah. Let me think . . .

I was a drunk man playing in the rain

But now I'm a gentle man trying to be brave

I sent you a telegram that came in my brain

But the fact remains . . .

You'd catch me at noon with my father's mandolin

Please shut down the music, you said with a grin

The harvest is over and now we can rest

Now we can worship the gods we forget

La la la la la look in my eyes

Look at the sunrise I saw when you died

I pictured us laughing and floating at sea

We tried to be us but I just couldn't be me, singing

Come Josephine

Come when I'm happy

Mountains and rivers and gold and the streams

I made the mistake of running away

And now I'm an old man in love . . .

The place I was raised was concrete and pain

Preachers and thieves were companions to me

Don't look out the window, don't ever get dressed

Now is as beautiful as you'll ever get

I came from a city where few of us talked

About the gallery of shadows at the end of the block

I gave up the privilege of driving in cars

And I've discovered your face in the stars, and sing

Come Josephine

Come when I'm happy

Mountains and rivers and gold and the streams

I made the mistake of running away

But now I'm an old man in love . . ."

Dale nodded. "That's the one. How the hell did you remember that?"

Charlie guzzled down the rest of his beer. "Eeaghh! This tastes like shit. We got spoiled on that good European Pils, eh?"

"Yeah, I think we did."

"Dale . . . are we getting a little old for all this?"

"What do you mean?"

"I mean look at us. We're full-grown men with bottles in our hands. Sucking on 'em like we're fuckin' babies."

"We're fine. We still got years before we gotta worry about any of that shit."

Suddenly, Charlie became noticeably dopier as the effects of the ghb kicked in. "While ago . . . We went to this casino with a couple work guys in Amsterdam . . . Those fuckin' pussies went straight to the poker room so I sat at the bar jus' kinda watchin' people, ya know? . . . So I'm jus' sittin' there, and this little fuckin' Nazi asshole—this obvious skinhead motherfucker—was jus' sittin' there at this slot machine called *The African King*, puttin' hundred euro after hundred euro in it, jus' hopin' for some big score. Fuckin' ironic racist piece of shit."

"That is irony right there. That's exactly what that is," Dale said, matter-of-factly. "How you feelin' over there, man? You look a little goosed. You all right?"

"Shit, yeah. I feel fuckin' great. And if I may, I'd like to quote the words of our great friend, Emmett Dorry . . . 'Fuck all you betrayers, lovers of guns and hollow-word sayers with your silver hammers—'" Charlie burped loudly.

Dale raised his glass, trying to hide the contempt he suddenly felt. "Whatd'ya say we pay up and head outside for a smokey-smoke, chum?"

Charlie was getting more belligerent up by the minute. "Fucksh, yeshhh . . . Let'sh goff." He nearly knocked over the table as he stood up.

"You're all right. Go outside. I'll pay the bill and we'll go party some more."

"Is your friend okay?" the waitress asked, handing Dale their bill.

"He's fine. He just got a promotion, so . . . Yeah, just put the whole thing on my gold card."

*11:49 p.m.*

"Where you chakin' me, chumsh?" Charlie muttered. "I shouldsh probably go to my hotelsh . . . I feel'n' fucksh up."

"Don't be a baby, Charlie. We haven't seen each other in ages. I thought we'd celebrate a bit . . . Driver? Take us to the St. Lawrence River Yacht Club, please."

"St. Lawrence? In Cardinal? Sure thing, boss."

"I thinksh—I thinksh I'm gonna be shick," Charlie said. His eyes were rolling into the back of his head.

"Not in my cab, man. Can't you hold it till we get there? Your friend better not ralph in my back seat, homeboy."

"He won't. He's fine. . . Aren't ya, bud?" Dale nudged Charlie, but he didn't respond. "See, he's fine. He's asleep now."

*12:42 a.m.*

When the taxi pulled up at the entrance to the St. Lawrence yacht club, Dale opened the door and pushed Charlie out. Charlie's head hit the pavement hard, and he vomited up a rancid-smelling brown liquid.

Dale giggled, but the cabbie looked like he was about to be sick himself. "That's fuckin' disgusting, man . . . Hundred and six bucks, homeboy. And tell your friend thanks for not puking in my cab."

Dale handed him two hundreds. "No sweat. Keep the change."

*1:51 a.m.*

"W-where are we?" Charlie asked, shivering uncontrollably as he stared out into the darkness of the St. Lawrence. "I'm f-f-freezing, chum."

"We're almost there, bud," Dale said, from under the hood of a thick winter parka. "I'm takin' us on a little boat trip, chum."

"Boat trip?"

"Yeah. You like boats, right?"

"I guess . . . I'm jus' . . . I'm jus' gonna lie down a bit, okay?"

"You do that. I'll wake you up when we get there. Hey, you cold? You need a coat or something?" Dale chuckled. "Oh shit. I only brought the one. Never mind."

*1:23 a.m.*

Dale shut the engine off and walked over to Charlie who was passed out on one of the boat seats.

"Charlie."

"Huh?"

"We're here . . . Wake up, man." Dale poked him, but he wouldn't move. "All right—have it your way." Dale disappeared below deck for a minute and came back holding a length of yellow rope and a large concrete block, singing: "*Come Josephine, come when I'm happy. Mountains and rivers and gold and the streams. I made the mistake of running away, but now I'm an old man in looooove,*" while fastening the heavy brick to Charlie's right ankle.

"That should do it," Dale said. "Sailor's knot, I think it is . . . All right, let's get you in the water, big guy."

"What the—? What ya doin', chum?" Charlie mumbled, half conscious.

"Why, you're going for a swim, ol' chum . . . What's it fuckin' look like?" Dale chuckled.

"No way . . . It's t-t-too c-c-cold."

"You'll be fine. Don't be such a pussy."

"Get off me, chum." Charlie tried pushing Dale away, but he fell backwards off the seat.

Dale burst out laughing. "Ah, c'mon, Charlie. Don't be like that. Otherwise I'm gonna make you do it."

"Just take me home. I'm f-f-fuckin' cold—and—I jus' wanna go home, chum . . . Please."

Dale grabbed Charlie by the collar and dragged him to the opening at the back of the boat.

"In. Now," Dale said, sternly.

"What's the matter with you?" Charlie cried, completely oblivious to the brick tied to his ankle. "It's fuckin' winter out here!"

"What's wrong with me? More like what's wrong with you . . . All I wanted you to do was take a little dip and you're making all this trouble for me . . . I pay two-hundred bucks for a cab, come all the way down here to have a little fun, and this is the thanks I get? Fuck it. I'll just turn us around and we'll go home. You fuckin' party pooper."

Charlie was high, confused and totally unable to comprehend the gravity of the situation; plus the ghb had made him virtually defenceless to the power of suggestion. "Arright."

"What was that?"

"I said arright . . . If I jump in, you promise you'll take me straight home?"

"Of course! Cross my heart, chummy-chum-chum." Dale made the sign of the cross on his chest.

Charlie looked down at the still, black water just a few feet below him. "You gotta pull me out quick, okay? I don't know if I'll be able to get myself back up. I—" Charlie nearly vomited again. "I think I drank too much, chum."

"Trust me, man. I gotcha. Don't worry about a thing. I got your back one hundred and fifty per cent." Dale grinned and motioned Charlie toward the frigid black water.

". . . Arright, fuck it." Charlie threw his body sideways into the frigid St. Lawrence River. The concrete block made scraping sounds as it skidded across the deck of the boat, plunking into the water behind him a few seconds later.

Dale looked down, and saw Charlie's hand reach up past the surface of the water before it disappeared forever.

The light of a full moon cast a long shadow of the boat across the sparkling water. Dale reached into his pocket for a cigarette, and let it dangle from his bottom lip as he unzipped his pants and relieved himself over Charlie's watery grave, all the while singing the same old tavern tune.

"*The harvest is over and now we can rest. Now we can worship the gods we forget . . . Singin' come Josephine.*"

A couple weeks later, Dale went home after a meeting with Metzger and Leeland, and noticed that a letter had been slipped under his door. There was no sender and no return address on it so he tossed it on the kitchen counter, and undressed to take a shower.

Later that night, he lay in bed thinking about Emmett and the cost he'd paid for *Concrete Grizzly* in those crucial final hours. He thought about Denis, his muscular body being pulverized inside a machine meant to dispose of ordinary, useless household trash. He smiled recalling the sound of Kalina's head being crushed in the same machine, and the last thing he'd said to her before her pretty little insides splattered on the white tile floor made him giggle. *You fucking whore.*

Poor little Lucia was just collateral damage.

He went over the details of his night out with Charlie and wondered if the pub had security cameras, or if divers would discover his body at the bottom of the St. Lawrence someday. Poor Charlie. Reaching up to the sky in hopes that some invisible hand might descend into that frozen black abyss and save him.

Dale lit a cigarette and snorted his bedtime Bafexatrin.

He closed his eyes and saw the crowd at the Guild Awards gazing up at him from the opulent hall. From time to time their applause would ring in his ears like the crescendo of an old love song, reminding him to laugh about broken hearts. He felt unstoppable.

For no reason at all, he remembered the letter on the kitchen counter, and that he'd forgotten to see who it was from.

He got up to retrieve it, then climbed back into bed, pulling the plush satin duvet up over his bare chest.

Dale,

Now that you've won, I hope your heart can rest easy.

Now that you've given them enough to pay the cost for their company.

I'm sorry. I want to say that I'm not upset about it, but that would be a lie.

I was there Dale. I was in New York for the Guild Awards. I watched you on stage, saying the things you said . . . Taking credit for that book.

Dale, I know you didn't write *Concrete Grizzly*. I know because I visited Emmett recently. He told me everything.

That is his book and he deserves the credit for it. Do you understand me?

I'm trying hard not to believe that you could have done something so awful to hurt your very best friend, but it seems like you have. I hope God puts it in your heart to do the right thing.

Please find me, Dale. We need to talk.

P.S. Don't worry. I haven't told anyone else.

Jane St. Marie

A long dangling ash fell from Dale's cigarette and splashed over Jane's signature like the tears of a dragon.

*Jane knows? How can it be?*

It didn't seem possible. He hadn't spoken to Jane since that morning in Prague.

Dale reached for the phone and dialled Gary Metzger.

"Hello?"

"Gary, it's Dale."

"Dale? What the fuck? What time is it? I was sleeping. What's wrong?"

"It's late, Gary. I'm sorry, but listen. I need Jane St. Marie's phone number."

"Jane St. Marie? The editor at *The Carriage*? What the hell do you want to talk to her for?"

"Don't ask me why, Gary. Just give it to me. I need it right now."

"You woke me up for this? I should come over there and kick your ass right now . . . And I was having such an amazing dream. This hot blond was riding me like you wouldn't believe and—"

"Gary, this is a fucking emergency."

"Okay, okay . . . Just give me a second, would ya? I gotta turn on my laptop . . . Hold on a sec . . . Okay, it's 555-8117. So why—"

Dale hung up and dialled Jane's number.

"Hello?"

It was Jane. It was the first time he'd heard her sweet angelic voice in over two years.

"Jane . . . It's Dale. Dale Potoniak."

" . . . I didn't expect you to call so soon."

"Jane, we need to talk about that letter."

"Okay, sure. Not over the phone. We have to do it in person."

"Fine. Where are you? I'll have Shayna book me a flight for first thing in the morning."

"I'm in Ottawa at the Creekside Hotel."

"Creekside? You're like ten minutes from me. What room are you in?"

"1710. Dale—"

"I'll see you in a half hour."

He hung up.


Jane answered the door wearing a cotton bathrobe robe over a pair of baggy flannel pajamas. Her face had aged a little, but it was just as beautiful as the day he'd left for Europe

"Hi," she said, softly. "Come in."

Dale stepped inside and sat at the desk. He looked around, nervously. There were papers scattered across the floor and several ashtrays filled with cigarette butts.

"Looks like you're working on a book," Dale said, trying to remain composed. "And you smoke now?"

"My latest novel," Jane said, sitting down on the edge of the bed just a few feet from him. "And yeah. I started when you left for Europe. Made me miss you less for some reason."

Dale cleared his throat. "What's it called? Your book, I mean."

"*The Betrayal.* I think."

Dale felt his eyelid begin to twitch. "Oh . . ." He cleared his throat. "What's it about?"

Jane reached for her cigarettes. "Why are you here, Dale?"

"Well, I guess to say sorry about what happened in Europe. I know it's pointless now, but I really wanted to tell you that. Especially before we get into this other stuff."

Jane didn't answer. She just held her burning cigarette and watched him carefully.

"Did you hear what I just said? I'm sorry."

"I really don't give a shit about that anymore . . . That part of my life is over and done with. I've moved on. So why don't we just get to the point and talk about that book of yours."

"Okay. So, I may have borrowed a couple ideas from Emmett, but I wrote it. He gave me permission."

"Dale, I've got a copy of Emmett's original manuscript right there and I've read it, like, five times."

"You do? You did?"

"Your *Concrete Grizzly* and Emmett's *Concrete Bear* are practically identical, word for word, so quit lying and tell me the truth."

"I wrote that book!" Dale shouted, pointing to the manuscript on Jane's bedside table.

"That book was his life, Dale! It's his story! Tell me the truth right now or so help me God!"

Dale jumped up in a furious rage. "You pompous cunt! You think because you went and prayed for him or some shit, you suddenly know him better than I do? I've known Emmett my entire fucking life. The guy lost his mind, Jane! I was there that night, not you. I wanted to help him. I didn't steal anything!" Dale took a deep breath. "I went to the hospital, and he was talking some crazy shit I thought would make for good writing. I was under the gun for a book, so I asked permission to use it in case he . . . Anyways, I'm not trying to exploit his suffering, or whatever it is you think I'm doing."

"A bestseller, Dale? Best work in contemporary fiction?" Jane shook her head in disgust. "The last half-decent thing *you* wrote was four years ago, drunk off your ass in some shithole hotel in Nicaragua. Then you went and had your little freak show in Europe and *completely* lost it."

"That was your idea not mine."

"*You* lost it, Dale. You had something so unique and special and you fucked it all up. If you would have just waited and let things happen naturally you could have written your own book!"

"Fuck that. If it wasn't for the way things are in this business then I wouldn't need to use someone else's ideas in the first place! You know what it's like when you get a book deal, Jane. They gave me a hundred grand! A hundred grand, Jane! Metzger was breathing down my neck and I had nothing!"

"That's no excuse for what you've done."

"I'm not making excuses!"

"Yes, you are."

"You want excuses, Jane? Huh? I gave my heart and soul to writing for over ten years—my life—and it didn't mean shit."

"You weren't rich and famous, but you had amazing friends. Charlie, and Emmett. And he still loves you, even though you took everything he worked so hard for . . . And you had me, Dale. We could've had such a good, simple life together if you hadn't—"

"Hadn't what? What, Jane? Say it . . . Say it!"

"If you hadn't gone to Europe and fucked around on me, you fucking asshole!" Jane started to cry.

"That's bullshit. You knew it would never work out between us in the long run, so don't pretend like you're some saint willing to take me as I was . . . I was a broke loser with no future, and that's why you shipped me off to Europe in the first place. And don't play the virginity card either. If I would've known it would end the way it did, I never would've—"

"I loved you, Dale! Don't you get it? After all this time, you still don't understand that?"

Dale sat back down, frustrated. "Fuck this. I came here to have a civil conversation about my book, and I don't want you to get upset, but if you're gonna keep saying that it's not mine, then we've got a huge fuckin' problem."

"It is not yours, Dale! It's Emmett's!" Jane was becoming hysterical now. "And you're not gonna get another interview in *Fairpress* or another award from the Guild until you tell me exactly happened in Victoria. That I promise you."

"I already told you! I've told everybody a million times!"

"Tell me what happened, Dale. What did you do? What did you say to him?"

Dale looked around, wishing he could disappear forever.

"Please, Dale," Jane begged. "Just tell me."

Dale remembered the look on Emmett's face. The sadness in his eyes the moment he'd said it.

"I told him . . . I told him . . ." Dale mumbled.

"What? speak up."

"I told him he was a goofy-looking fuck with a death wish or something, and if he was crazy enough to think that I'd fuck him in a nut house then he was probably better off somewhere people could keep an eye on him . . . It's not what you think, Jane. Emmett was bonkers, okay? I mean the guy's doped to the gills and what does he go and do? Tells me he's been in love with me since we were kids and he can't live without me for another day. Says if I don't give him what he wants, and you know exactly what *that* is, that he doesn't wanna live any more. He wanted me to—well, you know! Can you believe that? I said no, obviously, and he starts crying and begging . . . My best friend is lying there strapped to a bed in the fucking loony bin, and I told him—I fucking told him—if he thinks I'd do something like that, then maybe he is better off in a fucking cage . . . He was demented, Jane. Suicidal. He was suffering . . . I did what had to be done. I'm not cruel—I'm not like *that*."

"You're like—you're like some kind of mentally abusive animal . . . Why on earth would you say something like that to him?"

"Who the fuck knows?! Maybe I'm a piece of shit. Maybe I'm an evil genius . . . Why is Chet Cater marrying Ola Kant? Why did Bert Conrad's book get five stars in *Re-Think* magazine and mine—which was an absolute masterpiece—only get one? Life is fucked up, Jane. Shit gets crazy sometimes. Sorry."

"Bert's father owns *Re-Think* magazine, Dale."

"Yeah, and Bert owns one of the most successful publishing houses in Canada and makes a million dollars a year. The fucking prick. And *you*. So successful with your 'look at me, I'm so innocent, Jesus-loves-me, bullshit when I—Wait. Never mind. I don't mean that. You're different. Forget I said that . . . Honestly."

"You need help, Dale."

"No shit, Jane . . . Why do you think I took drugs and drank my face off every day we were together? Did you ever think that maybe it was the only way this goddamn world made any goddamn sense to me? Why did you have to be so clean, Jane? Why did you have to be so spotless and clean? You knew what I wanted. You knew what I craved and needed, and it wasn't help. At least not then. You just stood there in front of me every night, naked. It was right there, dripping wet between your thighs; and now you see I need help. Ha! Just now!"

Tears were pouring out of Jane's eyes. She'd huddled her body against the headboard of the bed and attempted to cover herself with a heavy down comforter.

Dale looked at her and laughed. "Fuck it, I'm sick of this. You want the truth, then here it is. The second I got to Prague I cheated on you with a Slovakian dominatrix because you, you prude, wouldn't put out. Plain and simple. I thought I could get you to come around, but once I realized that wasn't happening I got heavy into the femdom, and then shit started getting—oh, a teeny bit weird for me. The rest is ancient history . . . After Emmett told me about his book and made a move on me, I choked the little prick half to death and told him if he didn't tell me where his manuscript was that I'd kill him. Mind you I was a bit drunk when it happened; but a few minutes later, I snuck out of the hospital, broke into his apartment and got the manuscript. I went back to the hospital, and that's when I told the doctors he'd gotten loose and tried to kill me. Next thing I know he's in Victoria Correctional's psych ward for attempted murder. He's gone forever, I'm rich, and it was all that easy . . . Is that what you wanted to hear, Jane? Isn't that what you've wanted to hear this whole time? Now you've got your closure. Now you can go to church and pray for the big bad sinner, right? Pray for the evil shit who broke your precious little God-loving virgin heart? . . . All these years you've been lurking around the sidelines, watching me. Waiting for me to fuck up so you could rub it in my face. The whole time you've been thinking that Dale is a fucking failure. You've known it all along, right? Why are you crying? The world ain't all flowery-white and soft like you, Jane—and it should be me that's crying, not you! Do you know how hard it's been to carry this with me everywhere I go? To know what I did to my best friend for a fucking publishing deal? Well, do you? Do you know how hard it was to do what I did to Charlie?" Dale bit his tongue.

Jane was absolutely horrified. "What did you do to Charlie, Dale?"

Dale smirked and shook his head. "Well, I guess the cat's out the bag, eh? Surprise, Jane—Charlie's dead. And don't get all emotional about it. If Charlie read my book  he would've outed me in two seconds flat, so I drugged him up on ghb and dumped his body in the St. Lawrence River a couple weeks ago . . . Yep. We rode out in Gary's boat and I tied a fucking mason's brick to his ankle. Made Mr. Chummy-Chum go permanent swim-swim. I tied a fucking cinder-block to that Irish hick's foot and convinced him to take a swim in a frigid river on a pitch black night in the middle of an Ottawa winter. Is that what you wanted to hear, Jane?"

"You—you cannot be serious right now."

Dale moved closer. "Oh, I am. I'm dead serious, Jane. And I did it all for you, you stupid bitch. Do you know how long and how badly I wanted us to be together? You don't, do you. You'll never know, you know why? Because you're a selfish, manipulative whore and you'll never know how much I loved you all these years. Everything I've ever done was for you!"

"What the hell are you talking about? Who are you? Who taught you to act like this?"

Dale reached into his pocket for his Bafexatrin vile. He poured a giant bump on his hand and snorted it. "You're implying that something like this can be taught . . . I really hate to do this, Jane. But if you're not gonna play ball with me on this, then there's only one thing left for me to do."

Jane screamed for help, but Dale was already on top of her, squeezing her fragile throat with both hands.

"*She had demons inside . . . Dancing on her voice . . . Leaning out of the smoke bellowing from her lips and mouth . . .* Emmett wrote that when we were just kids. Fitting."

Dale whistled the melody to *Waiting On Nothing* as Jane's baby-blue eyes turned red and popped out of her head. *"Terror in her eyes . . . Misery in her ferocious stare. Precious angel, you'll forget how to breathe."*

Jane scratched and clawed and fought. Gasping for air, she she tried to break free. But Dale straddled her with his full weight, keeping his grip clenched firmly around her soft delicate neck.

Squeezing . . . Squeezing . . . . Watching her slowly fade.

"Our Father, who art in heaven—" Jane choked.

"Hey," Dale said, "since you obviously won't be needing it, I just figured out the name for *my* new book. I'm gonna call it *Betrayoooo*—shit! Now that felt fucking good! Do it again, baby. Why weren't you that freaky in Fitchburg, eh?"

Jane had reached down with her last ounce of strength and squeezed his testicles tightly in her right hand.

"See, why did that just turn me on? Oh what's this?" Dale noticed a lacy black negligee hanging on the bedpost. "I really think I should give up some of these absurd impulses, but if you're not gonna put that on, then I will." Dale bent down and whispered softly in her ear. "Sit thou silent and get thee into darkness. You like that one don't you?"

"Dale," Jane said. Her lips were a deep blue and she could feel herself passing. "What made you so sick? What darkness? What structure? What subordination? What lack of god to worship? What obedience? What falling into line? What all-encompassing sadness? What hardness? What numbness? What reaching out for help and no answers? What betrayal? What disappointment is it that made you hate yourself so much? And what is it that you love? What is it that you *would* love? That you would die for? What on earth is it? Dale? I really thought we would be together forever. Forever . . . Forever." Her eyes went dead and her body went limp. Jane St. Marie's throat had been crushed by the cold clammy hands of her only lover.

Dale stepped away from her lifeless body, positioned awkwardly now on the hotel bed. Jane's face had contorted unpleasantly as she died suffering.

"What a mess," Dale said, sighing. "Well, Christmas'll never be the same without ya, kid."

He reached for the negligee, which was still hanging on the bedpost. At first he held it softly to his cheek, like he'd held his favorite childhood blanket. The feel of the fabric against his skin made him feel safe and nostalgic and warm. A minute later, he'd taken off his clothes and put it on.

Standing in front of a large mirror, he examined himself.

"The kings of the past posed for pictures too, so the invisible future could one day dream of a world with heroes. They call me the one true hero . . . Regarding beauty in ugly women—I can see it, I can see it. I have always seen it . . . Oh, that looks perfect on you, Daley."

He wiped a pool of sweat from his forehead with the back of his hand, and picked a speck of dirt from his left eye.

Jane's head flopped sideways, hitting the bedside table, knocking the manuscript onto the floor. Dale walked toward her and brushed the hair behind her ears. He straightened her blanket and kissed her on the cheek.

"Strewn about your hotel room, in between us lies a book; and it's bound, broken and weathered, just lying around filled with crosses and question marks. God forgive us and avenge the fatherless. Idle hands will dig a grave, restless feet will find a hole. I am the bulletproof man, and life is hard to understand."

### THE END

# ABOUT THE AUTHOR

Josef Oteim was born in Sudbury, Ontario, in 1982, where he lived until his family relocated to Fitchburg, Massachusetts, in 1997. Josef left Fitchburg alone in 1998, and returned to Sudbury. The following years were difficult, but he eventually left Sudbury and began to travel extensively, writing several early versions of *The Opera House Ballet* while on the road and abroad.